Under
the North Star

Väinö Linna

(1920–1992)

Väinö Linna

Under the
North Star

Translated by
Richard Impola

ASPASIA BOOKS, BEAVERTON, ONTARIO, CANADA

ASPASIA CLASSICS IN FINNISH LITERATURE

Under the North Star
ISBN 0-9685881-6-6
ISSN 1498-8348

Published in 2001 by
Aspasia Books
R.R.1, Beaverton, Ontario
L0K 1A0 Canada
aspasia@aspasiabooks.com
www.aspasiabooks.com

Translated from the Finnish *Täällä Pohjantähden alla*
First published in Finnish 1959 by WSOY(Helsinki, Finland)

*Aspasia Books gratefully acknowledges the assistance of
the Finnish Literature Information Centre.*

Translator's Foreword by Richard Impola
Introduction by Börje Vähämäki
Aspasia Classics in Finnish Literature series editor: Börje Vähämäki
****

National Library of Canada Cataloguing in Publication Data

Linna, Väinö
    Under the north star

(Aspasia classics in Finnish literature)
Includes index.
Translation of: Täällä pohjantähden alla.
ISBN 0-9689054-0-4 (bound : v. 1). –ISBN 0-9685881-6-6- (pbk. : v.1)

    I. Impola, Richard, 1923- II. Title. III. Series

PH355.L5T3313 2001   894'.54133   C2001-901901-7

TRANSLATOR'S FOREWORD

The Finnish novelist Väinö Linna first attracted widespread attention with *The Unknown Soldier* (*Tuntematon sotilas*), which may be one of the best war novels ever written. It depicts the realities of war as experienced by soldiers in the ranks. Viljo Koskela, the quiet soldier in that work, is "unknown" in the sense that the background that shaped his character is a blank. It is as if Linna set out to remedy that deficiency in the trilogy *Under the North Star* (*Täällä Pohjantähden alla*), of which this translation is the first volume. In this, his major work, Linna traces the soldier's family back to the grandfather and continues the saga up to the time the novel was written. In the process he creates the single most important work of fiction to appear in 20th century Finland, a trio of novels that encompasses every important event in the country's history from the 1890s to the 1950s.

Finns apply the term "epic novel" to the form in which Linna writes, a designation that may puzzle some English and North American readers, who are likely to associate the term "epic" with legendary heroes and national myths. Jussi, the main character in this volume, may seem an unlikely hero, but Finnish writers prefer to present recognizable human beings rather than overdrawn heroes or villains.

In one sense Jussi can be described as truly legendary: his dedication to work. It is no exaggeration to call this first novel in Linna's trilogy an epic of work. It describes the manner in which a wilderness is turned into productive land. But there is little here of the romanticizing that often accompanies similar tales, such as the settlement of the American West.

In presenting the history of their country or region, Finnish epic novelists do not generalize or synthesize. Rather than focus on significant events, public personalities, or historical movements, they prefer to portray history as human experience. Linna does write from a broader historical perspective, but his chief concern is to show how historical events affect the lives of people, often quite ordinary people. In that sense, he is highly democratic.

One of Linna's virtues as a writer is a sense of comedic irony. Frequently the "reality" of an event is colored by the self-interest of those involved, with comic results. The romanticizing of the pioneer is parodied in the medal that the gentry grant to Jussi, while robbing him of some of the proceeds of his work. The vicar, although he first objects to his wife's proposal to take over some of the Koskela land, is able to rationalize her motives as a manifestation of mother love, while he views Jussi's desire to cling to the land as greed. Ironic contrasts between "reality" and its perception, between self-image and the judgments of others, are a rich source of humor in Linna's work. Halme, the tailor, is delightfully comic in his pretensions: the contrast between his socialist ideals and his efforts to realize them among the people is hilarious. The episode of the eviction might be pathetic, but given the nature of the Laurila family, it develops into black comedy. The distorted reporting of the scene in a socialist newspaper adds a further layer of humor to the event.

Like other Finnish writers, Linna manages to be simultaneously sympathetic and objective in his portrayal of character. He can be critical and understanding at the same time, and can poke fun at his characters without demeaning them. Despite Jussi's miserliness and his exaggerated humility, he is not an anti-hero, as some commentators suggest. His childhood experience of famine has been the key agent in shaping his character. And Linna is not being merely ironic in referring to Jussi as an idealist, for Jussi does believe in work. In the character of Halme, too, there is much to admire, despite the man's affectations. Readers who seek simplified characters to praise or blame will find few such characters in Linna.

I would describe what Linna writes as "experiential history." His goal is the realistic portrayal of human life, a goal that precludes the use of obvious plot devices and narrative tricks. But in the portrayal of character and emotion, in creating a sense of time and place, and in bringing history to life, few can match Linna as a writer.

One cannot but be impressed by Linna as a stylist. Critics speak of an author's voice. Linna has at his command a variety of voices perfectly suited to the character and event he is portraying. They range from Jussi's humble reticence to the highfaluting diction of Halme. The description in chapter nine of Akseli's state of mind on a bright Pentecost morning is a perfect marriage of style and substance.

The same is true of passage after passage, in which the nature and rhythm of the event shape the language of the narration and dialogue. In the area of politics, Linna has caught the tone of the different parties to a T. His work is both a joy and a challenge to a translator. I can only hope that the challenge has been met with some degree of success.

Richard Impola

INTRODUCTION

To understand Finland and the Finns
one needs only read one book:
Under the North Star by Väinö Linna
—*Esko Aho*

LINNA'S LIFE AND WORKS

Anong Finnish writers Väinö Linna (1920–1992) is universally admired. His two major works, *The Unknown Soldier* (*Tuntematon sotilas*, 1954; English translation, 1957) and the monumental trilogy *Under the North Star* (*Täällä Pohjantähden alla*, 1959–1962; English translation of Part One, 2001), were the top two choices in a wide-ranging survey conducted in 1997 on the 80th anniversary of Finnish independence. Both the cultural elite and the general public chose them when asked to select "the most significant work of art created during Finland's independence."

The son of a butcher, Linna was born into the working class of young Finland. After working several jobs on farms and in forest and mill industry, Linna settled in 1938 as a factory worker in the industrial city of Tampere. His tenure there, which lasted until he became a freelance writer in 1955, was disrupted only for service in Finland's Continuation War 1941–1944.

Linna received several literary awards, among them the State Prize for Literature in 1959, and again in 1960, as well as the Nordic Prize for Literature in 1963.

Linna's personal and literary development parallels that of several Scandinavian writers with a working class background. They were largely

IX

autodidacts and had gained a sense of perspective on their society through travel—in Linna's case the war experience.

Linna's approach to writing advanced from the extremely individualistic to the broadly and historically collective. His first novel, the painfully autobiographical *Päämäärä* (1946; The goal, not translated into English), was fashioned in the tradition of the working-class *Bildungsroman* represented in Finnish literature, for example, by Toivo Pekkanen's *Tehtaan varjossa* (1932; In the shadow of a factory'). *Päämäärä* depicts a materially and spiritually struggling young man who aspires to become a writer. Linna's second novel, *Musta rakkaus* (1948; Black love), a tragedy of jealousy and destructive forces, explores the depths and power of individual passion. The ethical and religious dimensions of human passion appear to have kept Linna preoccupied for several years until his religious crisis around 1952 brought about a great change in outlook; he discontinued work on his third novel, tentatively entitled *Messias* (Messiah), which was never finished.

As a consequence of this crisis, Linna's interest shifted from the individual to the socio-historical dimension of his characters and events. He came to realize that his strength lay in the genre of the historical novel. "In *The Unknown Soldier,* I found the springs of my inner self; now I wrote in my very own style; before, I wrote neurotically."

Linna's technique of focusing on a relatively small collective, a machine gun platoon in the case of *The Unknown Soldier* and a small rural village, Pentti's Corners, in *Under the North Star*, allows Linna to combine rich individual variation with historical relevance and representativeness. The effectiveness of this approach became evident by the enthusiastic, as well as controversial, domestic reception of *The Unknown Soldier,* which appeared ten years after the inglorious end of the Continuation War (1941–1944) against the Soviet Union. Finland had fought alongside Germany against one of the Allied nations and lost. She suffered the humiliation of severe peace conditions, war crimes trials, and the presence for several years in the country of an international Control Commission until 1947. Little public debate about the war and its aftermath had occurred in post-war Finland; the Finnish people tightened their belts, rebuilt the country, integrated into the remaining Finland over 400,000 evacuees from Karelia, which Finland was forced to cede to the Soviets, and paid the imposed war reparations.

This was the context in which the realism and the humor of *The Unknown Soldier* swept the country. The oft-quoted line from the last page of the novel,

"The Union of Soviet Socialist Republics won but the small and gutsy Finland finished a good second," is an excellent example of the kind of humor that permeates the novel. The quote does not reflect any of the gloomy atmosphere of the post-war years. The emerging Cold War and the precarious relationship between Finland and the USSR inspired self-censorship vis-à-vis unfavorable representations of Russians and the USSR, explain the omission of the above quotation from the English translation.

Buoyed by the success of *The Unknown Soldier* and empowered with the benefits of serious research into the history of Finland, Väinö Linna embarked upon his magnum opus, the trilogy *Under the North Star*: his insightful rendition of the historical forces and events that shaped Finland before and during the 20th century.

The novel sets out to examine, and explain, factors and forces at play in each of these crises. It does so, however, by depicting the lives of the people in a small rural village, Pentti's Corners, northwest of Tampere, Finland's most industrial city. At the center of attention is Jussi Koskela, a tenant farmer on the parsonage estate, and his wife and three sons. The larger society is experiencing an overall secularization and the advent and spread of socialist thought and labor activism. At the same time, the Russian Czar is attempting to reign in the Finns in a consolidated Pan-Slavic empire. Anxiety, unrest and suspicion, often for different reasons, permeate all social classes. This is the historical context for the first part of *Under the North Star*. The remaining two parts of the trilogy are published under the titles *The Uprising—Under the North Star, Part Two* and *Reconciliation—Under the North Star, Part Three*, respectively.

Linna's novel is, however, above all a testament to human experience and individual character. In fact, Linna's greatness as a depicter of collective phenomena rests on his rather Tolstoyan philosophy of history, which posits (1) the course of history is dictated by the ordinary people, not by the political leaders, and (2) significant historical change happens slowly and is largely unaffected by the intentions of individuals. Pentti's Corners serves as a location of historical projection and dictates the perspective that presents the village and its people as a kind of "Micro-Finland."

Both in style and outlook Linna harks back to Aleksis Kivi (1834–1872), "the father of Finnish Literature." Both authors are masters of humorous realism; both use humor as a means of penetrating through to the core of the characters. Linna employs humor also to present less than sympathetic characters in a favorable or at least understanding light.

Under the North Star is fundamentally a novel about people trying to survive under extraordinary hard times, people who are willing to work hard and unselfishly, and who, at the end of the day, ask only for justice, respect and human dignity.

HISTORICAL REFERENCES

Under the North Star makes explicit reference to numerous historical persons, places, literary works, and events. Although the homogenous cultural frame of reference for Finnish readers typically includes familiarity with such names and events, it may be helpful in an English translation to offer a few lines of explanation.

In 1884, Finland had been an autonomous Grand Duchy under the Russian Czar for 75 years during which era Finland underwent a series of transformations, from a society administered exclusively in Swedish—a remnant of 650 years as the eastern province of the Swedish empire—into one whose institutions and public life were run in Finnish. This "nation building" involved developing the Finnish language; creating a Finnish identity through the national epic, *The Kalevala* (1835, 1849); instituting primary, secondary and post-secondary education in Finnish; and generating a national, often nationalistic literature, and a Finnish press.

The "founding fathers of the Finnish nation," referred to also in *Under the North Star*, include four names above others: Elias Lönnrot (1802–1884), J.L. Runeberg (1804–1877), J.V. Snellman (1806–1881), and Zacharias Topelius (1818–1898). Lönnrot compiled the epic, *The Kalevala*, and its lyrical companion piece, *The Kanteletar*. Runeberg is Finland's "national poet," who wrote, for example, the *Tales of Ensign Stål*, which included Finland's national anthem, "Our Land," and the most well-known poem in Finnish literature, "Paavo of Saarijärvi," which all were designed to instill patriotism and idealism in Finns. Snellman was a philosopher, literary critic, and senator, who is credited with having gained official status for the Finnish language in

1963. Topelius, professor of history and rector of the University of Helsinki, wrote historical novels and plays, fairy tales and short stories, hymns and other poetry, and the legendary textbook *Boken om vårt land* (The book of our country, 1875), which was used in all primary schools for almost three-quarters of a century. One of his tales for children, "The Birch and the Star," is referred to repeatedly in *Under the North Star* and was, until recent years, read by all Finnish children in school. It is a simple tale about two siblings who are swept to foreign lands by raging war, but who, trusting in Providence, wander back home confident that they will find the birch under the star that marks their home. It is no coincidence that Linna's novel refers to the same star.

Other influential Finnish authors figuring in *Under the North Star* include Minna Canth (1844–1897), Finland's pioneering feminist playwright, and Juhani Aho (1861–1921), a trailblazer in Finnish realist prose.

The emergence of political parties and large national newspapers, for example *Suometar, The Worker* (*Työmies*), and the *People's Journal* (*Kansan Lehti*), is reflected in the novel. The *Suometar* people, the Old Finns, represent a more conservative approach to the language issue regarding the attitude of the Finnish-speaking majority toward the historically and economically powerful Swedish-speaking educated class, while the Young Finns movement took a more radical and hostile position toward the Swedish speakers.

One of the most important issues demanding reforms was the land-ownership question. Particularly in southern Finland, up to 70% of the rural population lived under contract on "torppas" or tenancies, for which rent was paid in work on the landowner's farm.

Matti Kurikka, editor of the socialist *The Worker* during the last few years of the 19th century, became a controversial figure in Finnish society in 1899 because of his position vis-à-vis the Czar-issued February manifesto. This inspired more than 500,000 people to sign a petition to the Czar to rescind the manifesto, albeit without effect. Kurikka urged the readers of *The Worker* not to sign the petition. Kurikka later became famous, or infamous, in North America for his role as founder of the Utopian Socialist colony, Sointula, in British Colombia (1901–1905).

In 1904, the Czar's representative, Governor General Bobrikoff, was dramatically assassinated by a young idealist Eugen Schauman, who instantly became a Finnish hero. In that anti-Czarist political climate and with the rise in socialist thought and agitation — in Finland as well as in Russia — the General Strike of 1905 became an initial test of the power of the collective. The characters Salin, Mäkelä, and Hellberg in *Under the North Star* were historical leaders of the socialist movement at the turn of the century. Finland's parliamentary reform, which offered universal suffrage as one of the very first in the world, was approved by the Czar in the summer of 1906.

Under the North Star was from the outset designed as an epic novel in three solid parts, covering the years 1884 into the 1950s. These years encompass several great crises in the course of the Finnish people: the tumultuous end of the era as a Grand Duchy under the Russian Czar (1809–1917), particularly the so-called Oppression or Russification years (1899–1917); Finland's path to independence (1917); Finland's Civil War (1918); the turbulent inter-World War years; the Winter War (1939–1940); the Continuation War (1941–1944); the German War (1944–1945); and the post-war rebuilding work.

Börje Vähämäki

Under the North Star

CHAPTER ONE

I

In the beginning there were the swamp, the hoe — and Jussi.
The swamp was desolate, its center an almost treeless marsh, from whose
waterlogged bed there grew only a few dwarf pines, tough-barked and flat-
crowned little oldsters. Jussi moved through the swamp, stopping, looking,
examining, and appraising. He picked up a rod, checked carefully to see that
no one was watching, and used it to dig a pit in the surface of the swamp. He
dug several such pits and examined them awhile, then covered them over carefully.
Now and then he stopped to look around as if afraid of something. Was he in
the throes of a treasure hunt? Old folk had indeed said that a will-o'-the-wisp
sometimes burned in the swamp.

Jussi walked slowly toward one side of the swamp. In one place, a small,
natural brook arose, carrying the muddy water from the swamp to a lake some
distance off. Here and there its banks were low, and the brook must have spilled
over them after winters of heavy snow, forming a kind of flood plain. After
following the brook a short distance, Jussi stopped. Here the stream cut through
a small rise, forming a gully over whose rocky bottom the waters rippled gently.
The place had long been familiar to him and a few others. It was known well
enough even to have a name, surely meant to be mocking, for it was called "The
Rapids." It was hardly that. In the spring it might bustle and babble a little more,
but at other times, the water barely speeded up here, as it sought its way among
rocks, brush, and turf.

Jussi picked up a pole, a stout one, and began to test the rocks with it. Some
of them moved easily. That pleased him; it was what he had been hoping for.

Finally he left, but he stopped again at the edge of the swamp and stood looking

3

back. His earnest, appraising glance once more circled the swamp, sunk in its silence of thousands of years. Then he turned to go and did not look back again. Along the old winter road-bed he strode, a man in his thirties, stolid and stern-faced.

The parsonage stood at the edge of the village on the shore of a small lake. The main building was large and painted a pearl-gray. It was sided with strong tongue-and-groove planking and the boards of its porch were decorated with carvings. Jussi did not go in by way of the verandah. He had never done so, even though he had lived at the parsonage since he was a little boy. For Jussi was no minister nor parish clerk nor even a minister's relative. He was the parsonage hired hand, and so he went in through the kitchen door.

He seemed to be leery of even this route. In the kitchen, he humbly took off his hat and addressed a maidservant, who was spending the early autumn afternoon leaning against the table.

"Is the pastor in?"

"And why do you wanna know?"

"I've got something to say to him. Would you ask if he'll see me."

The servant left and Jussi waited. He was obviously nervous. The girl returned and said lazily, "Go into the study."

The maid seemed at home here, but Jussi was ill at ease and embarrassed. He entered the parlor. Lace curtains were drawn over the windows, and a dim light prevailed in the room. He could see the furniture's waxen gleam and the flash of a mirror only vaguely. He did not quite dare to look closely at the room; it would have been almost like staring God boldly and shamelessly in the eye. He knocked at the study door and when he heard an indistinct sound from the inside, he went in. The pastor, the dean of the parish, had just risen from the sofa; on his face was the fuzzy expression of one just awakened from sleep, mixed with a trace of annoyance.

"Well, what is it, Johannes?"

The pastor was approaching retirement age. He was lazy by nature, increasingly so with age. On either side of his sturdy trunk his hands hung limp in a display of uselessness.

Jussi stood on the threshold. A humble timidity shone through his look of strained determination.

4

"Mr Pastor. I would like to... now since it's Sunday..."

Jussi found it hard to state his business, and the pastor's tired annoyance increased.

"I've been thinking... Being a hired man when you're married is not much of a life. If you, Mr Pastor, would let me have the swamp."

A slight impulse to laughter stirred in the pastor's sleepy being.

"But my good boy... What would you do with the swamp?"

Jussi was always "my good boy" to the pastor although a full-grown and recently married man. He grew more uneasy.

"I would clear it."

"You would clear it. What for?"

"I was thinking sort of... that a real farm... If you, Mr Pastor, would let me."

The pastor's expression became more and more annoyed, for his brain now would have to awaken from its half-sleep and start working.

"My good boy, don't talk nonsense... a farm in that raw swamp? And what's wrong with your staying here?"

Jussi waged an internal struggle. It was obvious he found it hard to do anything that might annoy the pastor, yet a look of determination appeared in his eyes.

"Nothing... It's just that with a family... And I would gladly take... You can't exactly get anywhere as a hired hand like this. You can't really get started. But as a tenant farmer, you can save more."

The pastor laughed. "Save more. You've held on to every penny since you were a little boy." Then he grew serious. "Well... That's right. I didn't mean... It's good. But have you really thought it through? How will you do it? It'll take years. How much money do you have now? You have in my keeping... well... less than a thousand markkas, and your wife has a little there too. The swamp won't yield you a living for years."

"This is how I've figured it... If Alma could come to work here and if I could be working out there. Except on my rent-days."

Jussi was relieved to see that the pastor was now awake and paying attention.

"I didn't mean... Why shouldn't I let you have it. But think about it... equipment, a horse... cattle... buildings. No, my good boy. Well, not that it hasn't been done before, and I'm sure you can do what others have done."

"If you just give me permission. That's all I need."

"Heh, heh... Well go on, my good boy. Do as you like."

5

Jussi's small, restless eyes gleamed, and his cheeks relaxed into a barely suppressed smile.

"Could I have the whole swamp? And the land along the brook?"

The pastor smiled benignly at Jussi's zeal and said, "Take it, take it... As much as you can. But just one side of it for now."

"What about a rental contract?"

"Later... later. I won't gouge you... Heh, heh..."

"Well...Thank you then...I sure will..."

The pastor became serious. "No need to thank me. But remember, work means nothing unless it is blessed. That is essential... for... it needs blessing... I say..."

Jussi's features drew themselves into a solemn expression worthy of the Evangelical Lutheran faith, and he mouthed the semblance of approval of the pastor's opinion. Then he left, and at the door he could see the pastor eyeing his sofa, Jussi and his swamp already forgotten.

Jussi went through the yard and across the road into his own cabin. It was an old structure with a birch-bark roof weighted down with poles. Its sides were no longer plumb, and it was otherwise decayed because of long vacancy. The bricks at the top of the chimney jutted out askew; one had even fallen to the roof and lay there slowly crumbling. The building had only one room with a small board shed at one end which served as an entry.

In that hut, Jussi and Alma made their plans that night. They calculated how far the money owed them by the pastor would stretch and found that it would suffice beautifully. For they too possessed an imagination, and despite the severe discipline of daily life, at moments like this it almost broke its shackles.

Jussi went out to the entry. There, behind the birch-whisks and the kneading trough were hidden a hoe and a shovel. And behind them, even better concealed, was an old, used wagon axle. It had been bought at an auction two years ago and carried in the dark of night to this corner of the parsonage. No one could see it, for it would have revealed something. Specifically this dream, which was now starting to come true, and which the existence of the axle proved to be no passing fancy.

Jussi took the hoe and tried its blade. He was impatient, ready to begin at once. Alma was five years younger than Jussi. She was a quiet, but nonetheless inwardly lively woman. She had warm brown eyes, and tonight they were warmer than before.

6

The two lay awake for a long time. Only now did Jussi reveal everything, even to Alma. How it had occurred to no one that deepening the channel of the rapids would make draining the swamp relatively easy. How the rise was exactly the right place for a building. And how the swamp was extraordinarily good soil. There was practically no moss on it. Directly under the water plants was rich black earth.

"But we have to get a contract before he notices that."

It grew dark that September night of 1884. The silence around the hut was unbroken. It settled in as if listening to their happiness.

Now what exactly would they do with it?

II

Before full daylight on a damp and misty September morning, Jussi arrived at the swamp with his working gear. An hour's thought is often the equivalent of a week's work, and Jussi stood for a long moment at the edge of the rapids, silent and meditative. The work itself indeed required no thought of him, for after the pastor had approved his plans, he had spent all his free time traversing the swamp. During that time he had sketched out a complete plan. A creator works according to a design. And Jussi's mind lingered on his design, measuring the distance between what was and what was to be. Matter was to be altered to suit the spirit's image; fate had led this man to the swamp and said: *Ille faciet.*

He took the heavy wooden shovel with its blade edged in iron and descended to the gully below the rapids. Thrusting the blade into the earth, he set his foot on its upper edge, and drove it down with his body's weight. Half-audible words interspersed with grunts burst from his lips.

"And so... here... it... begins."

And so it began. Smeared with clay, wet with sweat and drizzle, he drudged in the ditch. And gradually it deepened and cleared until a rocky bed lay revealed. That called for more than shoulders. Something was needed to raise the rocks, and Jussi was fully adequate to deal with the challenge. He made levers and poles for a skidway, and with them the rocks began to ascend the banks. If one appeared for which his strength was insufficient, it had to be dug in deeper or an attempt made to shift it to one side.

7

For the good-sized rocks, Jussi's strength was indeed sufficient. He was not really a big man, but his body was sturdy and compact. And more important, there lived and moved in it a spirit that could wring the last ounce from it. When the effort reached the breaking point, when the body's every fiber trembled, yielding its last bit of strength, and still another ounce was needed, that little iota lay hidden in some strange and secret store. A dark, settled look appeared in the man's eyes, his lips drew back into a kind of tight grin with a glint of ferocity in it, and the stone rolled up the bank.

At midday he broke for lunch, took his birch-bark knapsack from a spruce branch, and began to eat. There was bread and soured milk and half a medium-sized salt-bream. The fish was in a birch-bark butter-box, just like a better repast. Alma would indeed have provided butter to go with it, but even the timidly offered suggestion etched lines between her husband's eyes. The bottle of soured milk was diluted with water. For Jussi was tight-fisted. He had always been so and was even more so now that the swamp demanded years of unproductive labor from him. But there was black rye bread aplenty, and that he ate unsparingly. Not because he undervalued it, but because he knew that without it, the rocks would not rise from the ditch. While eating, he thought of these matters, and an unpleasant, annoying sensation passed through his mind. It came from the knowledge that people were aware of his miserliness, that they were even somewhat contemptuous of him because of it. But no one ever insulted him intentionally, for his laughable penuriousness was only another brush stroke in the mental picture people had of him. He was known for other things. For example, as a worker: keeping up with him entitled a man to boast. They also knew that Jussi would put up with a lot, but that there was a limit. One episode was enough to prove it.

One day he had witnessed a brawl between his own and a neighboring village. It had taken place on the main road. The two groups had already separated. Jussi was on his way from the village and had to pass through the band from the other village. He had had no part in the fight, but since he was from Pentti's Corner, they decided to beat him up too. Realizing their intentions, Jussi snatched up a pole from the side of the road and started through the group. The first two to set on him got resounding blows from Jussi's club and fell stunned. And as Jussi, his face pale and his lips quivering, walked unmolested through the group, he said in a surly, shaking voice that compelled belief:

8

"I don't... do anything... to anybody... But nobody lays a hand on me."

When younger, less than twenty, he had shown signs of a lighter life style and had even been drunk on occasion. But all that soon ended, and Jussi became an abstemious, and consequently a lonely young man. This had bred in him a kind of quiet antagonism toward the village and the villagers. So now too, as he always did, he responded to the embarrassing thoughts that had entered his mind as if in answer to the people's collective derision, "Where can my kind save, if not on food?"

And he was right. That's what it was like to be a Finn at one time.

Again he went down into the gully. At first his body was stiff and reluctant, but when the back of his flaxen shirt began to steam, the machine was at work again.

Before the frost set in, Jussi had the rapids cleared. That did not achieve his final goal, but it did avert the danger of spring floods overflowing the banks of the brook. Later he could gradually deepen the channel to drain the swamp dry. And still that same fall, he managed to clear a small plot of land along the brook. It was an easy job, for he could just plow it with the parsonage horse. There were no trees on the old bottom land.

There he could plant potatoes and even a little barley. Not that they amounted to much, but they would save Alma two days of work otherwise due in rent for a patch of parsonage land to grow potatoes on. Jussi gathered brush and leaves, burning it to ashes as a substitute for manure. Nor would he have been Parsonage Jussi had he not scoured the winter roadbed, shovel in hand, gathering rotted horse manure for his fields. Every little thing helped.

When frost halted work on the land, the felling of trees began. Jussi cleared the stream's bank to a point where the woods became too thick and then went on some distance into a spruce grove. There he could find timber for building.

From morning to night, day after day, the blows of the axe rang in the woods. At times they could be heard in the village, for the swamp was nearby. One person or another would stop by to look over Jussi's work site. Someone who fully realized his intentions would say, either in admiration or in a voice crackling with envy, "But that's a great place for a farm... How come no one ever thought of deepening the rapids before? And how come the pastor didn't clear it himself?"

Jussi fully admitted the advantages of the place, but he was also quick to

9

mention the work it required. Nor did anyone deny it. Then one day the old master of Kylä-Pentti came out to see Jussi as well. With others, a reluctant and indifferent Jussi grunted out his words as an aside to his work, but this man he greeted with respect, refraining from working while they talked. For the master of Pentti was not merely a person; he was a folk legend. He was known as the Czar of the Swamp, or simply as the Czar. He had, you see, turned the huge swamp of Pentti into a field with his hoe during his lifetime. For his feat, the gentry had given him a medal. Though he was still alive, people spoke of him as they would of St. George. In addition, his work with the hoe had already long ago grown in the people's imagination to proportions that far exceeded human capabilities.

When the Czar heard that Parsonage Jussi was engaged in clearing the swamp, he arrived to inspect the work, accorded inspection privileges by his reputation. Even in his late years the Czar was a tall, strong man. He asked questions and made observations. Jussi explained courteously.

"From there, I mean to go that way."

"That's not the way to do it."

"How then..."

"You'll do it this way."

And then the Czar explained how it was to be done. In his humility, Jussi was unaware that the change made no difference at all. But the Czar questioned, approved, and rejected.

"That's where you should run it through."

Such instructions Jussi would not have taken from anyone else. They were in fact inconsequential. Yet there was great significance in the Czar's next statement.

"In the spring, you'll come and get a calf and a pair of lambs from me."

"Thanks, but why would you, Sir... I'll pay for them..."

"You heard what I said. You come and get them in the spring."

After the Czar had left, Jussi worked more feverishly than before. The thought of the calf and the lambs warmed his heart, but he was also stirred by this legendary Finnish hero.

"This is the only way to do it... It will take a good man to be his match." Jussi was a great idealist.

Little by little, the clearing along the banks of the brook grew larger. But the man's face grew correspondingly leaner. His gaze darkened and the lines

10

around his mouth deepened. Sometimes he would stop working and stare blankly before him without seeing a thing, until his eyes spotted a squirrel wriggling its way through a spruce tree. At such times, not a sound broke the silence of the swamp. Only the squirrel moved. For a time it would freeze in place, then again it would circle the tree and find a new branch, where it sat and wondered at the man, who had come here to raise a commotion. The squirrel had something almost human about it: it was quick, curious, and wondering.

The furrows in the man's face relaxed and his eyes narrowed almost imperceptibly, as if lighted up by the barest trace of a smile.

III

The snow had melted from the log pile. The last of the spring storms would cover it from time to time, but the new snow melted before noon and steam rose from the bare logs. As spring advanced, Jussi hewed the logs. Alma wondered at their length, as did other spectators who stopped now and then at Jussi's work site. Not even to Alma did Jussi explain his building plans. He was terse and evasive.

"Why do they have to be so long?"

"For the walls, of course."

Alma smiled a small, secretly wise smile. Jussi intended to make the main building larger than the usual. Alma understood that the size was really not for their own sake, but for its effect on the villagers. Sometimes even Jussi lapsed into a slight impracticality. It would mean more work, but that he had never shunned.

The stones dug up from the rapids supplied the footing, and before sowing time, the bottom timbers were in place. They revealed that the building would be sixteen meters long and seven meters wide. Rather large for the main structure of a new tenant farm. At one end would be the main room, at the other end the bake-room, and in between the hallway and another room. Thus the house conformed completely to the established pattern. The majority of Finnish people were housed, lived, and died in such homes.

"Wouldn't a smaller one do?"

"Why not... But even in this one you can hear a person talk from one corner to another... And it's no harder to build."

11

When the days grew longer and Alma had a little daylight left after her work was done, she came to help with the building. She set the moss on top of the timbers, and as the walls rose higher, each evening the two of them lifted up the timbers for the following day.

As the summer evening darkened, they started for home. At times, however, they stood near the building as if observing a short moment of devotion. The brief words they exchanged then were always about entirely practical matters, but their minds were not on them. They were enveloped in a feeling of quiet joy tempered by bodily weariness into something akin to devoutness.

In between, they planted potatoes, and lastly Jussi sowed barley on the remaining land. Later, when a violet-tinged green began to spread over the land, they gazed at it and said that nowhere else were the shoots up so high so early.

The manor was the very center of the whole community. Even the parsonage had to bow to its greatness, for the manor was large and old, and was owned by a real baron. The main building sat by itself in a grove of trees. Surrounding the grove were household buildings of different kinds and vintages. Their outer circle was made up of small cabins belonging to the hired hands and farm workers. Beyond were the tenant cottages, each on its small speck of land, and outside this ring were the independent farms: Töyry and the two Penttis, Kylä-Pentti and Mäki-Pentti.

Jussi stood by the roadside, awaiting the approaching baron. A sense of reverence mingled with fear filled his mind, for the baron was not really in the same class as other human beings. He was somehow just one step below God. His demeanor was a little in that vein as well. He was straight, stiff, and dogmatic, somewhat like his grandfather, "Finland's War-Major," a harsh, stern man. Old people still remembered bits and pieces about him, particularly that he had been extraordinarily gifted at cursing. The grandson was not a soldier, but a quite ordinary lord of the manor.

From afar, Jussi regarded this large erect man and his heavy beard. After the death of Czar Alexander II, the baron had changed from side whiskers to the full beard favored by Czar Alexander III.

The only one to rank above him was the Czar of Kylä-Pentti. Jussi had a vague notion that the manor people had a family legend of their own. In some German war, a rank of nobility had been bestowed upon their ancestor, even though he had been an ordinary commoner, a common farmer and a cavalryman. Later he had been given a couple of farms by the king as a gift, their owners having been evicted for delinquent taxes. Their ghosts lingered on in the names of a couple of fields.

The baron was annoyed when he saw from a distance that Jussi intended to speak to him. He did not wish to be disturbed, for he was thinking. And when Jussi took off his hat, bowed, and began to state his business, the baron stared at him from round, unblinking eyes.

"I hear they're going to tear down the Vakkeri cabin. So, if the manor doesn't need those bricks, I'd like to buy them."

The baron spoke Finnish poorly. As the language struggle in Finland heated up, he spoke it ever more poorly, and if annoyed at something, he pretended not to understand anything at all. Jussi had chanced to stop him at a bad time and got back a question in place of an answer.

"You tear down Vakkeri place?"

"No, but those bricks I... if I could have that fireplace."

"You tear down Vakkeri bricks?"

"No, but I would buy them. Since the cabin is being torn down."

Now light began to dawn for the baron. He condescended to understand, looked at Jussi for a second, turned his gaze in the direction he was taking and said, "You get bricks. You cut rye four days."

And the baron left without a backward glance or a thought to Jussi's opinion of the bargain. In any case, Jussi did not consider the price a high one, and although offended and angered by the baron's conduct, he was also pleased.

That took care of the bricks. And the breeding stock for the farm the Czar of Kylä-Pentti had promised were fetched. They were a handsome gift in themselves, and they had a consequence. No actual contract had yet been drawn up, and the pastor would answer Jussi's anxious questions only by saying he would come and have a look first. When the spring weather turned warmer, he did come. Owing to his laziness and his labored breathing, he walked slowly and had already sized up Jussi's accomplishments from a distance. He was amazed at what he saw, for his mental picture of the whole enterprise had been of one much more modest in scope. A shadow of displeasure crossed his mind; the project was too grandiose.

"But Johannes, now really...."

13

Gasping for air, the pastor sat down on a log and looked around.

"You have big ideas, don't you. Are you planning to build a real farm house out here?"

"No, not really... but since the firs were like that... the logs were... well, so long."

"Well, how much of this do you plan to clear?"

"I've been thinking... along the brook as far as the swamp, and then the swamp..."

"The whole thing?"

"Well, yes. If I have the time and strength."

"But isn't that too much?"

"I don't think so... It's not so much. I'll need hay fields too. If we keep any livestock at all... The master of Kylä-Pentti gave us a calf and two lambs as a start."

A small cough escaped the pastor. According to custom he should have been the one to give such a gift since Jussi had been at the parsonage since early boyhood.

"Did he really? Why?"

Jussi averted his gaze slightly. "Well, I don't know... Alma did work there one year as a servant... But probably because... Because he's cleared so much land himself."

The pastor cleared his throat twice more.

"Well you can clear as far as you're able to. You can go up to the edge of the swamp. But no farther along the brook than you've already gone. The trees are big from there on. I am only the holder of the benefice; I don't really have the right to let it be cleared."

"I'll stop there... Can I go by your word?"

"That's really something... It's going to be a regular farm house... You could have settled for a more modest one."

Jussi had noticed the pastor's hemming and hawing, and said quietly, drawing out his words, "Well that's true. But then there's the cattle too... lambs and cows... Since I've already got a start... as a kind of help..."

A slight sense of annoyance stirred in the pastor's mind. He would not have wished so much for Jussi. He was a victim of the basic human emotions of envy and greed. Jussi was getting too much. But then the pastor conquered the feeling,

14

influenced decisively by the Czar's gift. His basic sense of propriety told him that helping his hired hand to get a start was not a matter for outsiders. The pastor swallowed his bile, and once over the threshold, he slipped into an absurdly compliant attitude. The work in lieu of rent would not begin until a year from that autumn. First a day a week on foot, the following year a day a week with a horse, the year after that a day a week with a horse and one on foot, and finally, two days with a horse and one on foot. The rent would not exceed that amount, at least not while he ruled the parsonage. And a proper document would be drawn up that would apply until his death.

As he spoke, the pastor's breathing became labored. He suffered from shortness of breath, and lately the threat of death had begun to settle in his mind.

Jussi was pleased. He explained his plans to the pastor, but he carefully emphasized the many difficulties involved, for the pastor must not be led to believe that this would be easy. And even the pastor's sluggish imagination revived. Upon leaving, he was fully in accord with his tenant's plans. On his way back he even reflected briefly on the matter from a broader perspective.

"Such men are needed... This country needs such men... He must be helped. Indeed... why not... What would I gain from him... Why should I any longer... uh, uh..."

IV

Jussi built the timber frame of the house by himself. But summer was drawing to a close, and it grew more and more obvious that if they were to move into this building come fall, he would need help. Putting up the roof trusses by himself would be difficult, and in any case he needed a stonemason, for he had never done such work himself. Jussi pondered and worried over the matter. There was a man whose value as a helper was self-evident as far as the work was concerned: Otto Kivivuori. But Jussi hesitated.

Alma also recommended Otto, but Jussi muttered, "He talks too much."

"Let him talk."

Exactly. If it was true that Otto was good at talking, he was even better with his hands, and at last Jussi yielded. He went to Kivivuori.

Kivivuori ('Stone Mountain') was a tenant farm on the manor. There was no mountain here, but there were plenty of stones. The living quarters were small and gray, but somehow well-proportioned. The frames of the small six-paned windows were painted brown. Behind the building was a rocky slope gnawed bare by goats, a potato-cellar, and a mountain-ash tree. In the yard were berry bushes and a vegetable garden with hop vines at one end. A shiny bottle had been slipped over one of the stakes. A touch of contempt fizzed in Jussi's mind as he looked at it. It was supposed to scare off the birds and keep them from stealing the berries! First they grow such useless stuff and then they even protect it. But that was Anna's doing.

Otto was lying on his back with his feet resting on the headboard. When Jussi entered, he rose with a demonstratively lazy yet strangely expedient movement and sat on the bedside, elbows resting on his knees. He was fairly tall and blond, but his eyebrows were thick and dark, and a pair of sharp, yet lightly smiling blue eyes looked out from beneath them. His mouth was sharply etched and the tip of his upper lip, which was covered by a blond mustache, pressed firmly down on the lower. He seemed to have been awakened by the visitor's arrival and drew a pained look from his wife when he said, "Plant your ass over here."

Anna was a shapely, slender blond woman. Her face was pretty, but always a little somber and somehow sad. Everything about her was neat and groomed— her hair, her clothing—and a careful cleanliness and order were apparent in the cottage. Playing on the floor with his wooden horse was a boy a year and a half old, in whose face his father's features were plainly evident.

Jussi sat down on the bench a little uneasily.

"We've had a nice summer."

"We sure have. Will that palace of yours be finished soon? People are telling the wildest stories. They say the main room will be big enough to drive a team of horses into."

"Heh, heh. First I'd need a horse to drive in the fields, before driving one into the living room."

"Well, horses can be bought. You just go to the fair and get one."

"What would I buy a horse with?"

"With the money you've got hidden away. They say you've got money in a sock in your attic."

Jussi's face stiffened.

"Could be. Though I don't know anything about any sock. I'd be glad if I

16

could find that myself. But I came here because I need help. There's mason's work. Need help with the trusses too. Thought I'd ask if you would have the time."

Otto did not answer immediately. He told Anna to make coffee, and she began to do so, but she was a little disgruntled. They could not afford to serve coffee to just anyone who dropped in. Otto pretended to think about Jussi's question for a while. Then he began vaguely to agree.

"Well... I don't really know. Here I would have... though hay-making is done now. But there is always something... But I guess I can find time now."

"What do you think your wages should be? If you take into account there's no food out there so you'll have to bring your own."

Otto stole a look at Jussi, and a sly expression flashed in his eyes. Then he began to ponder and agonize, seemingly in dead earnest. He knew Jussi was hanging on his every word in fearful suspense.

"Well... I don't know now... I wouldn't be asking all that much. I should really... There's plenty of this kind of work. I've got a job at Kolu Corners too. But let's let it go. We can decide on the pay later."

But Jussi would not agree to any delay. He would not live with uncertainty. And who knows what the man would ask when the work was done.

"No. Just name your price."

Otto could gauge Jussi's state of mind exactly, and irritated him further by hemming and hawing and pondering, until finally he said, "What do you think? Would one markka a day be too much?"

Jussi breathed a sigh of relief, but he understood that the low wages too were pure deviltry. A stone mason could have asked twice that, since he was providing his own food. But what of it? Let him mock. "Well, I'll pay that all right, since that's what you're asking for."

And to escape the awkward subject, he turned to the boy playing on the floor.

"Now that's a frisky horse you've got there."

The boy looked intently at the visitor for a moment, began to jounce his wooden horse energetically on the floor, and cried excitedly, "Whee... doddamn horty..."

His father laughed, but Anna looked distressed. She had the suffering look of one long since resigned, but it was in part affectation, as was her tone of voice when she said with a sigh, "Well, that's nice. Laughing at an innocent child's cursing, after he's been taught so well."

17

Her remark was apparently meant to explain the child's ungodly behavior to Jussi, but her hopelessness indicated that she must accept it, as indeed she, unable to do anything else, had done. The real cause for her slightly affected sadness and melancholy no longer existed; her pose reflected a time when gloom had been the outward sign of genuine pain and grief. Her intense love for the man who sat laughing on the bedside had made her thoroughly miserable. The daughter of a nearby small farmer, she had fallen in love with the handsome Kivivuori boy. Unfortunately, that young man was completely carefree and casual in matters of love. That he was a tenant cottager's son was a further obstacle, for although Anna's home was no larger than the average tenant's cottage, she was still a landowner's daughter. Not only that, hers was a strict household; her parents could have agreed to her becoming the mistress of a cottage, but not the wife of "a godless cheat," as Anna's father dubbed his future son-in-law.

But her parents' objections were not the worst of it; her suitor's own behavior was. Serious-minded, already inclined toward religion while young, Anna had fallen deeply and madly in love. But during their courtship, the young man would stop off at any available maidservant's quarters. Nor did the pain his behavior caused Anna bring about any twinges of conscience in him. When in tears she reproached him for straying, Otto, completely cheerful, defended himself.

"Well, I have to go somewhere. Seeing that you guard it like a jewel."

At that moment, Anna had unleashed a scream of anguish, an eruption of despair from the depths of her soul. It penetrated even Otto's thick skin. At first he merely cut down on the side-trips, keeping them a close secret. Before the wedding, they had stopped completely.

Anna's pain softened into a fine melancholy. Yet even after three years of marriage and the birth of their first child, she was still secretly afraid of losing Otto, although without apparent cause. He remained faithful and became a good father. His disposition, however, did not change. He laughed at the child's cursing and made fun of things Anna held sacred.

Even with regard to their housekeeping, he was not as serious as Anna thought fit. He kept up the cottage poorly. On the other hand, he earned good money doing bricklaying and construction work: at times it paid to hire someone to do his rent-work while he himself worked for wages. Although they were not needy, their money drained away as easily as it came in. Coffee, for example, had to be served to every caller, witness Parsonage Jussi, who never gave anything

18

to anybody, who deprived poor Alma of coffee, and probably kept her on the verge of starvation.

But of course Anna, who was always polite, concealed her thoughts from Jussi. She questioned him about his work on the building and he responded, happy to talk about matters of fact, for Otto was always poking fun at him because Alma was still childless.

Therefore, Jussi left as soon as he had drunk the coffee. He was in a good state of mind because of his cheap stonemason, not even bothered by the knowledge that Otto would say something about him to Anna as soon as he had left.

And Otto did just that.

"That Jussi would stand all day in the slime by the roadside if you gave him a markka."

The roof trusses were soon in place. Although Jussi disliked, even condemned, some of Otto's traits, Otto was clearly his superior in one crucial way. Otto could work.

Jussi himself labored furiously, with total concentration, while Otto worked casually, as if the work were some kind of sideline. And also, in his own casual and self-confident way, he took charge at the work site. Before long Jussi had to acknowledge how right many of Otto's recommendations were, and opposed only those that would cost money. Even there he had to give way, for a couple of gibes from Otto would force him into a position where only yielding would save face.

In the masonry work, Otto handled the bricks a little too roughly. He would pick up a brick, rap it with his hammer, and when the old, moldering lump fell apart, he would pick up another. For a long time, Jussi looked askance at him but said nothing. Finally, he began to sigh meaningfully. "How will the bricks last? How in the world will the bricks last if you break so many?"

Otto pretended not to hear and struck a brick so that the pieces flew. Jussi raised a hand and said, clearing his throat, "If you could be a little more careful... watch out a little more... so they won't run out."

"It just so happens, my good Jussi, that if it won't last in my hand, it won't last in the fireplace either. Besides, you have to buy chimney tile for above the roof. These rotten, old, weather-beaten bricks won't last two years in the rain."

19

"They'll cost too much... They'll cost money... If you'll just use these."

Otto stopped working, looked at Jussi, and said sharply, "The devil I will. It would really cost money if you had to do it over in a couple of years."

Yes. It was the truth, and Jussi had to admit it.

Otto's presence at the site put an end to the atmosphere of silent drudgery characteristic of Jussi at work. Though Jussi was a poor talker, Otto chattered on by himself, and all else failing, he talked to the squalling young magpies in the spruce grove nearby. "...spoon-stealing devils you..."

Whenever Alma appeared at the site, he would start in on a series of thoroughly Finnish double-entendres, suggestive and shameless. Sometimes even Jussi smiled, although such talk was entirely foreign, if not distasteful to him. Alma would laugh quietly, which inspired Otto even more.

"Look at the good mortar I have."

Otto scored a shape in the mortar with a sweep of his trowel, then flipped it upright from beneath, causing Alma to blush.

"That's what makes it good."

"You seem to have the right touch."

"I'm pretty damned good at it. That's why I'm such a nice guy."

But he was good in many other ways too and always did things casually. He borrowed a horse to haul the bricks, brought his grindstone to the work site, and prescribed where and how to get bricks most advantageously. He took care of everything with no fanfare and without pay, with the same light touch. And just as naturally, he went to borrow a drill from Kankaanpää's and stayed there the rest of the day drinking Kustaa's city booze.

It was Otto who thought up the roofing bee too.

"You can hammer away at it alone for two weeks, but make up a barrel of home brew, spread the word, and it's done in one go."

"Would anyone come?"

"Hah! Where there's beer, there are drinkers."

Jussi was of two minds. Home brew alone wasn't enough; there would have to be food and that would cost money. Doing the work by himself would be cheap, but on the other hand valuable time would be lost, and he still had to turn over some land this fall.

Alma was enthusiastic about the bee, but her flights of imagination were soon brought down, wing-shot.

20

"We're not giving any banquet here. Just so they get something to eat."

"But we have to have something. It would be a shame to give them poor food."

"Cook up a potato soup. They'll eat that all right."

But Alma bargained a little more and got Jussi to make some small concessions. And she exceeded her limits on the sly, buying bits and pieces without his knowledge.

They decided to hold the feast at the new building even though they couldn't eat indoors there. If the weather was nice—a prerequisite, for they couldn't put up a roof in the rain— they would eat outdoors. Jussi and Alma's hut was too small, and because of the home brew, they couldn't ask for the parsonage parlor.

Jussi had been at the parsonage since the famine years. He was originally from a neighboring parish, but on the death of his father, he had taken to the road with his mother to wander at the tail end of long processions of beggars. His mother had died in the parsonage parlor. When the pastor asked about relatives to whom he might be sent, the boy sat beside his mother's body without saying a word. Not knowing what to do, the pastor finally ordered that he be kept at the parsonage. There he had stayed in the care of maidservants until he was old enough to be the year-round hired hand. The pastor had taken it upon himself to search out the boy's origins, but although he located a few relatives, he kept the boy, who had by now become accustomed to the parsonage.

The naturally introverted and serious Jussi grew up in this atmosphere, somewhat apart from other boys of his age. Because he had had such little contact with his peers, Jussi wondered if anyone would show up to work. When the day dawned and he saw how many had appeared, he realized he was wrong. There were plenty of them for the number of spaces between rafters, and more than enough for the food and home brew available.

For starters, Jussi offered them tobacco—chewing tobacco and some pipe tobacco from the village store. He knew that the size of his offering would already have been a matter of some interest to the work crew, so he proffered the treats casually, his mind braced for possible comments. All the men were interested too in what he had accomplished and he was given many compliments, for in those days, work was the only honor among these people. Not only was it their honor; it was also the absolute and sole condition of life.

Then they mounted the roof. Without being bossy, Otto directed the work, dropping a word here and a suggestion there, throwing in little gibes that raised competitive fervor to a high pitch. Otto was born for such occasions. Knowing his own superiority, he manipulated the others into a state of mind where only keeping up could preserve a man's honor.

"Preeti, go next to Antto so you can help him in case he can't finish his row on time."

Preeti was a day laborer at the manor, a tongue-tied incompetent, whose whole being had evolved around an inborn helplessness. Antto Laurila, again, was a tenant of Töyry, a tense man, consumed by a constant, low-burning anger. He was so affected by defeat that it would send him into a fit of rage. This happened often, for despite his shambling body's strength and his compulsive nature, Antto's labors bore small fruit. Under pressure he became confused, and resorted to a blind and frenzied use of force.

Otto's remark laid the basis for the whole competition, for the assignment to the two was also a challenge to the others, even though it brought a malicious laugh from them.

"Hey tailor. Tie up the bundles of shingles, since you know how to make knots."

Adolph Halme, the tailor, had also come to the working bee. Not that he was interested in the work or even capable of doing it. The men were well aware of the meaning implied in his assignment as in that of Preeti and Antto: he was unfit for anything else. Halme was something of a gentleman, a lean, dry fellow, who had learned tailoring in Tampere, and who had become so enlightened there that he now passed himself off in his home community as the model of an educated person. He read the newspaper *Suometar*, and "took part in people's movements" or rather he talked about them to the indifferent people. And it was with such talk in mind that he had come to the roofing bee. Later in the evening when the beer was going round, he would have a chance to sound off on matters of importance, a prospect which made a short stint at bundling shingles worthwhile. He worked ineffectually, laughably clumsy, lifting the shingles as he would fragile decorations, highly fearful of getting splinters in his fingers.

Two more of the manor's tenants, Kustaa Kankaanpää and Victor Mäkelä, were present, along with the fourteen-year-old son of Priitta, the community's masseuse and midwife, and one or two others.

The work began. The tempo was regular and even at first, but it quickened from row to row until the slower workers began to fall behind noticeably. And

22

infuriating, mortifying, Otto's taunting cry would penetrate the ears of the hindmost.

"Nailing strip!"

His voice was always the first to be heard, notifying the others that his segment was finished and that he was ready to start a new one while they were still hammering away. He worked with exasperating ease, his long, supple fingers dealing out the shingles like a gambler's fingers dealing out a deck of cards. And though he grabbed up the nails helter-skelter, they always appeared head up between his thumb and forefinger out of the revolving cluster in his palm. While waiting for the others, he would gaze up at the sky from time to time as if bored and annoyed at not being able to go on immediately. Then he would glance appraisingly at the others' work and wait, tapping his hammer handle on the nailing strip.

Preeti and Antto worked side by side. The helpless Preeti was regularly last, but that was no consolation to Antto, for no one took Preeti into account. Antto began to rush, and the more he hurried, the less he accomplished. When Otto, in a tone of utter malice, cried, "Nailing strip!" Antto broke out into strangled cursing and reddened with rage, but then tried to control himself, knowing that anger would make his defeat shamefully laughable.

When he had finished his segment, he tried to set the nailing strip in place immediately, even though Preeti was still not done. "Bang away, goddammit, so we won't have to wait."

But Preeti, unaggrieved, answered in an even, humble voice. "Just set it down there. I can easily get the rest from above."

Aware of all this, Otto craned his neck as if he had just noticed, and said, "Ya-ah. Preeti should hurry up. He's making Antto nervous. Antto is in fine form."

Antto snorted, bitterly and contemptuously. "Damn it! If I had my own hammer I'd show you. But I picked up this bloody worm-smasher when I left. I didn't pay attention. It belongs to the house, and it's the same kind of dud as the old man himself."

"But the old man's tool is better than that hammer. He made Kustaa there in his old age."

They all turned to look at Priitta's son, for Otto in his entirely shameless way had spoken the truth. Kustaa was in fact the illegitimate son of Priitta, the

23

masseuse, begotten by the father of Töyry's current master. But they waited in vain for any sign of embarrassment in Kustaa.

He was a headstrong boy, with a freaky sense of humor, and it was his nature to do the unexpected. He never worked, and his appearance at the roofing bee was a minor miracle. In response to Otto's words, he merely bawled out, "Ya-ah, and goddamn well made he is too."

But when the work resumed, Otto found himself hard pressed; Kustaa finished his segment before Otto. Even though it was partly accidental, Otto took the matter seriously. He stopped whistling and lit into the work, still without any wasted effort. The work seemed to fly under his hands, and before they reached the peak, Kustaa quit upon noticing that he was squarely beaten.

When they shifted sides, some of the men suggested a pause, but Otto moved the scaffolding at once and said, "There are no breaks at working bees. We keep going to the last drop of blood."

And so they began to work on the other side. There was no party spirit in the work; it was deadly, merciless competition. There was no joking. The only sound was the continuous rapid-fire hammering as each man tried to outdo his neighbor. In the midst of the hammering, Otto's cry rang out from time to time.

"Nailing strip!"

Antto hacked away. The evening sun shining on the shingles bothered his eyes and the sweat running down his forehead made them sting. He hammered nails awry, threw them away, and now and then tossed down a bundle of shingles, growling, "Goddamn junk. Is wood so scarce here that you have to use bark strips for roofing?"

He found fault with the nails in the same way, seeming almost to challenge Jussi to argue. But Jussi made no attempt to defend his materials. He went on driving nails in the middle of the group, for he did not shine at this kind of work, where dexterity and speed were trump cards.

Halme, however, was upset when he saw the shingles being thrown down. He had his hands full getting enough of them up to the roof. And being careful was no help; he already had splinters in his fingers. In his shirt sleeves, he scurried to carry shingles from the pile and tie them to the rope. Sweating, almost pitiable in his clumsy scrambling, the man of intellect suffered his defeat on this hostile foreign ground.

"Why are you permitting the shingles to fall, Antto? It is evident that raising

24

them once is difficult enough."

"Just... up... goddamn... those sticks... damn... mm-mmm... umh... damned..."

Antto's voice trailed off into unintelligible mutterings, but he had taken note of Halme's unusual and prim rebuke.

As they approached the peak on the opposite side, Halme saw that they had enough shingles up above to finish the job, and, relieved, he went to wash his hands. Then he joined Alma, who was preparing the food at the primitive summer-kitchen. It was much more pleasant to chat with her here, praising her food as if in gratitude for the occasional delicacy he sampled in advance. He would pop the food into his mouth, not in a greedy or gluttonous way, but advisedly, deliberately weighing the choices, then taking a piece with the very tips of his fingers and conveying it to his mouth. As he chewed, Halme wore the look of one turned inward, concentrated on judging, and he concluded the tasting with a nod of approval to Alma.

"Truly exquisite."

Alma was pleased, for women considered Halme a great authority in many fields. He was also knowledgeable about foods, for his wife Emma cooked for banquets.

Preeti finished driving the last nails in the last row. Jussi would put on the capping boards later, but otherwise the roof was covered. The men climbed down. Their minds, numbed by the competitive frenzy, began to revive. Only Laurila continued being testy; he glared curtly, almost menacingly, at the others. The Lord had not even granted this poor man the gift of language as a means of escape from his shame. For in this company, a few appropriate words could have lessened the sting of defeat.

Otto's banter annoyed him particularly, though it no longer had anything to do with the competition. It was his easy, careless superiority, his all-encompassing glibness, that gnawed at Antto's mind.

For his part, Preeti was not the least bit upset. He had long since adjusted to his circumstances. He was humble and well-wishing and took a joke at his expense as a favor, not an insult.

As for Jussi, he was content. His house had got a roof. From the corner of his eye, he had kept watch to prevent waste in the heat of the competition. He had even managed to keep track of the fallen nails, determined to gather them up from under the eaves in the morning.

25

Alma had set up a table of boards laid over trestles of Jussi's making. She invited them to eat, and Jussi urged them on.

"So let's go now. Although it's nothing special... But what little there is..."

On the table were foods he hadn't even guessed at. Eggs and other things. For a second he frowned, but then his forehead cleared. Since the roof had been finished so quickly, Alma's trifling disobedience seemed acceptable. Actually, in hindsight, it seemed to be a good thing: the crew would have nothing to complain about now.

And Jussi became positively lordly. "Help yourselves. There are eggs... Eat them up."

Nevertheless, he was pleased to see food left on the table when the men rose.

V

The sun was setting.

A warm dusk suffused the new building's environs, but on the opposite horizon, the rim of a huge July moon promised new light.

A continuing rumble of talk rolled through the summer night.

"That's the way it is, all right. I pay two rent-days a week with horse for those goddamn strips of rock, and have to put in gift-days besides... It's real bad. You can just about scratch a living from them, and it's not much of a life, and money's so damned tight. If you get to take a kilo of butter to the village now and then, it all goes for coffee and sugar anyhow. Things've got to ease up or we're done for. And I still have to pay for food — a man has to take care of his parents — even when there isn't always enough food for a man's own table."

"We-ell now... It's different with Jussi. When this is done, he'll have it made."

"Goddamn it. I don't know. They're always bitching. That piss-ass had the nerve to come and tell me my horse couldn't keep up with his... I told him if it wasn't good enough, then goddamn, he could do without it. I can always leave, if nowhere else, then hit the road. And his old lady whining that the wool is no good. Five kilos we have to give them every year. She's a knucklehead too. But she takes after the family, those goddamn Hollo devils. They bleat out hymns on Sunday, and the rest of the week they whine that the help is eating them out of house and home and doing nothing. I wish lightning would strike that snooty

26

bitch."

This outburst from Laurila was directed at his landlords, the Töyrys. There was bad blood between them. Töyry had often threatened to evict Laurila, and would doubtless have done so already if he had not been deterred by a kind of family obligation: the Laurilas had been tenants of the Töyrys for generations.

Laurila was otherwise in a bad mood, and the brew had gone to his head, aggravating his temper. Preeti was drunk too, and while the better-endowed discussed matters that were beyond his reach, he kept up an endless jabbering.

"That's the way it is with men like us... with me and with you..."

His chatter was addressed to the more quiet and withdrawn among the men, those he felt to be his equals. While others spoke of their dwellings, their rent-work, their horses, Preeti's flat voice could be heard at intervals, repeating, "That's the way it is with men like us... with me and with you..."

Priitta's Kustaa also drank the home brew. Since the boy was only fourteen, Jussi was undecided at first about letting him drink, but Otto purposely served him.

"You didn't single him out from the crew on the roof, so he belongs at the barrel with the rest of us."

This wasn't really the cause of Otto's zeal; he simply thought it would be funny to get the boy drunk. But if he hoped to be amused, he was disappointed. Kustaa drank along with the others, but did not get as drunk as they did. There was also something manly about him in spite of his age. What little he said was addressed to the grown-ups as if he were their equal.

Jussi drank too, but only for the sake of appearances, so little that it had no effect. He responded to the drunken talk with the indifferent and evasive behavior of a sober man trying to hide his annoyance.

Halme also drank cautiously, each time gravely wiping his mustache. He spoke with such phrases as "taking this point into consideration" and "on the other hand." His efforts to initiate discussion of his pet topics were fruitless. The men did not respond. Only "the woman question" had just awakened the people from a sleep of centuries. But God help us, these men did not find it worth their while, and soon were bawling out such debasing comments that Halme could only cough and attempt a forced laugh.

When the tone of the conversation began to exceed Halme's level of toleration, he retreated into his dignity and tried to squelch the louts with a restrained,

27

condescending smile. When he spoke, he spewed out the "cultural questions of the age" over their burry heads. On that warm and dimly moonlit summer night, in the middle of a spruce wilderness in Finland, he beat his scurrilous foes about the ears with the "great Norwegians." But Ibsen and Bjørnson, mighty as they were, had more than met their match here. "Norwegians, heh, heh... the Norwegians are a small race that live in mountain caves and fish for herring."

Minna Canth was no help either, neither was Runeberg, although Halme recited a poem of his, one hand held high:

> My father was a soldier
> Young and handsome too
> At only fifteen years of age
> He stepped into the ranks.

Kankaanpää interrupted his poem by starting to sing:

> When I had scarcely reached fifteen,
> I killed my grandpa with an axe.
> And ever since, my home has been
> This famed hotel in Vaasa.

"I know only one woman who's in jail... That's Liisa of a Thousand Thrills from the village. She took Mellola's money, that is, she took a little extra. If the Norwegians want to liberate her, then let them, for all I care."

"Nowadays, the liberation of women means the shattering of the many prejudices that keep them enchained in modern society. Furthermore, it is only a part of the great social task of freedom and enlightenment that is occurring throughout Europe... It has now reached even these northern fringes, "these ragged border regions," as the great Elias Lönnrot says."

"That Loonroot guy died last year already ... that reciter of poetry...

> And the maid sat on the stone
> and the stone was smooth
> and the water washed over it...

"Free women. How in the hell are women any more slaves than anyone else?

28

Tenant farmers are bigger slaves than any women."

"Consider, for example, a woman's right to choose a marriage partner. Among the poor it's not such a sensitive question, since property plays but a small part there. But a landowner's daughter is married according to the amount of land owned."

"That stuck-up Hollo sure as hell didn't marry anyone of our kind... Those two of a kind found each other without any outside help."

"I'm speaking of women in common."

"Why not speak of common women?"

and when you knock three times on my coffin lid,
then I'll rise up and drink... tara-rara-ra'...

"Where's that jug that's going round?"

"Why shouldn't I speak of common women? They too are society's victims. Any number of poverty-stricken girls have been forced to sell their innocence for a piece of bread. But change is imminent. A tidal wave of nationalist uprising will smash the rotten rule of the Swedish-speaking landlords and businessmen. A new national education will create a new society."

"You damned fool, do you think your Finnish lord and master will squeeze you any less? If you get nowhere by working, is it because you're lazy and good-for-nothing? That's what they say. Aiee, by God... if I could only read the stars for those bastards just one time..."

"That's right. Everything stems from the lack of enlightenment. An uneducated people is helpless to defend itself. It's strange to imagine that young men who have the courage to fight with clubs, knives, and rocks, heads all bloody, don't dare go into a dark barn because they believe in ghosts."

Preeti laughed sagely, as if commending their sense of superiority from his own even loftier perch. Now he joined in the discussion.

"They say there used to be a house in Sääksmäki that had this ghost. If you stuck your ass into the chimney corner, it would hit you a smashing wallop with a block of wood. That's what they say. I don't know how true it is."

"And in Pouru too, this hired girl, they say she heard something ask 'What?' when she went into a dark room to close the damper. All she heard was 'What?' But the girl, who was a spirited one, said, 'Nothing at all. Just closing the damper.'

29

That's where they get the saying, 'Nothing at all. Just closing the damper,' said the hired girl from Pouru."

They laughed, for it was moonlight and they were not alone. Suddenly Priitta's Kustaa blurted out, "On Hell's Hill there's a naked man walking around with his head under his arm."

"Who ever saw anything like that?"

They were doubtful, since they were hearing the story for the first time. But Kustaa looked at them in a sullenly knowing way and said, "I don't know, but he sure is walking there."

Otto asked Kustaa if he had bought a gun yet, as he had been threatening to do.

"I haven't found a good one yet. I've got to have one that'll do the job. A popgun is no good on a bear hunt."

"Where are you going to shoot bear around here? The Czar of Pentti killed the last one thirty years ago."

"Maybe I know where to find them... and maybe I'm not talking... I think it's a good business. You get a big bounty for killing them and the hides are worth money too."

Laurila listened with a suspicious look in his face until he was sure the boy was joking. Then he growled angrily, "Stop it, boy. That's all just rubbish. Nothing but hot air."

The talking went on. The tenant's "sun" shone in the sky. It gleamed on the hewn wall timbers and the freshly shingled roof of the house. The clean, pleasant scent of fresh wood and pitch hung in the air, mingled with the fragrance of moss and new mortar.

A pale white mist floated over the swamp.

Halme was becoming fed up with the direction of the discussion. It always went astray. He tried once more to bring it back on the right track.

"The woman question views women chiefly as social beings. That women are also men's wives and mothers is another matter altogether."

"You seem to be keeping Emma only because of the woman question, seeing she's got no kids yet. Now Antto and I, we've settled our women's question the right way."

It was Otto Kivivuori speaking. Halme laughed off the joke, but Antto gave Otto a suspicious look.

30

"What's that supposed to mean?"

"You heard me, didn't you?"

Antto's anger suddenly boiled over. He had been in a foul mood all night. Now he started openly to pick a fight with Otto. A few threatening words followed. Otto's attitude of calm indifference added fuel to the fire.

"I mean... I tell you straight, I'm not going to listen to any more of that... You shoot off your mouth a little too much. I'll answer for my own children... If one of them isn't right, it shouldn't bother you."

"Of course not. You're the one who made him. Why should it bother me?"

Antto rocked his shoulders back and forth as he sat on the bench. "But you've blabbered around town that some piss went into his making. Or will you answer for your words?"

"I answer for my words all right, but I can't testify to that. You must know what stuff you made him of."

Otto was smiling, but watchful. The smile robbed Antto of his last shred of self-control. He rose.

"Goddamn it... don't you..."

In the dim moonlight nobody could see exactly what happened. Antto threw himself at Otto, but fell flat on his face as if his feet had been cut out from under him. Otto stepped back and let out an odd, strained laugh.

"Don't, Antto, don't... I mean it now."

Antto rose and renewed the attack, but Jussi appeared before him like a shadow. His voice shook slightly, not out of fear but anger. He was obligated, as master of the house, to play a part he detested.

"Calm down now, Antto... it... it's not right to start fighting here. Let's behave now. Drink your beer and go home."

Antto let out a smothered curse and tried to get by Jussi, whose arms held him fast. Then Kustaa Kankaanpää and Victor Mäkelä came to help him out by grabbing Antto's arms. They spoke soothingly to him but held on tight. Otto stepped farther off to avoid provoking Laurila by his presence. The men grunted with effort as they restrained Antto. Alma stood up and fluttered around nervously, but said nothing. She was afraid for Jussi, but understood that it was his duty as man of the house to stop the brawling. Halme stood hemming and hawing at a distance that was safe but not far enough off to be interpreted as flight. Trusting to his reputation as a mediator, Alma urged him to go and talk sense into Laurila, but Halme replied, "I believe words will not have the desired effect in this situation."

Preeti joined the group as well. Like one in authority, he took Laurila by the hand and said, "Listen now Antto, calm down and we'll go home together. I'll take you."

Preeti acted as if he had given the others a chance to do what they could, but seeing that their efforts were hopeless, had stepped in to settle the matter with a couple of words. But Laurila got a hand free enough to push Preeti away. "Don't you... goddamned lamebrain..."

Preeti's hat fell off. He picked it up and drew back. Frightened, Alma said to Preeti, "Don't get into it... stay away."

"I wouldn't care to touch him... I would have... by talking..."

Finally Laurila settled down enough to promise that he would go home, with Victor and Kustaa as escorts. It helped that it took three men to hold him. That, after all, made his position honorable in a way.

Priitta's Kustaa was still bellowing, "Hit him, goddamn, nothing else will do any good." But the boy's spirited words could be ignored.

The men left. Two or three others followed them. Otto and Halme still remained although Halme was saying his goodbyes. He took Alma by the hand, dumbfounding her with such gallantry.

"Thank you enormously. It was most pleasant. I wish you happiness as mistress of this home."

For Jussi's benefit, he delivered an actual little speech, hat in hand, and striking a pose whose dignity showed that despite the rabble's clamor, a gentleman does not forget his obligations. He left as a clergyman leaves the pulpit, making his departure an event, and not just slipping out the door like any common person.

"And thanks to you as well. It is my pleasure to wish good fortune for your new home. You have taken as your task pioneering in the material arena, so to speak, which is no less worthy than work on the spiritual level. Both are necessary, for hand in hand they lead people toward a brighter future."

Jussi grunted something under his breath, keeping a serious face so as not to hurt Halme, but fortunately an outburst of shouting some distance down the road spared him from answering.

"They're at it again."

The pacifying voices of the escorts reached their ears as a confused murmur,

32

but Antto's voice could be heard clearly.

"Goddamnit... You've no idea how much I've suffered... Son of a bitch. I'm attacked by lice and the world hates my guts, but I keep pushing right on."

Halme put on his hat and left. Otto took his leave too, but drank the remaining beer before going.

Halme walked toward the village through the woods, following what passed for a road. The moon was at its brightest since it was past midnight. The thick fir woods darkened the road, allowing only a few bands of light to fall across it. He found a stick suitable for a cane by the roadside. It fitted his mood at the moment. The moonlight lifted his spirits. The emotion he felt was an acquired one, a by-product of his erudition, created by the edifying and poetic spirit of the time. It was long ago that he had roamed this region as the Mäki-Pentti cowherd, a child who had been auctioned off. Somewhat timid and helpless, he had been a poor cowherd. Nor had he been given to horseplay with the local gang of boys, where a nose could be quickly bloodied. But the lady of the house took good care of her foster-child, for he was an exceptionally handy serving-boy. He even learned how to knit stockings and was clearly enthusiastic about the work, undisturbed by the laughter it evoked. His mistress had arranged for him to learn the tailor's trade, sending him all the way to Tampere, for the boy's skill and aptitude showed him to be fit for higher things than the career of an ordinary village tailor. Women said he would have been an even better preacher than a tailor, to which his days at the vicar's reading examinations, his days of glory, testified.

But he did not remain in Tampere. When his apprenticeship was over, he returned to his home village to be a tailor, bringing with him great skill at his trade, and in his head complete confusion, the mixed enlightenment gleaned from the library, the People's Society, the Friends of the Finnish Language, the Temperance Society, and from every possible free admission lecture series intended to educate the people. There were two reasons for his return. In Tampere, at the lectures, he sat completely unnoticed in a corner by the door, and since even greater men had been willing to go to the provinces first, why should not he, Adolph Alexander Halme, do so? The second reason was Emma, a skillful and humble girl, who revered her husband's erudition in full innocence, unaware that others found it slightly comic.

Well. Were the swine worth the pearls? Did it pay to speak of women's rights

33

to these people? They could think of women only as... Halme avoided the brutal popular phrase even in his thoughts, for his modesty was no product of education, but a genuine schoolmarmish sensitivity. What did the idea of nationality mean to them? The state of the Finnish language? Civilization?

But the moon shone beautifully.

> *In every hollow, on every point and islet*
> *I would like to build a home.*

Yes. Work for the future's sake was indeed worthwhile.

There happened to be a small hill near the parsonage main road, from which one could see the lake. Halme paused and stood there for a while in a statue-like pose. Something great and sublime stirred in his mind. A calm, serious, "world-historical" expression spread over his face.

> *Here, here is the land*
> *We can see it with our eyes.*
> *We can stretch out our hand,*
> *And point to the sea and the land,*
> *And say: Our beloved forefathers' land.*

Halme kept standing there. His hand, thrust straight out to one side, rested on the knob of his cane.

Then he started off, but suddenly he heard the hubbub of the drunkards ahead on the main road. He stopped, not wanting to meet them. He could hear Kankaanpää urging Laurila to go home, but Laurila was objecting.

"Goddamn, I'm not going home. Can't you fix me up with a woman now? I need a woman now."

"Now don't... Let's just go to see Aliina."

"No, let's go find a woman. I need one now."

At last the men got Antto to go with them, and their voices faded away. Preeti's was the last to be heard.

"That's the way it is with us. We can only suffer..."

When quiet was restored, Halme continued his journey. He humphed away the feelings caused by the men's talk and returned to his former mood. And his

34

expression, and the moon's, had something in common. An all-knowing, all-seeing, self-satisfied peace.

After Otto had left, Jussi and Alma went to bed. They spent the night at the new building, for it was warm and they did not want to leave the dishes and the other things unguarded. They carried bedding from the haystack at the edge of the swamp and spread it on the dirt floor of the main room. But before lying down, they looked over the building once more. They even walked a little way off to get a better view of the whole scene. It had not a thing wrong with it.

Alma gazed at the place almost dreamily, her hands thrust under her apron. She was in full bloom now. Her body was a little stocky; it was sturdy but not shapeless. The buttons down the front of her flaxen blouse were pulled taut, and the tightly-drawn sash of her apron accentuated the breadth of her hips. Her colorful summer head scarf was down around her neck.

"But it doesn't have a name yet."

"It does."

"What is it then?"

"It's Koskela." ('The Rapids')

Alma accepted the name. Even if she hadn't liked it, she would have accepted it, but she found it as fitting as her own choice, wisely kept and now forever to remain a secret: Kuusimäki ('Spruce Hill').

Lying in the hay, the couple exchanged a few words about the events of the night, mildly disapproving in tone. They were interrupted by Otto's song, echoing far down the road.

> *Matti's wife all weak and weary*
> *Wore her life out, passed away.*
> *Matti went to seek the pastor,*
> *To preach upon her burial day.*
> *If you bring a handsome cow,*
> *We'll find a fine grave for your wife...*

"Oh my goodness. And right in front of the parsonage."

"Where else?"

"But in other ways, he's a good man."

"I guess so...But the fight was his doing too. He should have known Antto

35

from way back. Teasing him for no reason, a man who doesn't understand the first thing about joking."

"Well. Here we are, sleeping the first night in our new home. A prayer is in order right now."

And Alma prayed, voicelessly mouthing the words. While she did, Jussi was silent out of respect for the prayer, but he did not join in.

CHAPTER TWO

I

The part of the house in which the main room was located was in livable condition before autumn. The other rooms could be completed when there was more time. A small temporary shelter was erected for the calf and the lambs. It was quite primitive, made of unbarked poles and roofed with sod.

New cropland came into being, a sizable plot, for Jussi worked only on the easily tilled deposits left by the brook. He grubbed away at the rapids for a week, a week of hard and heavy work. After raising a stone or two, his limbs twitched limply, and he was forced to sit down. It was a good thing no one was there to see.

But at last the rapids were conquered, and Jussi began to open a drainage channel, a task that was less strenuous. Still it was exhausting, killing work because it took so long. The job was so huge that he could not afford to think about it. His mind a blank, his whole being concentrated on the dull, repetitive rhythm of the work, he kept on digging. The channel advanced toward the swamp, reached it, and began to trench through it. Without taking grade levels, judging by sight alone, Jussi went on digging, and the water's cheerful flow showed its satisfaction with the result.

It was good that Jussi's mind was dead to any breadth of thought. He saw only the ditch, the black and muddy ditch, and noted, without conscious thought, that it grew longer day by day. His features were lifeless, a tired, taut furrow their only sign of expression. The blank stare of his eyes seldom showed a spark of life. Evenings he grunted monosyllabic answers to Alma's questions. There was no response to the last questions she asked in bed. He would fall asleep immediately.

One day an elderly man came out to see the work. He looked around and praised Jussi, but also gave him a sober warning.

"That's not the way to do it, my boy. You'll kill yourself before long. You won't feel it now, but wait until you get older."

Jussi did not argue. He may even have voiced agreement with the man, but only to make conversation. There was no conviction in his voice. Nobody knew what the future would bring so what point was there in thinking about it. He went back to digging, threw a clod to the edge of the ditch, and drew back the shovel more slowly than usual.

"Umh... well. That may well be true... who knows..."

Then he concentrated completely on his digging, a sign to the other that his presence was unwelcome. But even Alma began to cast worried glances at Jussi.

"You've gotten so terribly thin. You really ought to take it easier."

The only response was an irate mumble, not a word of it intelligible. But Alma was able to piece together a kind of answer: that Jussi in no way enjoyed abusing himself, but that making a go of the tenancy depended on one thing alone, and that was work.

Despite this assertion, Jussi derived some inexplicable sort of satisfaction from punishing himself. As he dug from morning till night, repeating the same rhythmic motion, he felt as if in some mysterious way his overtaxed body demanded that he continue. If he sat down from time to time, he was nervous and unable really to rest. He had to start working again. He was pleased, too, that Alma took note of his pain. His irritability in answering her questions was a mask for that feeling.

Before snowfall, the drainage ditch traversed the whole swamp. Black ridges of turf on either side showed that someone had been swinging a shovel there. And winter meant relief for Jussi. It was true that he spent the daylight hours felling trees in the swamp, but the days were shorter and the work easier. He had bought a carpenter's table and a few of the more important woodworking tools to work with in the evenings. First, he roughed out a sled with them, and then he started work on a wagon. He even bought an oil lamp since it made night work easier. The wheel of its wick, however, was in constant use. If, at any time, only a little light was needed, the lamp was turned down low. If Alma failed to do it, Jussi got up and lowered it, with a look and in a way that were a warning without words.

Winter passed and spring came. Jussi was again hewing timbers, this time for an outbuilding. During the summer it rose: barn, stable, wagon shed, and hayloft, all under one roof. There was no roofing-bee this time, but Otto was there again to help. The interior of the stable was left unfinished, for the horse would fit into the barn with the heifer and the lambs.

It soon became time to buy a horse, for it was not easy to borrow one during the summer, even from the parsonage. Otto knew of one that was for sale, but Jussi didn't exactly want to follow his advice in the purchase. Otto's own animals were an indifferent lot. The horses at Kivivuori had always been little mousy bays; Otto's father's had fed them sparingly and Otto didn't always see to it that there was fodder for them. And Otto's harnesses had already achieved a certain notoriety for being so patched up with rope.

Besides all that, the horse was being offered for sale by Victor Kivioja. He was a tenant farmer at Mäki-Pentti, although farming seemed only a sideline to his horse-trading and marketing jaunts. "I don't dare buy a horse from such a swindler," said Jussi.

"You're buying the horse, not the man. You may get it cheap... Check out the price first."

Well, they could certainly go and look at it. The two of them set out together. It occurred to Jussi that Otto might be an agent who had set things up in advance. He would have to be on his guard.

In fact, Otto had made no such arrangements. His reason for going along was much simpler. There would be entertaining talk along with the horse-trading, and a visit to town was a pleasant respite from sawing and hewing timber.

Victor Kivioja was still a young man, a boastful, fast-talking busybody, who punctuated his words with pointless floods of profanity. Between bursts of talk, he would suck on his mustache.

"This is such a damned good horse, you can't find a better one. I mean, look at her legs. Not the least thing wrong... And her disposition is like a human being's, by God. If you understand anything about a horse's teeth, then look at her mouth. She can chew roofing nails with that set."

Jussi ignored Victor's talk and looked at the horse. It was a quite ordinary-looking, medium-sized brown mare. Its stomach was slightly distended and its hoofs enlarged as if they wore wrappings. There were no external faults apparent in the animal, and its walk was completely normal. It seemed calm and submissive, even though Victor was tugging and jerking at its halter to make it seem spirited. It suited Jussi, who needed a work horse, not a bit-gnashing, head-tossing terror. Victor was mistaken in pushing the sale like a market swindler. His behavior awakened a healthy resistance in Jussi, to counteract the liking he was beginning to feel for the horse. The mare seemed exactly right to him.

"What kind of price do you want for it?"

Victor sucked on his mustache, pondered a minute, and said in an artificially hearty voice, "Two hundred and thirty. Count out the money and take it away."

A convulsive fit of laughter seized Otto. He roared as if he had never heard anything so funny in his whole life. When he was finally able to speak, he managed to say, "Well, no wonder you fleece so many at the fair. This shows you're no beginner at selling horses."

Victor was at a loss for words. He winked to his own detriment and began to bluster. "As I said, goddammit, you won't find a better horse. At two hundred and thirty I'm giving it away."

Otto laughed again and winked in turn at Victor to show his understanding of the latter's horse-trading ploys. A slight shake of the head signaled his astonishment and his downright admiration for the man's talents.

Jussi bent down to test the horse's hoofs. The animal submitted to his touch without the least bit of shying. A smile crossed his face. "Let's stop joking. Knock off a hundred. One hundred and thirty. That's more like it."

Now it was Victor's turn to explode. He let out a torrent of sound—scornful, indeterminate noises without a single intelligible word. He waved his hands and jerked at the halter to make the horse rear its head.

"They sell goats at that price, not horses. I mean, look at her mouth. If you buy this horse, you can say you're in the driver's seat."

"In the driver's seat, mmhmm... A hundred and thirty, though."

"Forget it...But let's say a hundred more."

Otto circled the horse slowly with a knowledgeable air, then looked askance at Victor as if looking for the key to this bargaining.

"Where would you really start talking seriously?"

Victor had warmed to playing the role of a hustler and made the first significant drop in price.

"I'll drop it thirty, but it's for a friend and I'll just break even."

Otto laughed again, but a shade less forcedly, to match the reduction of thirty markkas. But he still acted as if he knew that Victor was beginning with an unreasonable price, which he would later reduce in order to make the buyer think the horse was cheap even though the final price would be a stiff one. After some minutes of dickering, the price fell another twenty, and then still another ten. Jussi said little, but Otto, on the other hand, spoke up even more. He beguiled Victor into boasting about his shrewd deals. The prices he asked were made to seem mere showmanship, exhibitions of his art, not meant to be taken seriously.

"Toward the end, prices were really stiff when the Northerners started buying. Niittumäki said we should leave, that it didn't pay to buy at those prices. But I told him not to worry, that we should stay till the end. I noticed right away when the square began to empty. They had been working together, selling, but not buying, and they fixed the price as high as they could. And so they were left with horses on their hands. I said to Niittumäki, 'Now, Ansu, we'll get ourselves horses for nothing.'"

Otto shook his head and laughed, and Victor blustered, "I'm telling you, goddammit, that Victor Kivioja knows the score."

After that, the price dropped another ten marks. Then, following a serious and confidential exchange of words between Victor and Otto, the difference was split and the horse went at a hundred and forty-five markkas. Victor made a big show of the sale. He slapped his hand into Jussi's with tremendous force and said to Otto, "Let's clinch the deal. Break them apart."

Otto separated the clasped hands with a blow. Now the deal was official and irrevocable. And now Victor, still acting the horse trader, began to moan about the favorable deal Jussi had made. Under the influence of the groundless enthusiasm Otto had kindled in him, he still believed that he had led Jussi by the nose. He even imagined that Otto had been his agent in the matter.

"Now, Jussi, you made a deal you won't regret but I've done a stupid thing like I've never done before. This is the only time I've ever taken a loss. But let it go, since you're a friend. I'll get my own back at the fair."

Jussi mumbled something unintelligible about his satisfaction with the deal, but Otto waved aside Victor's words as if to say, "You can talk all you want, but we know you, Victor Kivioja."

That was Victor's last recompense. When the partners disappeared around the corner leading the horse, the sad and heavy knowledge that he had lost twenty markkas began to settle into his mind. He had known it all along, he hadn't forgotten his purchase price, but why had it seemed so insignificant?

"Well, let it go... I did the man a favor since he's so hard up."

Thus Victor settled the matter, approving it as a purely good deed. For he was a true tradesman.

Along the parsonage road went Jussi, pleased with the deal and the horse, which followed along without a single pull at the lead rope. It matched his pace as if it really did have a human mind. And Otto brought up the rear, whistling. Wherever the road ran close to the lake, he would skip stones, shouting, "By God, Jussi, look at that one. It hopped at least twenty times."

Jussi would grumble internally, "Hmh... just think of it... a grown man."

He had, however, slowly become aware that it was Otto who had made a success of the purchase. For a long time, during which they traveled at least a kilometer, he debated with himself about buying Otto a quart of liquor. He had already opened his mouth to speak several times, only to be cut off at the last second by the thought of all that the money could buy. Then the horse drew near and nuzzled his shoulder. Jussi felt a huge wave of well-being surge through him. That's a man walking there, leading his own horse. He's not just any old hired hand, but a man who owns a horse, a horse all his own, to whom he can say, "Well... don't get so close now."

"I... uh... I don't think I got such a bad deal on the horse."

"Think? I know you got him for next to nothing."

"Well, not all that cheap. But I could have paid more."

"You can't get one anywhere for that price now."

"Your talking helped me so much that I'm going to buy you a quart as commission..."

"Well, I'll be damned!"

Otto's voice and smile were so slyly knowing that Jussi was a bit offended. No matter what you said to him he was always the same.

But the bottle had been promised and Otto would get it.

II

Very little came of the work that evening. They tethered the horse, but frequently untied and walked her about. They could find no fault with her. For the rest of

42

the day, an inward smile lingered on Jussi's face. Alma brought out a piece of bread, and the horse nibbled it gently from her hand. She patted it, and the horse gave a lazy little whinny.

"So-o... that's our Liisa. Wha-at... Liisa...Wha-at..."

Jussi probed the horse's muscles again, an appraising look on his face. He was getting to be more and more satisfied.

At bedtime Alma asked, "Shall I make the bed?"

"Go ahead. I'll just go and move the horse's tether once more."

The master of the house was gone for an unnaturally long time. As he returned, he stopped in the yard for one last devout moment.

There she was, cropping the grass.

As Jussi stepped inside, they could hear, through the open door, the sound she made in blowing through her muzzle.

The sound made the half-finished home almost complete.

The wagon wheels were now shod with iron. Jussi enjoyed passing by the shed where he could see the wagon from the door, new and business-like. Some days he would pick up the shafts and pull the wagon out into the yard. What a sight it was for the two of them to look at.

And soon there could be heard around the house the inspiring sound of the wagon jouncing along, laying a track over the uneven ground, the base for what would later be the road.

A plow and a spike harrow also had to be bought, old ones to begin with. Everything cost money, and Lord knows what else they would need. A cow, certainly. Starting out with only one was hopelessly slow. The heifer would not calve before the following spring, and her offspring only after another two years. If it happened to be a cow. The dairy end of things would be expensive, no matter how much they cut costs.

The money held by the pastor had been turned over to them. What was left they had in safekeeping, not in the cottage, but under the sod in a cubicle of the potato cellar. As a container for it the pastor had given them an extraordinarily beautiful cigar box, with shiny pictures on the lid.

Much of the money had already been spent. Jussi kept counting the remainder over and over again, but the total did not increase. How could it possibly be enough? A plaguing, depressing anxiety took possession of him. Entering the cottage he saw Alma pouring milk into a pot of boiling potato chunks. The surprising anger in his voice made her start.

"Don't pour it out so recklessly. It's something we have to buy."

A hint of fear mixed with dejection appeared in Alma's eyes.

"Well, you can't call that much... You might as well leave it out altogether."

"Leave it out then... Soon all our money will be gone down that long blue road and that will be the end of our buying."

Alma did not answer. She gazed in silence at the fire, and Jussi left the room. But soon she was her usual placid self, and when Jussi eventually re-entered the room, he found her calmly setting food on the table. Nor did she mention what had occurred. As they ate, Jussi stared into his cup. His conscience bothered him a little, precisely because Alma was so calm.

Such exchanges were not very frequent, a fact which was completely to Alma's credit. She would fall silent rather than sustain them, and that usually made Jussi go off somewhere. In addition, there was much in life to celebrate, so that ill humor found only a small foothold in it. For example, the sowing of the rye, now taking place. It was the first at Koskela, a field of about two acres. Jussi looked upon it as his start in farming. Potatoes and last year's barley didn't count. Such crops could be seen around any shanty.

The pastor's offer of seed grain was a futile gesture of goodwill. Jussi was not about to plant the parsonage rye. The Vallén strain grown there was not good enough for the Koskela land: it had to be Töyry rye. Whatever that family might be, they knew their rye.

So it was with the Töyry variety in his basket that Jussi set out for the sowing. He hesitated a long time before taking an axe with him to the field. At its edge, he checked carefully to see that no eyes were watching. Then, as if winking at his own deed, he struck the axe, blade up, into the earth. Of course, there was nothing in that... but since it was the custom...

He always gave a little grunt of assent when someone made fun of the old ways, but he could not bring himself to ignore them. He would observe them, if only for the sake of custom.

Then he took off his hat, knelt, and clasped his hands. His prayer was improvised, its words a soft mumble. It was not an act of true devotion but there was great respect in it. The hope for a good harvest was no laughing matter. It was best to do everything possible to assure its success.

After the markers were in place, the seed began to fly out over the land. Its distribution was neat and even. The slight, nervous twist of the sower's mouth showed how seriously he took his work.

Then he looked over the sown land. He had done all he could.

Now it was God's turn.

During the course of the summer, the pastor had begun to nose around Jussi's work areas more and more. In his own lazy way, he had become enthusiastic about his tenant's projects. Lately, he had been experiencing life increasingly as a process of slow decay, a journey down a dead-end path, but now he seemed to revive. The familiar routine of the parsonage no longer interested him, nor was there reason for him to exert himself. An assistant had taken over his duties almost completely. On special holy days he preached flat, almost absurdly monotonous sermons, at which the parishioners secretly laughed. Yet he was generally popular just because of his benign and indulgent idleness, which spared them excessive harassment.

His children were full-grown and had risen to good positions in life. They no longer needed anything from him. One was a vicar, another a judge, and a third a railway engineer, busy building the railroads that were now reaching out in every direction. His daughter was married to a high official and living in Helsinki. They were all of higher status than he, in truth a member of an educated and clerical family, but now rusticated in his parish, a process his natural indolence had greatly abetted.

Indeed, without his rank and office, he would have been, even in Jussi's eyes, a slack old man who suffered from shortness of breath.

But it was pleasant to sit here and watch how things progressed. Something new always turned up. Yes indeed... that's how this country of ours... indeed.

And to all of Jussi's questions and requests, he gave an invariable answer: "Johannes can go right ahead and do it. Of course you can... Do as you think best."

And Johannes did. He had learned to be indifferent to the pastor sitting there and continued to work while he answered questions. The pastor's nearness no longer bothered him or interfered with his labor. His eyes devoured the extent of the swamp greedily. Since he had permission, he would take it all.

But he had to concede some of his time to the pastor, who would peer out toward the edge of the swamp through his failing eyes and ask, as if talking

45

to himself, "What's that now... what is that? That can't be a fox."

Then Jussi would have to look and explain, "No, it's our heifer."

"Is that so... Is that so. Now I thought... How could it look like that... My eyes are getting weaker... So. I'm getting old. I'm getting old."

"So it is... That's the way it is... for sure."

"So it seems... How old are you?"

"I've turned thirty."

"Is that so. You were just over ten when you came to the parsonage. In those lean years. It was the first one if I remember... It's almost twenty years ago." The pastor paused to breathe heavily. "Do you remember those times?"

"Ye-es.... Very well. There was so much snow. Up to my armpits in some places. Then I found a dead body by the roadside... I could see only some bright-colored cloth, and it was a woman with her child. They were both dead..."

"Well, those were terrible times. Almost twenty years ago, now. Ya-ah. That's how the years pass... into eternity, or wherever they go."

"That must be... for sure... they...."

The hoe rose and fell; the words were only tangential. The pastor rose to leave, but must have moved too suddenly, for he clutched a birch sapling and sat down again.

"Oh dear, what's this?"

The pastor pressed his hands to his chest and gasped. Jussi stepped closer to him and asked in an uncertain voice, "Is the pastor sick?"

"No-o... not really, but I felt dizzy. And my heart... What can it be... I must have eaten too much."

The look on the pastor's face belied the understatement of his words. He avoided Jussi's eyes, a strange, inward stare in his own.

"Can I help you?"

"No. I think I can... Or maybe just to get me started..."

Jussi took hold of the pastor's arm and helped him to rise. He felt very strange leading the man he was used to looking at from a distance with almost fearful respect. He was nearly ashamed to find himself acting as guide and leader on this journey. By now the pastor's attack had actually subsided, but Jussi's support afforded so much relief that he was allowed to continue, half carrying the old man, who leaned limply against his shoulder. It came to Jussi as an almost staggering revelation that the pastor was only a fat and gasping old man. As he led him, the individual features of the pastor's person were revealed in all their mundaneness: He had extraordinarily small feet for his large and sturdy trunk, and they were barely noticeably pigeon-toed. His legs were bowed just enough to match the toe-in. His fat cheeks sagged loosely under his beard, and at the corner of his mouth there glistened a drop of saliva.

These perceptions frightened Jussi, but they seemed to demand his scrutiny. The pastor's words were commonplace too, meaningless babble punctuated by gasps. They were intended to ward off silence, which would have heightened the odd feeling born of such close contact.

It was not, however, necessary for him to drag the pastor all the way to his destination. Halfway there, he said he could go on alone, and Jussi stood still long enough to make sure that the old man could manage. When he had disappeared around a bend in the road, Jussi returned to his work. The pastor's recent loss of dignity made him seem more of a human being, and what is more, an old and sick human being who could die at any time. The thought gave rise to anxious uncertainty. Until now, he had somehow overlooked the fact that the land did not belong to him. Now he realized that it was not even the pastor's land; it belonged to the congregation. The pastor's words and promises, even the papers he drew up, were binding only upon him. They would in no way bind his successor.

Once begun, the worry afflicted him continually. Back at work with the hoe, Jussi felt its weight. The work itself seemed somehow uninspiring now. But then by itself his mind began to build pathways to hope. If he were able to save the money, he could some day buy this land. If they would sell it. Somehow he propped up his hope with the notion that congregation land would be easier to buy than private property, that the elders might agree to sell it.

At first the idea was only a compulsive antidote to the worry and discouragement that had possessed him. Then gradually it began to sprout and grow into a secret plan in which he could take refuge when assailed by doubts. And why should a new master of the parsonage treat him any differently from this one? However, he could not be sure, and the hidden doubt continued to gnaw at his mind.

At any rate, one thing was certain. The work had to go on, and Jussi did not let up. Yet, little by little, the doubt became a fixed attitude, a background pressure affecting his entire life. The pastor's health became as constant a concern for

47

Jussi as for the pastor himself.

Nor did the pastor succumb to death quickly. He still came often to Jussi's work site, but each time Jussi could see that his step was short and his breath even shorter.

Autumn brought more ditches and more tilled land. The clearing spread along the brook, and the first open patches appeared along the edges of the swamp. A cow was purchased, one with calf and therefore expensive, but that sting was soothed by the birth of a she-calf. There were now three cows in the barn, and the sheep's pen already supplied them with wool. There was no lack of fodder. The brooksides and the flood land grew abundant hay.

The sense of belonging grew stronger.

III

The third year, a threshing barn and sauna were built. And now the most indispensable buildings were up, although not actually completed. The bake-room was still without a floor, as was the room back of the entry, but little by little what was missing would be supplied. The heifer calved in the spring and there were now two milking cows in the Koskela barn. They carted butter to sell in the village, and that was the extent of their small income, except for Alma's wages, which scarcely sufficed to buy food. A suckling pig was acquired that year, but they had no grain to feed it. They gathered water plants from the brook for it, and the result was a long-haired, tough-skinned beast.

The cigar box had already been brought indoors. It was no longer worth hiding since it was empty. Although Jussi had tried to make everything he possibly could by himself, many things still had to be bought. A horse, a cow, hardware for the wagon and sled, a harness, tools — they all cost money, and the cigar box had been emptied for them. And they still did not have everything they needed. To top it all off, Jussi's rent-work began that year, and though it was actually only one day a week, and that without a horse, it was a day lost from his work at home.

There was cause for joy as well. The first rye crop succeeded extraordinarily well. The virgin land poured its long-dormant strength into the first crop despite scanty manuring. Although Jussi lay awake on every coolish night his restless

48

mind jumping between hope and prayer, what he feared most did not materialize. Despite the nearness of the swamp, which was only beginning to be drained, they were not visited by frosts.

The rye ripened in abundance. After they had set aside the seed-grain and judged how much they would need for food, they realized they could sell a little. Jussi made frequent trips to the threshing barn, ran the grain through his fingers, and studied the kernels.

"Never in my life have I seen kernels like that," he said to Alma.

"Well, are you satisfied now?"

"Oh, we could have gotten more."

Yes. A silent gnawing greed followed Jussi to the grave. But Alma found in his words a pretext for a revelation she found hard to make.

"There won't be too much of it... if we have more mouths to feed."

For some reason, Alma blushed as she spoke. At first Jussi did not understand what she meant, but then it dawned on him.

"More... mouths..."

"That's right."

It wasn't really a surprise. They had talked it over often and decided to take no precautions, as Jussi reluctantly gave in to Alma's wishes. He would have liked to postpone things, so that Alma could go on working. Finally faced with the fact, he was not entirely happy. Her face a blank, Alma waited for his reaction.

"So... Are you sure?"

"I'm positive."

"When do you think it'll come?"

"Some time in the spring."

"Mhmm... Mhmm... Well, you can still work pretty far into the winter."

Alma's breast shook slightly with a laugh that she wisely concealed. She had expected a warmer response from Jussi, but realized how absolutely characteristic his remark was. She said calmly, "Why not? Of course I can."

In bed that night they reopened the discussion.

"Does it bother you?"

"What?"

"That... that we're going to have a child."

"No-o... Why should it... It's about time."

Once accustomed to the thought, Jussi was perfectly happy with it. It was

49

pleasant to think of a child, and as a pioneering farmer he could think of it only as a boy.

"And Liisa is finally going to have a colt. Seems to be catching around this farm."

Alma rocked with laughter. Her laugh always came easily but almost silently. She said nothing more. It was as if she were alone with her happiness. Her laugh was usually simple and innocent like that, a spontaneous overflow of happiness, which was not at all marred when Jussi said in a worried voice before they fell asleep, "What are we going to live on without your income?"

Alma was not one to take things lightly, but she was confident. Life would not come to an end with the birth of a child; only then would it really begin, she thought.

Now and then the couple heard what people in the community were saying about them. Someone even tattled to Alma about a woman who had asked Otto if they had any furniture in their home. Otto had replied, "She has Jussi and a whittling block."

Alma did not repeat the story, but began to press for a chest of drawers for the back room. At first Jussi did not even consider her request worth a grunt, but as her pregnancy advanced, his opposition weakened. He had started to ask about her health more and more apprehensively. Finally he agreed to buy the chest.

The secret power of the pregnancy had bowed Jussi's stiff neck. He feared it as a child of nature fears those powers against which he is helpless. The chest of drawers was an outright sacrifice to a phenomenon developing under its own power. It neither asked his permission nor cared about him. So Alma got her chest, the cabinet-maker his money, and Jussi some kind of temporary relief.

For a while that winter he worked for wages. They were cutting logs in the Kylä-Pentti woods, and Jussi got a job hauling them to the shore with Liisa. And that same winter the Czar of Kylä-Pentti died. He had had a number of heart attacks but refused to rest or seek a doctor's care. Growling and cursing, he banished the son who suggested such measures. The younger man, brought up under his strict regimen, humbly obeyed, his age and status as the head of a household notwithstanding. At the logging grounds the old man prowled around and observed. He kept asking Jussi questions and growling his approval.

"Is that mare there going to foal?"

50

"She is. She finally got that way after four tries."

"Is that so. And your wife too. Or what's this I hear."

"Well... heh, heh... Well... yes... something like that."

"I'll come out to see in the summer."

"Do come. Or come right away... some Sunday."

"I'll come in the summer like I said."

The old man barked a little when Jussi tried to set a time himself, but two days later he died. Standing alongside a logging road, he saw a young hired hand drive so carelessly that the sled caught a runner on the side of a tree.

"Look what you're doing, you goddamned bull-calf. Can't you drive a horse yet you bastard?"

The old man took two angry steps, but dropped at the third, and died right there. Afterwards, Jussi would gladly talk about the dead man. "There aren't many of his kind left. His hoeing and shoveling were really something."

In Jussi's opinion there was really only one of his kind left.

Liisa was in fact with foal, and Jussi drove her carefully. During the day he was afraid for his horse, and going home at night the fear that something might have happened there gnawed at his mind. By now he was used to expecting almost anything when he opened the door, but he would sigh with relief when he saw that his fears were unfounded.

Not until Easter Sunday did it happen. Hat in hand, Jussi started out for the village on the run, with traces of rye porridge at the corners of his mouth. The onset of labor pains had interrupted their eating. Nevertheless he stopped running when the first houses came into view.

Luckily Priitta was at home. She was a somewhat mannish woman, gruff, and outspoken. Jussi's agitation was mixed with a slightly fearful awe of her as he stepped inside.

"It's... could Priitta come over right away?"

Priitta gave him an appraising look.

"Well, what's going on there?"

"Er... I think... I think it's the time now. If you could come right away... so that nothing..."

"Hmhh... Don't choke now, my good man... They don't come through that gate in such a hurry."

"Well... heh, heh... but if something..."

51

"Well, when did the pains start?"

"Just now."

"Then what are you jabbering about? You go on ahead. Don't worry. I'll be coming."

Priitta was in no hurry, and Jussi started for home. Once in the woods he started to run again, but his eyes were on the road, watching for the horse manure that had come into view with the thaw. Only at home did he look up, trying to decide by the building's appearance what had happened there.

But nothing had. Alma was sitting in her usual place on the bench.

"Doesn't it hurt any more?"

"Not all the time... light a fire and fill the pot with water."

Jussi started to fuss with the fire, but it would not kindle. Now what was the matter? Alma came over and said impatiently, "Go away... I'll do it."

Jussi tried to help but was completely inept. Little by little Alma's pangs increased in frequency and severity. Jussi kept asking so incessantly how she was feeling that he finally made her nervous. Then he began making trips to the corner of the threshing barn where he could see farther down the road.

"Where is that woman dawdling?"

Peering down the road for the third time, he saw Priitta trudging along, her hands thrust beneath her apron.

"If you could hurry... they're getting worse."

Priitta threw him a scornful glance.

"You've really been mucking around here. I haven't been here since the first summer. That threshing barn is all new."

"It is... they're getting worse... all the time."

"And you've rooted up the whole swamp like that. You're quite a badger."

On the one hand, Priitta's calmness soothed Jussi. But even so, this was not the time for these questions.

Priitta stepped inside.

"A-hah.. Quite a room you've got... So you finally got what you wanted."

Alma tried to smile, but the pain twisted her face into a grimace. Priitta sat down and looked around.

"Grumpy there seems to have got things done, all right. I didn't think the devil of a burr-head could make a baby, but it sure looks that way."

One had to smile at that kind of talk. It was Priitta's prerogative. She was raw and direct, but without malice, and people sensed it. To answer in kind would have been useless, for she had no weak spots.

Even otherwise, Jussi could not in his present state of mind take offense. Priitta's arrival had eased his fears. She seemed literally to be some kind of guardian angel who dispelled his own sense of helplessness.

Between pains, Alma tried to talk to Priitta, who was starting her own preparations.

"Where are your scissors?"

Somewhat abashed, Alma looked at Jussi.

"We haven't got any scissors. We use the sheep-shears for any cutting we do."

"Hmh... Well, get them at least."

Jussi brought the shears to her. When they squeaked as she worked them, he felt a nasty shiver run through his whole body, and he muttered in an embarrassed voice, "The way it is... we didn't get any... we need so many things..."

Alma looked down at the floor. She was a little ashamed of having no scissors.

"Uh-huh. You get into that bed now. And you go outside and stay there, but within shouting distance in case I need some help."

For a long time, Jussi paced around the yard. He cleaned the manure from the stable, turned the sled around, and busied himself with a variety of needless tasks. He heard no sounds from inside, for Alma considered it a matter of honor to give birth without crying out. When Priitta appeared on the threshold to summon him, there was a touch of gentleness in her stern and severe voice. "Now, come on in."

Alma lay exhausted on the bed. She responded wearily to Jussi's shy smile.

"Which is it?"

"A boy."

Alma's reply was a whisper, and the word trailed away. There it lay in its wrappings by its mother's side, its eyes closed, not making a sound.

"Is he healthy?" Jussi asked Priitta.

"He is. And a real bull-calf. He must weigh at least ten pounds. Hands like a lumberjack and balls big enough to go courting right now."

Jussi felt like laughing, not so much at what Priitta said as from a sense of relief and release. Priitta ordered him to leave Alma alone and to help her with the household chores.

53

"I suppose I have to milk the cows too," Priitta said.

"Well, if you would, though I guess I could do it."

Priitta prepared a meal, grumbling at Jussi about the scarcity of ingredients. "A woman who's given birth needs something to eat."

Then Jussi began to explain. "We don't happen to have any coffee right now."

"Don't happen to? 'Happen' has nothing to do with it. You damned skinflint, you could buy that poor woman a pound of coffee now and then. You work her like a horse, and the poor thing doesn't even get a drop of coffee to put in her mouth."

"Well, if I got some tomorrow...you could come and have some."

"I have coffee and I always do. But I'll have Kankaanpää get some; he's going to the village. You just give me the money."

After having eaten, Alma revived a little and was even able to take part in the conversation. The setting sun of Easter day gilded the room. Outside, the crust of the snow began to harden with the evening cold, but the icicles on the eves were still dripping. A dazzlingly bright blue sky foretold the coming of spring.

When Priitta had left, Jussi sat down at the foot of Alma's bed. The child set up a faint wailing and waved his fists.

"What is it, Akseli?"

"So, he has a name already?"

"He's had it for a long time. It's Akseli Johannes."

Alma did not argue. She soothed the child as naturally as if she had been doing it all her life. A smile flickered constantly across her pale and sunken features. Jussi sensed that the smile was not for him, no, not even for the child, but was completely self-contained. It had no reference to any ordinary, sensible fact. It had in it something that resembled the spontaneous bright bliss of that translucent Easter night.

The fulfillment of her long-cherished hopes shone in Alma's brown-eyed, country-girl face. A half-undone braid lay on her breast, which swelled mighty under her flaxen blouse.

"Now, look at that little fist."

Jussi smiled. A silly, bewildered smile.

54

The following days were spent in a rare flurry of celebration. Priitta brought coffee, and that in turn brought the womenfolk to see the child. They were Alma's acquaintances from the days before her marriage. They came rather shyly, avoiding Jussi, for he had created a breach between them and his wife. Alma, on the other hand, was pleased. For once, she was on the same level with the rest. She could offer them coffee, and lying there in bed, she could talk to them in her calm, level voice about everything under the sun. The women praised her, the child, and the fields to the heavens, doing justice to Jussi in the latter.

Jussi was something of an outsider in this group and was not happy with the situation. But he had to put up with it for Alma's sake. In addition, Priitta stayed at the house those first days, and in her presence it was best to behave the way she would expect him to. Priitta had worries of her own. Her Kustaa was full of the devil. He had bought a gun and talked nothing but strange hunting stories. He had quit confirmation class, and the pastor had even threatened her.

"I'm having such a hard time with that boy. Why did I get mixed up with that damned old man when I was already an old woman. I had gotten along fine without him until then, so what lighted that flame? He just kept on petting and patting until he coaxed me into that last craziness."

In a few days Alma was up and around. And as Priitta's visits ceased, so did Jussi's offerings of coffee. He reverted to form and took tight control of their household affairs. The visitors disappeared, and he took the bag of coffee into his own keeping.

"There's got to be some left for the christening, too."

It didn't matter much to Alma. The child was more important to her than a bunch of old women and a bag of coffee. Humming contentedly, she went about her chores, and Jussi's displays of temper could not draw from her more than a few indifferent words. And the boy brought them closer. He was like a channel through which many familial emotions could flow more freely.

Then began the discussion of the child's godparents. They thought of the pastor but did not have the courage to ask him. Finally, they settled on Otto and Anna, although Alma had some doubts about Anna's attitude.

"Because she's a bit high-and-mighty. She thinks she's a little better than others because her father owned a farm."

They decided on Otto and Anna in the end, and Anna's pride was nowhere to be seen. She was completely friendly, and Alma's slight shyness, caused by her sense of inferiority, soon vanished.

On their return from the parsonage, however, Anna was in a sad and silent mood. She gave no reason for it, but Jussi and Alma guessed Otto to be the cause. Anna refused to speak to him, and the looks she sent his way were hurt and angry. Otto must have been sounding off to the pastor.

When, as was natural at a christening, they spoke of children, Anna sighed:

"Yes, we bring them into this world, but this is a difficult path to travel to God's kingdom."

"Is there some kind of shortcut then?" asked Otto, but Anna only pursed her lips as a clear indication of her refusal to answer.

When the godparents had left, Alma sighed. "It can't be easy to live with that Otto. There was so much talk when they got married. Everybody said Anna was lucky to get such a good-looking man. But good looks can cause problems too."

"No question. But she looks as if an angel's breath would blow her over. And a tenant's wife sighing like that... Nothing at Kivivuori was good enough for her. They started to slap paint on the window frames and to dig up the yard like a chicken had been scratching there. Root-crops and flower-bushes around every rock."

"Is it some kind of sin to have nice things around you?"

Alma's tone of voice displayed a slight hint of the women's question.

"He's such a good child," Alma would say, which was partly true, but not completely. Akseli might lie for hours in his bassinet, following with his eyes the little happenings that fell within his range of vision, a fly's progress across the side of his bassinet, for example. But when he gave vent to his anger, the fit was long and violent. At only two months of age, his little body would rise in an arch and jerk rigidly, showing how completely his rage possessed him.

In such circumstances, Jussi was at a loss. At last he would growl, in spite of the fact that the boy was still in his diapers. "Stop yowling now, or there'll be trouble."

For the most part he wisely avoided being a nursemaid, but he had to be one when Alma went to work. Fortunately, no one was present to witness his fussing

56

with the child. Singing, for example, had never been one of his strong points, but in a panic, he would try even that. If the boy listened, it was only because the noises he made were so astoundingly peculiar. He did not take the boy up into his arms lightly, and when he did, he held him clumsily, afraid of dropping him. When Alma appeared, he handed the boy to her as if freed of his greatest burden.

In the summer they had to take the child to the fields with them. They kept him nearby in his basket and checked from time to time to be sure that no snake would enter his mouth and go down his throat—such things were said to happen.

Whenever they found time from the field work, the building of fences, the hay-making, and other urgent work, they cleared new land. Jussi dug ditches and Alma hoed. The strips along the brook lengthened. Clearing the swamp was left for later; right now they needed food grains, and for those, the brook's clayey banks were suitable. Closer to the woods there were stumps, and these they had to pry up together. They sometimes called on Liisa's strength for help. Both the woman and the mare had offspring along at the work site, for a colt exactly like Liisa wandered the fields on his clumsy, tottering legs.

They took their noon-hour rest at the work site, for to save time Alma brought their lunch with her to the fields. The family gathered in some shady spot for the meal, and Liisa was turned loose to graze nearby with her colt. The meals were monotonous, and when they were nearing the end, with only scraps remaining, Jussi would stop eating.

"You finish the rest... I'm not hungry."

"No, you eat it... I don't want any more."

"Eat, just eat... We're not going to take that amount home."

Neither of them found the last bits of food tasty, and each tried to palm them off on the other. Their fencing continued until Jussi was on the verge of anger. At that point, Alma would finally eat them. Afterwards, Jussi would lie down to rest, and Alma would lean against a tree, her child at her breast, gazing off as if in a dream. Work had aged her. Her once round cheeks were weathered, sunburned, and angular. The translucent white of her full breast, which the child's fingers were squeezing, formed a sharp contrast to the brown neck and face. Perspiration had traced grooves in the dust from hoeing which had settled on her neck.

What was she dreaming of? Of nothing. Her eyes took in images of the

57

surrounding scene, but those images gave birth to no thoughts. Her weariness actually felt sweet. At times like this, Alma's being seemed withdrawn into itself. Contentedly it accepted itself and the world around it and found them good. She responded to the tranquil summer day with the same quiet restfulness as the earth itself breathed out. Over there the drainage channel ran through the swamp, its dirt banks now covered with a thick growth of hay. At the edge of the swamp were a few strips with a cover of thick green oats. On the other side of the ditch stretched the rye field, and nearby was the new clearing with its turf, its half-dry ditches, and its piles of stumps. The wooden fences surrounding the fields shone in their newness; only the older sections showed a touch of gray from exposure to rain and sunshine. The buildings formed a group of their own at the edge of the woods, and Alma's eyes seemed almost to be conscious that no one was there. Around the buildings and the yard reigned the stillness of a summer noon, broken only by the soft buzzing of the flies.

Nearby could be heard the stamping of Liisa's front hoof when she stopped eating and raised it to scare off the flies. Vilppu, the colt, was lying down. Somewhere beyond the fence were the cows and the calves. The boy was nursing, but lazily now, stopping at times, then eagerly starting over again, only to slack off shortly. His small hand was now using the breast only as a plaything which had to be pinched a little.

Then the boy stopped sucking altogether and let the breast fall from his lips. His mother started and began to gaze into the child's eyes, her expression changing from a dreamy to a smiling and soulful one. Akseli watched her for a time with a child's peculiarly searching, almost appraising look. Then his mother's smile was reflected on his face, and he began to intone busily, "Brrr... rrr... brrr..."

"Ye-es... he's driving a horse... mama's little boy is driving a horse... the little man is driving Vilppu... mama's little man... darling little horseman..."

Jussi awoke from his stupor and the mood changed again. Akseli was taken to the bassinet, where they managed to pacify him, and the grown-ups began to work. Sluggishly at first, their bodies still slack from their lunch-time rest, but soon tenaciously, relentlessly toiling. When Akseli began to whimper after sleeping a while, Alma dropped her hoe, hurried to the bassinet, and gave him suck.

Tirelessly, rhythmically, and by now with the precision of a machine, Jussi opened the ditch. Alma returned to the hoe, settling her breast beneath her tow shirt, stretching her back a little, but with her eyes already fixed on the hoe handle.

V

Thus their life passed in isolation, although they actually lived close to the village. Except for rent-days, Jussi Koskela seldom appeared among the people and Alma even more seldom. On occasion, he was seen driving through the village, sometimes toward the mill with his few sacks of grain on the wagon, sometimes hauling some other kind of load. Children ran eagerly to the roadside, for a colt was bounding along behind the wagon, and that was always a source of interest.

"What's his name?"

"Vilppu."

Jussi answered in a kindly voice, for he was pleased by their interest. And the colt stood tossing his head and sniffing at the children. Sometimes he would let himself be patted, but then he would start off suddenly and gallop to his mother's side with his hindquarters bobbing. The children shrieked with delight, and Jussi's stubble-bearded face wore a pleased smile.

The two cared little about the community, which in turn was unconcerned about them. Sometimes they saw Priitta's Kustaa passing their work site. He was halfway to manhood already, a big lout who did no work at all. Out of her scanty funds, Priitta had bought him a shotgun. With the weapon slung on his back, he wandered around hunting, not bothering to ask if it was hunting season or whose land he was hunting on. He would pass Jussi and Alma about twenty meters off, his lips pursed importantly, and disappear into the line of trees opposite as if heading for some great and meaningful destination.

News from the village gave rise to only brief exchanges between Jussi and Alma. Each topic was quickly pegged in its appropriate place. A maidservant had had a child. They agreed that such things happened. The baron had imported a bull and two cows from abroad, from England supposedly, although some said from Sweden. The more knowledgeable said that they had really been brought in from Sweden, but that the breed was originally English. A new steward had arrived at the manor, he too from Sweden. All the manor's farming and dairying practices were to be modernized. This news caused the community to grumble in sullen malice.

"It'll be the same kind of modernization as with the pasture rule. The tenants can pasture their cows only on that damned rocky hill. They eat and trample the seedlings in the woods... Well, I guess... And that goddamned Swede rides

59

around spying on you behind your back... If this kind of modernizing goes on for long, who knows where it'll end."

The Koskelas were spared such harassment. They could live almost as they pleased on the parsonage back land. The pastor still came to see them now and then, but he dismissed questions of wood and pasturage with a wave of his hand. All such matters had lost their importance in his life.

But one day the north wind blew, and died down completely in the evening. That night the couple did not sleep, and toward morning they saw the ground blanketed with frost and a white mist hovering over the swamp.

Jussi stood in the yard looking out over the field. Alma did not grieve for the rye, which was now dying. The grain was at the milk stage and there was not the least doubt about what would happen. She wept as she looked at the expression on Jussi's face. It was an inward, silent, unseen weeping. If he would only say something. But he didn't. Nor did she dare to speak.

She went inside and stood looking out the window. She could hear his words plainly when they finally came. They were words like "hell, goddamn, son-of-a-bitch."

Then he came in. Without saying a word or looking at Alma, he went to the bed and sat down. She watched him in secret and pitied him, sitting, staring into the corner with a stiff, strained face. She hoped he would say something; she herself did not dare. Finally, the bitter words came, "It's the end for us."

"But we haven't lost everything." Alma tried to speak as calmly as possible, afraid that contradiction would anger Jussi. And indeed it did. Knowing that her effort at consolation was meant to make the loss seem less than it was, he began with a caustic snicker:

"Sure... Very likely... Certainly not. It's easy for you to talk. But think about it a little. It's the only income we have. It would have brought in a few pennies, but now we'll even have to buy our own bread. And what will we buy it with, with no income? That's a fine way to talk."

"But we'll have to make do somehow. You'll have to find work somewhere."

"Yes. And when I'm gone who will do the work around here? It won't do itself."

Alma knew that Jussi was exaggerating the misfortune. She looked down and murmured quietly, as if to herself, "I don't think there's reason to be so downhearted. And we'd better not complain about God's decrees."

"God's decrees? What harm have I done to God? Haven't I tried to do my best? Does he have nothing better to decree than taking everything from someone who's worked himself half to death?"

Alma looked up. In a calm but decisive voice, she said, "Say what you will, but that's going too far. You'd better think about what you're saying."

She rose from the bench, went to the stove, and started to light the fire. She no longer looked at Jussi, but concentrated her whole attention on the chore. Jussi was silent for a while, then went to the window and began gazing out. Akseli woke up. Alma took him into her lap and began to prattle as if deliberately putting what had happened out of her mind, in a tone of heartfelt intimacy that carried this message: let's leave him alone; we don't care whether he sulks or not.

Finally, Jussi gave in. Cursing God was an action too drastic for one of his nature, and he began to qualify his recent words, blaming the swamp as if it were that which he had been cursing.

"What do I know about God... It wasn't God's decree... It was the swamp that did it... But if it thinks I'm going to quit, it's mistaken..."

Then he went out, but said from the doorway as if to punish Alma, "It means we have to match our mouths to the size of the sack, that's what it means."

Alma became even more absorbed in fondling the child.

That entire morning he was silent. The two did their chores, ignoring each other. Only toward evening did he ask, "Is that rake missing any teeth?"

"Yes, a couple of them are gone, I seem to remember."

Alma's reply contained no reminder of what had occurred, and so they made a fresh start. That whole evening her voice was unusually gentle, which softened Jussi's state of mind, even though the day had confirmed the almost total ruin of the rye.

Jussi's deep embitterment had sought strength from the very bottom of his soul. Man builds his world on the foundation of his defeats. The household's expenditures had already been cut to a bare subsistence level, but now Jussi set out to keep an even closer watch over them. Alma did not resort to quarreling, but tried in her own way to keep the frugality from becoming insane. They still had to eat if they expected to work.

That fall the snow came late, and Jussi ditched the swamp. He dug as long as he could see at all, with no pity for himself, drawing extra strength from a

61

kind of bitter defiance. The season left permanent marks on him. Prying out a stump, he felt a stabbing pain in his back. Although it subsided after a time, it always returned in a milder form if he moved his back in the wrong way. From that day on he could never stand completely straight. But he had to go on working, nor did he feel the pain as much then. At night, however, he was reminded of it.

The more time passed, the thinner he became. He could no longer straighten his fingers. They were covered with thick callouses, and only in the sauna did their sole-leather consistency melt and soften. In the evening he stumbled home in the half-dark toward the flickering light of the oil lamp. Often, he could see many-colored auras around the light that shone through the window. Sometimes, when he leaped over the ditch he felt as if the earth was not firmly in place. It seemed to be swaying. And sometimes he could not stay on his feet. His limp knee would give way and he would fall. It was tempting to stay there a while, to listen to the buzzing in his ears and his own heavy breathing. But he would get up, outright angry, and crow, "Hmh... there... pits everywhere..."

In the house, he ate and sat up for a while before going to bed. He was unable to speak, and even Akseli could get only a tired, twisted smile from him.

Alma sometimes watched her husband covertly. Seeing him so exhausted, she felt pity but she was afraid to say anything, for she sensed that any admonition would only anger him. Otherwise, she freed him from all the household chores. She chopped the wood and fed the horse, even drove it for work around the yard, often with the reins in one hand and her child under the other arm. She braked and scutched the flax herself, and even at night she carded and spun when Jussi and the boy were already asleep. Not infrequently, he dropped off to the whisper of her carding and awoke to the hum of her spinning wheel. The warning given by the frost had steeled them to do their utmost: Jussi gloomily and defiantly, Alma calmly and steadily, even cheerfully.

Her work habits were the complete opposite of his. All her daily chores were accomplished without commotion and without visible haste. She would come and go, bring and take. Never did she feel Jussi's burning desire to finish a job, nor did she throw herself as completely into her work as he did. She went about her duties humming to herself, planning at the same time how to dovetail her chores. When she went to get one thing, she took another along. And in that calm, workaday deliberation, her labor was blessed. Once her loom was set up,

62

even her weaving was done in between other chores. Every moment not needed for other work was devoted to it. She would say to Jussi, who watched in wonder as she ran the shuttle through a couple of times, while waiting for a pot to boil, "I'll be that much ahead of the game. And time would pass anyway while you're waiting for the food to cook."

And so they were now better able to survive. Their "capital" steadily increased, for they produced more than they consumed.

CHAPTER THREE

T he log walls of the building had already turned gray. Here and there on the roof could be seen the white gleam of replaced shingles. Paths and roads traversed the yard in well-established patterns. Beneath the window on either side of the stoop was a rose bush. The plants had come from Kivivuori. On the fringes of the grass-grown yard area, rotting stumps here and there bore witness to once heavy woods. Along the fields an occasional pile of twisted roots told the same story. There had not yet been time to burn them.

On either side of the brook stretched fields ringed by fences, and beyond them, a large area of tilled land extended into the swamp. At its edge stood a gray log barn. There was still much untamed swamp beyond the clearings, although it was crossed by a drainage ditch and some of the trees had been cut down.

Green shoots of rye shone brightly in the evening sun, making a splash of color against the background. The plowed fields emerging from the snow were black, but the hayfields still wore the brown of frost-killed grass. At the edge of the swamp, in the shade of spruce trees, some snow banks still persisted.

Seven-year-old Akseli was walking in the yard. He had just got out when his mother came back from milking, freeing him from watching his younger brother, Aleksi, who was going on three. Or so they said, but the older brother didn't care. The only thing of concern to him was that he had to watch Aleksi while Mother and Father were away. And now a sister would be sent to them. That's what Mother says. But Father says you can't know ahead of time. And you weren't supposed to ask a lot of questions about such things. Of course, Akseli knew the sister wouldn't be sent from anywhere, but that she would come from Mother's belly.

64

Mother had let him wear his leather mittens. They were like real choppers. They even had rings for hanging on the damper to dry — only in play, for you weren't allowed to get them wet. And you couldn't touch anything dirty with them. Auntie Kivivuori had given them to him on his seventh birthday. Uncle Kivivuori had made them. They were his godparents. There was a sister at Kivivuoris: Elina, Janne's and Osku's sister. He and Aleksi would get one like her, though it would be better if they didn't.

He was the one who would have to take care of them. He had to think up pastimes for Aleksi when they were together. He couldn't go out then. All he could do was kneel by the window and look out at a thousand tempting things.

Mother had come at last and he was free. It was fun to turn the puddles into streams by ditching them with his boot heel, but he had to stop because the door opened and he heard his mother's voice.

"You mustn't get your boots dirty. Out of the puddles."

Akseli obeyed. Then he started walking down the road toward the main road and the threshing barn. Its door was open and its blank darkness stirred a slight fear in him. There are ghosts in such barns because that's where they put the dead people. Of course, no dead man had ever been kept in theirs, but a threshing barn was a threshing barn. In back of the barn was a spruce grove where magpies nested. Wolf-Kustaa could just as well have shot them to stop their racket as prowl through the woods with his gun for nothing.

He had shot a wolf and thus got the name. The wolf had been somewhere in the world of Tiilisali. He had no idea where that world was.

He went farther along the road and looked at the boot tracks pressed into the sand that had been freshly spread there. Father had just done that, from the sand that had been hauled in and piled by the roadside during the winter. Father worked on the road every year and it still wasn't good. It must be that work never ends. Father had to work three days at the parsonage to pay his rent, two of them with a horse. And Vilppu always did all the work. He was part of a team, but the parsonage horse was lazy. Liisa had died or been killed; they had to get rid of her when she got old. Mother would not let her be sold. Father would have sold her all right, but no one would pay anything for her. His boots were made from Liisa's hide.

The boy stopped and stood by the roadside. He dared go no farther. He was forbidden to go beyond the beggar's spruce. The beggar had fallen asleep at its root. He had been taken away with a horse and died in the village. Akseli remembered him dimly. He had stopped at their house a few times because he came from the same place as their father.

Then he heard the clunking of the wagon wheels. Father was coming home from rent-work.

"Nobody seems to know anything about the spring chores there now that the pastor is deathly sick. And his wife is of no help."

His father said the overseer was a filcher. Akseli didn't know what that meant, but judging by his father's voice it must be something despicable. And father didn't want to butt in, not knowing how things are going to turn out there.

When his father approached with the horse and wagon, Akseli stood stock-still at the roadside. His father thought it was bad manners for a boy to dance and run to meet him. He was a little shy of his father, who had a quick temper. When he was next to Akseli, his father stopped the horses.

"Ya-hah. Wanna get on the wagon?"

Father's voice was mild, but his face was serious. Akseli climbed up and settled himself near his father on the piece of board which served as a seat. Father handed him the reins, at the same time noticing his mittens. A peevish note entered his voice.

"Now what are those mittens doing on your hands? They won't get cold at this time of the year."

Akseli looked down and mumbled, "Mother gave them to me."

Father did not reply. The slight tension between them marred the joy of holding the reins. Vilppu moved with sturdy, driving strides now that he knew he would soon be home, and the wagon teetered so much they had to hold on to keep from falling.

"Well, now he died."

"Oh."

"We'll see what happens now."

The boy did not answer, for the tone of his father's voice did not call for a reply. Having passed the threshing barn, they drove past the window, where they could see Aleksi's head. Father let Akseli drive to the very end.

"Well, what do we do now?"

The boy pulled on the reins, leaning well back, for his arms were too short to draw the reins taut otherwise. He turned the horse so that the rear of the wagon

66

was at the door of the wagon shed. Now and then his father's hands rose anxiously toward the reins, but he did not have to take them even once. Now came the hard part: backing the wagon in.

"Back up, Vilppu, back up!"

It went rather jerkily because Vilppu tended to rear in backing up. But they did not scrape the door jamb.

"That's the way... But hold the reins tighter so you can stop more quickly if it goes askew."

Affected by his father's praise, Akseli leaped down in a manly manner and went to unhitch the horse on one side. As they lowered the shafts, he held on with all his strength so that his father could tell he was not just pretending. Then his father pulled the harness from Vilppu's back and the horse made his own way into the stable. He snorted as he went and wrinkled his withers as he sniffed the earth, but he did not rear. They followed him into the stable. As his father fastened the halter, Akseli watered the horse.

Then his father fetched some hay from the loft. His habit was to take a sizable armful at first, and to keep cutting it down so much that he finally had to start adding more. At each step, he would gauge the remaining pile with a glance. As they left the stable, father and son would give the horse an approving pat on the flanks. Vilppu would glance back uneasily and turn again greedily to the hay.

Father and son entered the house in tandem, the father in front, stooping, one shoulder slightly higher than the other, and the boy following, manfully swinging his mittens on the ring hooked over his forefinger.

Jussi's homecoming followed an established pattern. Nothing was said, the parents merely exchanged inquiring glances to confirm that everything was all right. Then Jussi would set his hat up on the end of a beam. In most instances he would remain silent, but now he said, as if to himself, "He's gone now."

It was no shock to Anna. They clearly considered it a matter of due course.

"How did he die?"

"At three in the afternoon. He asked to sit up, saying he couldn't breathe on his back. They raised him up, but he dropped dead in their arms."

Alma was silent for a moment, then spoke the familiar words the living use to console themselves and ease the hidden anxiety death always brings, "It's better for him to be gone at last. He suffered so much."

67

And she added a feminine eulogy, "He was such a good man... even to us... may he rest in peace."

"Yes... I wonder what'll happen now?"

"Things'll go on like before. Why would they change?"

"Why? For whatever reason. The contract is good only during Vallén's lifetime. The successor isn't bound by it in any way."

"You should have talked to him then. When it became legal to draw them up for fifty years."

"I did talk to him, but he was so unwilling..."

A few years back the law had granted stewards of church property the right to make rental contracts for up to fifty years. Hearing of this, Jussi had asked for one, but the pastor had been reluctant, assuring him he had no need to worry. The pastor's disinclination arose in part from the knowledge that the parish congregation and the parish council were covertly critical of his management of church property. Therefore, he had been leery of imposing such a long-term contract on his successor, particularly since he knew the council would oppose it. When Jussi, in his panic, had pressured him, he had acquiesced. But he had procrastinated. When he took to his bed, Jussi didn't feel it was right to ask him again. It would have seemed equivalent to announcing the imminent death of the pastor.

So he was now without a contract or guarantee of his rights under the next pastor.

Alma, however, was more trusting, by nature, but also owing to the fact that the landlord would be a clergyman, who could not be expected to treat them poorly.

"Surely a churchman won't be unreasonable."

"You can't tell about preachers or parish clerks."

Nothing more was said about the matter that night, but it filled their minds. When the boys tried to voice a complaint, their father's irate warnings were sharper than usual. Therefore, a sober Aleksi had to whisper his questions about the pastor's death to his older brother. From the answers, he wove a fantastic picture, for he had no clear idea of the pastor or of the parsonage, much less of death.

Usually the Koskelas went to bed early. They no longer needed a light in the evening, for even after bedtime, a dusky summer twilight prevailed in the cottage. The boys slept in their own bed, and went on whispering until their mother's gentle but firm voice sounded.

"What kind of evening prayer is that? Do you have to be told every single night?"

The boys mumbled their prayers and fell silent. Akseli, however, lay awake for a long time. The pastor had gone to Heaven. But he was not the same as while alive. There he didn't have a black coat that came down to his knees, or bands under his chin, or trousers worn outside his boot tops. But surely he still had his cane. Only the soul goes to Heaven; that's why all the clothing is left on earth. The soul has only a white shirt and a long beard and queer laced-up shoes on its feet. Akseli had seen pictures of Heaven, and that's what it was like.

But why should they be afraid of the new pastor? He wouldn't come to live in their cottage; he would live in the parsonage, after the widow's year of grace was up... And the engineer gentleman had promised to take her away at once. But there must be something wrong; otherwise, Father wouldn't be so cross.

The boy fell asleep in a troubled, uncertain, restless mood, not to mention his parents, who lay awake even longer.

During the night Akseli awakened. He saw the white floorboards of the room beginning to redden near the window, a sign of dawn. He became aware of his father, who sat groaning on the side of the bed, and heard his mother say, "Maybe I should rub it a little..."

"No, no, that'll only make it worse."

Father's back was aching again. That, however, was such an everyday thing that the boy immediately fell asleep again.

II

The funeral activities caused a great stir even at the Koskelas'. Some sort of clothing had to be made for the boys, who would have to go to church. The tenants had even been invited to the funeral coffee. Jussi had to do a lot of rent-work in advance; the pastor's wife had asked him to attend to many things. The pastor's son and daughter, who had not made it home before his death, came during the days that followed, and Jussi had to drive them from the station. He also went to pick up the coffin. It was shipped in from the city by the son who was a judge, since none of the coffins in the parish were deemed worthy enough. The judge, whose official title in the parsonage was Master Carl, but whom the tenants referred to as Charlie, also arranged that Jussi should drive the hearse. He was intrigued by the romantic notion that an old and loyal tenant should drive the old pastor to his grave. Jussi was only in his forties, but grinding work had aged him, and he looked the part.

Jussi did not object, but he explained, stammering a bit, "The... uh... Master Judge... What about clothes?... You can't wear any old thing... And mine are sort of..."

"Wait a minute... My brother is your size and he has some old clothes here just as I do. We can scrape up a passable suit for you."

By pooling their resources, the brothers finally managed to get Jussi outfitted. As a final touch, they clapped on his head the old top hat belonging to Master Erik. They smiled covertly as they gazed at the results but nevertheless, they were satisfied.

Jussi was aware of everything, but he swallowed the insult, knowing that the brothers would not want the clothing back. He had also decided to ask the judge about the rental contract.

"Did it apply only during my father's tenure?"

"Yes, that's right."

"Why didn't you make it for a longer period?"

"The pastor didn't want to bother and then he got sick and I felt I couldn't bother him."

"But permission was given to establish a tenancy?"

"It was. The congregation did approve it."

"Well, there's no need to worry then. No doubt my father's successor will confirm the contract. He can, of course, change the rental terms, but there's no need to fear eviction. What would he gain by that? Only in the event that the property is badly managed can the inspectors order an eviction, and in your case that would be unthinkable."

"Would the judge write some sort of recommendation on behalf of the pastor's wife?"

The judge did so, for it cost him nothing. He wrote an absolutely glowing recommendation, declaring that Jussi was totally honest, industrious, temperate, and absolutely irreproachable, could be trusted implicitly and that the pastor's

70

wife, at her husband's dying request, had recommended to his successor that he kindly confirm the rental contract, "taking into account that the aforementioned Johannes Vilhelm Anttisson has single-handedly and without the least bit of help from the parsonage, cleared the lands and erected the buildings, whereby the right to their use is in all justice irrevocably his, although the pastor had not wished to bind his successor legally."

The pastor's wife signed her name to the paper and the judge gave it to Jussi.

"Give this to my father's successor. You don't need to worry about the interim trustee because he is not authorized to deal with such matters."

"Thank you..."

"No need to thank me. But you need a haircut for the funeral."

And Master Carl joined a noisy group of visitors who had taken over the parsonage, so filling it with their bustle that only the nearest relatives remembered the pastor's body which rested in the "cold room." The other guests had their own sentiments and topics of conversation, which had very little to do with the death of the pastor.

The paper calmed Jussi considerably. Alma, who was a better reader than he, read it aloud many times, for its contents were pure music to their ears. Jussi tried to appear matter-of-fact and indifferent at the downright hymns to his honesty, industry, and temperance. As Alma put the paper between the pages of the Bible with the rental contract, she smiled with pure pride and said, "Are you still afraid? Who would dare change a single clause of the contract after reading this paper?"

Jussi was largely of the same mind, but speaking as one more worldly-wise, he said, "You can never tell... about people of the world."

"Just think. You've done all of this all by yourself. You deserve a medal, just like the Czar of Kylä-Pentti."

"We-ll... I'm really no match for him, yet..."

But he had to get up from the bench and walk to the window, where he stooped slightly to look out and said in a genial voice, "Ya-ah. If the weather continues like this, we'll be able to get to the other fields in a week. We haven't had such a good spring in a long time."

Although the pastor was buried on a weekday, a crowd of people watched the funeral procession from the roadside. Jussi drove the hearse solemnly, tophat

71

on his head and an ungodly whip in his hand. The strange horses made him nervous, for in addition to everything else, they were of a quite skittish English breed. They had been borrowed from the manor, for the parsonage had none that were impressive enough. There were two of them, taken from a four-horse team, spindly-legged beasts with cropped tails and manes.

The funeral procession followed the hearse, and then came an unofficial convoy of the merely curious. Otto and Anna were among them, followed by Victor Kivioja, who whipped his horse at intervals so that he could then rein it in sharply. Completely ignoring the circumstances, he shouted to Otto, "I wouldn't make an even trade for horses like that. I mean, those skinny legs aren't worth a damn. They pull a gentleman's coach a little way, and that's it for them. But if you wanted to go as far as Tampere, say, their bobtails would be sagging before you were halfway there. Take something like that to the market and they'll offer you a few pennies for it, and not a bit more."

The procession moved on. People at the roadside bared their heads, both at the pastor's body and at the baron, who was riding behind the relatives. Wherever there were children by themselves, they would draw back and hide behind rocks and bushes, whence they gawked out, shy and timid.

Although it was a weekday, the church hill was also crowded with people. Among them were parishioners and visitors who had come directly from the railroad station. Jussi drove to the main entrance of the church and remained waiting there until the gentlemen who were to act as pallbearers could get organized.

A considerable hubbub arose on the hill as the visitors greeted one another, the voices speaking Swedish echoing more loudly. The curious natives wondered at the shamelessness of the gentry, who shouted out loud in public places. They kissed hands, and whenever two women met, they even hugged and kissed each other on the cheek. Was that considered acceptable behavior now? But then, it had always been known that the gentry had no sense of shame.

The pillars of the parish, especially the council and the municipal officials, circulated among the crowd. Some of them belonged to both groups — Master Yllö, for example, was a juror as well. The largest landowner in the parish, he had inherited his posts from his father, although still a youngish man. Members of the parish council also stood there, among them Töyry and his wife. The local dignitaries hemmed and hawed red-faced as they bowed to the visiting notables,

72

for despite their power, they were nonetheless rustics. Töyry's thin, tense-looking wife curtsied humbly, twisting her face into a smile that suited her nature as poorly as did humility. In contrast, the behavior of Yllö's pretty wife was natural and dignified, although she was only a country wife. She reserved her curtsies for the elderly. Her husband was more nervous. He held his head erect after bowing, perhaps too forcefully, as if to indicate that the only thing above him in this village was the church tower. A further badge of his status was the exchange of a few words with the baron, in a half-casual and therefore more noteworthy way.

The rest of the people stood by and watched from the sidelines, exchanging whispered remarks:

"Look at that weird hat."

"Is that woman in black limping?"

"The man with the big beard is an official of the Senate... a real bigshot... the pastor's daughter's husband."

"What a fatty, the one in the top hat. Belly like a lard barrel."

"Seems he's afraid it'll split, since he's got a chain around it," said Otto, referring to the gold chain draped over the gentleman's stomach.

Such were the remarks they buzzed and whispered to each other, always retreating a step or two when any of the gentry came within earshot. The upper class was at home in the churchyard, but the people stood flattened against the church fence along the roadside, the shyer ones even peering out from behind rocks and bushes. Just as the pallbearers were getting organized near the hearse, a disturbing incident occurred. Down the road came an old, crook-backed woman with a bundle of brooms on her back. It was the well-known broom woman, Viinu Roopeti, already bent double by nature, but bowed even more by her load. She could see only about to a man's knee, and did not know exactly what was going on. Through the group she moved, licenced by her age and her simple-minded innocence. The gentry, their faces clearly showing their displeasure, had to make way. Viinu stopped and tried to raise her head farther, twisting it backwards in an effort to see just what was going on.

"What in the world is this? Such fancy shoes..."

She spoke wonderingly to herself, and the master of Yllö, seeing how matters stood, grasped her by the arm.

"Let's go now, Viinu."

73

In his effort to smooth over the distraction, he spoke in a whisper, but only succeeded in making matters worse. Bewildered and confused, Viinu was like a frightened hen.

"Huh... now what... what in the world's going on..."

"It's a funeral... now go away... out of the gentlefolk's way."

"Jesus Christ... Are they really gentlemen? Who in God's name has died?"

The gentlemen became embarrassed, and a few others joined Yllö in his efforts to get rid of Viinu, which only made the situation worse. Viinu darted here and there, emitting confused sounds. Angry shouts began to ring out, and bystanders started whispering advice to the masters.

Some of the gentlemen frowned, but others had to struggle to keep from smiling, and the country people began to titter openly. Viinu circled around, trying to look up. Finally she saw the hearse and coffin, and had the presence of mind to get out from among the gentlemen. Off she went with her brooms, babbling to herself in her agitation. A short distance off, she stopped and turned her body halfway round; only then could she see the entire picture. With a rush, she took to her heels, and from the distance they could still hear her shocked prattling.

The coffin was lowered from the hearse and borne to the altar. Jussi drove the vehicle over to the church stable and returned just in time to see Akseli snatch up a lengthy cigar butt discarded by a gentleman and carry it to Otto.

"What are you picking up, boy?"

"Easy now... I had him do it because I was ashamed to. If pastors would only go on dying, it would keep me in tobacco."

A pastor high in the councils of the church gave the funeral sermon, praising the deceased shamelessly. A man of fiery word and spirit was gone. The congregation had lost a good shepherd, through whose intercession the Lord had done His work among them. The women wept, believing the speaker's every word, and the men approved them as appropriate to the occasion.

After the service, the wreaths were deposited. Words of commemoration in Swedish resounded throughout the church, which echoed the words and the sobs back from its walls. There were even Finnish words on some of the wreaths, one of them from the judge. Unlike his brother, his sister, and her husband, he was active in the Finnish cause. The wreath from the congregation was set down by Yllö and his wife.

74

The coffin was carried to a grave near the church wall, close to those of many other pastors of this mother parish. On their iron crosses, without exception, were inscribed these words in Swedish: "*Här vilar...*" ['Here rests...']

The parish council closed up the grave, after which the wreaths were brought out to the mound from the church.

The visitors gathered again on the church hill to wait for their transportation. As the pastor's widow stood leaning on her son's arm, Halme stepped forward from the ranks of people and approached her. His action stirred a movement in the crowd. "What's he doing now? Is he going to speak to her? He sure is."

Victor Kivioja was absolutely furious.

"Look at him... Look at that son-of-a-gun... Is he going... He's taking her hand... Well, I'll be damned... That's all I can say."

Halme did indeed go up to the pastor's widow with calculatedly slow steps, head erect, drawing his gloves from his hands. He was even dressed like a gentleman, perhaps better than many of the local ones, for he wore a suit of his own making, and as a tailor he was beyond reproach. He doffed his hat, bowed deeply, and said in a clear voice, "Honored lady, permit me as one member of the congregation, but surely on behalf of many, to speak unofficially and express my deepest sympathy in your great grief."

Moved by his words, the widow thanked him, and Halme bowed again, put his hat back on, and returned to his place as calmly as he had left it. The incident caused a stir of whispering in Swedish among the guests. They looked closely at Halme, while the widow's son answered the questions they were asking. The word "gentleman" was repeated often, but although Halme understood it, not a flicker of awareness marred his dignified expression.

The people standing close by nearly succumbed to a warm feeling of respect for his deed.

"Who would have believed he could go up and offer his congratulations like that," grumbled Victor, and even Otto had to admit, "He's smooth all right..."

Then they all stepped into their conveyances and began the return journey to the parsonage. Jussi brought up the rear with his team and his top hat.

The lower orders were served coffee in the hired hands' quarters while the gentry ate and drank in the main house. The pastor's wife came to exchange a few words with the former. She even patted the Koskela boys on the head, and Alma flushed with pleasure. Then the Master Judge and his wife appeared, to distribute black funeral confections with inscribed Biblical texts.

After coffee the guests wandered around the yard, talking in a lively fashion about everything except the deceased. Jussi had managed to change his horse and buggy, for he was waiting to drive away the first guests to leave. He too stood in the yard listening indifferently as the judge argued with another gentleman.

"Words, words... you can always find words when you need them. I always make myself perfectly clear to you, as you can see, or rather, hear. Even you can understand, although in your laziness, you haven't fully learned the language."

"But how do you feel about the fact that it's a social issue as well. A popular awakening is not a question of language alone. A little bit of education is worse than none at all... It causes unrest."

"Perhaps. But what are the consequences if things go on like this? Do you really think this stagnation can continue forever? That nothing will change and that you with your language can live separate from this people forever? In your opinion, it's enough if the people are barely able to write their names, read a few passages in Finnish about their duties, and add two and two to get four. But don't ever believe it'll stop there. Before long they'll add four and four and get eight. And it's better that we teach them than let someone else do it."

"Just as Wright is doing, you mean. But those people are already at odds."

"Why not? But I'm not thinking about socialism. That isn't our problem. That belongs to industrial countries. Ours is a political question. Our position is becoming more and more critical, and we are indeed helpless if the country people go on living in darkness. They can be fed just about any propaganda by the Russians, which is exactly my point. We have to take things into our own hands, and that can happen only with the help of their language. Without the Finnish language, there is no reaching them. For the present, they are mute. Look at that man with his horse. He stands there as if there were never a thought in his head, but he may awaken, and, it matters a lot who awakens him."

Jussi could tell from their glances that they were talking about him, although he was unable to make out the words. He began to blink as he looked at the ground.

"But I find his hat more amusing than the thought of anything that may awaken him."

76

"Ha, ha, ha... It's my brother's old top hat. We had to dress him up because he was driving the hearse."

Jussi sensed the cause of their laughter and turned away in shame, not for himself, but for the gentlemen, and he tried to conceal the fact he understood who was being discussed. At that moment Alma arrived on the scene with the boys and said, "They seem to be enjoying themselves even though it's a funeral."

"Some gentlemen's nonsense... whatever they're babbling."

Two women approached the gentlemen, and the conversation lost its serious tone for good.

"Do tell us the subject of your interesting and heated discussion."

"It must surely be Carl's Finnishness."

"Carl is bringing civilization to the people, and as is only proper he is starting with the head. He has given his hired hand a top hat."

The women laughed. Although married, they shaped their lips into an enticing pucker. The conversation then turned to the pointless social chatter remarkable throughout the ages only for going on endlessly without a shred of subject matter.

"We should be going home with the boys. The cows will be lowing already."

"You just go. I won't get out of here until night. I've got two loads for the nine-o'clock train."

Alma left with the boys, each one clutching a black funeral candy in his hand.

"Mother, can we eat them now?"

"You can eat them at home. But you have to save the wrappers. Father will make a wood filler for them, and we'll keep them as a souvenir of the pastor."

"Will he go to Heaven from the church grave?"

"On the last day, when everybody rises from the dead."

"When is the last day?"

"That's when Jesus comes."

"When is Jesus coming?"

Alma tittered. "My darling child, only God knows that. You can feed the lambs their twigs."

"I'll give Vilppu his hay."

"You both can."

A little worried because their home had been left alone, the mother approached it with the two boys. When it came into view in its calm, gray repose, she said in a tone of relief, "That's our home. There it sits all alone waiting for us...

77

wondering where we've been loitering... we've taken so long..."

"Is the new pastor going to live here?"

"Where did you get that idea?"

"Because father is afraid we'll have to move."

"He's not coming here. And we won't have to move. God will surely let us keep it."

III

None of the preachers giving the trial sermon was aware of the searching pair of eyes focused on him from one of the church benches, sharply and severely judging him. Jussi was not in the least concerned about the kind of preacher the man might be, but judged only with his private ends in mind. The first one he judged harshly, presenting his opinion to others in a quite uncharacteristic manner. He was clearly agitated.

"It doesn't pay to pick that kind of ranter. He's an angry man through and through. You can't know what his idea of mercy may be... He's too rigid."

The candidate was indeed a man who spoke in a firm and commanding voice, whose entire personality exuded power. In general, the men liked him, and Jussi would have too, had he not been the parsonage tenant. He would be too strong a landlord — no telling what scheme he might concoct.

The second candidate was exactly suited to Jussi's ends. He was a young man, a twenty-eight-year-old gentleman-preacher from Helsinki, a man who only just met the age qualification for vicars. Since the women's preference weighed heavily in these choices, Jussi might have known in advance there was no cause for worry — there spoke the next vicar of the parish. He might even have known it without the knowledge that the man had just written an extremely meritorious theological study and that he belonged to the inner clique which held most of the power. If not a relative of the powerful, he was well known to them. There were bishops he could address familiarly as "Uncle." There were even senators he could greet with a "Good morning, 'Uncle'" and to whose wives he could say: "Very well, thank you, 'Auntie.'"

Of course those things helped only up to a point, in becoming a finalist and the like. The final decision was to be made here, in this old country church,

78

before these coughing and sniffling people, their brows furrowed in judgment.

At any rate, the handsome young man with the gentle voice was a clear favorite. He looked so candidly into the eyes of the congregation as he spoke, his language a pure Finnish refined by a Swedish accent.

"...for in love and mercy is Christ's own sacred being. He comes to us not in thunder and lightning but in gentleness and consolation, a friend even to the most wretched, in the light of love and mercy."

The women were already thinking of the impression he would make at the buffet table during the annual literacy tests, a Helsinki gentleman, a preacher from the larger world. He was different from old Vallén, who was likely to have said anything under the sun, who had sometimes got names wrong at christenings, once erring so badly as to name a child "Carl Christina."

The man seemed as if made for Jussi's purposes. Such a refined young man would never wrangle with a tenant; he would consider it beneath his dignity. So as difficult as it was for Jussi to voice his opinion, he joined the discussion in support of the young preacher.

Halme was of the same opinion, if for a different reason.

"He is an educated man, and as far as I know, a friend of the Finnish cause. Those are my prerequisites for the position. The Word alone will not suffice; a spiritual shepherd must devote himself to the people's earthly enlightenment as well. And we can expect this man to do so on the basis of his theological writings."

How was Halme to know that the young man had written those studies precisely with an eye to increasing his merits for the appointment.

The Töyrys voted for him, casting another vote for the Laurilas as well, that right being reserved to them in the tenancy contract.

The end result was the appointment as vicar, by majority vote, of Lauri Albin Salpakari, formerly Lars Albin Stenbom.

The vicar came to the parsonage alone at first. His family was to remain in Helsinki until the place could be made ready for them. In the inspection that accompanied the transferral, the run-down condition of the parsonage became evident. This was particularly true of the farming sector, but in upgrading that, the parishioners agreed to repair the main building as well.

The vicar was an unusually friendly and courteous young man, who presented his requests so timidly and modestly that the directors consented to them immediately, especially since there was money in the building fund.

"My good fellows, do not believe that I, for my part, consider the matter very important, but wouldn't it be better to complete the repairs now during the changeover, since in any case they will soon need to be done. For the sake of the building itself, to keep it from deteriorating."

The rooms were checked one by one, and the projected repairs entered in the register. The benevolence of the elders began to cool a little when they realized that satisfying the vicar's expectations would completely change the appearance of the old parsonage. The parlor's slightly sagging parquet floor was to be taken up and renewed, new drapes provided for all the rooms, every floor, ceiling, and window frame painted, and the rather battered bedroom tile stove done over completely.

The vicar presented his requests in a slightly troubled and shamefaced way, a clear indication that the repairs were not for his sake, since he found it so difficult to ask for them.

The elders did accede to the requests, but looked at one another surreptitiously, thinking that all this would hardly reduce their tithes. They offered no objection, however, merely exchanged a few brief words which revealed much more to one another than to the vicar. He could not catch the nuances with which the shrewd landowners made known their real feelings.

"Well, Vallén was like that... He didn't care much about such things."

Then they inspected the tenant farm.

Töyry, as a member of the community, was the expert on the Koskela place, and explained things to the vicar.

"How was it now? Your agreement was valid only for Vallén's tenure?"

"That's right..."

Sensing a latent threat in the question, Jussi looked from one man to the other.

"Uh... I'd say it's an open matter now. You'll have to make a new agreement. If the vicar plans to continue the arrangement."

"Of course I will... Why should it be discontinued?"

Jussi very nearly straightened his bowed back.

"Uh... well... I've been thinking... If I'd be allowed to continue... Since I've tried to take care of it with that in mind.... And since I started from nothing... I've tried my best to keep it up."

"So you've cleared and built all of this?"

80

"That's right... In a raw swamp. It's thirteen years now since I dug the first shovelful."

"Thirteen years, and such large fields already."

"Well, there are fields all right, but the land isn't all that good . But if the vicar would go on with the agreement, we would ... since we have nothing else... and we've lived here with that in mind."

"Don't worry, we'll certainly come to an agreement, but later. Until then we'll leave things exactly as they are."

They explored the buildings and the land. Little sounds of astonishment escaped the elders. When Jussi and the vicar were not present, they were able to speak freely.

"This is better than many a landowner's farm. The son-of-a-gun even has five milking cows."

The master of Töyry stood with hands in his coat pockets. He was a lean, sinewy man, thin-faced and tight-lipped, who always thought for a long time before he spoke.

"It seems to me that the rent there is really nothing. Vallén gave him a free hand because he considered him a sort of foster-child. Not that I want to interfere—the vicar can do as he sees fit."

The master of Yllö looked around at the swamp.

"Yes, it's true—a very low rent, but remember that all this was cleared from a swamp. An already cleared farm is another matter. Thirteen years... thirteen years, and everything in such good condition."

The vicar too marveled at the size of the farm, and Jussi admitted it was big, but the land was not very good, that it had taken great effort to achieve anything at all.

Then they went in for coffee. The boys fled from the visitors into the chimney corner, and when the vicar urged them to come out, they retreated even farther. Alma told them to come out, and they finally dared to do so, Akseli in the lead, Aleksi following. Eyes riveted to the floor, they approached the vicar.

"Well, what's your name?"

"Akseli."

"Is that so? Is that so? And this other young man?"

"Aleksi."

"Well, well, Akseli and Aleksi... And that little one in the bed there?"

81

"That's Akusti."

The girl Alma had been hoping for had turned out to be a boy and had been named August Johannes . He was now half a year old.

"Three boys... well."

The vicar was friendly, but Jussi did not trust his friendliness. It was unfamiliar to him, too glib, too genteel. The deceased Vallén had been different. You could know and understand the workings of his mind. This man was completely concealed behind his amiability and courtesy.

But at least the worst of it was over. He had promised an extension. The agreement would have to be made quickly, before he had a chance to change his mind.

"The uh... the agreement, Master Vicar... When would it be all right with you?"

"Well... I'll let you know. There's so much to do right now. Let's leave things the way they are... for the time being. We'll get back to the matter later."

The visitors left, having confirmed that the property was well cared for, the land and buildings in proper condition, and raising no objections to extending the lease. The vicar was free to make any rental agreement he wished. As a person above reproach and a conscientious farmer, Jussi satisfied the conditions laid down by the law.

On the return trip, they explained Jussi's past to the vicar.

"There's no denying he's a decent man," said Töyry. "You can get along with a tenant like that, but I have problems with mine. It makes no difference whether he shows up for the rent-work or not, the work he does is worth nothing. There's no real benefit from these tenancies anyway — It's better to take them over yourself. And if my tenant doesn't change his tune, that's just what I'll do. I would have done it long ago, but I put up with him because he's the fourth... and even a relative of sorts."

"Is Laurila related to you?"

"Well, only because the tenancy was granted as a daughter's dowry a long time ago... four generations back... so he's no longer really a relative. But his grandfather's mother was a Töyry."

At the parsonage, the parish board took leave of the vicar.

"And since you live so near here, you can help me with everything and explain whatever needs explaining."

82

These last words were spoken to Töyry, who then remained after the others had left. As the vicar was very much in the dark about agricultural matters, Töyry promised to help him when he began to manage the property.

"Thank you very much. I'm very happy to get help. My knowledge of the country and farming is limited to summers spent on my relatives' land. For the time being, I won't start anything until my wife arrives. She has the background and experience and has eagerly followed the practices on her home farm."

"Is your wife from a country farm?"

"Well, not exactly. Her father was a judge, and his last post was in Helsinki, but they had a country estate near there. She is Judge Sointuvuori's daughter. You've heard of him, haven't you? He was a well-known supporter of the Finnish cause, as are my wife's brothers."

Töyry coughed and said somewhat uncertainly, "I can't say I have..."

He was embarrassed that he didn't know about such matters; apparently he should have kept himself better informed. In actuality, Töyry's vision did not extend beyond local affairs, into which he had been led not by his aspirations or talents, but by the size of his property. He was merely a narrow-minded, dry-faced farmer, whose world centered around his home and property, or "proppity," as he and his wife termed it.

The position of advisor did tickle his vanity, although he was not prone to vanity. On the other hand, an innate, deep-seated caution warned him against interfering in the affairs of the parsonage. At home he and his wife discussed the matter in their expressionless way. His wife was especially wary.

"It's no good meddling... in other people's business. You never know what will happen. And then they'll blame you."

"Oh, I'm not going to... that much really..."

The inspection had aroused in Töyry a feeling of envy toward the Koskelas. There was no real reason for it, since he lacked for nothing, but his greedy mind did a slow burn at the thought of Jussi's success. He sought some kind of rational grounds for his feeling: he was, after all, a member of the church council and thus not supposed to remain indifferent to the affairs of the parsonage.

"That Jussi Koskela has grabbed up a lot of property in no time at all."

"Hmh...that's what they do all right. You can see it on our own land too... living for free on someone else's property and bleeding it dry."

"That's a ridiculous rent to pay. I wonder if this new one knows anything at all about things like that. For a place of that size on the manor, they work three days a week with a team of horses and a fixed number of extra days. Koskela does two days with a horse and one on foot, and not a single day more. I meant to explain a little of this to the vicar, although what's other people's business to me... But when you think how the congregation is bled dry... No wonder the parsonage is half in ruins."

In this instance his wife was not restrained by her usual caution. She hated the Laurilas so much she would gladly have tightened the conditions for all tenants out of pure malice toward their own.

"You should really let him know. It'd be better to evict that bunch from our land. We'll have to finally do something about it. That woman passed me by today without so much as giving me a look, but then she let out a nasty laugh behind my back."

IV

The vicar seemed to have forgotten his tenant completely. For a long time Jussi waited for him to bring up the question of the contract he had promised, but nothing happened. When the uncertainty became unbearable, he mustered up the courage to inquire about the matter.

The vicar was visibly annoyed, but since he could think of no reason to refuse the request, he told Jussi to come to the parsonage and bring the old contract with him. Before the appointed day, he discussed the matter with Töyry.

"That Koskela wants a contract now. How does one deal with tenants here? How long do these contracts last?"

Töyry pondered the question for a long time and then explained. "It varies a lot. Some can be canceled with a year's notice, others with five or ten. There are even lifelong contracts."

"What is the case with church property? I'm not too clear on that."

"The last law says you can make a contract for fifty years. An officer of the church can't make one for longer than that."

"How should I proceed with this Koskela?"

Töyry's reply was dry and evasive. "That's the vicar's own affair. He has complete authority in all contractual matters except for the fifty-year restriction.

And the tenant farm must be well run, and the tenant not convicted of any crime in a court of law."

"Koskela hasn't been convicted, has he?"

"No-o. He's a proper man in every way. But in Vallén's time, there were people on the council who opposed agreements for longer than the incumbent's tenure. A new man would sort of have to be free to make his own agreements. But like I said, the vicar has full authority to name any period up to fifty years."

"Well... I would hardly make it that long. For my own part, certainly, but it would really be out of line to bind one's successors. It would be direct interference with their emoluments."

"Well, it's up to the vicar, like I said before. As a rule I don't favor long-term contracts myself. I'm not talking about the Koskela case, just in general terms. It's like this: give a tenant a long-term contract, and he lives like an animal in the fields. The threat of eviction is the only thing that keeps them a little bit in line. But as I said, this parsonage tenant is a first-rate worker... so that's not... I won't get mixed up in the matter... I'm just saying what I think, in general."

"I'm not considering eviction since they are decent people... or what's the word... not decent, but... well yes, decent. But what about the rent? I don't know anything about that. If it's too high, I can reduce it."

A small, dry smile creased Töyry's cheeks.

"Well... ah... er... I... I don't know. It's the vicar's business. But if you're asking me, I wouldn't consider it high, given the situation. But it isn't my place, as I said."

The vicar noted Töyry's smile and his evasive tone. He felt that the elder was laughing at his stupidity and lack of experience in such dealings. He was embarrassed and even blushed. His handsome, clear face was prone to flush easily, for beneath his smooth and courteous fine gentleman's ways lay uncertainty and shyness, especially since these things were so completely new to him.

To cover his confusion, the vicar said quickly, "Are the old terms too easy then?"

"Ahem... that depends... they are light, considering the size of the place, but the fact is that the parsonage invested nothing except the logs for building, and they were standing. So that's one side of it... one consideration, I would say. But as I said, the vicar can do whatever he pleases."

The vicar was left uncertain as to what he should do. He had heard only occasional comments on the tenant question and had no understanding of it. Töyry's laughter troubled him; there must be something wrong with the Koskela rental. Perhaps it was laughably small. While still a child, that Koskela had been some sort of servant boy to the former pastor. Töyry had probably been amused at the way his inexperience would be taken advantage of.

The matter troubled him somewhat. There was something distressing in it. He was not greedy, but he was afraid of making a stupid mistake that would make him a laughingstock. And in the background lurked a much graver threat. Mrs. Ellen Salpakari had told him, "You are to do nothing until I get there. You must not hire servants or make any decisions about the household. I want to choose my own help. You know nothing about such things."

Lauri had to admit the truth of her words. He was as helpless as only a shy young man brought up in the city can be. For that reason, he had put off making the contract until he had succumbed to his tenant's pressure. He was sure that Ellen would have no objection to continuing the arrangement, but its terms were another matter. If he did something foolish, Ellen would be angry. So now, while waiting for Jussi, he decided to make some kind of loose temporary arrangement that could be rescinded should Ellen not approve.

The long separation from his wife brought her to his mind with a warm, passionate surge of love. Many disagreements and even painful quarrels vanished from his thoughts, and he remembered only his wife's lovely and sensually attractive being. He had fallen in love with her some ten years ago, in a humiliatingly mindless way. And humiliated he had been. Ellen was the daughter and sister of the "wild Sointuvuoris," a proud and arrogant family. She had indeed fallen in love with him, but true to her nature, in a demanding and capricious way. He had been under her thumb from the start, and remained there. It began with his name. Her father, who was still alive at the time, had declared to him abruptly and brutally.

"You will become my son-in-law under the following conditions. You are to learn the Finnish language thoroughly. We won't listen to that pig-German you gabble. Secondly, you will change your name, first and last, to Finnish. The middle name Albin you can keep, since there is no Finnish cognate for it; Alpo, which some recommend, is unnatural. Then you will give your word that any children you have will be given Finnish names. I won't meddle with your opinions themselves, but if you start opposing the Finnish cause, you won't find

86

it pleasant to be a member of this family."

He had consented. The issue itself was not of importance to him. He was a liberal and would have preferred to see the language groups at peace with each other. Because of his family traditions, he would have favored Swedish as the language of education, but would have granted the people the right to use their own language in all situations where it was indispensable. As a preacher and theologian, he was unable to judge the question from a worldly point of view. In his opinion, it had to be solved in accordance with practical demands.

But the way in which the conditions were presented hurt and humiliated him. Yet what could a shy young man in love do? Only to Ellen did he reveal how deeply the lack of consideration had wounded him.

"Yes... It is a bit regrettable in a way. But you don't understand father! You don't know how he's been hurt and ridiculed because of his Finnishness. He himself has said that he had nothing against Swedish at first. As a judge, he only wanted to be sure that people would understand what was being said about their cases in court. He said it was terrible to sentence men who had to have the decision itself translated with their own meager means. But as a result, father suffered so many terrible indignities in his public career that I can fully understand his attitude."

And the lovely Ellen pursed her lips tightly and said with her head held high, "And I completely agree with him. If you really love me, then you must love the people I love."

"I do respect your father. He is at least forthright and fearless."

"I didn't mean only my father. I meant the Finns, the Finnish people."

"I don't consider myself a stranger here in spite of my native language. I've always thought of myself as a Finn. And I believe that racially I'm a purer Finn than you."

"That doesn't mean anything."

Her last words were spoken in a brief and offhand way. The truth of the matter was that in spite of their landed background, Ellen's family had often intermarried with families of German and Swedish origin after they had joined the ranks of public officials.

But no matter... he could not bear to give up the proud, erect, and pretty Ellen, and he tried to shut out the whole language question from his mind. He gave lukewarm support to her family's Finnishness. There had been problems aplenty, and his sitting here now, waiting for his tenant, was an upshot of them. For a long time, he had been looking for a good parish as a means of escape from the quarrels in the capital city, and now he had found it.

He would have been able to leave earlier, but only as a curate or an assistant. Until now, his age had excluded him from a vicariate. Ellen would not hear of a lower position, and her view was understandable.

Now everything was well. He had got away from all that. His family life would also improve, since troublesome side issues would no longer affect it. The abrasive relationships which had made life unbearable would be a thing of the past...

... because of his refined sensibilities. It was his phrase to describe one of his character traits, but the thought of it worried and fretted him. He could not be ruthless and unwavering. He found it difficult to oppose the wishes of others. He thought of his brothers-in law, and even here by himself, he felt a nervous frustration. They treated him in a playfully friendly way, but he sensed in their attitude a slight contempt. Especially the older brother offended him with his behavior. When they met, the brother would thump him on the shoulder, laugh and say, "So, what's new, Topelius?"

He used the name in a demeaning way, because of the vicar's his sensitivity and his conciliatory nature.

How senseless it was to quarrel about language. How had it all begun? Surely his father-in-law had meant well at first. But when he met with criticism and opposition, the issue became a personal one. One dispute led to another and in the end it no longer mattered what was best for the people; now it was merely a question of anger. The Finnish cause had become for them a question of thwarted careers, of personal injury, of alienation for the family. They met all this with unyielding pride and arrogance, seeking honor even in boorishness. As students, his brothers-in-law had been quick to use their fists since it was Finnish and folkish to do so. It was dashing to leap up on a table and shout, altering Bismarck's words:

"A Finnish Finland will be created not with words, but with blood and fists!"

What hope is there for us when such things bring honor, thought the vicar. There is only one lasting value. That which Christ wrought. How brilliantly Tolstoi had shown things in their proper light, when he presented Napoleon as a small and laughable creature. But perhaps I think so because I'm unable to cut a dashing figure.

He moved uneasily in his chair.

A secret, gnawing vexation sought to re-establish itself in his mind. Suppressed and therefore dimly sensed fragments of thought wandered through his consciousness. He had never been able to think them through and they were still unclear.

Was mine a genuine calling for the ministry? Surely it was. It wasn't only that... Perhaps I took refuge in those values...unable to succeed at anything else. Because I couldn't jump... Certainly not... I didn't reject them out of shyness and sensitivity.

I have prayed for peace in all sincerity... And for truly free faith. It will be possible to find it here.

The vicar looked out the window at the small lake and its few islands, shining in the late spring light. If only Ellen and the children would get here!

Ellen was beautiful. Especially when she let down her full hair for the night. He hoped she would be satisfied with the parsonage.

I should, however, think of her more as a mother. At least as a mother she was splendid. How lovingly she dealt with the children.

Everything would be different here. That Koskela... he's somehow distrustful; he's disturbingly withdrawn. I should have put off this matter until Ellen's arrival... I wonder if he's hurt his back somehow, since he's so stooped?

At that moment Minna entered to announce Koskela's arrival. He always thought of the housekeeper they had brought with them from Helsinki as Minna, although Ellen again went to ridiculous extremes in insisting she be called Miina.

Jussi entered. His shyness made him nervous, and concern for the success of his mission further heightened his tension.

The vicar stood up.

"Good evening... Welcome."

The vicar extended his hand in greeting, but Jussi did not at first understand that he should grasp it. Despite his unpretentious ways, Vallén had never shaken hands with his tenants, any more than other gentlemen in Jussi's sphere of life. He blinked at the vicar's hand, became completely flustered, finally extended his hand and then withdrew it fearfully. Then he seized the vicar's hand in a kind of panic, shifted his feet restlessly, groping for some kind of bow. Uncertainty turned the effort into a jerky bodily movement. Incomprehensible sounds issued

89

from his mouth.

"...mmm.... nnn... ning."

The vicar became flustered as well. Red-faced, he seized a chair hastily, and offered it to Jussi. His action only aggravated their mutual nervousness, for that too was completely contrary to old custom. Jussi did finally sit down on the very edge of the chair in such a position that standing would have been easier in the end. He did not dare rest his whole weight on the chair, but supported half of it himself, putting a strain on his knees.

"Okay... so... about the contract... Have you kept the old one?"

"Ye-yes, I have..."

Jussi dug frantically through his pockets and handed the papers to the vicar.

"Uh... there's a paper there... a letter of commendation. From the former pastor's wife... Or actually from the young master of the parsonage."

"Is that so... I see..."

The vicar read through the paper nervously.

"Indeed... This is a very good paper. They recommend continuing the rental rights, and, as I said, we will do so, of course."

"Well... That would be real fine... Since it's like our home... and we've lived there thinking we'd live there a long time..."

"Precisely... We'll make a contract. But ah, I've been thinking... for the time being we'll make a temporary one. We'll keep the present contract in force, but not for a very long period."

Jussi did not immediately understand what the vicar meant, but he realized that what he feared most, the uncertainty, would be intensified.

"Well... uh... Master Vicar... why... when..."

"Look, I have to admit that, coming from the city, I'm completely ignorant of these matters. There is an ordinance dealing with church property, but I don't know it fully. And for the most part, I know very little about rentals —I don't know at all what to charge for rent. We'll make a permanent arrangement when I'm better acquainted with things. This one will be only temporary, to keep you from worrying..."

"But... It's just that... It's hard to live when you don't know how long you can stay... and... there's still the work to do on top and all..."

The vicar's torrent of words warded off Jussi's doubts — or was meant to.

"No, no, no. Don't think that way. You can live there as long as I have the pastorate. That isn't the question at all. But look, this is church property, and I'm not completely in charge of it. I have to sound out the parish council in all questions that concern it. But under no circumstances do I intend to impair the agreement, so you can rest easy."

The outburst did not completely reassure Jussi, and he asked uneasily, "Exactly what kind of arrangement does the vicar have in mind?"

"Well, I've been thinking of something like... sort of... You can have the tenancy while I'm the incumbent, but not for longer, since I can't bind my successor. That clause of the contract gives you assurance that you need not fear eviction. As for the rent, we can keep it as it is for the time being, but we'll make it a condition that it can be changed every two years. Only with the consent of both parties, however."

"But at least we can live there..."

"The contract guarantees that."

Jussi sighed, somewhat relieved. Then he embarked upon a confused explanation.

"About the rent... I'll do as much as I can. Since the boys are so small, I'll have to do it all myself. It's not so much, but considering that in Vallén's time, I started from scratch... But I'll do whatever I can."

The vicar was troubled again. It was hard for him to endure the other's apprehension, and the appeal to Vallén's benevolence made things even harder to bear.

"No... look... The thing is this stipulation is because of the parish council... You see..."

The vicar hesitated a moment. He wondered if it was proper to talk to Jussi about Vallén's mismanagement and the council's comments, but since it offered the easiest way out of his predicament, he began to explain.

"Some things came up in the inspection... not about your place... it was praised extraordinarily... but the parsonage is in bad repair. That is undeniably true, and there were complaints about it. It was understood that Vallén was an old man and therefore neglectful. But his... this isn't my affair only... Vallén was an old and respected pastor, and the congregation couldn't say these things. But it is my duty... We'll leave the rental clause open so we can refer to it in case of complaints, but be assured that for my part I won't change the terms. Do you understand? It's just a formality."

91

Jussi did not exactly understand. But he was not in a position to do anything but accept any conditions offered. The vicar began to draw up the document with joyful eagerness now that the troublesome situation was finally resolved.

Then he read the text. The contract guaranteed Jussi the right to live on the land unless the council should find that the good of the benefice required otherwise.

That was an additional condition, and Jussi shifted in his seat.

"How come... I mean... that makes it worthless..."

"Not from my point of view... But this is only a formality. And no matter what agreement we make, we are in practice subject to the council's decisions, whatever the law requires."

"Well... that's the way it is, of course. But if the vicar himself..."

"I already told you... On my part, this is of course valid."

The amount of rent was to be set for two-year periods, by agreement of both parties, at which time it would be taken into account that the tenant had developed the property by himself, which entitled him to a lower than usual rent.

Then followed the bureaucratic clauses which Töyry had explained to the vicar, and which, despite their apparent insignificance, declared the landlord's absolute and sole power with regard to the agreement. They stated that the tenant was to be of good reputation, was to till the lands well, was not to damage the forest property, was to have no lodgers without the landlord's consent, could have no meetings without the landlord's permission, was to behave virtuously and irreproachably, and was to satisfy the rental conditions scrupulously.

Each one of these general stipulations meant that the landlord, by resorting to any pretext under the sun, could nullify the agreement. Even the failure to greet a landlord was considered bad behavior. One tenant had been forced to leave his farm in the church village area for that reason.

But Jussi was not afraid on such grounds. He felt his behavior was respectful and his tenancy exemplary.

The vicar wrote out a second copy of the agreement, after which the two men signed the documents. Relieved and happy, the vicar parted from Jussi, trying with an excessive display of friendship to gloss over a fact they both understood: the agreement had been greatly changed for the worse. Jussi's reaction to the effusive show of friendship was nervous discomfort. Another handshake followed, as clumsy as the one on Jussi's arrival.

92

"Well now, Koskela, I hope we will live in harmony as good neighbors. Nor do I doubt it in the least. If any of my actions seem strange, you must understand that I am completely inexperienced in all this, heh, heh... I'm just one of those Helsinki farmers, who don't know which end of a horse to hitch up. Any real farmer would laugh at me. And with good cause, heh, heh... with good cause... Well then...We'll be seeing you... And don't worry... We're sure to get along."

Jussi left, turning in the doorway and shifting hat and papers from one hand to the other in an effort to free one of them so that he could close the door. After lengthy fumbling, he succeeded, but now the vicar came rushing to his aid, which upset him even more. He closed the door with his free hand just at the moment the vicar was reaching for it. Then he opened it again, sensing that it would be wrong to close it in the vicar's face. The door swung back and forth a couple of times, the vicar alternately raising and lowering his hand, and the two of them emitting unintelligible sounds as each perceived the other's intent. Finally, the door was closed between the two and they separated, one as flustered as the other.

The pastor's sigh of relief was followed immediately by a feeling of depression. Uneasily, he put the paper into a drawer, feeling his behavior had been unworthy.

Jussi walked toward home. Step by step, his mind settled down from its agitation into a state of calm appraisal of the event. The conclusion was disheartening: the agreement had indeed been made worse.

"We'll have to see when I get home. Alma is better at reading."

He tried to hope that a new reading would bring out something reassuring in the agreement. Alma could tell from looking at Jussi that things had not gone well.

"Looks like we got ourselves a real landlord this time."

"How so?

"Read this... But slowly..."

Alma read, but the text told her no more than that things were as they had been.

"But this guarantees our right to live here."

"So it does... if the good of the benefice doesn't demand otherwise. Isn't that what it says?"

"But the old one was no better. This paper won't protect us, whatever it says. No matter how strong the language, you know for sure that we have to leave if they say so."

Well, it was true. It seemed to bring relief when you thought about it. The paper wasn't so crucial after all. It was indeed strange that consolation should come from the knowledge that they were unprotected in any case.

Once again the Koskelas spent a night of concerned silence. Again the boys had to be quiet because of their father's gloom. The only bright spot was their mother's voice. She spoke calmly, almost happily, as she rubbed machine-oil on their calloused feet.

"As for that rent-work, they can't think up so much of it that in a couple of years these two can't do it... these mother's favorite men..."

V

For the most part, life is resilient. Whether we rise or fall, once the motion ceases, we soon adapt.

So it was with Jussi, too. Life went on even under these circumstances. The increased uncertainty gradually became the normal state of affairs, and it was no longer constantly on his mind but affected his attitude toward life below the surface.

He was assigned the task of fetching the vicar's wife and children from the station. Another horse and driver were borrowed from the Töyrys for the nursemaid and the luggage.

"But how will I know her? Your wife, I mean."

The vicar laughed happily. He was almost exuberant, and his behavior, in Jussi's opinion, was highly improper.

"You'll be able to single her out easily enough. Two children—a boy and a girl—and a nursemaid with her. There is no danger of error, there are so few travelers here."

Jussi mounted the buggy and started out.

"Listen, Koskela."

"Master Vicar."

"If you don't recognize her otherwise, pick out the most beautiful woman. It's sure to be her."

Jussi did not immediately understand. His hesitation made the vicar turn bright red. The excitement of the moment had perhaps made him speak out of turn. But the thought of Ellen's passionately awaited arrival wiped out the humiliation, and he continued.

"It's a sure way to know her. But remember, the most beautiful—without question."

"Heh, heh... I'll try... If only I understood such things."

There truly was no danger of error. Only few people got off at this country station, and since the choice was between gentry and other people, the matter was crystal clear. The vicar's identifying clue was valid and would have been so had a whole trainload descended on the station. A beautiful young woman with an erect carriage stepped onto the station platform. Behind her veil, Jussi could see boldly arching brows and eyes whose slight protuberance served only to accentuate their beauty. A high, tight collar covered her neck and kept her head sharply erect. Her close-fitting dress made clear to any observant person why the vicar had swallowed the stinging humiliation administered to him by his father-in-law.

Jussi was oblivious to all that. He saw only a face, which instantly evoked a fearful respect in him. He approached her, hat in hand.

"You must be the vicar's wife... Good day... I'm... that is... sort of... to meet you."

The woman gave him a passing glance and had already looked away when the truth dawned on her. In a tone of wonder, she said, "You? Are you from the parsonage?"

"Yes I am... I'm sort of... to meet you here."

"But where is my hus... the vicar?"

"Well, it's... We were supposed to come together... But the vicar told me to explain... But the buggy is so small we wouldn't really fit... And the vicar said too... that he doesn't really drive... that I was to do the driving."

"Well, that's really too bad. Children, come now."

Following her were two children, led by a nursemaid. The boy was about five or six years old. The girl was too small to walk, and the nursemaid had to carry her. The vicar's wife was clearly disappointed, and Jussi, sensing her ill humor, grew nervous. She fussed with the baggage in apparent confusion, for she kept asking about a basket which the nursemaid claimed had been left behind.

Eventually they were settled in the vehicle. The woman's ill humor persisted, for she had evidently expected a different sort of reception. The station was small and surrounded by only a few dwellings since the section of track on which it stood was quite new and located at some distance from the more heavily populated parts of the parish. Near the hitching rail stood a twill-coated old man who regarded the vicar's wife with the steady, unflinching gaze of a backwoodsman. Ellen Salpakari was quite accustomed to heads turning as she passed by, but this was a scrutiny of a different sort. An odd, inward smile flickered over the man's face, and when the vicar's wife was seated in the buggy, he said to himself as if confirming a thought being born and shaped all this while in the imperturbable depths of his being, "Pretty lady... heh, heh..."

After a pause long enough for every corner of his mind to register the sentiment, he added, "Even a veil... over her eyes."

The vicar's wife could not hear his words, but she could still feel his stare on her back. A subconscious fear stirred within her, of the kind one feels in the presence of the insane. She was relieved when the vehicle set off.

The wife and the children rode in Jussi's vehicle; Töyry's day laborer was bringing the nursemaid, and the baggage. The little girl sat silent, but the wife had to grab the boy from time to time when he teetered as he shifted restlessly on the seat. Before they had traveled half a mile, Jussi realized that her prohibitions meant nothing to the boy. He always had his way in the end. The very tone of voice in which she uttered her commands was routine; it was clear that she did not take them seriously herself.

"Are there vicious horses at the parsonage?"

"No. Right now there are no horses at the parsonage."

"Ilmari, don't ask silly questions."

"But are there any vicious pigs there?"

"There are no animals at the parsonage yet."

"Ilmari... Don't you ever listen... But whose horse is this then? You're one of the parsonage men, aren't you."

"That's right. But this is my horse. I'm the parsonage tenant."

"Indeed. There is a tenancy on the parsonage, is there? Why is it that we have to start from scratch? Are there cows and horses available in the area? Good cows, I mean..."

"Well, you can always... But not all that many. The manor has its pure-bred stock... But the baron doesn't seem to sell them... he always keeps the good

96

calves for himself... Now and then he sells a calf or two to the landowners as seed stock. The spotted ones... with the big horns... those 'Airesies,' or whatever they are called."

"But why is the parsonage so far from the church?"

"It's been that way since old times."

The questions asked by the vicar's wife were curt and abrupt, prompted by whim, and Jussi's answers were stiff. He felt she was an alien; everything about her was unapproachable and repellent. He knew from the tone of her questions that she was oblivious of the person answering them.

They drove through the parish. The road wound uphill and down. The gray hamlets with their dwellings, storehouses, and people were left behind. Although most of the houses were gray, nearer the village some of them had been painted with red ocher. The larger houses, such as Yllö's, had even been sided and painted with oil paint.

Children standing at the roadside withdrew into hiding as soon as they noticed a gentlewoman sitting in the buggy. Some old woman came toward them carrying her shoes over her shoulders, curtsied deeply, but turned to watch from behind. They met a load for the mill, and a substantial landlord riding in a chaise, his weight depressing the springs to one side, giving the vehicle a ludicrous, lop-sided appearance. A large wicker-encased bottle balanced on the chaise... What was he doing with oil in the middle of the summer? Oh, that's right, Järvelin had lowered his prices for the summer months.

At the foot of one hill there might sit an indefinable creature beside a pushcart packed with a mixture of junk, rags, and the like. A buyer of bristles, ragman and part beggar.

Suddenly, from over a hill, they heard the clatter of jouncing wheels and shouts urging on a horse. Two young hired hands were racing their hay carts now that they were away from the farm and out of the landlord's sight. Not noticing the vicar's wife seated in Jussi's buggy, one of them shouted back to the other just as they drove by.

"Goddamnit, just wait till we get to Uotila's straight stretch. I'll make him go so fast he'll leave a streak of shit in the sky."

Dust rose in the wake of the carts, and the boys jounced and swayed as they strove to keep their balance.

A Finnish high road near the turn of the century.

The vicaress took refuge behind her parasol from the dust and the shock caused by the shouting. She asked Jussi a question prompted by the recent encounter.

"Is there a public school in the parish?"

"There is one in the church village and one in Salmi. They're supposed to build one in Pentti's Corners. They're talking about it. The baron has promised the lot and the timber."

"It's none too soon. But what are the people like? Are they patriotic?"

"Well... I can't say..."

"Do they hate the Russians?"

"Well... Not really all that much. There aren't all that many of them around here... maybe a gelder or a peddler once in a while. Nothing unusual about them. Oh yes, they did beat up a Russian once."

"Why?"

"Well, the thing was he sold bricks ground to powder as cockroach poison. They beat him up the next time he came around. And even then mostly because he laughed... He asked why they didn't catch the bug and put the poison in its mouth. So they gave him a little beating... But that's about all."

The vicaress sneered vaguely and stopped asking questions.

The parsonage came into view, and the vicaress examined it from a distance with keen interest. When they turned from the road into the yard area, the vicar came running out the door and straight up to them. The children shrieked in a single voice.

"Daddy!"

The vicar lifted them down, kissing each one on the forehead. When he kissed his wife, Jussi turned his head away. It was only a kiss on the cheek, not owing to shyness at Jussi's presence, but because of the children. Jussi could hear the vicar's voice choke with emotion as he said, "Welcome home...darling..."

And for the first time Jussi sensed a human being beneath the armor of pride when she said softly, "Yes, at last... at last..."

A commotion of mutual greetings followed, while Jussi stood by uneasily, feeling himself superfluous. Still he had to stay because of the baggage.

Once it was inside the house, he prepared to leave. The vicaress thanked him casually and said, "Just a minute, here's two markkas."

"Thank you, but the... I'm doing rent-work... so you owe me nothing."

98

"Oh, of course..."

The vicar addressed Jussi. "I have to ask Koskela if he can work for wages a couple of days. The furniture is at the station already and needs to be driven here. I'll ask Töyry to lend us a couple of horses."

"Yes... That'll be all right."

Jussi had the hay-making to do at home, but he understood the furniture had to be driven from the station.

"Your name was Koskela?"

"It is... It's my extra name."

"Extra name? What do you mean?"

"Well, it's like a place name. In the church records, I'm just Anttisson."

"Lauri, you'll have to enter Koskela as this man's family name immediately."

"Yes, of course..."

The vicar's laugh was amused and yet tender as he said, "Right away, my little Fennophile."

Jussi left.

Feeling somewhat uncertain, he walked toward home. There looked to be tough times ahead. Only now had the master of the house arrived. Why had she brought up the name? It couldn't be some kind of trick, could it? Since the contact was in another name?

CHAPTER FOUR

I

It appeared that the fears inspired by Jussi's suspicious nature were unfounded. The vicaress turned out to be extremely friendly, so friendly, in fact, as to become oppressive. "How is Koskela feeling? Don't we have a beautiful lake here? How many children does Koskela have? Isn't it great to get up so early on a summer morning? I sometimes ask to be awakened very early just to enjoy it."

Jussi, of course, had to respond to the woman's saccharine friendliness, and his face wore an outlandish smile as he tried to accommodate her moods. Her behavior did not diminish his uneasiness, but rather heightened it. Over-familiarity on the part of the gentry did not bode well; worst of all, it forced Jussi into an extremely awkward position. He would trot, shambling, to open a door for her, behavior which seemed unnatural even to the vicaress in whose smile of appreciation a shade of annoyance would occasionally appear. Coming to terms with the boy was for Jussi the most difficult of all. He embodied everything that Jussi could not tolerate. He was lively, disobedient, and irrepressible, rushing headlong into everything. But in his mother's presence, Jussi had to hunt enthusiastically for his ball, and when he found it, he would hand it to the boy with an unnatural smile intended as a show of friendship, but with an angry look of disapproval in his eyes.

The couple laid the foundations of their household at the parsonage with great enthusiasm. They enjoyed the novelty of their position, but the work crew was on its toes, apprehensive at their zeal. They spent too much time at work sites, and followed things too closely. But worst of all was their attempt to establish friendly relationships with the people, not only with their recently hired help,

100

but with the people of the community as well. It was strange to hear a beautiful, aristocratic lady discussing the prospects for the rye crop. People would have been glad to talk in practical terms, but the vicaress was inclined to introduce something metaphysical into the discussion as well.

"Our bread is safe this year from the frost, that old enemy of our fatherland. The people of Finland have three enemies: the Russians, Swedish speakers, and the frost."

At that point, the eyes of old parishioners would wander to some vague, distant point, and they would give an answer so round and slippery that it offered nothing to seize on.

"Yaah... I guess so... That's the way it is... with many things."

Sometimes such encounters would lead to tension and offended feelings, whereupon the gentry would say with a sigh that the education of the people had to be improved. Although the task of refurbishing the household's economy called for great effort, they turned their attention to the stagnating issue of the public school. A visit to the Kiviojas to buy a horse gave them the final assurance that a school was indeed indispensable.

Generally, they depended upon the expertise of their overseer in buying their cows and horses, but this time the two of them went to the Kiviojas. Victor had received word of their coming and was half-drunk with enthusiasm. Horse-trading with the gentry was a new experience for him.

The Kivioja place was a complete shambles. An incomprehensibly large number of buildings leaned every which way, small coops, built one next to the other. A passerby would have been hard put to sort out the mess — he might have guessed one coop to be a stable by the horseshoe nailed over the door. Strewn around the yard were vehicles of various sorts, a number of them in different stages of disintegration. Some were sprawled without wheels at the corner of the barn, thick growths of nettles sprouting through their broken boxes.

Victor ran out to meet the couple. Confounded by his zeal and anxiety, he greeted them at least twice. His wife and children peeped out from near the window frames. One of the boys followed his father out; he wanted to be in on the dealing. On his head was a ragged felt hat, through one of whose rents a tuft of hair thrust itself into view. His cheeks were caked with dirt; only beneath his nose were two streaks of white skin visible. The boy was the vicar's namesake, as became apparent when they asked the usual question:

101

"And what is the little man's name?"

"His name is Lauri... I gave it to him... the old lady wanted something else. Get inside, boy... get away from under the gentlemen's feet. Let's take a look at a gelding... I'll get him right away. I left him all ready in the stable... no need to go to the pasture."

And Victor ran into the stable with the boy at his heels. What they did and what they whispered in the stable could not be discerned from outside, but some kind of buzzing went on in there. Soon Victor and the horse burst forth through the doorway, so abruptly that the door frame rattled. Lauri came running behind them. He had obviously been whipping the horse, for it lunged out of the stable in a fright. Victor ran it around the yard, shouting to the gentryfolk.

"Look at him... You can see he doesn't limp. Look at the way he plants his feet... Every joint flexes."

Lauri ran after the horse, emitting a buzz like a horsefly, whereupon the animal quickened his lumbering trot.

"That boy... He's speeding him up!... He's going to be a horseman. Look at him closer..."

Victor brought the horse to a stop in front of the couple.

"Look in his mouth if you know anything about teeth."

"Well... maybe we'll look from here..."

"Take the reins and walk him... You can see for yourself..."

The vicar actually did take the reins and began to walk the horse. A sly gleam flashed in Lauri's eyes, and he began to trail the vicar with great ado, repeating, with one hand raised in a gesture of warning, "Don't let him have his head... don't let him have his head... don't let him tear loose..."

Slightly startled by the boy's upraised hand and his animated bustling, the placid horse dodged to one side and tossed his head. The boy went on teasing.

"Hold on... so that he can't... He might get a notion... Be careful... Don't let him have his way..."

The vicar stopped the horse, and they began to look it over. Victor circled around the animal and the boy followed suit. It was apparent that every one of his tricks had been learned from his father. He ran beneath the horse's belly, slapped its sides at intervals, lifted its tail, and even pried its mouth open.

"They're strong... You can tell his age..."

The vicar's wife looked at the horse as well, and said, "But isn't he too small

102

to be a work horse — we need strong horses."

The boy shoved his rag of a hat to the back of his head and declared expansively, "Better a pound of sugar than twenty pounds of shit."

At first Victor burst into laughter, but the gentlefolks' smile was so tortured that he waved a hand at the boy and began to explain.

"That boy... don't pay any attention to him... don't bother to listen to him. The son-of-a-bitches teach him those things. Keep a clean mouth in front of gentlefolk, boy, or you'll go inside. But he knows horses... he talks a little rough, but common people's children... Don't mind him."

The couple tried to gloss over the matter, but their enthusiasm for horse-trading had been dampened. Victor still tried to bustle and rattle on, but the vicar's wife cut short his fussing.

"The horse is unsuitable for us. We won't buy it."

The gentry departed, but on the way they could hear Victor ranting at the boy as he led the horse into the stable, "You goddamned boy, you had to go and say that in front of a lady... they don't like it... If you'd only said manure... But what the hell, it was well put... Where did you learn it anyway... Better a pound of sugar than twenty pounds of shit..."

Then Priita, the masseuse died, and the vicar and his wife had to deal with Wolf-Kustaa. Kustaa had built a coffin himself and placed his mother's body in it, unwashed, on bare straw. Half by force, the vicar's wife had the parsonage servants prepare the body properly for burial, for Kustaa would not let anyone into his hut. Learning that he had not been confirmed, the vicar took up the matter with him.

"You're over twenty and you haven't attended confirmation school. Can you read?"

"No. But there's nothing to read anyway."

"But you have to know how... and you should be confirmed."

Kustaa glared at the vicar in his uniquely sour way and said, "The latest law says that anyone who isn't married doesn't have to be confirmed."

The vicar's jaw dropped for a second.

"When was such a law passed? I've heard nothing about it. It can't... that's... how could such a thing... You have to be confirmed in order to be married, but confirmation is mandatory even without marriage."

103

"Ya-ah, I don't know about that... Who is in the right, the Czar or the vicar? Anyway, the Czar had passed a law like that. We have to sort of follow the laws laid down by the authorities... I don't know. Maybe the vicar has his own laws, but I have to listen to the Czar."

The vicar was left standing there, stunned, as Kustaa walked off. Later on he learned about Kustaa from others and understood what was involved. He tried once or twice to bring pressure to bear on Kustaa, even waxing indignant, but with each effort, Kustaa was firmer in defense of his own contrived law, which he still affirmed to be of the Czar's promulgation.

The matter of the public school had to be expedited. The baron had already announced he would donate the lot and the timber if the community would undertake to build it. He had even promised money to pay for work that required skilled labor, work which could not be done by volunteers.

How should they approach the baron — should they invite him to the parsonage? The question was difficult for reasons of etiquette — well, not of etiquette exactly, but of language. When she had first heard of the baron's Swedishness, Ellen had immediately turned cold toward him. They had, of course, met him at the official gathering arranged by the parish elite and the big landowners to welcome the new vicar. But they had exchanged only a few words there, particularly because Ellen had been annoyed by the humble demeanor of the lesser elite in the presence of the baron. For his part, the vicar would have resolved the matter simply by inviting the baron and a few of the landlords to the parsonage. In any case, the matter first had to be straightened out with the baron. Without him, the school could not be built. Yet it grated on Ellen that the baron should ignore them.

"Well, we've already been introduced. What's to stop us from broaching the subject, on the public highway if need be?"

But the matter was resolved very simply. Walking past the manor, the vicar and his wife ran head-on into the baron. Near the road that went by the manor was a fenced-in area, in which stood a handsome, purebred cow. The baron was standing near the fence, face-to-face with a maidservant who was obviously pregnant. Their voices were raised, and the couple approaching could make out what they were saying.

"Why not with calf... why you not... you know that Ursula... every time till now ... nothing wrong her... you let go by... you not watch... you let breeding time go by."

"That's a lie. She was bred at the right time. I can't do anything about it. I can't very well breed her myself. If a bull can't get it done, that's it." The maid was sobbing with anger. She had already reached a state in which she had forgotten who was master and who was maid.

"What you say? You breed... You watch... it your job."

The baron pointed to the maid's elevated stomach with his cane and said: "You bitch, you take care Ursula get it as good as you get it yourself..."

"Goddamn it... I wasn't bred by the manor's bull, that's for sure."

"What you say... what you say... what you mean those words? Not bred by manor bull... speak slow..."

Then the meaning of her words seemed to become clear to the baron, and he loosed a torrent of jumbled curses. Then he said, "Go to paymaster. My order. Put pay in pocket, time up, go long way from here. You miss best cow's time many time. She barren, you fool around. Go away. No good."

The maid left and the baron turned angrily away. At the same moment, he noticed the couple from the parsonage, tipped his hat, and started toward them. Only the slightest trace of amusement crossed his features when he realized the visitors had seen and heard the encounter. It was erased by the courteous and respectful smile with which he greeted them.

"Good day. The baron is at work. Pardon us for troubling you; we meant only to pass by. Please don't let us disturb you in any way. You probably have important business on your hands."

"Good day. Nothing important... they not watch... how they can when always lazy? But I ask pardon, I so poor speaking Finnish language. Could I please use Swedish?"

"Please do... I just thought the baron might know Finnish since he lives in such completely Finnish surroundings."

"Madam knows that if I used the local language, I could not converse with her."

From then on the conversation flowed in Swedish without a hitch, for the couple too spoke it more fluently than Finnish, in which they still suffered from the occasional awkwardness and gropings of a speaker of a language learned by studying.

The baron ushered in the visitors. The conversation was lively, but they avoided mention of the language question. The baron did know that the vicaress was the daughter of an ardent Fennophile, a member of a radical group which had pushed the language question to extremes in the seventies and eighties. In the baron's circles, Sointuvuori had been described as wild merely for being a trifle outspoken in polite company. The baron had not known him, but had read his articles and snorted with contempt.

The school issue brought them perilously close to the language question, but even there they managed to bypass it. They spoke only of the need to educate the people in order to eliminate their immorality and barbarity. The baroness took little part in the conversation. A small, delicate woman who seemed to have no understanding of such matters, she looked like a small flower of some sort to pin to her robust husband's lapel. She made shy efforts to turn the conversation toward the couple's success in the parish, but the baron drowned them out rudely with his own preoccupations. The parish needed a cooperative dairy, and a public school was needed to awaken the slack and lazy people to an understanding of the importance of the economy. Tenants were so thoroughly shiftless that unless he forced them to keep up their tenancies, everything would go to rack and ruin.

The couple prepared to take their leave. The baroness did at least take them to see her flowers, which she said she loved. And so she did. Nor did she do anything else but look after her husband's health and knit innumerable scarves for him, scarves he never wore. Her concern for his health was strange, for the baron was as sound and sturdy as a green tree. "Now, Magnus, don't catch a cold. Dress more warmly."

It was clear that the small and delicate baroness had only two things in life: the baron and her flowers. When the visitors admired the plants, she beamed with pleasure and explained in detail when each one of them had begun to bloom.

On the way home the vicar said, "It was a bit gauche to address him in Finnish. He surely realizes we know how poorly he speaks it. He may think we did it on purpose."

During the visit, the vicaress had completely forgotten her grudge against the baron, but the vicar's words brought her back at once to her battle station.

"It is not tactless of me to speak Finnish. It is tactless of him not to understand it."

The vicar did not dare to disagree.

106

II

Little by little, the Koskelas came to realize that the course of life had changed. Not only had the terms of the agreement become vaguer and the uncertainty of life correspondingly greater, but in addition, they were now exposed to the full misery of a tenant's predicament. The rent-work, those three days, two of them with a horse, were still fairly easy, but there was now added the so-called "compulsory work." One landlord in Häme had once written into the contract with his tenant: "You are to report for work whenever summoned, and if you don't appear, then out you go." Almost every contract contained a decree of this sort. It was a kind of fundamental law for tenants. There was no such clause in the Koskela contract, but that did not free Jussi from such work. He had to go when called. Tenants did get paid for the extra days, but the wages were poor, since they were unaffected by any shortage of labor.

Fundamentally, however, it was not a question of money. For the wages paid him, plus a little extra, one could hire a replacement. But a rural village economy can support only a limited reserve work force, which was always otherwise occupied at the time the compulsory work was required. The demand came when everyone, down to the last child capable of field work, was busy with the haying and the harvest. At other times, there was a surplus of help, but then even the tenants had no need of it. During harvest time, the tenant either had to harvest his own grain at night or see it fall off the stalks.

It never occurred to the vicar that Jussi might have work of his own to do. By Wednesday evening of each week, Jussi had completed his rent-work, but now they were harvesting the grain on the parsonage land, and he had to work for wages the rest of the week. And even that was not enough.

"Couldn't Koskela's wife come for a couple of days? Can she leave the children yet? The oldest boy is able to take care of them now, isn't he?"

"Well, I guess... for that part... But we really can't, because of the cows."

"Is that so? That's too bad because it might rain, and we really should get the grain in."

Then Jussi would begin to yield. All it took was an expression of dissatisfaction on the vicar's face. That is where he read the terms of the contract, not in the paper they kept between the pages of the Bible.

And so they worked late into the night at the Koskelas. Since Alma after all didn't have to work at the parsonage all that often, she did what she could, with Akseli helping her with the housework. When she was at the parsonage, the boy had to do it alone.

Now Aleksi was tending little Aku nearby. Once in a while, Akseli had to chase Aleksi back to his charge. Aleksi had a tendency to stray from his post. Akseli himself was not much better, but circumstances forced him to play the father. And his own father's anger was the kind of threat that kept him at his work. But sometimes he would defy Jussi, morosely and stubbornly.

Akseli resembled his father. The same rustic Koskela features, the same slightly protruding cheekbones, the small deep-set eyes, and the same serious expression, which seldom softened into a smile. His body already showed signs of his father's strength and solidity, but he was clearly going to be somewhat taller and more slender. Aleksi, however, was completely different from both his mother and father. He was delicate — thin and a little pale. He was also serious and sober, but somehow softer than his older brother.

The oldest boy had already given cause for discussion between his parents. They were worried about the outbursts of temper and the fits of stubbornness he sometimes exhibited. His last thrashing had been of a sort that shook them both. Akseli had found a bright blue jay feather, and Aleksi wanted it. When the older boy refused to give it up, his mother said, "Now, let him hold it for a while."

"No, I won't. Because it's mine."

The words came with such defiance the matter could not be ignored.

"Give it to him right now!"

The boy was silent, but showed no sign of obeying.

"Father, you have to do something."

Jussi looked at the boy. "Did you hear what your mother said?"

No answer.

"What's that above the door?"

Still silence. Jussi took down the switch from above the door.

"I'll ask you once more. Will you do as your mother says?"

The boy retreated behind the stove and crouched there. Jaws clenched, he crushed the feather in one hand and lifted his nightshirt with the other. His father was taken aback, but then began to whip him. After a couple of light blows, he asked, "Will you open that fist?"

The boy refused to answer, and now Jussi struck him out of anger and without mercy. Red welts rose on the boy's lower back in the wake of each blow. But the boy made no sound. Finally his mouth opened, and in a voice crackling with pain and rage, in rhythm with the blows, he said, "Not... even... if... you... kill... me."

Aleksi and Aku began to cry. Frightened, Aleksi grabbed his father's arm and shouted, in panic, "No more, Father, don't hit him... I don't want it."

Tears welled up in Alma's eyes too. "Not so hard..."

Jussi was bewildered by Akseli's words. He stopped beating the boy and began to pace back and forth, angry and flustered.

"Well now, the world is in a fine state when you can't get a pup like that to obey. I've never seen anything like it in my whole life."

The parents realized, however, that the boy would have to be whipped to shreds before he would bow. He was still crouched against the wall. His body quivered with pain, but no sob escaped his lips.

In gloom and depression, the day wore on into night. Akseli would not even agree to eat supper. At bedtime, he disappeared. They found him in the loft of the stable, and his father carried him to bed by force. He did not hit him again, but overcame his squirming by squeezing him so tightly in his arms that he could not move.

The following morning, the mother and father talked it over.

"The beating will have to stop," said Alma. "It's just too awful. Those welts were almost as thick as your finger."

Then she wiped her eyes.

"Well, I'm not beating him for pleasure. But where will it end? If he goes on like this, he's going to have a hard time of it. The world doesn't spare its blows. It lays them on without measure."

"What if we tried with kindness... He's just so quick-tempered. And there's more of goodness in him. If you praise him, he's so pleased, even if he doesn't show it. And he tries all the harder. That's how we should talk to him... He might soften."

"All right, why not... But you can't make any concessions to him just because of work done. A man has to work, just the same as he has to wear clothing."

After that, Akseli was no longer whipped, yet his parents saw no increase in his stubbornness. He did as much work as he could, and sometimes at night his mother pitied him when she saw his exhausted little body. Food was also a source of friction. Their mother wanted to give better food to the boys, but for the most part, she had to do so without their father's knowledge. She managed to see to it that they could eat the black rye bread freely. They had to ask for it, but it was never refused them, although Jussi's nagging usually accompanied the gift.

"What on earth kind of stomach can grind up all that bread? I could live for two days on a piece that size."

But Jussi was not always irritable. At times he was actually in a good humor, and then his words were kindly. He praised the boy occasionally, sometimes even going so far as to feel proud of him. As in the incident with the ram.

When the Koskela sheep were driven into the barn one fall, the ram eluded capture and escaped into the woods. They tried to catch him, but he would let no one get near him. He often came close to the house, but ran off when he saw a human being.

One Sunday, Akseli had stepped outdoors for a little business around the corner. He did not so much as have shoes on his feet, even though the ground was already frozen. But there stood the ram, in a clump of junipers on the hillside in back of the threshing barn. The boy began to creep up closer to him. But the ram scented his stalker immediately and became restless. He stamped his hooves and tossed his horns, but he did not flee. Akseli came right up to him, reached out a hand, and coaxed the animal to him. The ram eyed him, but each time he took a step forward, the ram backed off a step. When the boy saw that the animal was about to bolt, he threw himself upon it. The ram fell to the ground with the boy holding tightly to his horns.

The struggle was fierce. Boy and ram rolled through the junipers as one mass. They were about evenly matched, so the issue was not about to be resolved. Inside the house, the boy's father heard shouting and ran outside. From the hillside came the crashing sounds of a struggle and the boy's shouts, repeated at intervals: "Fa... ther... the ra-am..."

Jussi could hear the boy sobbing and ran as fast as he could to get there, but on his way there came to his ears sounds the like of which he had never heard before. In between sobs, the boy cursed the ram, the thump of his fists beating a rhythm.

"And... for... God... damn... sure... you'll... stay... here... you bastard... you'll see!"

In the heat of the struggle, the father was not concerned about his son's cursing. Coming to Akseli's aid, he bound the ram with his belt, and the horned beast's dreams of further adventurous jaunts were over. Only then did the father turn his attention to the boy, and he was frightened by what he saw. Akseli's clothing was in tatters, and blood was running from his mouth and hands. Sobs shaking his body, he suddenly threw himself upon the bound ram and began to hammer it with his fists, weeping violently and croaking the while: "I'll show you... I'll

110

show you... no matter what you are... I got you..."

"Now, now... You mustn't beat Alpreeta like that," said his father gently.

"Why did he kick me then?"

When the boy had calmed down a bit, the father threw the ram over his shoulder, and they started toward the barn. Akseli, walking behind, continued to threaten the ram in the intervals between his now subsiding sobs.

"I'll beat him some more in the pen."

"No, no, go to your mother and get your cuts washed."

"God help us, what happened?" The mother was shocked at the sight of the tattered, bloody boy, but began to minister to him at once. One tooth was loose, and the ram's sharp hoof had split his lip.

"That rascal of a boy. There's many a man would have let go, you can be sure of that."

Luckily the cut lip left no scar. But the often-begged-for and the equally often-refused knife appeared on Akseli's belt.

"But you have to let Aleksi whittle with it once in a while."

Akseli did let him. Now and then. And he would always watch sharply, scowling as his brother whittled.

"You can do that one more piece and then you have to give it back."

Jussi too had to get involved in volunteer work on the school, first on his own account and then on behalf of the parsonage. He was supposed to donate money to the building fund as well, but that he managed to avoid. The vicar was in charge of the fund. The baron had made the initial contribution to it, and the idea of a collection from the poor remained for the most part an expression of idealism.

One day Master Tailor Halme appeared at the parsonage.

"Pardon me. Would you gentlemen please grant me the opportunity to do my own small share to help in this effort toward public education in the spiritual awakening of which I have had the pleasure of seeing you honorable gentryfolk show initiative."

The sentence had been carefully formulated in advance, although his learnedness had even otherwise infused Halme's speech with literary expressions which had become so deeply implanted that he used them even at home.

The couple was immediately charmed by Halme, not least because he gave them two hundred and fifty markkas for the building fund. For a man in Halme's position, it was a large donation, and he had been accumulating it for a long time.

111

The discussion soon turned to questions of enlightenment and nationalism, and although the pair had to suppress a smile now and then, they were pleased to have made his acquaintance.

"Excuse me, but has Mr. Halme worked with the *Suometar* Party?"

"I'm not a member of the party, but the national aspirations and the language question are near to my heart. Since they are, so to speak, the preconditions for the awakening of the masses."

When he was asked discreetly where he had acquired his knowledge and learning, he responded vaguely, "When I was in Tampere studying for my profession, I was quite active in the cause of popular education. But having reached the conclusion that such activity is most crucial precisely in the rural areas, I returned to my home village. From a strictly professional point of view, the decision was disadvantageous, but great causes cannot be advanced unless lesser ones are subordinated to them."

A long and enthusiastic discussion ensued. They talked of elevating the masses, and although Halme emphasized the importance of a concomitant achievement of social justice, no arguments arose. The vicar and his wife took the idea of social justice to mean some kind of sewing-circle and charitable activity. The conceptions were vague on both parts, and so could be dovetailed excellently in the discussion.

Departing, Halme bowed deeply, and in shaking hands with the wife, raised her hand as if to kiss it, but stopped the gesture midway. He would like to have done so, but instinct warned him where to draw the line.

"What a curious character! Who and what is he?"

"I've heard that country tailors and shoemakers are philosophers. It comes of their having to sit so long at their work."

"But this was no shanty philosophy. He's a weird mixture. A real treasure. Just think how much closer we can get to the people's mentality through him."

At the school building, the people's mentality was running riot.

"Goddamn charity work. I should be propping up the barn roof before it falls on my cows' backs. But you can't stay away, or you'll be in their bad books."

"But on the other hand, it's good that the kids will have a chance to learn."

"They learn their lessons well enough. As I went by Kankaanpää's place and their boy was standing in their yard, he was barely able to talk, but he yelled out anyway: 'Ith there thit in yer panth cauthe you walk tho careful?' I said there wasn't in mine, but that he might find something of the kind in his."

112

The supervisor of the construction work was a self-made master-builder named Hellberg. Since the town would take over the building when it was completed, it was also in charge of the construction. Hellberg's pay was its share of the cost.

This church-village carpenter had recently moved into the parish. He was above average height and dark-complected. Behind his back, they sometimes referred to him as "I, myself." He was, in fact, uncompromising and dogmatic. While speaking, he looked a person directly in the eye in an oddly penetrating way. If an argument arose, his glance slid aside, and a low grunt emerged from the corner of his mouth. Thereafter, he would frequently busy himself with another chore as if to show his opponent's insignificance by forgetting all about him. He rarely smiled, and when he did the smile was usually a sarcastic one. One encounters people of his sort at every turn, but his uniqueness in the parish was not based on those traits. He was an "organized" carpenter, had worked in construction far away, and had joined some kind of union there. He was also known as a socialist, and subscribed to the socialist paper called *The Worker*.

At the school site, his most distinguishing trait was his behavior toward the baron. When others had to speak to the baron, they were in agreement even before they understood what he was saying. They stayed a respectful distance from him, and anyone he addressed would stand at obsequious attention for the entire time of the discussion. But when the baron spoke to Hellberg, he sometimes had to wait for an answer if the master-builder happened to be looking at some detail in the plans.

"I want other way. Why so big entry? Teacher may have big family. Kitchen now chicken coop."

Hellberg looked at the baron as if weighing his opinion, and said, "Ya-ah. There may be something in that, but anyway it's too late."

"Why? Still easy can change. I want."

"I can see what the baron wants, but the men who approved the plans didn't want. They should have been told at the time. I didn't draw up the plans, and they didn't ask me. If they had, they would make some sense. But the town gave me these plans and told me to build according to them, and that's what I'm doing. The baron can talk to them if he has something to say."

And Hellberg withdrew to one side, turned his back to the builders, and continued to study his papers. It was not an intentional provocation. He simply took no more notice of the baron than of anyone else.

Halme was often seen posturing around the school site. He took no part in the work, having made such a large donation. He now had a cane, which he handled half playfully, as if to blunt people's criticism. Nevertheless, it was his inseparable companion. Hellberg found a discussion partner in Halme, but one as assertive as himself. Nor could he annihilate him with a snort. Halme was just as good at saving face as Hellberg. One day Halme stood leaning on his cane, looking on as the men were notching the corners.

"Uh-huh. There it rises. A beacon of enlightenment. A star of hope for the Finnish people."

They could hear Hellberg snort. "There's little hope for the Finnish people under such stars."

"I cannot share your opinion. Obviously, you're not being serious."

"Listen now, Halme. When a baron like that, and a vicar like that, together with their wives, put up a public school, you can tell what kind of stars will shine on its roof."

"In the vicar and his wife, I have detected nothing but a sincere striving to stimulate the people's desire for education."

"Of course. They're educating the backwoods for the benefit of the *Suometar* people. Drawing the rural people into the masters' sleds. Or rather, hitching them up in front of those sleds."

"As far as the poor are concerned, without enlightenment, they will remain forever poor."

"A poor man will remain a poor man, even if he sing-songs his way through *The Birch and the Star* from morning to night. Listen, I've been to public school. I know."

"Perhaps you do. I haven't attended public school, but I have read *The Birch and the Star* and I consider it a very beautiful story. That it won't satisfy anyone's hunger is a reasonable and self-evident truth. But I stand by my opinion that the social conditions of the people will be improved by means of enlightenment."

"Slavery can be ended only by cutting the chains that bind men."

"Enlightenment will cause those chains to break with its own power. That is the cornerstone of my world view, its charter, so to speak, upon which I build everything."

"Hmph... As for building, you'd better get out of the way now. They're bringing a timber."

Some of the men laughed, but Halme shifted to another spot, leaned his hip against his cane, and shouted, "Listen, Otto. Since you are the life and soul of this work, its true leader, so to speak, would you take charge of noting who comes to work most often. The vicar has asked me to find out so that those men can be given special thanks at the dedication."

Otto promised to do so, and declared himself to be the first. He truly was, although everyone treated his comment as nothing but a joke. Otto excelled at these group projects, and since Hellberg was often absent, the role of leader of sorts naturally fell upon him. Underlying his zeal, however, was realistic calculation. The work on the fireplaces would be paid for, and he was determined to snatch the contract for himself. Hellberg's word would weigh heavily in the matter, and Otto tried to curry favor with him, although his tongue was preparing poisoned barbs for Hellberg's arrogance.

The workmen listened in on the debates between Halme and Hellberg without being able to take part in them. But there was much in Hellberg's talk that appealed to them. Actually, they had held the same opinions as he all their lives. Tenants were slaves, the hired hand and the man who worked for room and board were also slaves — that they had known for a long time. The tenants felt their lot most keenly. The man who worked for food could always change masters, but getting a new place as a tenant was a risky matter, and tenants were further tied down by their cattle and dwellings. True, they fared better than others, but the difference was negligible.

Terminology and programs went buzzing over their heads, but the central issue was clear.

"What can be done then? We really need some kind of law."

"Whatever would life be like if we were to have some kind of protection?"

When Halme noticed that the men listened to Hellberg with particular sympathy, he agreed in principle, but argued questions of interpretation. The "great masses" had always been the focal point of his sympathies, but he viewed socialism as only one aspect of enlightenment. He discussed the subject as if he were thoroughly familiar with it, but was irritated at not knowing everything, since he could not stand anyone knowing more than he did.

Hellberg promised to bring him the works of Salin, Tainio, and Kurikka in support of his position, and Halme said indifferently, "Why not? I'll be glad to become acquainted with their opinions."

But, at home, he pursued the subject avidly. Hellberg brought him all possible kinds of leaflets and clippings, which he accepted off-handedly:

"You can bring even more. In case you order these booklets from Helsinki, ask for extra copies for me. Lately I've been reading mainly history, but whenever I have the time, I'll squeeze them in."

115

Halme read late into the night. Gradually, the men began to listen to him more.

"'I myself' is often stuck for an answer."

Halme's quick grasp of ideas and his innate facility for making things his own soon gave him clear sailing, and before long he was better grounded in socialism than the more sluggish Hellberg. Their differences were now only minor, for Halme had no difficulty adopting socialist positions. He had always considered questions of language and nationality issues to be social issues as well.

No one noticed that in Hellberg's absence, Halme became a more rigid socialist than he was in their debates. The men now listened to him, and he was even the cause of a small incident at the job site.

One day, the masters of Töyry and Kylä-Pentti were there. Halme was discussing the question of the underprivileged. Antto Laurila began to grumble.

"Yaah, goddamn it... we've got to get some kind of democracy... Otherwise there'll be no end to this misery."

Töyry laughed and said, "I don't know... It seems to me that work is the only way to fight hunger."

"Goddamn it: work doesn't end a tenant's hunger."

Töyry began to hew furiously at a timber, saying, in time to the blows of his axe, "Not a... single one... of us... has had... to die... of hunger... yet."

His words were followed by silence. The men bent to their work, hiding their smiles. Those nearest examined the timbers, or studied their saw-blades intently. Halme tapped a log with his cane and said, "An election reform would surely open up possibilities."

"Halme will have to go to the Legislature himself. Since no one else there seems to know how to do anything. That is, if he's gotten wise from Hellberg's books."

"I don't need the wisdom of Hellberg's books. The need for election reform is apparent simply through local research, so to speak."

An embarrassed silence ensued. Otto stood by the wall, tested the blade of his axe, and said, "There are a lot of programs, but if I got to go to the Legislature, I would start out by fixing the women's question."

"A most urgent matter."

"You can say that again. Number one priority. That's where we would start."

Halme snorted, but comments began to ricochet from wall to wall, about which the brotherhood of the Finnish populace had always agreed, from Hanko in the

116

south to Petsamo in the north.

The master of Kylä-Pentti gave a landlordly guffaw and said, "I tell you... When you hear that kind of talk, you're on a real job site, I tell you."

Halme alone smiled condescendingly. Preeti Leppänen was afraid to join in the laughter because he could see it was displeasing to Halme, who had just promised to take on his son as a tailor's apprentice. Preeti was married to Henna, who looked after the chickens at the manor. She was as helpless as Preeti himself. They had two children, a boy and a girl. Their household was wretched, and they went hungry at times. As the Halmes had no children, Emma had advocated adoption, but Halme had opposed the idea. Instead, he had decided to take on an apprentice. Valenti Leppänen was still too young for such employment, but nevertheless Halme had decided to engage him. He had several reasons for doing so. An apprentice would enhance his reputation and free him from such slightly demeaning chores as chopping and carrying firewood, and from other petty duties which he performed most unwillingly. Not out of laziness, but out of reluctance to see himself lugging in an armload of wood. The books Hellberg delivered to him had also deepened his sympathies for the deprived, and although his fellow-feelings were fundamentally theoretical, he offered them as his motive to his doubtful wife.

"Precisely because he is so dirty and hungry. That's why we have to take him on. Water and soap will overcome your opposition. We'll be able to save at least one human being from dying of hunger and lice. We have the resources to afford him a livelihood whether or not he has an aptitude for the trade."

The event eased the Leppänens' burden markedly and elevated their status as well. Another coincident occurrence worked to their advantage: Henna's mother died of starvation. The sickly old woman lived in a shack by herself at the edge of the village, and although Henna took whatever she could to her, it was not enough to keep her alive. She would have died sooner if some of the neighbors had not helped. The town had refused its aid because it felt the woman had someone to care for her. She left behind three molting hens, which actually were not laying. But, as Preeti put it: "We're even getting some livestock."

Nor did they begin to lay eggs for the Leppänens, for they themselves lived as gatherers at the mercy of their natural economy.

Bit by bit the school was completed. Otto achieved his end and got a good contract for the fireplaces. Working as his hod carrier was his oldest boy, Janne, who, people said, was building a school for himself. The boy looked exactly like his father.

117

"And he has the same kind of mouth," people said.

The Kivivuori boys were an unusual phenomenon in the community. They were the only ones to use the familiar address with their parents and were never beaten for it. Their father was unwilling and their mother too soft-hearted to whip them. So it was that even at the construction site, Janne's shout rang out: "Hey old man! You need some of this slop?"

Through Hellberg's agency, Halme subscribed to *The Worker* and spoke more and more frequently of socialism. Hellberg found himself increasingly eclipsed by him. But Halme's brand of socialism contained many planks of his own contriving, and in opposition to Hellberg's rigid programs, with their absolute class bias, he would speak with respect of some necessary reforms.

"Even the ruling classes will recognize their necessity, at which point they will be effected by mutual consent, so to speak."

Hellberg laughed scornfully, with all the effect of a dull knife on rock.

The people's attitude toward Halme began to change. Until now they had viewed his programs for enlightenment with some degree of sarcasm, but now they were willing to concede.

"That son-of-a-bitch is a smart man. He even puts Hellberg in his place sometimes. Not many could've gone up to the parson's widow and spoken to her the way he did that day on the church hill. Now he's got a cane. But why the hell shouldn't a common man swing a cane?"

Once, when returning from the building site, Antto Laurila asked Halme, "Did the frost kill all your potato plants?"

"Well, I can't say all of them. But I'll have to buy some."

"Come and get some from me in the fall. I'll be getting a good crop. If I only get a chance to dig them up."

"Thank you for the offer. But of course I'll take them only if I pay. You've got enough hardships of your own to endure."

Antto had always been the harshest in his attitude toward Halme.

Whenever Halme happened to come in contact with the couple at the parsonage, references to social issues appeared more and more often in his discourse. But since they still appeared as theories only, they were discussed with mutual understanding, and Halme maintained his unofficial position as a link between the pair at the parsonage and the people.

118

III

Late in the fall the school began to function. A gala opening was held, at which all the elite of the parish and the biggest landowners were gathered. From the home village itself even the less influential were in attendance.

The master of Yllö gave a welcoming speech and thanked the builders on behalf of the town. It was the vicar's wife, however, who delivered the official address. She spoke with fervor of a Finnish fatherland. Every new public school broadened the base of Finnish education. From that base, the Finnish movement would spread to wider frontiers, until it had completely conquered the heights as well.

Every sentence was an attack on the baron, but he gave no sign of noticing, which was for the most part true, for he understood not one word that was spoken. He could make something of the hired hands' and tenants' dialect utterances, but the Finnish of the educated was totally foreign to him.

Even Jussi was there on one of the back benches, trying to remain invisible. He would rather have been anywhere but here, and had come only as a result of the vicar's prompting him as one of the builders. His fears regarding the contract had become so acute that he humbly obeyed even this casual exhortation with no attempt at refusal.

While drinking coffee, Halme had made his way to the dignitaries' table. People exchanged glances and whispered, "Look at Aatu. Good God — does he look like a gentleman, or what?"

Halme's fine hands, with their shapely, long-jointed fingers, wove an elegant accompaniment to his speech. Everything about him was stylized — his speech, his gestures. His dry, long-limbed figure that seemed to have more than its share of joints — everything about him was of a piece. Above all, his beautifully arching, rounded brow caught the eye. His fingers attached themselves to everything gracefully, surely — to the coffee cup, to the creamer, to the coffee bread.

The vicar spoke mainly to the baron, but Halme and the vicar's wife carried on a lively discussion of drinking among the young, of their brawling, of their unchastity, which Halme referred to as "the non-spiritual union of members of the opposite sex."

The vicaress proposed the establishment of a Youth League, but Halme had another remedy.

"Madam's recommendation is certainly most worthy of note. But a deeper examination raises doubts. At this time, too much culture is perhaps improper. I know this people, and I am of the opinion that they must be fed things gradually.

119

Let's consider, for example, the establishment of a fire department. As an active, functioning organization, it would attract the young men, and they are precisely the object of our concern. The female sex is by nature already on a higher moral plane."

"Ooh, we women thank you for those words, Mr. Halme. But I believe you have just settled the whole question."

"Well, let's also take into account a fire department's practical value. Just think of these wood-shingled roofs of ours."

The baron seized upon the subject with extraordinary enthusiasm. He promised financial help, although his only thanks for establishing the school had been abuse. In that respect, his poor command of the language had been a genuine advantage.

"But you. It was you, Halme. People with you. I get manor men, sure."

"Indeed. You do have influence among the people."

It was the vicaress speaking, and Halme answered with great seriousness.

"I have tried to spread about me the idealistic spirit of the age. But the young would still rather hold a knife in their hand than a book. Well, why would we do this work, if it weren't necessary for that very reason. First the spirit, then matter. By way of the spirit, we can undertake even fundamental social reforms."

"But of course. I can see before my very eyes how we can build a new Hellas here in the north. And the old one will shrink to a mere fable by comparison."

And so it was decided to establish a fire department. Halme would undoubtedly be a key figure in the endeavor.

The celebration came and went. The kids in the community would have been glad to see the building burn down, but that did not happen. A teacher arrived, and a very typical one at that. He wore spectacles and even sported a Vandyke beard.

Akseli Koskela had to go to school too. The joy of wearing new boots and woolens hardly compensated for the anxiety of this farm boy coming among villagers. So far, he had had little to do with other children. Only the Kivivuori boys were better known to him, and it was to them that he turned for refuge. Not to Janne, but to Oskar, who was younger. Janne was not an easy type to befriend, for he remained aloof from the others behind a mocking front no one could penetrate.

Oskar was more accessible than his brother, and Akseli turned to him in his isolation. He knew the Kivivuoris because Otto and Anna were his godparents.

120

In the new school, age played no role in the organization of grades: a seven-year-old might sit next to a seventeen-year-old. Attendance was not compulsory — children could go as long as their parents wanted them to. Jussi had decided to limit his son's attendance to a couple of years.

The school day opened with draggy hymn-singing, mingled with the sound of coughing and nose-blowing. The nose seemed to be a crucial item on the teacher's agenda for popular enlightenment, for on the first day he decreed that everyone was to have a handkerchief. These were cut from new bed linen, old linen shirts, and from every conceivable fabric. There were periodic checks, and then a fuss was raised about the kind of handkerchief, for there emerged from the boys' pockets unrecognizable pieces of rag, black with the tar from skis, from dust, and from all the junk a young boy carried in his pockets.

After the hymn a reader with knitted brow would stammer his way through a passage from *The Birch and the Star* to be rewarded by titters for words he had guessed at. His nose would start running too, and naturally he would wipe it in the old way on his coat sleeve, already stiff from earlier wipings.

"How are you wiping your nose? Quiet back there! You uncivilized bushmen! I'll teach you to act like human beings, you sons of mitten-noses."

If the teacher had ever possessed a sense of humor, he had lost it in wars waged in his previous positions. Seeing only glowering looks and veiled sneers as he watched from under his brows, he lost his self-control. But since some of the pupils were almost grown men, a display of temper might make matters worse. Of medium height and slender to boot, the teacher would try to drag some of the older boys into a corner. The boys would not resist actively, but would spread their legs and stay rooted to the spot. One such boy once said, "What wind can move a stone?"

"Detention. Detention. Two hours every day. The entire school, without exception. The impudence. Your parents have labored to provide you with a school, and you act like wild animals. You are the shame of this country, you hooligans. I'll get together a force of your parents and we'll hold a mass flogging."

The worst malingerer was Janne Kivivuori, but the teacher had to admit that he was also the sharpest student. He learned everything easily and effortlessly, which was all the more remarkable because he was never seen to study. His knapsack often lay unopened at home until lunch was put into it the next morning.

But Janne studied before class periods and even during them. He was a master at bluffing, and when he was unable to answer a question, he would bring up a side issue with such earnestness that the teacher would say, "...well. That's

121

right. That's absolutely right. But that isn't what I asked."

Akseli was well-behaved, but he was a completely mediocre student. Only in arithmetic did he do well, but that did not compensate for his other weaknesses. His written compositions, in particular, were so wooden that the teacher read aloud from them to teach the other pupils how not to write.

He had tried a couple of times to sing by himself. The pupils each had to take a turn, and Akseli made the effort, too. He was shy, but since there was no alternative, he began to intone lustily.

"Oh, fountain lo-ovely, near thy side..."

"Stop...stop. Sit down."

When during the springtime the pupils were required to sing individually for the assignment of grades, the teacher absent-mindedly told Akseli to try again, but before the boy could open his mouth, he remembered the earlier incident and said, raising his hand defensively, "Sit down...sit down. You already have a grade."

Reading was hard for Akseli, and reciting from memory even harder. Haltingly, word by word, he recited a piece about the Finnish war: "...on every side... the cannon roared.... On every side, blood ran... Blackened by powder-smoke... ummm... without medical supplies... and, and... and... dressed in rags... often without food.... ummm... to satisfy their hunger... but always... uh... the menacing rifle on their hunched shoulders... the...ar...army marched once more... toward umm... the deepest north..."

In the middle of it all, the class broke into laughter. Janne had been wagging his jaw and making faces behind the teacher's back, but he was too slow in putting on a serious face, and the teacher realized who the culprit was.

"Kivivuori , you hedgehog..."

He began to flog the boy with his pointer.

"You... you ape... you... ass... Haven't you heard what your ancestors were like? They... were men... who knew... what it meant... to sacrifice... But you, you grin like an ape... You're not worthy to be called Finn... What will this country come to with the likes of you... You vagabond louts..."

On the following day, Janne walked with his side askew and a look of pain on his face.

"What's the matter?"

"My side hurts."

"Why?"

"Because the teacher hit me."

122

"You're lying. I hit you lightly. It hardly hurt you."

"It didn't hurt much. Not even later during the day. It only started at night. And it doesn't bother me except when I move... It feels like a broken rib... Although my father says it isn't broken."

The teacher eyed him doubtfully, but for a time he stopped using the pointer, and he never again hit Janne. At recess time, however, Janne was perfectly well.

The next pupil to be flogged was Akseli. He was not ill-tempered or badly behaved in school, but the beating resulted from a fight. The episode really began with Oskar. Akseli had no skis. He was still not able to make them for himself, and got only a growled response about a useless waste of time when he asked his father for them. Oskar sometimes let him use his skis, and when one of the bigger boys took his friend's turn on the hill by force, Akseli felt duty-bound to go to his defence.

"It's Oskar's turn. You shouldn't count it as his turn when I use his skis."

It was a question of sharing a slope with a jump on it. Because of their numbers, the boys had agreed to take turns.

"What business is it of yours?"

"It was Osku's turn."

"Yes, but it wasn't yours. It's no skin off your back."

"It just might be."

Akseli's voice was quiet, but his old, explosive temper was beginning to boil.

"Shut your mouth. You're not so tough, even if you think you are."

"Tough enough to take care of you any time."

"Poor thing. You don't even get enough to eat at home."

Akseli had heard innuendo now and then about his father's stinginess, but he ignored it because he was sensitive on the subject. But this was too obvious to be ignored. He struck out, but not to the body, as little boys do. Instead, he went straight for the face and head. Panting, he kept on hitting, even after the boy lay under him on the snow.

"You don't hit someone when he's down."

The others dragged him off, and he himself became aware of what was happening. Panting heavily, he wiped his bloody knuckles on the snow and left.

The boys kept fights of this sort to themselves. The loser had to keep quiet, for tattling would have brought on another thrashing, this time by the whole group. But the tracks of this fight were evident on the boy's swollen nose and bloody lips. The teacher questioned him for a long time.

"Who hit you?"

123

"No one."

"What happened to your face?"

"I skied into a tree."

It sounded suspicious. Then one of the girls explained, with expedient gravity, "He was fighting with Akseli Koskela."

Akseli stood looking at the floor while the teacher tried to extract information about the fight. The girls did not know what had started it, for they had been some distance away. The teacher next resorted to questioning Arvo Töyry, whose relationship to the other boys was somewhat different. As the son of a large landowner, he behaved better than most of them, as if he already knew as a child the obligations imposed on him by his status. He answered the questions factually, saying only what he had to.

"He took Oskar Kivivuori's turn, and Akseli told him so."

"Such matters are to be brought to me. You are not to take the law into your own hands. This is appalling. Look at the way you've cut up your friend's face. Ask forgiveness for your behavior."

The boy riveted his eyes even more firmly to the floor and pursed his lips even more tightly. The teacher shook him by the shoulders, but when he remained stubbornly silent, began to beat him. Clenching his teeth and grunting, Akseli took the blows. Had the teacher known the kind of thrashings he had received from his father without giving in, he would have understood how pointless his efforts were.

Again he was forced to shatter his pointer on the desk and scream himself hoarse: "Am I supposed to make human beings out of you, you tiger cubs?"

"It's asking a lot to expect a man to retain his faith in this people's future," the teacher was apt to say to his wife after a session of this sort. 'A Northern Hellas,' as we used to say in normal school. God help us."

Since Akseli had to stay for two hours' detention every day that week, the matter came also to the attention of his home folk. Jussi no longer hit him, but he had to listen to sermons enough, and he was threatened with going without food for a day or two.

"You're a real hooligan. Only through God's mercy will you stay out of jail all your life."

There was compensation as well. Otto Kivivuori made him a pair of skis. Not because of the fight, of course, but because of Anna. She took her position as godmother so seriously that when she learned that Akseli could not get skis at home, she demanded that Otto make them.

124

Akseli sometimes stopped at the Kivivuoris on his way home from school. Shy and quiet, he would sit on the bench near the doorway. At home the Kivivuori boys were more involved in their own activities, so he would sit orphaned on his bench. He was the most shy of Anna. To him she was something to be revered, something on a higher level. In addition, things were neat and clean here. At home there were no rugs on the floor. Here, one had to take off one's rag of a fur hat and hide it behind him on the bench.

He spoke only in answer to questions. He was pleased when he was given the skis, but at the same time he was troubled, for he knew the reason why. As he watched the family's actions and listened to their talk, he sometimes felt a secret urge to smile. His "auntie" scolded the father and sons almost incessantly for their foul language, for their misbehavior, for everything under the sun. They in turn teased and provoked her as much as they possibly could. Only the girl, Elina, was quiet and well-behaved. She was the apple of her mother's eye, always pampered and neatly dressed. The boys teased her whenever her mother's back was turned. Sometimes they pinched her, sometimes they pulled her braid in passing. When they did, she always let out an affected shriek.

A year or two back, the boys had smeared the girl's bottom with tar as revenge for one of their mother's punitive measures, which were usually something like the loss of butter for a certain number of meals. Anna could never bring herself to hit the boys. The worst she would attempt was a slap with a dish rag.

Feeling that he had sat there for the appropriate length of time, Akseli would start out for home. Only on his way did he give himself up to the full enjoyment of the skis. He was no longer troubled by the reason for which they had been given.

When Alma learned about the background of the skis, she said, "You really could have made them yourself."

"Why does he need them? And we don't have the money for such things."

Jussi did have money in a drawer of the secretary in the parlor. That room was otherwise pleasant as well, for the windows were curtained and there were rugs on the floor. But they did not live in that room. The door was kept locked, and it was heated only enough to keep it in good condition.

125

The vicar and his wife had made frequent promises to visit the Koskelas, but it was the following spring before they came. Even the tranquil Alma was flustered when she saw the gentry arriving.

"God bless us... greet them. They're waiting."

There was awkwardness at the start, but the friendliness of their superiors soon broke the ice. Again the boys had to undergo the ordeal by fire of introductions. Having answered a few of the usual questions about their age, they were permitted to take refuge behind the stove, where they peered out at the visitors, soberly but searchingly, with the shrewd powers of observation peculiar to such woods-bred creatures.

Before long, the discussion shifted completely to the vicaress's astonishment at the condition of the tenancy.

"Did you clear all this by yourself?"

"Well, you might say so... No one else has been here except for a few who helped a little with the building."

"And how long has it been?"

"Ah-mmm... It'll be sixteen years this fall since I came here."

The vicar looked out at the swamp through the window.

"Indeed. We should make an application for the Agricultural Society's Pioneer Medal for Koskela."

"You're absolutely right. We'll do it at once."

Jussi rubbed his elbows against his knees. For all his forty-five years and his stooped shoulders, he blushed.

"We-ell... Not really... The old man of Pentti... the one who died some years ago... he got one... But compared to his work, this isn't much. He hoed up more than thirty hectares in his lifetime... This isn't anything... It's small compared to his... So that as far as this..."

"This is certainly worth a medal. You have to be recognized for your work. That's how the wilderness in Finland has been cleared... But have you been hit by frosts?"

"No-o... not much. At first, before the swamp was cleared. The ground water kept things so cold... It still nips the oats sometimes in the fall, but they can stand it by now... It did wipe out one rye crop... We got only a little pig-feed from the chaff."

"Yes, that's the danger pioneers have to face. It's described so well in the poem *Paavo of Saarijärvi*. Juhani Aho also has some good portrayals of it."

"Well... That's the way it is, all right... It's no laughing matter."

"But you must be doing well now. With so much land."

Jussi nearly jumped. His old, ingrained tenant's instinct awakened.

"Ye-es... Well... our bread yes, with hard work... But we can't... I've never had to beg for food... But there isn't all that much land... And it's starting to get poor... in the spring, water is a problem in these swamp strips... doesn't pay to try to plant rye there, when even hay sprouts are likely to go... eats up clover altogether... So there is trouble too."

"Certainly there is hardship. But we Finns are accustomed to it, and we will not be discouraged. No other race could endure such conditions. Fate has not coddled us, and for that reason, here lives a people whose equal in strength and tenacity cannot be found. And you little pioneers of the future. Come here now."

Three pieces of candy materialized from the woman's pocket.

Alma urged the boys to thank her nicely, and they bowed to the best of their ability. Aku got a pat on the head to the bargain.

"There. It's nice to think of you carrying on your father's work. Your country expects you to give your all when your turn comes. And I believe that you will."

The vicaress refused Alma's offer of coffee.

"We don't want to put you to any more trouble. Some other time... It's such nice weather that I would like to walk a little. The road leading up here is so nice."

"Yeah... I guess it is... Still a few mud holes, tho' I've hauled gravel in every winter."

The gentry departed, leaving in their wake a feeling of total elevation. A medal. He had to snort at that — that wouldn't happen. But then Jussi thought of the money in the drawer. If they would agree to sell some day... It might have an effect on the congregation... In a few years, if we really bear down, I can manage it.

The couple walked slowly toward the parsonage. The vicaress leaned on her husband's arm, admiring the spring evening. They had been discussing the Koskelas in highly approving fashion, and the vicar, who had vaguely feared the encounter, was pleased it had gone so well.

Now his wife turned the discussion to the parsonage, and not for the first time.

"They are really in better shape than we are. The parsonage spends more than it takes in."

"Well yes... But let's wait until we're done with these initial costs."

"I'm not even taking them into account. I'm speaking only of day-to-day

127

expenses. I'm beginning to be afraid. Our resources are dwindling when they should be increasing. Ilmari is nearly of school age, and soon Ani will be too. It will be expensive, since I can't exactly have them on my brothers' hands in Helsinki."

"Of course not... That's perfectly clear."

The vicar was troubled. The question was a sensitive one, although he had tried to discount it. The cost of establishing a household at the parsonage had been paid out of Ellen's share of the family estate, given to her by her brothers. He himself actually had nothing, which was a source of embarrassment to him. Not because the money was Ellen's, but because he was so inept in its use. As a result, he had left many of the decisions to her. Especially since he believed her to have a good grasp of things economic as well as experience in farming.

Such an error in judgment resulted from the vicar's own ignorance of rural economy. Ellen's positive pronouncements had the appearance of being based on considerable expertise. "We have to devote all our efforts to cattle-raising. All the experts have recently come to the conclusion that the future of Finnish farming lies in dairying."

"...recently come to the conclusion." These dicta had such a weight of authority that the vicar could not bring himself to ask how and on what basis they had "recently" come to such conclusions. And Ellen was a modern woman. She scorned the old-fashioned ladies who thought themselves too good to understand economic matters that went beyond the boundaries of the kitchen. These vague pronouncements she had picked up from her father, who practiced idealistic husbandry by distributing iron plowshares and better seeds to farmers. Her superficial grasp of the women's question added emphasis to all this. In the country, her energies found no other outlet than in questions of domestic economy, so to them she applied herself, with the result that the threat of trouble became obvious. Something had to be done.

"Exactly how many rent-days does Koskela have?"

The vicar was roused from his gloomy thoughts.

"Well, you know that yourself. Two with a horse and one on foot."

"But isn't that really very little?"

"Normally it is. But the rent from developed holdings is different. This one is entirely their own work."

"But now it is developed."

"What difference does that make?"

"The difference is obvious. They no longer have to clear the land. Couldn't

128

we raise their rent a little?"

The vicar was upset and said uneasily, "It would be a little difficult... It doesn't seem right... and... besides..."

"What would be wrong with it? And they themselves would understand if we explained it in a friendly way. It's exactly why the parsonage is unprofitable."

"But why should we clamp down precisely on them?"

"Not only on them, of course. We have to look into the hired hands' and the maids' pay as well. I was too inexperienced. We promised too much. And I don't mean a lot. Just helping days during the summer. We won't increase the rent-days themselves. And they don't put in any pasture and wood-days at all. That's unheard of anywhere else. You'll see, they'll understand perfectly well. But we can't expect them to offer it on their own."

Thoughts he did not dare utter whirled through the vicar's mind. To do so would have involved criticism of Ellen's decisions. They had brought a nursemaid and housekeeper with them from Helsinki, they had hired a cook or inside maid in the country, had separate help to tend the cattle, and several hired hands. In addition, Ellen was planning to hire a coachman and get a team of horses. The estate in this old mother parish was rather large, but the vicar was aware that one could not live here on the same scale as on a manor.

But he could not speak his mind, and so he presented his doubts from a moral point of view.

"Indeed. Of course they will do it if we ask them. They haven't in all this time objected to anything we've asked. But that's exactly why it's so difficult. I feel absolutely sorry for him. His back is very painful, although he tries to hide it at work out of fear. I, at least, would find it hard to explain the matter to him."

A shade of annoyance at his opposition was apparent in Ellen's voice.

"But Koskela himself won't have to put in those helping days. They will be women's days, so his wife can do them. And the older boy can be responsible for them in a year or two, when he'll be up to it. Your qualms are pointless. You'll see that they won't mind. They are understanding people and will realize that the parsonage cannot survive without a normal income. But you're not aware of realities. Am I hardhearted? I don't think so. But in a couple of years we'll be penniless. We have to clamp down. How will we raise and educate our children? The Koskelas can easily bear a few extra days. They even have six cows."

"Listen... A cuckoo."

They stopped, and the vicar counted, "One, two, three, four, five, six... Six times. Did you hear?"

129

"I did... It was very beautiful... The cuckoo and springtime. They somehow belong to the Finnish landscape... They are the essence of its beauty."

Aroused to enthusiasm, the vicar took up her words. "It's true. It's at its height then."

"It is indeed. This really is a beautiful country... But listen. We have to break it to them gently. I'm sure they will understand. They'll realize that we are forced to do it. They are very good people... Exactly the best type of Finn."

Troubled, the vicar looked down. His recent joy had vanished, and he asked in a strained voice, "How many days were you thinking of?"

"Let's say six days."

The number had stayed in her mind from the cuckoo's call, so she chose it.

"Well, that really isn't much, but it won't help us a great deal either. We could just as well do without it."

"Don't start thinking that way again. That's only a part of the program. We'll take other measures as well."

The vicar was silent for a long time. He could not quarrel on an evening like this. Then he changed the subject.

"The meeting to establish a fire department will be held next week. Will Halme get the support of the people?"

"I'm sure he will, and the hired hands from the manor and the tenants will go along merely on the baron's say-so. But I have my doubts about that tailor. He gets that paper, *The Worker*."

"What significance is there in that? It's mere childishness. We don't have the conditions necessary for the success of socialism here."

His wife was not afraid of socialism either, but she found it otherwise offensive.

"But we don't need that kind of childishness either."

"No, we don't. But they are pleading a good cause."

"Some of them are. But have you read what the new faction is writing? That unbelievable Kurikka. And a shoemaker named Salin. For a shoemaker, he's incredible. He organized the shoemakers' strikes in the capital. He's an extraordinary ranter who makes the weirdest speeches... and he's a horrible drunk."

"There are always those original types... But there's something I wanted to talk about. When we are involved in dealings with the baron about the fire department again, I wish you would be more restrained. There is no reason to bring personalities into discussions of opinion. Forgive me, but some of your comments are insulting."

Ellen's hand shifted beneath her husband's arm.

"Is that so? Just what do you mean? I haven't referred to him directly. If he wants to take my criticisms personally, there is nothing I can do about it."

"I only meant that... perhaps too much militancy isn't proper."

The vicar noticed that Ellen's hand was beginning to stir restlessly under his arm, and he was beginning to regret his words. He could sense her rising agitation.

"But I haven't been at all militant... Who has aggravated the situation? The Swedes themselves. They haven't voluntarily conceded a thing. They have answered our requests with arrogance and bullying insolence. They consider everyone who speaks Finnish to be uncivilized... They have degraded and scorned us... almost...almost... how can I put it... How have they lived here? Like plantation owners in the colonies. As for civilization, you see the evidence of an enduring one in the Koskela cottage. What strong and humble people. Just wait until they are enlightened. I hear behind me the sound of thousands of footsteps... That's what my father always used to say. And soon we'll see how true it is... Why don't you ever get excited?"

"I do."

The vicar put his arm about his wife and kissed her. Almost moved, he smiled and said, "Sometimes I have to laugh at your enthusiasm. You talk like a child then, but I still love your capacity for exaltation. Don't ever lose it. But use it right..."

Ellen smiled in response. A consciously childish expression appeared on her face. She gave herself up to the embrace in the grip of the sudden rush of affection that held them both. It was completely characteristic of her. Whenever her husband held and caressed her, she seemed to contract inside and a wave of love and tenderness concentrated within her body. It caressed her whole being with its warmth, and brought her to a state of purring euphoria.

They completed the journey closely linked to one another. The spring evening chirped and warbled by the roadside in the voices of innumerable birds. Swarms of insects whirred above the road. Somewhere in the recesses of the spruce trees, a brook gurgled. The sun had still not set.

At the Koskelas, Aleksi came rushing into the living room.

"The cuckoo is calling... I heard it... Six times."

"Six times," grumbled Jussi... "That isn't very much... Why is he so stingy? He could have run off a few more."

When the two years mentioned in the contract were up, Jussi himself brought up the subject of the rent. Unprepared for the discussion, the vicar began to hem and haw.

Jussi could tell from his uncertainty that something was coming. The vicar began laughingly to explain.

"I uh... I've been wondering if Koskela could help me out a little... We're both farmers, but I have to admit that compared to Koskela, I'm completely helpless... Koskela has brought his farm into production and has kept it up, but I haven't been able to do as much with the parsonage. I'm in deep trouble... What would Koskela think if I asked him for help in my plight?"

The vicar spoke as if he were thoroughly amused at his own ineptitude and at the comic circumstance of having to ask Koskela for extra days. He also expected Jussi to laugh at the idea, to ask how much aid was needed to save the parsonage. Perhaps he might add some amused comment about a tenant's certainly having to help the parsonage if it would otherwise go to ruin.

But his laughter grew strained when he saw the suspicion on Jussi's face.

"Well, what kind of help would be needed then?"

"Well, not really any kind. I was just joking. But seriously, would Koskela find it objectionable if we increased the rent-days? Not by much.... Just some help-days during the summer... six women's days, for example."

Jussi stared stiffly at the ground. His thoughts groped quickly through the ramifications of the matter. The pressure on him was greatest during the summer, and the rent-days were certain to be required at that time.

"If it's the vicar's order, then we'll have to..."

"No, no... I want this to be a request, not a demand... And I'm not happy doing it. Circumstances are such that we are constantly having to put money into the parsonage. It doesn't bring in enough to cover expenses. We try to pinch pennies here and there, and it's a pity that we have to impose on you. But as a farmer Koskela can understand the facts of our situation. They are such that... Everything has its own laws... Since the contract specifically requires the agreement of both parties, this is only a request."

Jussi almost snorted: in this case, there was no difference between a command and a request.

"I'll try, of course... as much as we can... There is no... As long as we can live there."

The vicar assured him in a voice that sounded almost offended that the question of eviction did not even merit consideration. He even spoke vaguely of reducing the rent if the situation improved. "And how could we do without Koskela? Where else could we find a tenant like Koskela?"

Six days. In itself, the extra burden was not impossible for them to bear, but it was proof of the insecurity of their situation. During those days, Jussi began to suffer stomach pains in addition to his back ailment.

"Father has to take soda. Be quiet now. Your father's resting."

Now and then, his family began to hear bitter words from Jussi about the masters of the parsonage. The vicar's friendliness, which now overflowed, had no effect on him. Jussi saw through things clearly. "His wife gives the orders, and he can't buck her. And he's happy to put up with it; he's not even ashamed."

"Ya-ah. So now I have to start supporting the parsonage. Right. So they won't go completely bankrupt. Carrying another gentleman's family on my back. Easy enough, but not when you have to support an army of maids to boot. They're said to be looking for a pair of horses. Long-necked blacks, of all things. There's a lot to learn about him... The late Vallén used to load his sleigh with women on his way to church and hang on to the runners himself... Even when he was old. Now these people will soon be driving in a coach."

"Well, hardly to church," said Alma in a discouraged tone of voice. She herself was somewhat downhearted. Not because of the six days, but because of Jussi's bitterness. She was completely healthy and did not fear the extra work. She could stand it for a year or two, and then Akseli would be grown up.

"Surely not to church. But they say the children have to be driven around, and they have to take pleasure trips... that the children have to be brought up in a style that suits their class. I don't know what riding around has to do with education... But I have to go... And you boys have to spread the manure on the corner plots. You too will do work that suits your class... And it's got to be done by this evening."

Although Jussi said "boys," it meant only Akseli, for the work of Aleksi and Aku amounted to little. They were sent along to prevent Akseli's thinking he was being treated differently from his younger brothers. During the summer, the family was hard pressed. Not only did Alma have the six extra mandatory days; she also had additional wage-work to do, as did Jussi.

Twelve-year-old Akseli had to take up the scythe. The other boys raked, and when the three of them were alone, the younger brothers found out who was the boss. To Akusti, raking was a game, and he kept at it only as long as it amused him. His father had made him a toy rake, but Akseli insisted on taking the matter seriously.

"Just keep on raking... along the edge of the ditch."

"No I won't."

"Yes you will."

But Aku knew his brother would not use force to make him, since his mother had forbidden it.

"He's a child... He doesn't have to do it yet."

These words were sharply etched in Aku's mind, and he knew what they meant. When Akseli, muttering something about his being a baby, told him to go, he waggled his jaw behind his brother's back and hissed to himself, "Pig's-eye, pig's-eye... Koskela's bleary-eye..."

It was a nickname the younger brothers had given to Akseli, but there were times when it was unwise to use it.

Akseli was cutting hay. The scythe was heavy for him, and he had not learned to sharpen it properly, but he was learning the art of mowing with it. The phenomenal prowess that he showed in later years stemmed from these days. From his father, he had inherited an attitude of silent fury at work, but not his wearing, crushing drive. He was more flexible and, like his mother, knew how to supplement his strength with skill. His very arms sensed it. The slightest deviation in the angle of the blade made mowing harder. The scythe had to strike at exactly the right angle before it cut freely. In addition, he learned the importance of a proper rhythm. A particular tempo was best. Increasing it meant expending more effort without increasing the yield. A slacker tempo was just as unsatisfactory.

Evenings he was exhausted. But when his father went out to the fields after returning from work, Akseli had to go too. He was not ordered to do so, but the situation was similar to Jussi's when the vicar suggested extra days. He could not refuse when his father said, "You've cut down quite a piece... Are you still able to rake a little?"

Then it was back to work, where he went on raking in the dewy late evening, half asleep.

"If we did that strip yet... We'd be that much ahead... You should be able to do that much... I'll help you after I cut it."

He really wasn't able, but he had to.

During the day he had to take care of everything. The pig had to be fed on time, the chickens had to be guarded against foxes and hawks... Mother had

134

prepared food for them when she left for work in the morning, which they had
to heat for themselves. As they ate, they carried on strange discussions about
the outside world, the world that began somewhere beyond the threshing barn.
For the most part, the exchanges took place between the younger brothers, with
Akseli, who had even gone to school, playing the superior and condescending
arbiter of their disputes.

"No... a *ruuna* is a gelding... That's what the books call it... And the parsonage
gentry speak words that are in books. And it doesn't have to be brown, it can
even be black."

"Why is it called a *ruuna* then, if it's a gelding?"

"Well, I'm telling you, it's that way in books... But it's a castrated horse,
just the same. And keep your fingers away from there. There are three for each
of us, and you've already had your share."

Aku had a tendency to rebel against his oldest brother's rule. But when dark
clouds thrust their way into the clear sky above the spruce tops beyond the
threshing barn, they all watched uneasily. After the first clap of thunder, they
went indoors. Akseli checked to see that the dampers were closed; otherwise,
the lightning might come down the chimney. He sent his brothers to sit, each
in his own corner, far from the windows, and he himself surveyed the situation.
The boys sat without moving, legs straight out in front of them, and asked uneasily,
"Which way is it going?"

"It's coming right over us."

Aku was the optimist, and said, even though he couldn't see, "No, It's heading
for the parsonage."

Akseli was uneasy, and the groundless hope would irritate him so much that
he might bark angrily, "Well, I can see, can't I?"

When lightning flashed in the darkened room and the windows rattled a quick
response, they spoke not a word. Each one looked a different way, none wanting
another to see his eyes. Then a roaring wind sprang up, and with it the first drops
pelted the windows. Flashes and roars succeeded one another, and the three little
men sat like Buddhas, their breathing soft and tense. Gradually, the intervals
between the flashes and roars lengthened, and a relieved discussion arose. Father
and mother might even come home in the middle of the day, since they could
not make hay in the rain.

Sometimes it did happen. But that was worse than anything, for it meant the
day had to be made up by compressing two work-days into one. During rainy
days, they tried to find work for Jussi at the parsonage, but it was more difficult

135

to find it for the women. Alma often had to go home.

Jussi was making a playhouse for the girl at the parsonage. As it neared completion, the boy became intrigued by it, and demanded that it be made into a gingerbread house.

"Hmm. I can't make anything like that. What kind of house is it?"

"Its roof is made of pancakes and its window-frames of sugar."

Jussi smiled a twisted, angry smile. There were many things in the world of which he did not approve, and a boundless imagination was one of the first. The boy brought his mother to his aid, and she said in a resentful voice, "I'm at a loss with him. He has more strange ideas than he has the time to carry out."

Her tone implied that she and Jussi had previously commiserated with each other about the troubles of parenting, and he, of course, went with the current. "That's right. There's a lot you have to figure out, that's for sure ..."

"Why don't you cut out a couple of shapes like gingersnaps, even if it's only from cardboard, and nail them up to the wall."

Jussi did so and a gingerbread house of sorts was born. The boy also wanted to handle his tools, and that angered Jussi. He addressed the boy ingratiatingly, "Give it to me... It's just been sharpened... You'll hurt yourself."

But when the boy again approached the tools, he would watch unnoticed and fume within. "Take it... Go on and take it... I've never seen a kid like that."

Ilmari was not really an unusual sort of child, but Jussi could tolerate no excessive liberties on the part of children. The rest of the staff actually liked the spontaneous boy. Miss Aino, in turn, was already restrained in her behavior as a child. The two had been given really Finnish names, from *The Kalevala*, actually. The girl was known as Ani, however.

The vicar was giving the boy a kind of elementary schooling, and when he was called from the yard for his lessons, the people at work would see him run crouching for refuge in an alder grove, so fast that the leaves hissed. Most of them sided with the boy and said nothing of what they had seen.

Among other things, the boy was taught *The Tales of Ensign Stål*. One day he appeared at the work-place, and seeing Jussi's patched, threadbare coat lying on a rock, he put it on, leaving one sleeve empty. Then, standing on a rock, he held forth his hat extended toward the wondering crew.

> *Friends, men and women,*
> *Is there a listener here,*
> *Who will sit and hear the story*

136

of an old-time grenadier?
One hand lost at Umeå,
The other held out shaking here...

"What a weird leech he is..."

Because of the gingerbread house, Alma wound up taking care of the children one day. The rain had put an end to her work, and the overseer could find nothing for her to do.

"That's too bad," the vicar lamented. "Are all those sacks mended already?"

"Yes they are."

It never even occurred to Alma that she might be excused for the rest of the day. As if on cue, Ilmari appeared and began to demand a witch for his game.

"I haven't got time," said his mother. "Go and ask Emma."

"I don't like Emma. She can't do anything. She doesn't talk, she only laughs."

The boy's attention focused on Alma, and he began to ask for her. At first they refused, laughing, but then an idea occurred to the vicaress.

"But you can go with him. Stay until he tires of the game. That won't be long. That's how we'll finish out your day. It would be too bad if you had to come again tomorrow."

"But will I be able to do it?"

The vicaress waved her hand and laughed. "Just go. Sit there and rest now. That's all you need to do. It'll help me get a moment's peace. I've played witch long enough."

Somewhat ashamed, Alma left, for it seemed an unnatural way to do rent-work. But yet... It was so easy. Hansel and Gretel sat in one corner and she in another. The children ate pieces of coffee bread she fed to them. At intervals, she had to feel the boy's finger, which he duly put in her hand, bent at the knuckle. And she always had to wonder why they didn't get fatter.

Ilmari began to demand that his sister cry, but she refused.

"I don't feel like crying."

"You will cry. You're afraid of the witch and you will cry."

"I can't cry."

"Do it right now, lady... right now."

The vicaress liked to call her daughter lady because of her quiet disposition, but Ilmari used it as a term of abuse. The matter ended with Ani's crying, not out of fear, but because her brother had pinched her. Alma scolded him to the extent that a tenant's wife could scold her master's children, which had no effect

137

at all. Ani went indoors crying, and Alma, slightly uneasy, waited for the vicaress to appear. She was not angry with her, but Ilmari got a scolding and a declaration that his mother would no longer play with him on that day. "You won't have a bedtime story either, since you have learned your tricks from the trolls."

For Alma she had a friendly word, sensing her fear because the children's play under her supervision had ended badly. She even gave her the remnants of coffee bread to take to her boys.

At home, Alma laughed about the odd form of rent-work, but then she said seriously, "But what strange games. They play at eating people."

CHAPTER FIVE

I

Halme did not become chief of the fire department, but chairman of its auxiliary. The manor coachman was chosen as drill chief, nor would Halme have been suitable for the position. The auxiliary was entrusted with the task of educating the public and of organizing socials and entertainments. The baron, since he had promised to finance the department, was not in favor of such frills. But Halme, along with the vicar and his wife, believed that without them, the fire department would be devoid of all ideological significance. It would be a mere crew of hired hands, gathered together at the baron's for free.

Even Preeti and Henna came. "Because there weren't any tickets or anything."

Henna was a confused and compulsive babbler. She fussed and rattled on at random about things as they popped into her head.

"We came to hear Halme speak... the boy too... he's taken him in... My shoe is rubbing, too. They're bad... He's going to be a master tailor... We've got to listen, since he took in the boy like that... Jesus, can we really sit down here... People like us, really... and sitting like this..."

They were careful to avoid Halme this time, however. The boy, Valenti, had behaved rather badly. He had an unbelievable imagination, and had acted out the part of a horse. He would bite down on his bit, whinny, and kick. Playing with the other boys, he would say not a single word at times, for horses, after all, could not speak. The incident in question had been quite distressing. The boy had shed his clothing on Mäenpääs' hill, gone down on all fours in the middle of the road, and, snorting through his lips, begun to relieve himself of a double burden, as horses do. Otto Kivivuori, happening to come upon him from behind, had broken off a branch, silently crept up close, then suddenly and unexpectedly

139

struck him on the bare bottom. The horse had let out a shriek, run off naked, and hidden in the woods until Otto was gone.

Otto spread the story, and the boy received a comprehensive lecture on civilized behavior from Halme. He was spared a whipping because "We must reach people through their hearts, not their bottoms."

On this occasion, it was pointless for Henna and Preeti to avoid Halme. At the moment, he had no mind for such matters, but moved gravely back and forth, overseeing the scanty program. It contained his own opening remarks, the manor coachman's clumsy presentation of fire-fighting methods, in which the phrase most frequently repeated was "kind of," a schoolgirl's recitation of a poem, and his own speech.

The affair was held in the large classroom of the schoolhouse. Halme stepped gravely to the rear of the desk. He had no written text for his address. He had indeed written it many times over, but having read in *The Worker* of Salin's delivering a brilliant speech without notes, he had left all papers behind. First he measured the audience with a deeply penetrating stare, shifted his eyes to the classroom ceiling, and broke the expectant silence with his first words:

"Our forefathers, who have compressed their enormous life experience, accumulated over hundreds and thousands of years of existence, into those expressions of wisdom known as proverbs, have said: 'Fire is a good servant but a bad master.'

"And haven't we in this parish often been made aware of how true our fathers' dearly bought wisdom is. Numberless have been the times when families, even poor families, have had to flee into the night, amid the frost and snow, fire having destroyed their home, which although small and poor, was still the dearest place on earth to them, as our late, great Topelius has said. But how could it be otherwise in this fatherland of ours, where innumerable wood-shingled roofs arch over homes, people, and animals. Therefore, the ideal of the fire department has spread with extraordinary rapidity among our people, and today it is here among us, for which state of affairs we thank the master baron and our congregation's highly worthy vicar and his wife. We villagers note with joy this manifestation of the progressive spirit among our upper classes. The poor, especially, whose struggle to live is often so bitter, are happy to see these signs that they have not been completely forgotten."

The word "poor" caused a slight ripple here and there, but the courtesy apparent in Halme's thought dispelled its effect, even among the gentry. It was all clearly social doctrine of the *"Suometar"* kind. Halme's speech was a long one. At times the gentry were slightly annoyed when Halme presented even practical matters in the same ceremonial style. At the end of the speech there was another rhetorical flourish, and Halme concluded with an expansive flight.

"For hundreds of years this people has slept, but now it is awakening. Let this ideal rouse our people from its slumber. Let it swell in all hearts like the raging spring waters, procuring the good fortune and success of our fatherland. So growing ever stronger and soaring ever higher, long live the noble ideal of the fire department!"

Pursing her lips firmly and incapable of looking directly at Halme, the vicaress began to applaud, whereupon the public joined in with enthusiasm. Halme returned to his seat, and amid continuing applause, the vicaress stepped behind the desk.

"I would like to thank Mr. Halme for these words. But above all, I wish to inform you that he has completely ignored his own part in the birth of this idea. He is indeed its true father, and he deserves our thanks for it. And by way of thanking him, we must thank all those who do volunteer work among the people to advance their enlightenment and prosperity."

There was more applause. The celebration ended at that point, and the gathering began to disperse. Halme's cheeks were noticeably flushed. For the first time, he had made a speech in public, and it had been exciting. Still, he tried to appear as unruffled as possible in discussing a few further practical matters with the gentry. Plans were for a special fire hall to be built, with an assembly room to be used for the purpose of educating the people. The schoolhouse was really inadequate for that purpose.

Laurila, who had begun to favor Halme, muttered as he was leaving, "Those goddamn thank-you's could have been left unsaid. The poor get very few benefits from those fire departments... What does a poor man have to burn? There'll never be such a goddamned rush that a poor man can't get the few rags he has out of a fire."

"But he really has a way with words... He speaks so clearly."

At the parsonage, the couple exchanged a few listless words about Halme's presentation. They smiled about it, but praised it as well. They were not quite sure what to think of him. In part he seemed laughable, but at times he appeared in quite a different light.

"He does seem to be affected by *The Worker*. There were signs of it in his speech."

There was vexation in the vicaress's voice, but the matter seemed insignificant to the vicar.

Then two events occurred to which the community paid more attention than usual. Töyry and Laurila had had another fight. It was not the first, but the situation had become extremely tense by now.

Laurila was at his rent-work, mowing oats. Töyry's son Arvo was raking after him. Laurila's scythe struck a rock. He had just sharpened it, and so began to curse.

"Well, by God, that's it. They seem to try to get you at every turn... They don't even bother to clear the rocks from the fields... just to make it goddamned worse all the time."

And Laurila threw his scythe down on the bank of a ditch, sat himself down with an angry lunge, and took out a pipe and tobacco pouch from his pocket. He jammed the tobacco into the pipe so forcefully that the bowl was in danger of cracking. Arvo, annoyed, went on with his raking, and when he did not react to Laurila's show of anger, the latter growled, "Go tell your father he's smoking a pipe."

Arvo replied, half-mumbling, "What'll he do if I tell him?"

"I don't know what he'll do, but he must need to know, since he sends you out here to spy on me."

Arvo continued to concentrate on his raking, and Laurila rapped his half-smoked pipe against the scythe-handle so hard that the embers flashed. Although there was no danger of the fresh herbage catching fire, he stamped out the smoldering remnants of tobacco as violently as if he were trampling to death a litter of fleeing rats.

"God... damn... The same as... I'll bet you have butter in your lunch even if the hired hands get none. And Tehva had two god-awful lunch boxes yesterday. A miserable bite of cheese was hidden in one, and an old herring was stinking up the other... Why do men like that have to have these goddamned spies? No... I have to sharpen it again so that the oats will really fall... To really make money..."

After the incident, Töyry issued a final warning. "I'm telling you just this one last time. You even scared my boy at work. And you know from experience that I keep my word."

"Keep your word. You keep it goddamn well when you're dishing out rent-work. But remember that when you got this land from your father, you promised me lifetime tenancy."

"So I did. And on condition that you behave. So keep that word in mind, too."

On that occasion, Antto controlled himself, but the quarrels were soon renewed. Antto was in an agitated state of mind for other reasons as well. His oldest boy, an idiot, had grown too big to be allowed to run free. The boy was not actually violent, but was capable of doing harm on impulse and was liable to break anything at any time. Only when opposed did he become angry, and then Antto had all he could do to restrain him. So they had chained him to a wall, and there he lived and bellowed.

The town officials turned their attention to the matter when they heard that Antto sometimes hit the boy. A poorhouse had just been established in the parish, but it was filled to overflowing, and when Antto refused to surrender the boy "to be tortured there" the matter was pursued no further.

"Let him take care of him... We have enough on our hands as it is."

Antto was absolutely right. He did in fact strike the boy sometimes, but not after he was chained, and his treatment in the poorhouse would probably have been worse. There they tried to cure the eccentricities of hoboes and the half-insane with whipping. The superintendent of the place, a great psychologist, would say, "He's not crazy; he's just full of the devil."

Antto's situation was growing so tense that the threat of eviction hovered in the air. There was another verbal battle, and his landlord said, "Shall I say the word, or will you behave decently?"

"Go ahead and say it... But I won't leave..."

Then, when the baron evicted one of his tenants, Antto began to be afraid. He raged inwardly, but said nothing as he went about his rent-work, obeying commands without a murmur. The tenant from the manor was thrown out for stealing wood. The baron had grown increasingly strict about the use of his forests, for the tenants, when they cut down trees, were concerned only with serving their own purposes. Finally, the baron found it necessary to hire a forester to mark all the trees they were permitted to cut. Firewood had to be requested a log at a time. The tenant in question had stolen a couple of birches to build a sleigh. Since it was for his son, who was starting out life as a tenant in a

143

neighboring community, he had no right to ask for the trees. The baron was not concerned about a few birches, but the example set by the deed angered him.

"You steal. Why you not ask?"

"I didn't think it mattered."

"Mattered, mattered. I hear how tenant say when he ruin my woods... Not poor man he steal from... he say... Is it anything but one hooliganism? Why you get sleigh for other man's tenant?"

"I thought... as a gift."

"Gawddamn, you not gifter of manor's woods. You not even ask. You take... I not overlook no more. You go, others learn."

After notice was given, the tenant spent what was left of his time dawdling through his work, breaking what he could break, doing more harm than good. The baron became so indignant that when the tenant sought a new place, he went to the landlord with a report of his behavior and put a stop to that.

The matter came in for a good deal of discussion. The one who had the most to say was Halme. In his discourse, the word "poor" was often repeated. At times he gave voice to socialist ideas quite different from those conveyed in the expression "our mutual reforms."

Töyry had heard of Halme's talk and even spoke of it in passing to the vicar and his wife. They were a little surprised, even irritated, for there were strikes in Helsinki at the time, and threatening language had been used in connection with them. The labor movement had dissociated itself more sharply from the advocates of legislative reform and was becoming disturbing in its growing radicalism. The vicaress had once discussed the eviction with Halme, smiling and with no sign of antipathy, but the discussion had developed into a latently vehement exchange.

"But certainly the baron is not obliged to tolerate a thief in his service?"

"Has madam forgotten that the baron is an enemy of the Finnish cause?"

"But you amaze me. The language question is not at issue here."

"It just seemed to me madam's sympathies were on the side of the powerful baron in this case, and that surprised me. I wouldn't call the man a thief. He went a little beyond his rights, that's all."

"Is that what *The Worker* teaches Mr Halme?"

"Not really. These ideas stem from a consciousness of social justice, so to speak."

144

Neither of them wanted to bring the issue to a head, however, and they parted amicably. But the vicaress was left with a slight sense of pique. She had considered Halme a kind of tool. He, in turn, sensed her attitude and was offended. He was no errand boy for the *Suometar* people. On the whole issue, he would have to read carefully the writings Hellberg had secured for him.

"That's just it. The people are not accepted as equal partners in the work of building our society. Perhaps that talk of building it is only talk."

II

One February day, the vicar read in the *Suometar* a manifesto which began as did all the Czar's manifestoes:

"We, Nicholas the Second, by the grace of God Czar of All Russia and Archduke of Finland..."

Carelessly skimming the text of the edict, the vicar did not at first realize its full import, but on reading other sections of the paper where the manifesto was discussed, he became fully aware of what had taken place.

That same evening, the newly installed telephone in the parsonage rang. It was a call from Helsinki, from Ellen's older brother, who went into the matter at length, adding more information about the occurrence.

"But that is obviously a coup... It means the overthrow of the constitution."

"What else could it mean? It's no surprise here. We've been expecting it for a long time. But we won't just surrender. The patriots have held separate meetings here, and have decided to form a resistance front. We have no more detailed plans, but you are to be ready for any eventuality there. We must raise the people in opposition to this plan."

"But what can we do? How will we resist?"

"We will hold fast to our rights. Before long, our plans will be crystallized. I'll give you further details then. I got in touch with you only so you can be prepared. We must create a spirit of resistance in the entire country."

Ellen was completely carried away. "The people must rebel. We have to get weapons from abroad."

"Oh, you! What good would that do? We are facing the entire army of the Russian Empire."

The vicar was disheartened, but Ellen bit her nails as she always did when she was excited. "Must we surrender then?"

"That isn't what I meant... But weapons... What can we do with them? And things may not be all that bad. Perhaps the edict will be rescinded."

"There's no point in waiting for it to be. Their intentions have been clear for a long time."

Ellen paced back and forth nervously. She ordered the children to bed earlier than usual. Then, wringing her hands, she burst out, "I now rescind my oath of allegiance. The Czar, the Archduke, has broken his oath and I am now freed from mine. Finland no longer has a ruler. From now on, she is a republic, an independent republic."

The vicar, who was sitting in a chair looking at his wife, suddenly began to laugh. "Haven't you settled the matter a little too simply now?"

"No... There are no 'if's' or 'but's'...This country is to be declared an independent republic, or a king is to be chosen. By betraying their oath, the Romanovs have forfeited their right to rule in Finland. I cannot live under the rule of a perjurer."

"And if the Romanovs refuse to relinquish that rule?"

Ellen paced back and forth as if searching for an answer, but realizing the situation, she sat down on the sofa, pressed her cheeks into her hands, and burst into tears.

"Poor country... Poor fatherland... What will happen to you? What will happen to our work, to all our people's strivings? Will they make Russians of us?"

The vicar sat down by her side, raised her bowed head, and began to console her.

"Don't take it like that... We haven't lost hope yet... And we can never, ever become Russians... We may lose our laws and our status, but we lose our souls only if we surrender them ourselves. The situation is not as bad as it seems. Let's at least wait and see how things develop."

Ellen sniffled, searched for a handkerchief, dried her eyes, and calmed down gradually. But then she began to rage anew.

"Never... Never. This people will not be destroyed... What can they do to us... Pitiful slave-Czars and their slaves... Boors and barbarians... This people will stand firm and unyielding. What an idea... Assimilate us? How can a civilized people be assimilated by a nation of serfs? With one manifesto?"

146

She uttered a hysterical-sounding, contemptuous laugh. The evening passed, marked by alternating outbursts of weeping and threats on her part. The vicar tried to console her as much as possible, but his words had no effect. She was indeed deeply stricken.

With the passage of time, things calmed down. But the flavor of daily life had changed. They phoned Helsinki after a while to inquire about the course of affairs. When they learned about the petition of the people, it eased their anxiety to a degree. Perhaps the document would have an effect on the Czar.

With the children in bed for the evening, the pair discussed the situation heatedly. Ellen still suffered fits of depression and defiance, but the calm and passive-natured vicar tried to see as much hope as possible in the matter.

"Maybe the Czar himself, by means of the petition, will be brought to realize that Russia has nothing to gain by this?"

"The Czar is not behind this. He has no will of his own. The Pan-Slavists are pressuring him, and he is unable to stick to the path of truth and justice. How unfit he is to be a ruler. Should a Czar be concerned about the opinion of those around him? Is he not the Archduke of Finland as well as the Czar of Russia? What right does he have to act as Czar to the detriment of those whose Archduke he is?"

"He has the right of power."

"He has sworn his oath. He has signed a solemn pledge, as did his predecessor. Does that mean nothing? With that signature, he has affirmed our rights, and now he is destroying them. What cheap, what mean behavior. Do the weak have no other right than the right to succumb to violence?"

"Right always triumphs in the end. God will not permit the wrong to prevail."

Ellen was irritated by her husband's passivity, and she said half-angrily, "For many days, you've behaved as if you had not been robbed of your civic rights, as if your country's laws had not been trampled into the mire, as if despotism had not gained control."

"I know very well what has happened to us, but as a clergyman, I must believe that nothing happens except by God's decree."

"Violation of an oath is not of God's decreeing. It's wrong to think of God in a context so vile."

"You have never been particularly devout."

Ellen began to argue heatedly that she could not believe that God would sanction evil. It was all the work of the devil. "If you betrayed your sworn oath, would you think the act to be approved by God?"

"Certainly not. What I really meant is that God does not sanction despair. Despair is equivalent to disbelief. You have lost your faith, and that is wrong."

"I have not lost my faith in God, but I have lost my faith in the Czar. Tyranny has displaced justice."

When they went to bed that night, Ellen undressed by pulling her gown over her head, and there from inside her skirt, she declared for at least the tenth time that Finland was independent and the Czar had forfeited his right to the title of Archduke of Finland.

III

The horse trotted along, breaking into a wild gallop from time to time, for Victor Kivioja stood on the sleigh wielding a whip.

"Goddamn it, Timotei, I'm sure you've never had a proper ride before. I mean, look at his feet fly. I paid twenty-two for him, and left Lammilainen standing there with the money in his fist when I hitched up this trotter and took off."

Victor was returning from the market with a Russian pack-peddler, Timofei, whom he had picked up along the way. The man they all called Timotei tried to shield his cheeks from the chunks of snow flung up by the horse's hoofs, and urged Victor, in his poor Finnish, to slow down. That was enough for Victor; he sat back and let the panting horse slow down to a walk. Then he extracted a bottle from his bosom and offered it to his rider.

"It's Finnish vodka. I mean, take a drink."

"Tha-anks. Good goddamn vodka liquor."

"Sing Timotei, sing!"

"Cuckoo, cuckoo, coo-coo-roo-roo-coo, / Sigh-me-a, rhyme-me-a, mocking bird..."

"Let it out, goddamnit... You're a real singer... You're a helluva nice Russian. Want to buy brushes? I've got some. The pigs are like porcupines, goddamnit, but look at that horse...

Trot along now, horse,
The sky looks so dark,
And home is a long way off...
And why are they taking me off to jail,
And why are they binding me in chains,
When I have done no wrong
Tho' I've played cards to pay for my drinks...

"You sing too, Timotei... Let it flow. How does it go? 'O chee chornya...' Heh, heh... I can sing Russian and anything else. You're a businessman... Do you need a woman this time? I'll get you one."

"Fliduski, fliduski. Nje fliduski. I'm faithful Russian Timofei... That's all..."

"Kuksima plituski, vinski plituski kuksima... Tra-la-lal-laloo... But look, Timotei. I mean, look at his feet go."

The village came into view, and Victor made the horse trot for all he was worth again. Timotei was driven into town at a God-awful speed, which was really a form of advertising, for his arrival was the more noticeable thereby. He set himself up at the Kankaanpääs, where they boarded pack-peddlers, even though the baron looked askance at them. His grounds for rejecting them were moral rather than nationalistic. There was something suspicious about these itinerant peddlers. Rumor had it that some women paid for their yard goods with other than legal tender. Timofei was of another sort, however. He was married and missed his family and often gave gifts to children with his own in mind.

People gathered at the Kankaanpääs. Many of them had no money to buy anything, but stood admiring the packs of fabric. Anna Kivivuori bought pretty and expensive dress fabric for her daughter. Although she tried to make the purchase quietly, it drew attention to her. Halme also bought material abundantly, but that was to be expected, for he needed a supply of fabric on hand for linings and other uses. He did buy suit material for himself, however.

"And what about that other matter? I hear the Czar plans to overthrow the Finnish Constitution."

Timofei raised his eyebrows nearly to his hairline.

"That I not know... can't know... How could one little Timofei... Russian law another matter. Not Constitution. Only land law... Renters become owners... But Finland's lords don't like it."

"What Russian law?"

"That land law. The Czar gave it. Finland's lords don't like it. That the peasant gets his land."

Timofei went on explaining, but his poor command of the language left his listeners in doubt, which may well have been his intention. When the talk was of constitutions and manifestoes, Timofei spread his hands. What could "one small Timofei" know about the Constitution? He had heard nothing about it. But the Czar wanted to promulgate a land law, and the Finnish lords were opposed to it.

Could it be the Czar's intention to make the tenants independent? That seemed doubtful, and Halme said, "We hardly have cause to expect such action from that quarter. There has to be something else involved."

"How you know? It's not away from the Czar if those lands are given, but clear that the lords are against it. Got to be careful now."

"I'll get a better picture of the matter when I ask my comrades in Helsinki."

That night the people sat up late at the Kankaanpääs. There was discussion of other things besides the land law, for the Russian peddlers were a substitute for newspapers in a day when the common people's chief sources of news were rumor and ballad lyrics.

They laughed genially at Timofei's poor Finnish and made fun of the Russian's way of jabbering. Pack-peddlers and the occasional Italian organ grinder that strayed into the community were their only contact with the greater world. Such visitors were treated with a patronizing goodwill, a little like house pets. People laughed at their liveliness and their antics, admired their speed and dexterity, but if they felt the admiration to become excessive, they were quick to add:

"That is indeed something... But how would they hoist a pine log onto a sleigh rack? If you put someone like that into the woods, he would smother in the snow."

If a young and handsome traveler was involved, a show of too much interest by the women might lead to bad blood. Then a young man might be heard to say:

"Well, he can grind an organ, but you pull your knife and jab him once and it's goodbye."

No one wanted to have Timofei lift pine logs, nor did he need to fear knives. He was an oldish man and fairly well known; this was not his first visit to the village. There was kindly laughter and joking in his presence. Some tried to speak a Russian of their own concoction to him, and he responded with his triumphantly successful "Cuckoo, cuckoo, coocoo-roo-roo-coo, / Sigh-me-a, rhyme-me-a, mocking bird."

The Kankaanpääs's son Elias, a real imp of the devil's brood, as they called him, did his worst to harass Timofei. He would mock him and steal his goods, something Timofei took half seriously, although the boy would return them later.

The following day Timofei departed, but he left behind a rumor that spread from tenant to tenant and shack to shack. There would be a Russian law, and all the lands would be distributed. The tenants would be given their lands free of charge, and the rest would be given land from the manors and the estates.

Halme squelched this rumor quickly. He spoke to whatever people he met, explaining what had happened. "I'll keep an eye on the situation. I'm waiting for action by authoritative quarters. Perhaps I should send Hellberg as an emissary to Helsinki."

Halme did not have the undisciplined imagination of his apprentice. He did indeed plan to do what he said, but *The Worker* soon broke the whole story. Kurikka had attacked the petition in writing because no workers' representatives had been appointed to the committees.

Halme had got an inkling that something was brewing at the parsonage. People had been summoned there, and he had naturally expected to be called as well. Perhaps he would have been, but the Kurikka article provoked a fierce political storm, and the vicar and his wife were so affected by the stand taken by the *Suometar* that they did not invite Halme. He was rumored to have said Kurikka was right.

Although not considered particularly significant, the disturbances involving Töyry's and the manor's tenants were recent occurrences, and Halme had aired his opinions about them. Since Töyry and the baron would both be at the parsonage, it was thought better not to have Halme come. The baron, of course, was unaffected by Halme's talk, but with Töyry it was a different matter.

One night a secret meeting was held at the parsonage. People from throughout the parish drove to it. The baron was there, and there was no sign of a language quarrel. The vicar and his wife went out into the snow to greet him, an honor granted to no one else. The remaining gentry and their wives were met in the hallway. Only Halme had been ignored. He stayed at home and resentfully read through *The Worker*, looked again for the books he had received from Hellberg,

151

and became absorbed in them. Then he said to Emma and Valenti, "This country's masters don't seem at all interested in the feelings of the poor for their fatherland. For me, as a patriot, being forced to fear that my country has forgotten its poor is a bitter blow. I have tried to open their eyes to the country's perilous situation, for now, if ever, this must be one country, one people. Well. The best efforts may come to nothing... At this moment there is good cause to say: 'poor country.'"

He rose and walked back and forth across the living room a couple of times.

"Listen Valenti. I hope it won't be necessary for me to remind you again of the disorder that prevails among my tools and supplies."

Halme's voice was sharp, and the boy began a hasty explanation. "I haven't touched my master's things... Who has been mixing them up? Not for the whole day... not even yesterday... I put everything where my master told me to."

"You know that Mother doesn't touch them, and you also know that I never leave them lying around carelessly. And you know too that visitors don't touch them. You must be able to conclude from this that only you can be at fault. You must also now perceive that you are a liar, and that lying is contemptible, and in my presence, absolutely forbidden. I ask you to behave in such a way that from now on a discussion of this kind between us will not be necessary."

The uneasy boy's slightly parrot-like face was the picture of candid innocence as he assured his master that his hopes would be realized. The master himself gradually became detached from the matter, rose above it, and gazed deep in thought at the fires flickering here and there through the windows of the village, a gaze which went beyond them far into the future and his destiny.

There were heated negotiations at the parsonage. Who would carry out the collecting of signatures and in what districts? At length the canvassers were chosen. For Pentti's Corners, it was the vicaress.

Residents of the church village were assigned the task on their side of the parish. The gentry decided everything. The free farmers were the only ones to represent the people. They sat stiffly and said little. The owner of Kylä-Pentti kept looking at his boots as if he were wondering how they had materialized on his feet. The master of Töyry weighed his every word doubtfully and tried to be as neutral as possible. Quarreling with the Czar was not an everyday occurrence. "What were those rumors about the Russian laws? We may lose our land and the rest of our property if we offend the Czar."

152

Their wives drank their coffee shyly and quietly. It was hard to get used to having coffee in the presence of the gentry, even of the baron himself. It was the first time they had seen him like his, sitting among them, just like a human being. On all other occasions, he was a being of erect carriage, from whose mouth issued briefly worded fiats about those matters for which they had come into his presence. The baron had a handsome beard and was otherwise a handsome man. He explained in his broken Finnish that they must not yield: "Not one inch, not one inch space. Law stays. It obey itself, it command others. Also Czar. Czar not bad. Ministers bad. They speak Czar."

This opinion had won the day. The Czar had been blinded by his ministers, and now, when the will of the people was made known by the petition, he would yield.

The Baron had another reason for speaking as he did. He had close relatives in the Russian army, but they served the Archduke Czar, not Russia, and so it was nicer to think that it was not the Czar, but the Russian ministers, who wished ill to Finland.

There was still one difficulty remaining. One person had to be chosen for the delegation to present the petition. The vicaress had dreamed of getting the mission for herself, but of course that dream would again be crushed by the stupid prejudice that women were unfit to carry out the business of society. "One organization is lacking in this community, and that is a women's organization."

She got to keep her dream to herself. The baron was the overwhelming choice. One reason for the support he received was the intuitive realization among all landowners that he himself would pay for the trip to St. Petersburg. Fund-raising was beneath his dignity, but might have been necessary had some less eminent person been chosen.

Then they discussed their fatherland and its critical situation.

"But have you heard? They are spreading rumors about a general distribution of land."

"Yes, there has been such talk."

"They are Bobrikoff's tricks to confuse the people, but he won't succeed."

"But you have to wonder at Kurikka. He has written against the petition in *The Worker*, exposing the plan prematurely. It would be awful if he mattered at all. But the working people won't listen to him, and even other socialists have been critical of him."

153

"That half-crazy eccentric. Forget about him. He has been thrown out of the Arkadia, and rightly so."

"We have to do more enlightenment work among the people. Those rumors about the distribution of land are dangerous because the people are so simple-minded."

"Yes... That's the way it is... Soon a man won't be master of his own property."

Töyry's wife sat rigid and quiet, uttering only a word now and then. A courteous hostess, the vicaress moved from one woman to another, making appropriate comments. To Töyry's wife, she remarked, "We ought to establish a women's organization in our parish, since so much depends upon us women. The situation demands vigilance on our part."

"Yes... Those organizations sort of help... like the young people's association movement."

The meeting eased the minds of those who attended. At least something had been accomplished, and the activity invigorated them. They believed that the petition would bring results, and when the visitors were taking their tardy leave, the vicar suggested they sing the national anthem. The gentry took up the idea gladly, but only a few of the farmers knew the song.

When a parsonage hired hand, his bare feet curled up inside birch-bark shoes, stepped around the corner, he could hear lusty singing from the big house. Having covered the signs he left in the snow, he ran into the cabin and said to the other hired hands, "God help us... The gentry are drunk. They're bawling out so loud the window panes are rattling."

IV

The parsonage's black coach-horse with white stockings trotted from cabin to cabin. The coachman sat up front and the vicaress erect in the rear, wearing her husband's fur traveling coat.

She began with the Koskelas. Jussi had done his rent-work for that week, so she had to drive out to his place. The sleigh-bells, or *krassut*, rang so merrily that even the boys conquered their shyness and came out to see the wonder. The bells were something quite different from the tenants' single-toned *tumpelit*. There were many of them on either side of the fine leather breast band, and they rang softly

154

and harmoniously when the quivering pure-bred horse moved even slightly. By the side of this animal, Vilppu shrank into complete insignificance. The boys had never seen Star so close up. He had gleaming blue-black eyes and a soft reddish muzzle.

Alma went for the key to open the parlor door. "It's a little cold in there, but perhaps madam will be warm enough."

"Thank you. Don't bother. We can stay in the main room."

Because of their isolation, the Koskelas had not heard of the uproar about the petition, and they were uneasy about the vicaress's reason for coming.

"My good neighbors. I am here on an errand which is painful to us all."

Jussi flinched as if expecting a blow. His fear and suspicion of the vicaress had grown so great that he felt a threat to their home every time he saw her. His subconscious dread had sunk so deep that he tried to avoid her when working at the parsonage for fear she would speak to him about the tenancy. Not only had they been subjected to a poorer contract and additional work days, but he had also heard that the vicaress had spoken slightingly of the parsonage pastures and hay-fields. She had said that the establishment of a dairy cooperative meant nothing to the parsonage, for they could keep only a few cattle.

As the vicaress continued, it was soon clear to Jussi that the question was about Finland and not the Koskelas' land. He drew a happy sigh of relief and experienced an extraordinarily warm wave of fellow-feeling for the vicaress.

"You have surely heard of the blow that has fallen upon our land."

"There has been some talk of it... But not much out here."

"We have decided to present the people's opinion in the form of a special petition to the Czar. That is why I am here. I am asking for your signature on these papers."

Jussi hemmed a little, shifted uneasily, and said, "Well, yes, in that kind of matter. But... um... what kind of thing is it... It won't cost a lot, will it?... Although of course if we have to... But if it's a lot, things aren't too good right now..."

The woman's face flushed. Her voice, when she spoke, was half amused and half dryly curt.

"It doesn't cost anything... And any way... In fact, it's not a question of money. Money is worth little compared to this."

"Well... Then of course... I didn't mean..."

Jussi's concurrence was half fearful, for he had noticed the woman's expression and her tone of voice, as had Alma, who hastened to say, "Of course not... When

155

it's a question of that kind... those are important matters where Czars are involved."

The names were signed, and so Nicholas the Second was put on notice that Jussi and Alma Koskela were also of the mind that the world was not run on trickery, with all due respect, eternally obedient to their sovereign, but also holding fast to their own rights.

The vicaress took her leave, thanking them warmly.

"A ruler must realize that he cannot take a stand contrary to the wishes of an entire people. And you, boys, when you grow up to be men, remember that your country needs unwavering support for its rights."

The boys became timidly serious on receipt of such attention, but when the lady left, they followed her outside.

"Let's go and hear the sleigh bells ring."

Star stamped as the woman settled into the sleigh, and the silvery chime of the bells accompanied the horse's movements. Then he plunged forward with his head bent almost to his breast, and the eyes of the forest boys took as much joy in observing his pretty gait as their ears did in hearing the heavenly chiming of the bells.

The landowners had already signed the petition at the meeting, and so the vicaress's route included only the tenants' cottages and huts. Laurila's was the next, and it was with a feeling of uncertainty that she drove into the yard. She had heard a number of things about the family, the tone of which, given their feud with the Töyrys, may easily be conjectured.

Here no one hurried to meet her, and she had to open the door herself. Antto was at home. He sat on a bench in front of the stove, peeling birch wood for a wagon shaft. In the crib lay a girl recently baptized at the parsonage, and whose name the vicaress recalled: Elma. She herself had given the girl her name. The parents had wanted to call her Sofia, but the vicaress had managed to secure a name of Finnish origin for her, in truth only because Antto considered the matter insignificant.

Antto glowered at the vicaress from under his black brows, answered her salutation, and invited her to be seated. Voices could be heard across the hallway from the bake-room side of the house, and Aliina and her boys, six- and five-year-old Arvi and Uuno, appeared from that direction.

Aliina welcomed her, at the same time casting an inquiring glance at Antto,

156

as if wondering what the trouble was now. She was only a little over thirty, although her first son, the half-wit, now chained to the bake-room wall, was well into his teens. She had had to marry Antto as the result of an accident that occurred when she was of confirmation school age. The matter had caused a great stir in its time because of Aliina's youth. Continual quarreling with the high-strung Antto had aged her prematurely and made her harsh and tense. Mumbling a greeting to the vicaress, she jerked at a bedspread of sorts and disappeared behind the fireplace.

The vicaress sensed the coldness immediately, but nevertheless spoke in a friendly tone of voice.

"I have come to you on our country's business. You have surely heard that the Czar has issued a manifesto which subverts our country's constitutional rights. It has therefore been decided to put together a people's petition, and I am asking for your signature on it."

Antto had not stopped working. He continued to do so and said, as the knife slid along the wood, "Is that so? We don't know anything about signatures here. We haven't been taught the art."

"But Laurila knows how to write. I've seen him do it."

"Sometimes he does, sometimes he don't. I don't know what those constitutions do for me. I haven't gained anything from them."

"But you don't profit from a constitution. There is no visible profit in it for anyone. It protects our national and individual freedom."

"It hasn't protected me... And besides... Maybe we know the real facts about the law here. There will be a Russian law and a land distribution. All you need to know is why there's such a big panic."

The vicaress was genuinely astonished. "Who's told you that?"

"I don't know... Somebody said so. Somebody who knows."

"Well, I do know. It's a rumor spread by Bobrikoff. He intends to divide the people with it, and he has succeeded to a degree. How can you believe such things?"

Aliina spoke from behind the stove, "It's as easy to believe as any other talk."

"Do you mean to say that I am lying?"

There was a clatter of pots and pans being shifted from one spot to another, mixed with an irate muttering.

"I don't mean anything... It doesn't matter what people say... We have to go anyway... Czars and constitutions are none of our business. Our constitution is what old man Töyry says: 'Hit the road.'"

157

The vicaress began to breathe unevenly. She could never brook opposition, and this was doubly infuriating.

"Your relationship with Töyry has no bearing on this matter. It's a question of our country."

"But that's precisely the question."

"I'm not going to get mixed up in your quarrels. I only hoped that the common distress of the people would have moved you. But since that is not the case, I'd better leave."

The vicaress rose and glared at Antto scornfully from her prettily protuberant eyes. Her erect figure straightened further as she sent her parting shot from the door: "Our country doesn't beg what it is owed. It demands it."

Passing through the entry, she could hear the clanking of chains, the stamping of feet, and the sound of weird bellowing mingled with wild laughter.

The coachman could tell by her expression that this was the time to help her humbly and courteously into the sleigh. But despite his best efforts, the vicaress jerked the robes over her feet so abruptly that she tore them from his hands.

They continued on their way, with the coachman bent almost double, sensing the thunder at his back and knowing it was sure to be discharged upon him. Unfortunately, the next stop was Wolf-Kustaa's. At first the vicaress did not intend to stop, but then she decided to make the effort.

The situation was much the same as that at the Laurilas, for Kustaa was also at work. He was seated in one corner of the room, and a fishing line ran from his hands to a nail in the opposite corner.

"Good day."

"Yes, it is."

"I said, 'Good day.'"

"I heard you."

"I have come to ask for your signature on a petition of the people which is directed to the Czar."

"I won't sign my name to it."

"Why not?"

"You don't write against the Czar. That's as plain as a road sign."

"But the Czar has broken his sovereign oath, and therefore a petition is being circulated."

"Circulate away. The Czar can break whatever he pleases. He is the all-powerful

158

Czar and Archduke, and no one can object when the Czar tells us how small to chop the straw. The Czar even has the right to cut off every last head of ours."

"Are you then of the opinion that the Czar can break his oath?"

"Well, I can't say yet. I'll take the matter up with him when I see him next summer."

"Where will you see him?"

"Around here. He's sort of sent word that he'll go fishing with me next summer."

Kustaa looked closely at a twist in his line. The vicaress opened the door. "Goodbye."

"I heard you."

On the way to the Kankaanpääs, the vicaress snapped suddenly, "Why is the horse jerking? Don't you know how to drive?"

The coachman was at a loss, for Star was trotting along at a perfectly even gait. The stop at the Kankaanpääs softened the vicaress's mood, for there the petition was signed willingly. The readiness was made even greater by the fact that Kustaa Kankaanpää was slightly befuddled. He was in the habit of mixing a punch from the household's liquor supply during the cold weather. He became indignant to the point of reviling the Russians and declaring that "an axe in the neck is what they need."

From then on, the signatures were forthcoming in one cabin after another. Victor Kivioja signed in large letters and said, "This is written clearly enough. The Czar should be able to see what Victor thinks of Finland's laws."

The vicaress's bad mood was finally dissipated at the Kivivuoris. Respectable folk at last. For once a clean, neat house, where she could sit down without being on guard against scraps of bread slobbered on by children. She was completely delighted with Anna. And such a neat little girl, already schooled in good manners. She came out and curtsied so prettily.

The vicaress's good mood made her talkative. Anna was fearful the entire time that Otto would start in with his indecencies, but she was mistaken about his sense of decency. He did argue against the petition, however. In his opinion the Czar would pay no attention to it.

"But the Czar cannot ignore the opinion of an entire nation."

"He seems very well able to do just that."

159

"But what sort of man is the one they call Wolf-Kustaa? Is he some kind of Russian sympathizer? He refused to sign his name, and would not even start a serious discussion."

"Well, he's kind of a crank."

"Crank... What does that mean?"

"Sort of a grouch."

"Is that what a grouch is? Crank and grouch. Are those words part of the language of the people? Are they in general use?"

"Sometimes. People use them now and then."

"A crank is someone who won't talk seriously... So he's likely to be rude."

Otto laughed. "At least Kustaa is... He's other things as well. Tight-lipped, really."

"But that means using only a few words. It doesn't necessarily mean rude."

"Well, anyway, that's what Kustaa is... and has been since he was little. He has to have people bake bread for him now that his mother is dead, but otherwise he has very little to do with them."

The vicaress went on to praise Anna's household. Anna's face wore a devout and rather mournful expression. In the vicaress's presence one had to be even more pious than usual. When the vicaress admired Elina, Anna was about to melt with humility. In the pauses she managed to breathe a little sigh about God's kingdom.

As she was leaving, the vicaress stepped back once more from the doorway and said, "Listen... You must send this girl to school. We need a broad foundation of education, and it must begin at her age. It won't come all by itself... I can help her when the time comes... I can give advice you..."

Anna cast a humbly approving glance at the vicaress, but Otto said:

"You can't educate kids on these strips of rock."

The woman left, but they could hear her rebuttal from the entry.

"Oh dear! Don't say that. Think of Lönnrot and Aleksis Kivi. The learned of this country have often set out on the road to education with a knapsack on their backs. All it takes is a firm faith... A pack with a shoulder of lamb and a piece of hardtack in it, that's always been the Finnish way."

Halme sat at his low work-table in his shirt-sleeves. Valenti, who was still not able to help with the tailoring, was cutting carpet-rags from the remnants of old clothing, the best pieces of which had been used for patches. When the parsonage horse, Star, turned with the sleigh from the main road, Halme ordered Valenti to hide the carpet work, to go and sit by the kitchen doorway, and to stay there unless specifically sent for. He himself rose and shifted two of Hellberg's books to another table so that their title, *A Short Guide to Marxism*, was clearly visible.

Quickly he donned his coat, knotted a black tie around his shirt collar, and went to meet the vicaress, who was knocking at the entry door.

"Good day. A most unexpected and equally unmerited honor to my humble home."

Halme's bow was lofty and refined. The vicaress nodded, smiling.

"Good day. This house of yours isn't really all that humble. Is it your own?"

"Yes, it is."

"Really. But let's get down to business. You must know about the petition."

"Ahem. Thanks to my contacts in the capital, I am thoroughly familiar with it. And where else could I have gotten such information?"

The woman did not catch the implications in Halme's words or his tone of voice. She shed her coat with his help. Then they went inside.

"So. I have come to ask for your signature on these papers."

Halme had provided a chair for the vicaress and now sat down himself. He coughed lightly and looked out the window.

"In principle, I am in favor of the petition. It's just that a mistake has been made. The working people have been completely excluded from the matter. The writer Kurikka, who made that fact known, has been the victim of abuse, even outright violence."

The vicaress's face registered surprise, perhaps more strongly than the circumstances warranted.

"What do you mean, excluded? I have been driving all day from one working man's house to another. Everybody's name is being taken, the working people's as well as all others."

"I don't mean names. I mean the organization. The representatives of the workers have been completely excluded from all committees."

"But the committees have not been chosen on the basis of party affiliation. They are composed of individuals and are not appointed by parties. How can anyone even think that people would be excluded from this activity when the

161

intent is precisely to have all the people with us? Kurikka was assaulted because he opposed the petition, not because he is editor of *The Worker*."

"Ahem. Forgive my contrary opinion. Kurikka did not oppose the petition but the procedure. He wrote that the workers should not join in because they were not even considered worthy of notice."

"Oh no. That's going too far. Small as this nation is, how could we deliberately cut off a part of it when the odds are already unequal?"

"I've been very much worried about the very same thing. I think I dare say that my country has always been my guiding star on this earth, and I am crushed to see it wounded so shortsightedly."

The vicaress stole a glance at Halme and tried to conceal an incipient smile. Then she took the papers, set them down on the table, and said, "But we're not arguing about the main point. At least you can sign your name."

"As an individual I will of course sign. But first I want to read the text of the petition."

"Here is the copy."

Halme had read it earlier in a newspaper report, but nevertheless he perused it carefully and judiciously.

"Well. One or two things should be changed, but it's too late."

He took up a pen and wrote his name in the regular and painstaking script of a calligrapher.

"As I said, I have signed purely as an individual and not as a member and representative of the working class."

The vicaress thanked him and twittered as she was leaving.

"Not as an individual but as a representative of the people of Finland. So have we all signed our names. But where is Mrs. Halme? I should get her name too."

The quiet and withdrawn Emma had remained in the kitchen, for Halme had not called her forth. She was so completely dominated by her husband that she had not even come to greet the woman of her own volition. Halme was not a household tyrant; Emma submitted of her own free will. The master walked to the kitchen door and said, "Mother."

Emma entered, wrote her name, responded in a low voice to the woman's social chatter and disappeared, bowing, back into the kitchen.

Halme escorted the vicaress back to her sleigh, even settled the robes in place,

162

and said, "I hope you realize that when the next blow falls, only a unanimous people will be strong enough to withstand it."

"That is just the point... we're already agreed on it."

The vicaress's reply came back from the sleigh in the gay voice of one who tries to avoid a troublesome issue by treating it lightly. Halme went indoors, removed his coat, took off his tie, and returned the books to their original site. The vicaress had not even noticed them. Then he sat down to work, and Valenti was allowed to return from the kitchen and resume cutting the carpet-rags. He sat silent for a while and then said in a humbly respectful voice, "Did the madam ask the master's advice on things?"

Halme was threading a needle, looking at it against the light from the window. He answered in passing as he concentrated on the task, "What she had to say doesn't lead me to that conclusion."

The thread went through the eye of the needle, and the master's tone changed as he continued. "Which is not my problem, but theirs, and, sad to say, our country's."

The final stop was at the Leppänens. When she reached their turnoff, the vicaress paused again, but since the quantity and not the quality of the names was crucial, she entered. Although this farm-hand's hut belonged to the great manor itself, it looked so wretched from outside that even its holding together was a minor miracle. It had a birch-bark roof, and the planked entry was missing a few boards, which had been used for kindling wood. A pane was missing from the small window, and a sack and some shingles stuffed in its place. One part of the yard was used to dump swill, and the space around it also served as a latrine.

It was half-dark inside. Preeti was not home, but that fact had no bearing on the vicaress's mission, for Preeti was unable to write his name.

In the room were Henna, their ten-year-old girl, Aune, and two of the molting heritage hens. The baron's dog had killed the third. Remains of a meal were on the table: potato peels, bits of bread, and the bluish dregs of salted milk in a mug. The sickening smell of rotting dish rags and stale dish water invaded the woman's nostrils. Henna panicked. Seizing a rag, she swabbed at the benches with it, shooing away the chickens, which fled cackling, while she babbled an answer to the vicaress's greetings.

"Bless us. Come in... Welcome... I said that some higher-ups were coming

163

when I heard the sleigh-bells. And I haven't even cleaned up yet. I didn't have the time... Everything's strewn around... Won't you sit down... Although our kind of place... is kind of not... for higher-ups."

"Thank you. But I don't have time to sit. You have probably heard that the Czar intends to abolish the constitution. I have therefore come to ask for your signature on this people's petition. It is addressed to the Czar as a result of the manifesto he issued."

Henna stood dumbfounded for a while, rag in hand and head cocked to one side, like a hen mindful of a recent kick, which having squawked its fill, now stands listening, apparently waiting for the next development. Then she began to get a grasp of the matter.

"So the Czar's overturning the law... It's easy for him when he's so high up... When he's such a proud Czar that... But names like ours can be left out. What could such names... I'll just thank the Czar in church. That's the best thing for people like us to do."

"We do not mean to thank the Czar, but to present the people's protest to him."

Now Henna was completely at a loss. She could say nothing. Aune, who sat lolling against the table, wearing her father's ragged stocking feet, opened her large, slightly flaccid mouth to say, "That's not what the petition is for. They are not thanking him, but saying he can't abolish it."

Aune had heard about the matter in school and so was better informed than her mother.

"Exactly. The Czar has broken his oath."

"Is that what he's done. Those higher-ups can really do anything. So he's broken his oath... Don't step there... Those chickens... It's so cold in that wreck of a barn... So... He's really a merciful Czar..."

"Won't you at least write your name on this paper?"

"Well, if the lady wants me to. Although the names of people like us..."

Henna wrote laboriously, admiring the vicaress's pen, marveling that a person like herself should ever use this kind of thing.

"It didn't come out too good... But it will do for a person like me. We're all dust and ashes here."

The vicaress put the paper and writing implements into her bag and left, thanking Henna, who babbled on.

"...Bless us... The door by yourself. I'll open it for you... Fine hands, such

164

high-class hands... I said there were high-class people coming... When there isn't... in this kind of place..."

Stepping into the sleigh, the vicaress could still hear her confused, sporadic eruptions, which faded gradually to the sound of the bells and the hoof beats.

"And they're writing to the Czar, no less. A horse like one of God's angels... Stopping at a place like this... The horse must be a real thoroughbred... Don't try to rush out now because you won't stay outside anyway... You'll shit on the threshold... Such a pink-and-white lady... The devil take you if you don't stay put..."

V

The Czar refused to receive the delegation bearing the petition. Nevertheless, he let it be known that he was not angered by it.

Someone stood looking at a rabbit's tracks and pondering.

"That's the way he went. I ought to put a snare in that gap in the fence."

Snow covered the tracks and new ones appeared. The century approached its end.

Summer came to Pentti's Corners too. The fire brigade practiced now and then. The manor coachman had attended a course of some kind and so could spread his learning further. The baron had secured for them all a white cloak, a belt, and a helmet. Sundays they wore them in their drills.

On Mondays they went off to their rent-work. Toward autumn came the heavy harvest days when the whole hell of serfdom fell upon the tenants. On the manor, the mowing took the form of outright competition. A specially chosen overseer mowed a trial run to set the quotas, which had to be met , if in no other way, then by bringing in extra people or by working late. The baron was especially enthusiastic about this competition. He went around the fields offering up his opinions.

"Gawddamn good man... what man should be... Poor man... Faint halfway... not good."

And for the sake of honor they strove, even though they staggered home at night with flecks of dry foam at the corners of their mouths and dark circles under their eyes. There they had to start their own work. The August moon lighted the gray walls of the cabins where the younger children were already asleep. But from somewhere in a field beyond the well could be heard the swish of a

165

scythe. Sometimes the blade would ring on a stone and then a certain word would resound in the night, letting the world know there were Finns at work. Sometimes other sorts of speech were heard:

"You're not going to bed. You're going to keep on binding as long as I mow."

"I can't do any more."

"Goddamn, you have to. I have to keep going night and day."

About midnight they dragged themselves home. One of the more energetic ones might stop for a minute in the yard to look at the moonlit landscape. There shone the "tenant's sun," setting the stage for dreaming. Perhaps it had already given birth to the tenant's dream, the stolen hope that things would not continue as they were.

Bodily weariness weighed them down. The foot that groped for the threshold was unsteady, but one still had to turn in the doorway. The creaking of oars could be heard out on the lake. Was Wolf-Kustaa out there so late?

It wasn't Kustaa. Women's voices could be heard as well. They were guests of the parsonage. A man's voice was urging someone to sing, and after a confused exchange of words, there was a stillness, broken soon by the soft voice of a woman singing:

> Pennants waving, vessels glide the water,
> The glow of evening gilds the lovely scene,
> The splash of oars, the sound of trumpets ringing,
> Among the fragrant groves of Mälaren.

The cottage door creaked. The blessed hours of sleep were beginning.

> ....The hours are long
> Until the dawn.
> Now Erik plays the kantele...

Rent-work was made easier for the Koskelas by the fact that Akseli was now able to carry out some of Alma's tasks. Of regular women's days they had only the six left, but the compulsory days continued. The vicar himself had begun to realize how hateful they were to the Koskelas, and he would ask for them apologetically.

166

"Could your wife come again tomorrow? The foreman tried to get workers from the village, but they are all busy at the manor with wood and pasture days. If you could come this one last time? We'll try to get along with our own crew after that."

"This one last time" was soon repeated, so that it became a byword at the Koskelas. Leaving for work in the morning, Jussi was apt to growl, "I'm going this one last time. At night we'll work with our own crew."

But when the vicar asked again, Jussi would humbly answer, "Yes... Yes I can... If I'm needed..."

Jussi was paid a little for the work, which was some consolation. And when Akseli was able to take his mother's place, the household ran more smoothly.

In his lonely role as head of the house, the boy had become accustomed to hard work, and when he was praised a little, he strove all the harder. The vicar sometimes praised him, which pleased even Jussi. Akseli already drove the horses on his own, although his father sometimes said he would never make a good teamster.

"He's too hot-headed. You can't get along in the woods with a temper like that. He's going to break many a rig in his lifetime."

There was some truth to Jussi's comment. In the presence of people Akseli was shy and quiet, even stiff, but he was nonetheless capable of sudden rages. When a sled stuck fast on a stump or rock, the boy would latch on to a load weighing half a ton or more and try to lift it, oblivious to the senselessness of his efforts. And although words of the "Godfrey-Daniel" class were the coarsest the Koskela boys dared to use at home, the "Goddamn son-of-a-bitches" came easily to him then, not just out of mere habit, but as a manifestation of obstinacy and anger coming from the very bottom of his heart.

Attendance at school and contact with other people at work around the parsonage had awakened Akseli's interest in the life of the community. On Sundays he gladly went out with the other boys. That always caused some squabbling with his father.

"You'll only wear out shoe leather and clothing there, and learn all kinds of tricks from those budding hoboes."

The village and its people had become more and more the objects of Jussi's scorn and laughter. He saw little there deserving of serious consideration. To Jussi, the boy's interest in his peers seemed cause for condemnation, but after

167

grumbling at length, he accepted it. The sole cause of his acquiescence was that the boy's requests had in their favor his enthusiasm for work. It gave him license to display an independent will.

A more severe disagreement arose at New Year. Oskar had invited Akseli to the Kivivuoris to greet the new year. Other boys had been invited, and the "old man" had reportedly given his consent.

"Isn't that something. Starting to prowl the village at night at his age."

Finally his father agreed, since Akseli could attend to a matter of business at the same time. Otto was supposed to go to the church village after the holiday, and Jussi asked to have him get a jar of Sloan's liniment from the apothecary.

"Let him pay for it himself. I'll give him the money later."

Akseli promised to take care of the matter, although for some reason his father's back ailment seemed shameful to him. He was so stooped and twisted.

He left in the evening. That New Year's Eve the moon glowed dimly on the new-fallen snow from behind a veil of clouds. Snow-laden spruce boughs formed an arch over the road to their home. Passing the beggar's spruce, the boy felt a slight shiver. As a child, he had not been allowed beyond that point.

The first thing to come into view was the parsonage lights. Beyond them, the village began. The boy walked rapidly past the parsonage. He was afraid someone there would see him out late, heading for the village. There was no light in Wolf-Kustaa's hut. He was not asleep, but fumbled around in the dark by himself.

Farther off he could see the many lights of the manor, although not of the main building, which was hidden by the trees. "They must be having visitors there. I wonder if the lieutenant is there now, the one who always paws the maids when he's drunk and then remembers nothing of it when he's sober. The baron doesn't know about it, and the maids are afraid to tell him. And Uncle Otto says some of them don't want to. Because they like the lieutenant. But Vappu Mäkelä said that if he came to paw her, she would let him, and pee in his hand."

Uncle Otto always talked dirty. As did Janne, and Oskar too. Even when alone, the boy felt a silent and disturbing sense of shame rise within him. At home they could not even hint at such things. Even with animals such matters were only mentioned indirectly. The boys were not even allowed to see the cows being bred. He had seen it, though. On the sly.

Nevertheless, his mind revolved around the matter constantly. Janne was

168

already visiting the maids' quarters at the manor. He dropped hints about his visits and made jokes about them with Oskar. Uncle Otto laughs and says Janne isn't good for anything but teasing yet.

A few of the village boys were already at the Kivivuoris. Akseli greeted them with a shy mumble. He was uncomfortable with his aunt, although she was always friendly toward him. To be rid of the vexing business of the medicine, he dispatched it at once, and Otto asked Anna to remind him of it when he started out for the church village.

"Is your father's back worse?"

"No-o... It just hurts."

"Is that so. Tell him this now: What does it profit us to gain the world, if we break our backs."

Akseli laughed painfully. Uncle Otto had obviously been drinking. The fact became more certain as the evening progressed and he made repeated trips to the bake-room, returning more and more happy with each successive trip. And Auntie Anna looked more and more disapproving.

Janne was preparing to set off for the village. He had a new coat and boots, and he walked back and forth, saying very little to the younger boys. He had more important matters on his mind.

"Give me a little of that beer, old man, and don't hog it all to yourself."

"That's one thing you're not getting," said Anna quickly.

"That's right," said Otto. And to Janne: "Make your own beer and then you'll have some."

Janne wasn't really serious in asking for the beer. He still kept things from his mother, not wanting to hurt her. There had been times when he had had too much beer in the village, but no one had told Anna about it. Still, his mother worried about his running around for other reasons.

"You could stay home. What kind of century will this be, when it's brought in so rowdily. At times like this, you should think about your life a little."

"It'll be a fertile century," said Otto, and Janne laughed. Nor was his mother able to conceal a slightly sour amusement. As a matter of fact, her moral condemnation of her son's and her husband's behavior had become increasingly a formality. Sometimes she had to laugh when she heard the two jawing at each other. She was affected by the age-old maternal sense of gratification at the prospect of her son's becoming a favorite with the women. In actuality, he was

169

already one, despite his youth. He was the image of his father. As he postured there in his new gear, his pointed upper lip compressed into the lower just as his father's did, with the same look of mischief on his face, she could not resist the surge of pleasure that she felt.

As the boy was leaving, his mother said, "Come home in good time."

And his father, "Don't do anything you'll be ashamed of."

The boys' New Year's celebration began rather stiffly, since they were visitors. Gradually, Osku got them to unbend. Setting off explosives made from pieces of iron pipe stuffed with dynamite was to be the high point of the evening. In order to prevent any accidents, Otto had promised to prepare them.

The individual tug-of-war did not entertain them for long. Akseli easily jerked them forward one after another. He was older than the others, and also stronger. Acting as umpire, Otto bustled around as enthusiastically as the boys. In general, he treated adults and children in much the same way, perhaps because he did not take adults too seriously either.

Otto began to trade words with Valenti Leppänen, trying to catch him off balance. The boy would tell any lie that came to his mind, and when Otto confronted him with his outright contradictions, he would slide over them without the slightest embarrassment. He had an explanation for everything.

Otto laughed and said, "You can explain the shapes when we pour the molten tin."

The tin was poured, and the shapes it settled into were truly remarkable. Nor did Valenti's explanations fall far short of them in wonder.

"This is a man on a white horse."

"How do you know the horse is white?"

"It sure is. You can see it clearly."

"You can't see it at all."

"Yes you can. White horses have thinner legs than others."

"Hollo has a white horse, and its legs are the same as any other's."

"No, they're not, if you look closely. And even if they are, most white horses generally have weaker legs."

"You're just talking nonsense again, and lots of it."

"Well, okay, then. I don't know. But it really does look white. If you squint your eye a little, it looks absolutely white."

No one could argue with Valenti. If he was cornered, he would change the

170

subject, perhaps even to the gold fields of South Africa, where the possibilities were infinite. None of the others had read Halme's *The Worker*. "Maybe Valenti will go there when he grows up. The Boers are waging war down there, maybe he'll go as a volunteer."

But midnight was approaching, and they had to start making the explosives. Otto filled a section of pipe with powder, closed both ends, and attached a fuse. Among the many rocks in the yard, they found one with a cleft that was just right for exploding the device. When the clock neared twelve, they quieted down to listen. The moon, shining behind its curtain of cloud, made the night strangely misty. They could hear shouts of various kinds from the village.

"A new century is coming! Three cheers-hip-hip-hooray!"

"Hey you girls of Pentti's Corners. We've got some good idle equipment ready to greet the new century with."

The last shout drew comment and clarification from many quarters. Bathed in soft light, the Finnish heavens arched over its children, receiving the messages of their upward-striving souls. The new century was approaching from the east. At some point it would zoom overhead, but their clocks would not be able to indicate that.

The boys hid around the corner and Otto ignited the charge. After the blast, a small fragment of stone whirred through the air, but the stout sides of the stone did not split. The noise was like a signal for the outburst of firing heard in the village. Firecrackers soared into the air over the manor, and a rattle of shots echoed from the neighboring villages.

"It's the year nineteen hundred after the birth of Christ..."

"Hurrah! The whole world is exploding."

"Let it explode. Let's have more of the same."

"Hurrah boys. Fire away. That will make those Russians' shit run."

Having ignited the charge, Otto had retreated around a corner. Now he returned quietly and said, "Well, boys. Until this day, there was no way I could have gone so far no matter how much beer I drank... starting out in one century and ending in another... And now home, you louts, every one of you."

On the way home, Akseli walked quietly, listening to the haranguing of some drunks ahead of him. A couple leaning on one another appeared, going in the opposite direction. "It's Vappu Mäkelä and the manor hired hand, Yrjö. Better pretend not to notice." At the parsonage fork, there was a larger group, or rather

171

two groups, one of boys and girls and the other of boys only. From the latter came a shout:

"Is that goddamn Jussi's boy starting to go night prowling?... Then he hasn't become completely moss-grown out there in the woods."

That provoked a laugh, and Akseli hastened his steps. At first he was embarrassed and ashamed, but then the shout began to grate on him. He was tempted to answer it, but he did not dare. Not because he was afraid of the grown-ups, but because shouting was taboo. He had to continue on his way and snarled precociously to himself. "Just wait, goddamnit, until we've greeted a couple of more new years. You might run into something with your nose out here."

"They joke about father's stinginess too. That's well known. But one of these days they'll stop. And when I get bigger, he won't boss me around like that. Or else I'll go to work in the bush, logging... Out into the world. You can bet they won't yell then."

Bit by bit, his anger subsided. The silence of his own yard received him as if it were listening. The soft, warm dimness of the night caused him to stand out in the yard for a minute. There was a thump from the stable as Vilppu shifted his legs, and the clink of a chain, and the sighing grunt of a full-bellied cow from the barn. For some unknown reason, the boy felt an inexplicable sense of well-being.

He crept quietly inside, but he could hear by the grunting from the bed that his father was not asleep.

"This was this one time. Just so you know it. Your running around ends here."

"Ye-es... Is your back sore?"

"What would have made it better so soon? Will he bring the liniment?"

"Yes, he will."

"So what did you do there?" His father's voice was a little softer.

"We played tug-of-war and set off an explosion. Uncle Otto made a pipe and lighted it."

"Hmph. The life some people lead. Going through life setting off explosions."

Akseli went to the cupboard to look for some food and said, to divert his father's attention from what he was doing, "So it's a new century now."

"So it is. But leave that dish of meat alone before you empty it altogether. As far as I know, we'll have to eat in this century too."

172

CHAPTER SIX

I

First the herds were improved, which made a dairy cooperative necessary, and then the cooperative brought money, which made a savings bank obligatory. At the start of the century, the parish advanced on all fronts. The prime movers in these activities were the landowners from the church village, Yllö, Mellola, and Pajunen. From Kylä-Pentti, Töyry became a director of both the cooperative and the bank. The baron was a participant in both enterprises but did not seek positions of power in them because of his poor command of the language and the language struggle.

The fire department at Pentti's Corners was active, especially the auxiliary. Halme organized all kinds of summer festivities, about which people complained when their children begged five and ten penny coins to take part in them. But the master squelched such complaints with a few pertinent and carefully molded phrases, in which he made known what was to the common advantage of society, regardless of questions of status and prestige.

"As a socialist, I hold certain positions which, I hope, you have noticed but the idea that fire is an acceptable phenomenon, regardless of whose house it ravages, is not among them."

This was in answer to comments that poor people had nothing to lose in a fire. And so the summer activities continued. The boys ran sack-races, climbed poles, and "did other fool stunts," as Jussi Koskela said to his boys when they asked permission to attend.

At one of the affairs, Halme spoke out openly against the Czar and Russification policies. He was summoned before the bailiff and threatened with a charge of "lèse majesté" for agitating against illegal conscription. He set out for the village with a serious demeanor, answering the questions people put to him with the steadfast composure of one who goes to the gallows for political reasons.

To Halme's disappointment, no court case ensued. The bailiff merely issued a warning. At first he treated Halme amicably, but grew angry when Halme criticized him. He began by explaining sympathetically.

"It's a question of a public speech, at an event for which I have given permission, on condition that you speak only of the fire department. But in every speech at these affairs, you have dealt with political matters. If word reaches the ears of higher authorities, we are both lost. I wouldn't be able to protect you even if I wanted to. As a private individual, I share your opinions in these matters, but as an official, I cannot tolerate them."

"Master Bailiff, I have given public expression to the people's common opinion of these illegal measures. If you consider this sufficient reason to summon me to court, then here I stand."

The bailiff was rattled. He was in a difficult position. And there stood the tailor, calm, quietly intent, looking him straight in the eyes in condemnation.

Under his arm, Halme carried a cloth bag. In it were underclothing, writing implements, and some food. In spirit, he was already on his way to prison.

"I don't want to lock you up. But you understand that I cannot go on ignoring this."

"Master Bailiff, fate has granted to me, in my insignificance, some small measure of learning and wisdom, so I am aware that in asking me to submit, you are in violation of the law and your oath of office. For in this instance, I stand for the law, and you stand for lawlessness. I apologize for my words, but in this matter they are unavoidable."

The bailiff lost his temper. He berated Halme for making a public official's already difficult life more difficult.

"What's the good of unburdening your mind to these people, most of whom are minors, anyway?"

"Master Bailiff, it is difficult for me to ascertain the degree of good that may or may not be done by my speeches. I give that question no attention whatsoever. But the public proclamation of truth and justice is the duty of every citizen. How did the great Zola put it at the time of the Dreyfus affair: "One day France will thank me that one man was to be found to save her honor by speaking the truth.""

The bailiff gaped. The words came forth as if pronounced at the Last Judgment. But he concluded the matter by saying irately, "Go home now. But I'm giving you a serious warning."

"Master Bailiff, have no concern regarding me. You need not fear. When Fate grants me the honor to lend the least bit of service to justice, to my country, and to the people of Finland, you know where to find me."

At the next summer celebration, Halme did not give his usual welcoming speech. He stepped forward quietly, faced the audience, and spoke.

"For certain reasons, I am omitting the speech of welcome today. In its place, I am going to recite the poem *The Governor* even though I am not equal to the task of interpreting the great Runeberg's words."

There was obvious emotion in his voice as he recited the lines:

> *Your victory grants you the right*
> *To work your will on me,*
> *But long before I saw the light,*
> *Law was and still will be.*

Even when questioned, he gave no explanation, nor did he divulge what the bailiff had said.

After that, the vicar and his wife found it easier to tolerate Halme's socialist ideas than they had previously. They did laugh about the bundle under his arm, with which he had set off for jail, the bailiff having told the world about it. But they added, "Yes... but there is something of the true Finn's sense of justice in it."

The vicar had not forgotten Jussi's pioneer medal. Its bestowal had been delayed only because such awards were generally given in connection with some kind of celebration. This time they were to be presented at the provincial agricultural exhibition. Jussi refused to go. Under any circumstances.

"But you must go and accept your medal."

The very thought filled Jussi with dread. To go there and be gawked at by all those gentlemen and everybody. He fell suddenly very ill. He could go nowhere now.

Nonetheless, the medal arrived. Mention was even made of it in the newspapers, which people brought for the Koskelas to see. They never got any newspapers.

175

The gentry, for their part, did not treat the matter casually. There was a modest "gathering in honor of" at the parsonage. People were invited and coffee was served. Jussi had to get dressed up again in the Vallén boys' clothes. The vicaress pinned the medal to his breast and made a speech.

"This is the workers' badge of knighthood, and Jussi is a member of its high nobility. Throughout Finland, this badge honors the current generation of pioneers and the work of those who have gone before. Many dangers may threaten our fatherland. Its laws may be trampled underfoot and cheapened, but the work sacrificed on the bosom of this beloved land can never be stolen from us. That work has transformed a dark wilderness into a cultured land. It is the Finnish people's quiet, and therein stronger, answer to its oppressors."

The vicar felt a stirring of pity for Jussi in these circumstances. He was so helpless, so completely at a loss. There was no trace in him of the sober and somewhat brusque tenant, who did his daily work naturally and confidently. Torn loose from that routine, he did not know how to react and stuttered in his agitation.

Even at home, there was still a tinge of red on Jussi's cheeks. He held the medal up in his hand to show to the boys before it was stowed away in the bureau drawer to keep company with the wood-filled commemorative candy wrappers from the parson's funeral. He did not change his clothes at once but sat and then paced back and forth in the fine apparel. Alma checked to see that the moths had not been at them, she brushed them, and turned over the coat-tails:

"It's the finest of fabric. It's still like new."

"Ya-ah — If that back would only settle down now."

From time to time, Jussi was heard to wonder, as if incidentally, "But when you think about the late Czar. He did thirty hectares in his lifetime... This is nothing compared to that... Although there was the building and the rent-work here... With the Czar, it was all hoeing... He didn't have the other work... He had just the hoeing... He didn't care to be a landlord. Well, he was a man all right. You won't find a better."

Even people from the village came, otherwise a rare occurrence. They had to see the medal. The wives should really have been served coffee, but there was no sign of any. And Jussi droned away, "That Czar of Pentti, now... When he got the medal that time... That councilor, or whatever he was, he said it would take a whole row of ordinary men to equal him."

176

Again he counted his money in secret. "I should put it into that savings bank, but you can't tell about those places. How is that Mellola getting along with that sawmill of his, I wonder. They say he'll go bankrupt one fine day."

"If I could get a little extra piece of that woods — they should let it go for less than ten thousand. If I could get a couple of thousand more together, I might even risk borrowing the rest."

II

Ellen had bitten her nails to the quick. The feeling between the couple was strained. The vicar wandered from room to room. Ani kept to herself, quiet and expressionless. Ilmari was at school in Helsinki; his sister would go the following year.

"How can we ever get out of this bind?" Ellen looked at her husband as if demanding an answer.

"I can't think of any possibilities except for cutting down on expenses. Above all, reducing our number of servants. We have too many of them. The parsonage won't support them and we don't really need them."

Ellen looked thoughtful. "We can get rid of the parlor maid, and Emma can take her place now that she's no longer needed for the children. But that's a drop in the bucket. We won't get far with such measures."

"We've spent so much on this place. Machinery is so expensive."

"We've been able to reduce the work force because of it... But all our income is from your salary and the fees for your minister's duties. The land brings in nothing because there is too little of it. Our yields from the cooperative are laughable compared to Töyry's."

"But that's only natural. Töyry has a larger herd. You must take into account that these church lands are intended to be family plots, not sources of income."

"They are intended to be a part of your salary, but this one has been nothing but a drain on us. We've been paying the congregation instead of them paying us. We've been forced to renovate a building that was nothing but a run-down shack. There was brush growing in many of the fields. But I've been thinking — we could increase the dairy herd by four cows, for instance. If we calculate three thousand liters of milk per cow per year, that means twelve thousand liters. At current prices, it would come to fifteen hundred markkas a year, and the cooperative

177

may even increase the price. It would be pure profit. We won't need to hire more help; the help we have can handle it. The amount would cover the children's school expenses if they board with my brother."

"Wouldn't that be more than enough?"

"How so? Tuition, clothing, pocket money, other expenses — they are all absolute necessities in Helsinki."

"Well, that is a lot of money, but can we keep more cows?"

"Not as things stand. There is a way, though not an easy one."

"What is it, then?"

"The parsonage owns a tenancy, almost as large again as it is itself. If we could just take part of it back as parsonage property..."

The vicar shook his head forbiddingly. "It won't do."

"Then you have to come up with something else. You know this can't go on."

The vicaress didn't say anything further about the matter. At first the vicar refused even to consider her suggestion, but it lurked in the background. After some time had passed, Ellen returned to it. The vicar referred to the contract, but he found no refuge there. The unfortunate clause he had originally inserted for the benefit of the governing board destroyed the basis of his argument: "Unless the good of the benefice requires otherwise." It was now clear from the nature of Ellen's arguments that her recommendation was no sudden brainstorm, but a carefully premeditated plan.

"This qualification means that you have full freedom to make the decision. It's not a question of canceling a contract, merely one of returning some of the land to the parsonage for cultivation. I think Koskela will understand if things are explained factually."

"I doubt it. I don't believe you'll find an explanation factual enough to satisfy Koskela. He's an absolute glutton for land. What he has isn't enough for him, let alone a smaller place."

The discussion was taking place at the dinner table. Ellen swallowed a mouthful, and her head rose slightly, as if she had just shaken off the last bothersome scruple. Her tone of voice served notice that the wraps were off now.

"Why on earth do we have to take Koskela's feelings into account in this case? He doesn't assume that he has any right to the land, does he? You, with

178

your fine sensitivity, are starting from a completely wrong premise. He himself understands that he is renting another's land, which he will have to give up some day anyway. In my opinion, Töyry is absolutely right in saying that if one is to have tenants, one can't let them settle in for a long time; otherwise they begin to feel, on completely fallacious grounds, that they own the land."

The vicar removed the napkin from under his collar. His throat tightened. During their many years of marriage, he had learned to read the workings of his wife's mind in her posture and her tone of voice, and now he sensed the beginning of a life-and-death struggle. Ellen had made up her mind. That much was very plain.

"In my opinion he does have a kind of claim. The rights of a man who has cleared the land."

Ellen arched her brows in her own peculiar way. "Have you cleared the parsonage land that you now hold?"

"What on earth... What do you mean?"

"Give it up at once then. Go and find the man who cleared it and turn it over to him as soon as possible."

"You're just quibbling. That doesn't mean a thing."

"Quibbling, am I? Not at all. The right to ownership is derived either from purchase, inheritance, or receipt of land as a gift. Since the general re-allotment more than a century ago, there has been no such thing as a squatter's rights. Tell me how many people in this country have cleared the land they now own."

"Regrettably very few. We have no cause to add to the general misfortune."

"Oh, listen to that. I think you've been secretly reading Halme's *The Worker*."

The vicar did not laugh, although Ellen's remark had clearly been intended as comic relief.

"*The Worker* has nothing to do with this. On my part, it's not a legal question. I could in good conscience take the entire tenancy away from anyone else, but not from Koskela. During these years, I've grown to admire him without reservation precisely as a tenant. He has never caused any trouble. He dreads the rain on the parsonage hay fields as much as on his own. He has always been ready to help us whenever we needed help."

Ellen laughed benevolently. "But that's a question of good manners. Certainly no one wishes for rain on another's fields, and I have a rather different conception of the help he gives. I don't consider work done in return for wages to be help

179

exactly."

"But even so. It would be hard to talk to him."

"Of course it would be hard. I'm not asking you to do it. But we have to do something. You do know that."

It was true. The vicar knew that they were getting into insurmountable difficulties. They had just purchased mowing and threshing machines, but those large and conspicuous purchases were not the real cause of their predicament. The expenses took the form of innumerable little outlays that were draining them dry. The worst were the trips to Helsinki, which they made often, for Ellen wanted to keep in touch with her earlier sphere of life. Whatever their land produced, the servants' pay devoured. On occasion, they had been late with the wages, and once they had to borrow from Emma. This last occurrence was what had given rise to the current dispute.

The vicar imagined the scene in which he presented the matter to Jussi, and it was such that he adamantly refused to consent. The result was increasingly bitter scenes between the two.

"We don't have to live in such grand style. It isn't proper, both because of my profession and the office I hold. To my knowledge, I am the only minister in the church of Finland who has a team to draw his coach."

"My goodness. What are you saying? Are you going to start carrying out your duties in a sheepskin coat with a cord belt, like those northern Pietists? And remember that the coach didn't come from your earnings. It was bought with money from my share of the inheritance."

It was a low blow. But the vicar vowed to endure.

Ellen, however, had made the same resolve, and despite her superficiality, she was a strong-willed woman. Having set her mind on something, she almost always saw it through to the end. They returned to the subject from time to time, and the issue became more complicated. It was no longer merely a question of a tenant's lands, but a struggle between their opposing world views. The vicar wanted a modest, quiet family life, but that was totally contrary to Ellen's attitude toward life. Her energetic spirit suffered in idleness and constantly sought out new goals. The quarrels grew more and more difficult. They often spent days without speaking to each other, and Ellen wept frequently. Life was becoming unbearable. The presence of servants demanded an outward calm and customary demeanor, and it often happened that a knock at the door transformed bitter

180

expressions into strange, affected smiles.

The vicar suffered the most. He had always found it difficult to live in disharmony. He tried, often, to discuss the matter, but the only result was a verbal exchange that left Ellen in tears. One night she no longer came to the bed they shared, but slept in the children's room with Ani. Next morning, the vicar said reproachfully, "Ellen. This is getting laughable. The servants will soon suspect something."

"What did you say — laughable? And... and... I've just about run out of tears... I'm all alone... Alone with my children... who will be left homeless or abandoned to the mercy of relatives..."

Ellen went on sleeping apart from him. Ani became the object of her tenderness and care. The vicar often heard her address the child in words intended for his ears:

"Poor child. Mother's very own girl. Let mother braid your hair. Mother won't forget you."

The impassive girl accepted all this with a formal sweetness, not understanding the reason for her mother's assurances of fidelity. At bedtime, Ellen would sometimes walk through the parlor in her nightgown looking for something. Pained and depressed, the vicar would sit watching her. In the early days of their marriage, he had always admired Ellen in the evening, especially in her nightdress. She would always let down her lovely rich hair so that it covered half her back. The sash pulled tightly around her waist set off the curves of her body, and sometimes on those early evenings, he would say tenderly in her ear, "Darling, they call it divine, but what a weapon it would be in the hands of Satan."

Ellen was already over thirty, but her splendid beauty was at its height. The vicar looked at her. Her head moved almost imperceptibly, and her hair rippled down her back. There was something calculated in her walk and in her bearing.

"Ellen, really, let's at least talk... After all, we are man and wife... Why can't you try to understand me?"

"I can understand anything. But I expect support from my husband when it's a question of my children's life and future."

She left, and the vicar pressed his head into his hands. "God... Give me strength..."

The days went by. The vicar sought for other means, but there were none

181

to be found. He tried to write notes for a sermon, but nothing came of it. The subject was goodwill among people, a subject brought to mind by the Russo-Japanese war. In the margins of the note paper, numbers began to appear: the number of cows to the liters of milk to the price per liter at the cooperative. The total was a handsome sum.

Maybe Koskela would give up the land on one side of the drainage channel. It would be exceptionally good land for hay. We could reduce the rent in exchange. Make one of the days with a horse a day on foot. He's beginning to be old and sick, and there is actually too much work for him on the place. His life would certainly be easier. The boys have done none of the work of clearing the land themselves. There can be no problems on that score. Actually, it would be doing old Koskela a favor. He can live on less. And it's about time. He is fifty years old. He has the right to take things easier in his remaining years. But in his greed, he would wear himself out before his time. The tenancy is too large. A smaller one would suffice, and it would be easier for him to run. Yes indeed. The facts speak for themselves. I am not seeking my own gain, but the congregation's. I have obligations to the church property.

But the thought of confronting Koskela made him reject the idea once more.

He was still sleeping alone. Lying awake at night, he struggled with the question for long hours. During the day, the couple spoke only of necessary matters. This subject always provoked a quarrel. In the vicar's eyes, Ellen grew more beautiful day by day. The weeping only heightened her sweetness. Sometimes a warm surge of tenderness toward her welled up in him.

"Well... She's fighting for the welfare of her children... For their good, as she sees it... How much I loved her... How much I still love her."

A day or two later, they were sitting in the parlor. It was already bedtime, but Ani had asked her mother to play something. Ellen sat down at the piano and began, as the vicar looked on from the side. Again he felt a wave of love and tenderness. Sometimes Ellen sang as she played, and she did so now. Her voice was true, if a little harsh — the vicar did not like her tight vowels and almost unpleasantly thin liquid sounds. But the song she now sang was one he had heard often as a suitor.

Across the misty glow of eve there softly glides a swan,
She settles on a tranquil bay and fills the night with song.

182

She sings of Finland's heavenly joys, of her land's delight,
How yesterday brings in today, forgetful of the night.

Those bygone days were not on the vicar's mind at the moment. He saw only Ellen playing there, and his tenderness swelled higher with the song.

She who finds love here knows highest happiness...

"It's for her children's sake. It's the mother's love in her... Surely Koskela's desire for ownership cannot be a more worthy emotion."

Although your dream of life was short, let it suffice to say,
You loved and lived on Finland's soil, and sang her summer day.

Ellen rose. She started toward the children's room, but the vicar said in a low voice, "Ellen."

"What do you want?"

She looked inquiringly at her husband. He felt his throat constrict with emotion. Confused images of another lonely night of pain whirled in his mind. Only Ani's presence kept him from embracing his wife. "Ellen, let's stop this. I've thought about the matter. Perhaps we can come to an agreement."

Ani wondered why her mother was no longer going to sleep with her.

"My dear child. Mother slept with you only because you had a cold, and now it's better. Good night, little one. And now, a kiss for daddy."

In bed, Ellen began to weep.

"It's so hard to bear your thinking me a heartless, inconsiderate creature who cares only for herself. I understand your position and I respect it, but it still isn't right. We're taking only what is our own. Do you believe such a thought could even enter my mind if I didn't think it was right?"

The vicar kissed his wife, wiped away her tears, and said, "Well... Everyday life makes it impossible for us to fulfill the highest commandments... My darling... Please don't feel that I don't respect you. None among us is better than another. How could I look down on you? You must have come to realize that during these years together... You are a part of me... These days have taught me that lesson again."

The intimacy of the talk heightened the desire that had been repressed all

183

those days. The night was a partial renewal of their wedding night, made somewhat coarser by familiarity.

In the morning the vicar's mind was empty. Bit by bit, it began to fill with troubled thoughts. Once, he said aloud to himself in his office, "I'm a liberal through and through. I lack sufficient firmness... It's because of the way I was brought up... the way I was brought up..."

Gradually he grew accustomed to the idea. Breaking the news to Koskela was the only difficulty. For a long time, Ellen was humble and loving. She waited on the vicar, ran his errands, asked his opinion about every little thing.

"What do you think about this? Should we do that? Whatever you want. Mother doesn't know. You'll have to ask Daddy. He'll decide. Tell me what you want for dinner."

When things go exactly right, it seems as if God's sheltering hand takes charge of one's life and guides it through all difficulties. In a discussion of parsonage business with Töyry, he found clear support for his intent. As a matter of fact, Töyry's words were the very ones he could use himself:

"The tenancy is too large. It is to the congregation's advantage to return at least a part of it. Its size would not have been approved in the past, but no one had been willing to oppose Vallén."

The load on the vicar's mind grew lighter. The affair had taken a turn which made it a question not of his, but of the church council's desires. And when Töyry proceeded to ask the vicar's support in getting his brother a permit to open a general store, there was hardly need to do so.

"It's to the whole community's advantage. I've wondered why no one else has done it before. I'll gladly support him and try to get others to do the same."

"We already have the baron's support, and that of many others. The church village storekeeper will of course oppose it, but that can't be helped."

"Where does your brother intend to build it?"

"We thought at the fork of the road, where the Laurilas are now. We'll have to evict them from the place. Not just because of the store — I would do it anyway. But it's the best place on our land because it's nearest to the village."

"Well, of course, heh, heh. One has to go where the customers are. How does it go now? If Mohammed doesn't come to the mountain, then the mountain has to come to Mohammed, heh, heh. But as I said, I will do my best for your brother. The matter concerns us all, not him alone. It's one more step forward

184

here. Also, perhaps you'll speak to Yllö and Pajunen about the Koskela thing. It would be good to have a clear statement of the church council's opinion, since this is more their affair than mine.

"I already know their opinion. They are sure to agree."

III

Having summoned Jussi to his office for that evening, the vicar paced the room restlessly, waiting for the appointed hour. At times he was troubled by the task that faced him; at others, by the fact of being so uncomfortable and fearful.

Ani was asking about something, and he answered her absent-mindedly, not really aware of her question. Sometimes, the ramifications of the matter attacked his mind in the form of vague presentiments. I lost the battle. I lost the battle. Our life won't change. Everything remains the same... And why?

Only by vigorous bodily movement could he keep his mind from its clumsy probing at the sore spot.

The telephone rang and Ellen went to answer it. It was clear from the exchange of greetings that the call was from Helsinki. Soon he could hear her voice raised in exultant shouts of wonder.

"Really? Who? Did he die? How long? What will happen now? But yet, what a great... There are still heroes."

The vicar went to her side. "What... what? What's happened?"

Ellen silenced him with a wave of her hand, her expression showing she was not to be disturbed. The vicar listened in suspense until she replaced the receiver and said, "The Governor General is dead. They've shot Bobrikoff... God, pardon me, but I thank you."

"Shot. Who shot him?"

"Some Schauman... Eugen Schauman. General Schauman's son. He shot himself, too. And there was a letter addressed to the Czar in his pocket, asking for an end to the oppressive measures."

Excitedly they mulled over the situation. Ellen could not remain seated but rose from her chair time after time and repeated, "The tyrant is dead... the tyrant is dead..."

The vicar was stirred, but he was also well aware that murder was not exactly

185

to be applauded. He said soberly, "We have no right to take a life. But Schauman has paid for the deed with his own, and that changes the situation... There is something sacred in it... something morally exacting..."

Even as he spoke, a smile played about his features. He tried to suit his expression to his words, but without success. Before long, his enthusiasm was as boundless as Ellen's.

They went on talking for a long time, until the vicar suddenly remembered: Koskela was coming. His expression darkened, but only for a moment. The whole Koskela matter was now of such little consequence.

Jussi was sitting in the office, suspicious and uneasy. It had to be about the tenancy, otherwise he would not have been summoned here.

The vicar could not sit still, but paced up and down as he spoke, "Although in principle a murder is always murder, this case is different. He is not an assassin in the Russian style, but a deeply moral person."

Jussi watched the pacing vicar furtively and said perfunctorily, "That's the way it is with those big officials. If you start shooting at them, you lose your life."

"He himself died at once, but Bobrikov lived for some time."

"Well... It's good he didn't have to suffer long."

Jussi was unable to summon up any interest in the subject, for he knew he had not been called here to listen to a discourse on Bobrikov's assassination.

The vicar was now more subdued, but he was plainly still in the grip of enthusiasm.

"How is Koskela's health?"

"It gives me enough to think about... The back is so-so and the stomach keeps acting up."

The vicar's mind was still in ferment with the deed and he felt himself elevated to a higher plane of humanity, where small, everyday affairs had lost all significance. His state of mind showed in the erectness of his carriage. In a friendly manner, almost smiling, he said, "I wonder how Koskela would feel about... The church council has voiced the opinion that the parsonage should get back a little of the Koskela land... not much... just a part..."

"Ya-ah ..." was Jussi's only answer.

Now the vicar became serious. He hastened to explain.

"I know it seems unpleasant coming so suddenly... But it isn't a question

186

of much land, only the section of swamp by the woods... starting from the drainage ditch. The conclusion has been reached that with it the parsonage would be more self-sufficient... What would it amount to now? About four hectares... no more than that."

"That's a full one-third of the land. And a half of the best land."

The vicar coughed. There was something challenging and offensive in Jussi's voice. Thinking about the encounter earlier, the vicar had secretly hoped he would be angry. That would have made his task easier.

"Is that really true? Isn't the land along the brook really the best? The swamp is good for oats and hay, of course, but you can't, for example, plant rye there at all."

"Well no, not really... But we won't be able to sow much rye along the brook... and we'll have to get rid of some of the cows..."

"But Koskela will have more than enough left. It seems to me that Koskela would be better off with less work to do... When his health is so poor..."

Jussi tried to straighten up and look vigorous. "Well. There is that... But I can still... And the boys will soon be big... But if it has to go, then what can I... We'll have to give it up... I only thought... since I worked on it... that it would... But there's nothing to be done... If it has to go..."

"Koskela understands that I am, in a manner of speaking, only the congregation's tenant. Therefore I do not have the power to decide matters. And the church council... They all feel that the good of the benefice demands it."

Jussi sensed that all discussion was fruitless. Trying to control himself, he rose and said, "Well... What has to be done... I suppose we have to renew the agreement."

"That won't be necessary... Look, we're not renewing the agreement, just returning a part of the land. Its boundaries weren't clearly defined in the contract anyway."

"Uhuh... We'll let it go, then."

"Ye-es... Oh, but I almost forgot. Of course we have to change the agreement. I meant to change one of the days with a horse to a day on foot, since a decrease in land calls for a decrease in rent. But we can do that later. Since the land won't be returned until the next planting season, we'll make all the changes in the spring."

Jussi took his leave. The vicar accompanied him to the door, still trying to explain how much easier things would be, that he would try to arrange lighter

187

rent-work for Koskela. "For you have slaved enough in your lifetime."

For a long time, he watched the departing Jussi from the porch. A knot formed in his stomach, and he stared down at the dried fir branches in front of the steps. Then he went indoors only to hear Ellen on the telephone making more detailed inquiries about the assassination.

"Well, surely he must be dead. No official information has been released, however."

"Tyrants rise not against people but against God, and God's arm is long and heavy," said the vicar.

"And let them build their fire hall. We won't go. It doesn't matter what we do... Our land has been stolen. There isn't much more for them to take."

No indeed. Jussi Koskela would not be seen working on that fire hall. Akseli, who was seventeen, had intended to go, but Jussi forbade it.

Although the boy was at an age when the young are often indifferent to house and home, the loss of the land affected Akseli deeply. Hate began to sprout within him as he watched his mother weeping in the chimney corner with her apron pressed to her eyes. His father's distress did not touch him as deeply; he did not like Jussi's despondency and was becoming more and more estranged by his penny-pinching and greed, to which he attributed a large part of his bitterness.

He wanted to console his mother, but since he was a seventeen-year old son of a man from Häme, the consolation shrank to a reproach, delivered in an almost angry tone of voice, "What are you bawling about? That won't make things any better."

Alma dried her eyes and said, "I wasn't really... But for your father's sake... Can't you see he didn't sleep a wink last night."

The boy stared to one side gloomily and said, "I don't think lying awake will do any good either. What's gone is gone."

"You can talk... But if you had done all this as your father has... If you had trod that path yourself, you wouldn't talk... I've seen it all from the beginning and I know... But you don't care about this place because you don't remember how it was built."

His mother's criticism was unreasonable, for the boy cherished the place as his home. His attachment was even stronger than his parents', having begun in early childhood. And what was happening now had happened before. Since

188

he was never able to say fully what he felt, his brusque effort to comfort his mother led to something more like a quarrel. But she rose now from the stool where she had sat slumped over and dried her eyes completely. She was calm once more and went on with her chores.

"Yes. We must learn to be content with what God decides. Arguing about his intentions does no good... What he judges to be right, we must accept."

The boy flared up. "Don't drag God into this. God doesn't need our swamp. God doesn't ship milk to the cooperative... That goddamn preacher is the one who does. Don't go and blame everything on God."

"Don't you swear. The day will come when you'll believe in God's will... They say Hellberg is teaching in the village that there is no God, and Halme says the same thing. If you spent less time there, you wouldn't be talking that way."

"I haven't heard Halme say one thing or the other about God, except that He is used to explain every crooked trick under the sun. You can see for yourself how true it is. And you won't see this boy raise his cap to this parish's vicar from now on... That's the goddamned truth."

"Don't start speaking your mind or we'll soon lose what's left. And your cursing is beginning to go too far. It's time you learned to control that temper of yours. No good will come of it."

"Come what may, the world is going to hear about this swindle. And I can always earn a living elsewhere. If it comes to that, an army uniform is good enough for me."

"Is that so... And you'd leave your poor father alone... At least, try to think a little."

"But I tell you this neck will not bow to those thieves. It's a good thing I'm through with confirmation. At least I won't have to listen to the bleating of that lamb of hell."

"Now don't... really. No matter what, he is still the servant of God."

"Hah... He's the servant of the devil, and the very top devil to boot."

The boy went out. Near the woodshed, his father was making poles for haycocks. The younger boys were helping by whittling on inserts. Jussi looked in disapproval at his oldest son. "Have you quit working altogether?"

"Not quite yet. But I may soon. It doesn't pay to sweat for someone else."

It was only the purging of a seventeen-year-old mind, and Jussi knew it, but

189

it gave him a convenient excuse for being angry himself. As he sharpened a pole, the swing of his axe accelerated in tempo to the accompaniment of an angry grumbling.

"Yaah... What good is quitting... We really have to start working now... Let them steal it... Let them take it all... Let them take the ashes too... But it doesn't help to let up..."

Twelve-year-old Aleksi whittled away soberly, trying to second his father's mood with his seriousness, but Aku smiled covertly at the grumbling.

Shovel on shoulder, Akseli went to clean out the pasture ditches for the summer. Soon the thudding of clods of dirt could be heard behind the barn. Akseli's lower jaw, with its few straggling bits of down, was tightly clamped to the upper. And with every shovelful of dirt that flew up the bank came an angry grunt.

At the Koskelas, you vented your anger by working.

IV

"And remember not to start acting up there... We'll soon be driven out on the road if you do."

Akseli was setting off to do rent-work. The vicar had advised them that from now on, he could substitute for his father. It was meant as a show of consideration, but in fact Akseli was as good as his father at most tasks and even better at some.

The boy did not answer and left without saying a word. His parents took up their sparse dialogue about his attitude, the mother siding with Akseli.

"It really has to hurt him, too. He's worked like a slave ever since he was a child and now this happens."

"Ya-ah... But it doesn't pay to fight the reins too much... You can't trust the gentry's show of friendship... They were so sweet, yet they were already laying their plans."

Akseli was harnessing a horse at the parsonage stable. The vicar appeared from somewhere and said in a friendly tone of voice, "Good morning... We have a very nice day again."

There was no sound from the other side of the horse. The boy merely jerked angrily at the harness.

190

"Good morning."

Akseli drew the reins taut and leaped up onto the wagon. His face was red but his lips were tightly pursed. He was clearly determined to persist in his defiance. The vicar looked wonderingly at him, and then said, in a hurt tone of voice, "Why doesn't Akseli answer?"

"I don't know... Surely saying good morning isn't a part of rent-work."

The vicar was baffled at first, but the boy's impudence caused him to respond sharply, "Certainly not. But it is a part of good manners."

The vicar did realize the cause of Akseli's behavior, but although he felt that he had wronged Jussi, he did not think the boy had any right to such a demonstration. For one thing, he was only a youngster. So he went on, "I expect proper behavior from Akseli, if for no other reason than for his parents' sake. It will be difficult if Akseli continues to act this way."

The boy jerked at the reins and left. The vicar looked after him and turned toward the main building. He related the incident to Ellen, and she recommended telling Koskela about it.

"I don't want to make the old man feel bad. But the boy must be made to understand what good manners require. I could understand old Koskela's being bitter, but what right has the boy to complain? He has no share in the tenancy. If anyone has some right to it, it is his father. He surely can't think of the place as an inheritance."

"I don't think he's angry about the land. He has an otherwise very difficult disposition. Who was it once wrote that a man's nature is revealed in his treatment of horses? I've noticed that the boy treats them very harshly. I told him about it once, when he was hitting a horse. He has a violent disposition, and I am afraid we will have trouble with him in the future. It's wise to be on guard. We will have no rental agreements with him, but if the Koskela contract is to be continued, let the second boy have it. He is better in every way."

The vicar, however, did not take any action. For a long time, as if by mutual agreement, he and Akseli avoided each other as much as possible. Finally, stiffly and testily, Akseli began to greet him, and so a formal accord was established. But the relationship remained strained and never did improve. Nevertheless, the boy's performance at work improved noticeably. He strove beyond his strength, making the rest of the crew scramble to keep pace. They complained bitterly.

"Why are you working like crazy? The rest of us have to keep up with you."

191

"The gentry won't get by otherwise."

The boy was angry with almost everyone. If an acquaintance met him on the road and asked, "Where are you going?"

"To Port Arthur," he would snap.

Such odd behavior was the object of wonder. But gradually the boy's anger settled into a silent and scornful bitterness toward the masters of the parsonage. He no longer demonstrated it overtly, but the pair sensed it. The vicar was sincerely hurt.

"It is sad that our relations have become so strained, but we must put up with it for old Koskela's sake."

"I, at any rate, don't intend to put up with insolence," said Ellen. "If he starts to show signs of it, he'll have to be taught good manners."

"Lately, his behavior has not been out of line. And I have to admit one thing. As a worker, he is extraordinary — as good as his father, if not better."

The new mowing machine also helped to thaw the feelings between the two. It was supposed to be driven by the overseer, but he was unable to install the blade properly. Akseli, who was keenly observant, immediately understood how. He grew to know the machine in other respects, and was soon completely familiar with it.

"You can drive it yourself, since you understand it better."

It was a rare position of trust for such a young man. Agricultural machinery was new and scarce, and its operation was generally entrusted to the dependable older men. When Akseli drove the machine, it ran unusually well. People in the community heard about the matter and discussed it.

"That Koskela boy is driving a mowing machine at the parsonage. Not many boys of that age know anything about machines. But it doesn't seem to help them, no matter how much work they do... They still took their land away... I wonder how long we'll be here..."

Joy and pride in his new position wrought an improvement even in Akseli's attitude toward the parson. Intrigued by the novelty of the machine, the latter followed the hay-making, and praised Akseli's work. The boy did not acknowledge the praise, but he might explain magnanimously, "There's nothing to it when there aren't any rocks."

Ilmari was home on vacation. His uncle had given him a bicycle as a reward for passing a grade, something which during the course of the school year had

192

been a matter of some uncertainty. The boy was bright enough, but his uncle had to exert the full weight of his authority to see that he did his homework. Ilmari cycled enthusiastically around the community, scaring old women off the roads far into the woods, where they kept up an incredulous mumbling long after he was gone.

Ilmari promised Akseli that he could ride the bike, but Akseli dared not touch it.

"Can you ride it on the streets of Helsinki?"

"Yes, you can. But we go on bicycle trips to the country anyway with the boys. It's bad if there are cobblestones on the streets. They shake you up."

"What kind of stones?"

"That kind. Fist-sized. One next to the other."

"Did you see Poprikoff get shot?"

"Of course not. That happened in the Senate House. But the Cossacks were riding up and down, and everybody stayed inside. But we were outside, and we were throwing stones at the Cossacks from the gateways. They couldn't get over the board fences, and we would run around to the next yard... But remember not to say anything to mama and papa."

"No... Why would I?"

Akseli was left pondering over streets which had stones the size of fists. "I should really go to a city. But that won't happen because it costs money, and Father will never give it to me for anything of that sort."

That summer they built the fire hall. Akseli would have liked to take part in the work, but then the land issue intervened. His father forbade him to go, but that would not have stopped him had not his own anger dampened the inclination. Halme had asked him to go many times.

Watching the training sessions, he had been secretly attracted to them. The hose drills were especially appealing. He would really have liked to join in.

But still, it was the gentry's affair, not his. "Halme talks about socialism, all right, but he pals around with the parsonage masters." Sometimes he did hear the tailor arguing with them, but what was the use of empty talk? He bows and scrapes before them anyway.

"Goddamn. I won't go and take part in their business. Bustling around with the gentlemen in a fire department isn't going to free the tenants. The manor workers listen to Halme talk and say yes-yes, that is so, but when they catch

193

sight of the baron's beard, they scurry around and snap to attention with their helmets on their heads. And Halme goes to meet him with his cane flying. He's the same way with that pair from the parsonage. Goddamn, let the whole world burn, for all I care. Let it burn till there's not a single coal left."

The following spring a boundary fence was built along the drainage channel. The vicar had the parsonage workers put it up; he could not bring himself to have the Koskelas do it. He was often depressed by the matter. He was unusually friendly to Jussi, and tried to be so to Akseli, but the boy's cold response made it impossible, and he was forced into the realization that the silent bitterness at the Koskelas was deepening and setting roots. At times the fact seemed almost liberating. He was hurt. Hadn't he always done his best? How did most people of rank relate to the common people? As if they did not exist, as if they were an inferior breed. But hadn't he been different? Hadn't he often gone to visit his tenants? Hadn't he discussed things with them as equals and always tried to explain things in a friendly way?

He suggested to the church council that Koskela be paid the value of his work on the land returned, but though there was some support, the majority were opposed.

"Is there any such provision in the agreement?"

"No."

"Then there is no issue. We can't start making such payments from congregation funds. Everyone who moves will demand such payment, but if we started doing that, it would be an impossible situation. Landowners would be paying for their lands all over again. And Koskela has lived there with his family for twenty years. Their living certainly hasn't come from anywhere else. That in itself is payment enough. And he still has most of the land."

None of them had anything against Koskela. The congregation could easily have afforded to give him some compensation, but many of the council members were landowners with tenants themselves, and the land question was an imminent threat. They had therefore taken a stand on principle. It was a precedent they could not set.

"Agitation is spreading among the tenants. If we start being too soft, landowners will soon fall prey to thieves."

And behind the scenes, they said, "If the vicar wants to pay, let him do it from his own pocket. He is the one who profits from it."

194

The vicar spoke to Jussi about the matter.

"I tried to get compensation for you, but the council wasn't willing."

"That figures... That's what they are like... those councils."

And Jussi quickened the pace of his work as if in defiance. The vicar walked away, crestfallen.

"How wretched everyday life is. How mean people are in pursuit of their daily necessities. And I am no exception."

But thoughts of a different tenor soon followed. The vicar had gradually lost the sensitivity of youth. Everyday life had dulled his tender conscience, and rationalization had assumed a larger role in the shaping of his opinions.

"Essentially, this is not my fault. The question arose from existing conditions. The land belongs to the congregation; there is no getting around that fact. Since the men of the congregation believed the tenancy to be too large, the land would have had to be given up in any case under the next incumbent. Why do I torment myself with this question? The underlying cause of Koskela's bitterness is nothing more than greed and acquisitiveness. Are they to be approved? No...no... The whole question doesn't even rise to the moral level... It has resulted from the barbarity that resides in all of us, and one side is no better than the other... In Manchuria they are killing people by the thousands... Of what consequence is this matter... If we were only once free of all this... that... that... ownership and land question... The solution lies elsewhere... in our hearts... If we did as Christ bids us, such questions would have very little meaning. Greed is greed, regardless of who feels it..."

The baron had promised to sell them a good cow as a breeder. The manor herd was in fine condition. Groups on field trips from the agricultural school came to study it, and the newspapers wrote of the baron's pioneering efforts in the improvement of agriculture and dairying. The vicar had to admit that the agricultural methods employed at the manor were excellent. Even at the parsonage, things were headed in the right direction. The land was being brought into condition, and now they could increase the dairy herd, for the swamp would supply them with plenty of fodder. There was no doubt about that.

The Russians had been defeated in the Far East — everyone knew that, although newspapers were not permitted to print the news. Halme received information from Hellberg, who had his own sources, and the tailor gladly imparted the news to others.

"I can give you the happy news that the oppressor has lost one of his fangs. You can feel joy at the success of the Japanese, for every victory of theirs is a victory for Finland."

And raising his cane, Halme uttered a strange word whose meaning he refused to clarify, no matter how often he was asked: "Banzai!"

Valenti, on the other hand, was all the more eager to explain. He was beginning to imitate his master in speech and behavior, nor did Halme disapprove. With regard to Valenti's talents as a tailor, Halme had long since given up hope and gave him only the most rudimentary tasks to do. But the boy served as a listener to his master's discourses, and were it not for his totally undisciplined imagination, he might have been a partner in the discussions.

It was a habit of the boys in the community to stand at some central crossroad on Sunday afternoons. They were fifteen- and sixteen-year-olds. At that age, they would make their appearance in the village about noon and leave for home at a suitable hour in the evening. The older boys would not show up until about six, and no one was ever witness to their homecoming.

Akseli did not exactly belong to either group, but his friendship with Oskar kept him with the younger boys. There was still a third group of younger boys, the "punching bags," who were the enemies of the other two. They carried on campaigns of petty harassment and were sometimes punished for it. A "culprit" was seized and his neck wedged in the crook of an elbow.

"Ox or loafer?"

The pressure was increased until the captive admitted that his was not the neck of an ox, but of a loafer. In such a predicament, Uuno Laurila could be extremely tough. Osku Kivivuori once caught him and began to squeeze. The boy grunted, but answered every query with the word "ox." At the end, he could only wheeze, but he would not surrender. Osku had to release him, and once at a safe distance, Uuno began to shower them with pebbles.

"Goddamn shithead... wait till I grow up... You might get a knife in your lungs..."

They stood and they stood and they stood. They kicked at rocks and they

196

talked of many things. Small tests of strength were a regular part of the program. Valenti gave speeches about the great world. Banzai! Didn't they know? Banzai was the Japanese war-cry. They were little people, about a meter and a half tall, they were completely yellow, and they had slant eyes.

"Don't lie, goddamn. There are no such people."

But Valenti was good at explaining. He knew about such things, for Halme got *The Worker* and, in addition, had assembled a sizable library, which Valenti could explore without asking permission. On the contrary, he was under some pressure to use it. Valenti kept his sources to himself, very likely not the last such occurrence in the history of Finnish culture.

The women's organization founded by the vicaress gave the boys extensive subject matter for discussion. The group knitted stockings to supply the needs of missionaries and held enlightening discussions. In them, the boys sought out new materials for obscenities.

They also paid some attention to the girls who walked by. At their age they still traveled in groups, and what little exploration they carried out was still a collective affair. A particular girl might already be the object of special attention, which they showed by saying, "That's a pretty chick."

Akseli took no part in such doings. With girls, he was stiff and withdrawn. If one of them looked at him with more than usual interest, he was inwardly embarrassed, but his face took on a stony and withdrawn look to hide his inner confusion. Since he was already seventeen, some of the older girls would give him an appraising look. Not that he was outwardly remarkable; it was the girls' mothers who had stirred their interest.

"That Koskela boy is different from those other good-for-nothings. He's even driving a machine at the parsonage... Ya-ah... That's how the time goes by... And him old enough to marry soon. It'll be a lucky girl who gets into that nest of money... When Jussi keels over..."

Jussi Koskela's wealth had become a legend in the usual folk way.

"They'll find plenty of money in that nest..."

If people had been told the amount of money that Jussi actually had, they would simply have laughed.

"Heh, heh... Don't try to tell me. Nobody knows but Jussi himself. I wonder if he even remembers all his hiding places."

Such mothers' talk the girls stored away in their memories according to their preferences. So some would look at Akseli as they passed by, but the result was likely to be that familiar feminine toss of the head and the comment to a friend walking arm-in-arm:

"Pooh! He's nothing special. He stands there like the wooden god at Piikkiö Church. His face looks as if he's just eaten one person and is ready to start on another. What has he got to boast about, when he doesn't even have a decent suit to wear?"

He didn't, and that was a problem. He had gotten a confirmation suit made of store-bought material, but it was too small for him now and was being saved for Aleksi. His father refused his requests.

"Home-made clothes are good enough. We're going to need what little money we have if they throw us out onto the highway."

Otto appeared as his savior. He and his boys had a contract to build a brick storehouse for grain in Kylä-Pentti. Being short of time, he offered Akseli a sub-contract to dig the foundation. Even though the work would be over and above the rent-work at the parsonage and his work at home, where they were badly rushed, the boy agreed willingly.

To get money of his own, he worked almost the whole night through. There were nights when he did not actually sleep at all, but his young body responded to the demands. His eyelids reddened, his mouth felt tacky from the lack of sleep, and his rather prominent cheek-bones began to stand out farther. Otto paid him handsomely, more than was profitable, and for once he was serious and said, "You're a real demon..."

Akseli was pleased by the remark. He really could not show his pleasure, but the tempo of his work accelerated to the limits of possibility.

He bought good fabric for a suit, and there was even money left over, although he had given some of it to his mother.

"What is this... I have enough money to run this household."

"It's not for the house, it's for you. Get something for yourself for once."

"Oh, you poor boy... What do I need? I have everything."

She didn't and the boy was painfully aware of it. He forced her to buy dress material. His father did not interfere, for the boy had a full right to his first money, but he could not refrain from a muttered complaint or two. Jussi's stomach was worse, and there were traces of white around his mouth from a constant dosing with "soda."

198

Akseli took the fabric to Halme to have it made into a suit. The tailor snapped off a piece of thread, burned it with a match, and said, "You haven't been cheated. It's good wool. I could already tell just by the feel of it."

And he began again to solicit Akseli's membership in the fire department.

"I don't know if it's worth the trouble to put out gentlemen's fires. They stole our land. Why not let everything burn."

"Listen. You have the wrong idea of socialism."

"What is it then?"

"That is a broad and difficult question. For the moment, I will say only that its aim is not to burn and destroy, but to create and preserve. Thus a fire department is vitally necessary, regardless of the gentry. In addition, it provides us opportunities for the promulgation of good activities among the people. But with regard to socialism, one of the primary issues facing us is the resolution of the land rental problem."

Halme spoke for a long time, while the boy listened. Although most of the presentation was beyond his comprehension, there were many points in it that he could seize upon with enthusiasm.

"That was well put. All that talk about the free purchase of land is pure bullshit. Who's going to sell the land? They won't even let you keep it when you pay rent."

In the end, after a bit of praise from Halme, he agreed to join the fire department.

"You're a spirited young man. Exactly the kind we need."

During the fittings for the suit, he enthusiastically discussed socialism with Halme, especially the land question.

"The case is clear. Nothing will end this but complete liberation. We even had to get rid of three cows. You can't rent hay fields anywhere. But the preacher is adding to his herd. Let them say what they like; they can't fool me."

"I'm happy to see you so enlightened about these general questions. When I think of our country's future, I put my hope in young men like you."

During training sessions for the fire department, they often discussed the question. But when Halme chatted with the gentry at the festivals as if he had forgotten about all the others, Akseli would feel a slight contempt for him.

"Why the hell is he fawning on them. They won't be any help in this matter."

Halme tailored his suit with extraordinary care. The boy's grave earnestness had pleased him so much that he treated him in an altogether friendly and respectful manner.

199

"There. It's a pleasure to see it on you. I sometimes have to heave a heavy sigh on behalf of Finland's tailors. How seldom it happens that one can find fulfillment in clothing this rickety people. The deforming effects of hunger are so often apparent. If I weren't a socialist on other grounds, I would become one for that reason alone. The Grecian physique is every tailor's dream. Yours approaches the ideal. The poetry of our time has put the female form on a pedestal, but I have read that the Greeks considered the masculine figure more perfect. I share their opinion. So. This Northern Hellas we are building is apt to forget that a more varied diet is crucial in forming the bones. I've read up on the subject. Nor can a healthy soul reside in a rickety body... Uh-huh. Forgive me if I praise my share in the success of this suit. Indeed. Tailor's work of the highest kind is an art. Equally sensitive and therefore as demanding... No matter where you wear this suit, I have no reason to be ashamed."

Although the national spirit had elevated tattered apparel to a sacred virtue, the suit attracted admiring attention in the community. People came to see it as they once had come to see Jussi's pioneer medal. "We're on our way to see Akseli Koskela's suit," they would say to people they met on the road. Even a few from the neighboring village who knew the Koskelas somewhat better came. They looked at the suit and fingered it.

"It really is nice looking. But Hollo's hired man got one cheap in Tampere. He bought it from a Jew. He was careful to be the first one in the shop on Monday morning, and he bargained for it. Jews won't let the first customer of the week go without making a deal, so he got it for almost nothing."

They knew a lot about the great world.

On that Sunday, Akseli made a wider swing than usual through the community. He even went to the Kivivuoris with Osku. Janne, of course, had something to say about the suit, whether in truth or mockery is hard to tell, but Otto and Anna praised it.

Akseli tried to be matter-of-fact about the new suit. In that house, he dared show no sign of awareness that it meant anything to him, for a quick thrust always lay in wait for any hint of vanity there. It could be delivered so casually that you might miss it at first. He was well aware of this, and tried to forget what he was wearing.

But in the solitude of the woods road on the way home, he opened the coat buttons and let the tails swing comfortably on his haunches. The spruce wilderness

200

was the only witness to the way in which poverty can enrich life. A certain Finnish tenant boy had got a new suit.

At home a cow was sold. There had been a long period of dickering over the deal, for the buyer, Tilda Vuori from the neighboring village, was a would-be expert herself. Milk-veins were probed, and the animal's condition had been both praised and questioned. Jussi finally got his asking price, not out of superior salesmanship, but by exhausting the buyer. He yammered and yammered until Tilda thought it best to give in. She did not have the full price to pay for the cow. Her husband worked partly for food at the Hollos, and they could not get enough money together from his wages. They got part of the payment from the forced sale of their old cow to the slaughterhouse, but Jussi would have to wait until autumn for the rest. The Vuoris were raising a pig. They would sell half of it and use the money to pay the remainder.

"How are you fixed for feeding a cow?"

"We're allowed to make hay along the ditches. He charges twelve women's days for it, but at least we can get it. Last summer I had to put in eighteen days because I was short on account of rain. But what's life if you don't even have your own cow."

"We can't get hay from anywhere... We still have to get rid of two more... We do have that straw... But nowadays you need to get a little milk... It doesn't pay to keep them just for the manure."

Tilda left, leading Kielo at the end of a rope. Alma went with her for a short distance, patting the cow's side and giving Tilda instructions.

"If you give her a little of the oat bran... She's used to it... steeped in warm water..."

Kielo let out a last low of farewell as she disappeared around the corner of the threshing barn, and Alma turned away, drying the corners of her eyes with her apron. Of late, tears came easily to her. Her once robust health showed signs of weakening. Moods of depression she had never known before kept trying to surface. She had begun to speak of God and death in a different, more serious tone. Often, she sang hymns to herself. She was approaching fifty, and the older women said that she was beginning to feel the effects of the "granny's disease."

Jussi did not mourn the loss of the cow. He calculated how long it would have taken to earn Kielo's selling price with her milk.

"Well... Here are these few miserable pennies now. How is this all going to end?"

Akseli was so full of his new suit that he offered no opinion.

Aku laughed to himself for a while and then had the audacity to say, "No one ever knows what lies ahead, but behind you there are always tracks."

Jussi looked angrily at the younger boy and growled, "Don't crack jokes, boy. We'll see which way your mouth turns when there's nothing to put in it."

The community began to draw Akseli more closely into its circle. He was breaking loose from the isolated life of the tenancy. Although the new suit soon lost its charm and did nothing to alter his relationship with girls, a restlessness he had not known before drove him to the village. And when his friends disappeared, one by one, on excursions which drew a slightly exaggerated snort of manly scorn from him, he became more attached to the fire department and to Halme's activities.

Akseli became an enthusiastic fireman. Before long, his performance in the drills was outstanding. Sometimes the manor coachman, who had grown weary of the chief's duties, let Akseli take his place. The boy's enthusiasm had anything but an idealistic foundation. That kind of hanging out at the crossroads and the frame of mind it required did not agree with his nature. He could not excel in that, but in the fire drills he could advance his talents.

When, out of general indifference, they lost a competition with the church village, he was angry. "Why go at all, if we're not even going to try? One or two men can't do it all alone."

"Don't get all steamed up. It's not that important."

The boy fell silent, but his anger smoldered all the way home.

Halme made note of it.

"When you are older, I will consider the position for you. Just between the two of us, the present chief has no commitment to the ideological mission of his office. He works only because of the baron's commands. My influence in these matters is not insignificant, and when the obstacle of your youth is removed, I will use it to effect certain changes in the practical training of the department. Learn things well, keeping precisely these changes in mind. But for the time being, we'll keep this between the two of us. When the time comes, my hand will be at work, and it has some power."

CHAPTER SEVEN

I

One dark November evening, Valenti Leppänen raced from hut to hut and cabin to cabin. Out of breath from running and fired by zeal for his vital mission, he delivered his message: "I am on my master's errand. He is calling a meeting of the people... tomorrow at the firehouse... at seven o'clock. Great issues are at stake."

"What in the world is going on?"

"Great issues... A general strike. The whole country is on strike. We are planning to strike here too. We are demanding new representation... And the land will be divided. The tenants will be freed..."

"It can't be... who said so?"

"The master has read it in the paper. And he went somewhere to call up about it."

"Then where is the strike?"

"In the cities. The people are marching in the streets and singing. Remember to come. The master said I should tell everyone that when your country calls, rheumatism and gray hairs must not be allowed to stand in the way."

The news was not a total surprise. It was known that there were strikes and disturbances in Russia, and Halme had recently predicted that there might be some in Finland as well.

"The land will be distributed and the tenants will be freed. There will be elections and the poor will vote, as well as those with land and money."

"Well, Halme can talk, but what will the masters say. Indeed."

Many speeches by Halme had stirred them to enthusiasm, but when they thought of the baron's power and might, for instance, it gave them pause.

When Valenti brought the news to the Koskelas, Akseli caught fire instantly. "We'll strike here too. Not a forkful until the lands are freed."

"Don't go mouthing off around there. We're not too safe as it is. You've started to talk like that Aatu. A talker like that won't get us our land."

"Maybe not. But when the people start marching, I'll be surprised if that boundary fence by the ditch doesn't come down."

But Akseli had a slightly different idea of the strike than Halme. The tailor had already been at the parsonage to consult about starting the strike. The vicar and his wife had expressed doubts, but promised to attend the meeting.

"Why should we go on strike against ourselves?"

"It's a general strike. Isn't it the duty of everyone to support it?"

"That's true. We'll certainly come to the meeting. It'll be best to decide things there."

Halme left in a satisfied frame of mind. At one stroke, the strike had opened up a whole series of possibilities. Although his relationship to the couple had cooled of late, he still wanted to organize the strike in conjunction with them. That was the most remarkable thing about it. He was in the grip of a socialistic-patriotic fervor of some sort, and believed that all problems were about to be solved at one blow — the entire social and national quandary. When he heard that the nationalistic bourgeoisie had been drawn into the strike, he decided to move swiftly. The gentry would accept the strike, but it would have another leader. On his way home, he was already drafting the first words of his opening speech: "Citizens. Great events..."

At the firehouse, a surprise awaited the people. They were assembling under the banner of land distribution and freedom for the tenants, but the landowners and the gentry were also there in force. Only the baron was missing from the ranks of the mighty. "What do the landlords and the parsonage couple have to do with the partition of land?"

Furthermore, Halme greeted the elite with unusual courtesy, leaving him little time to pay attention to the rest. He seated the parsonage couple in the front row, making room for them by ejecting some young people from the seats.

He was not aware that the two had held a long telephone conversation with Helsinki that day. They had been urged to calm any strike activity and, if possible, to prevent a strike entirely. There was hope for the defeat of the February manifesto, and that would be enough for the present. Law and order must be restored before further reforms could be discussed. The workers' strike objectives had taken on a disturbing character. They had established a "People's Guard," which was responsible for maintaining order, but it was controlled by the workers, and the situation could become threatening. Reform of the legislature was to be supported, but by lawful means, through action by the old Diet of Estates.

Halme took his place behind the speaker's table.

"Citizens! Our people are being swept along by a tide of great events. Bloody oppression, which answered the appeals from the people in St. Petersburg with machine-gun fire, made the pot boil over in Russia. A huge wave of strikes has paralyzed the whole Empire. In concert, all the people of Finland are demanding the return of the rights stolen from them. But no longer content with those rights alone, they are also demanding those reforms, whose absolute necessity is known to all of us."

Halme went on to explain the demand for suffrage, the reform of the tenancy law, and restrictions on the hours of labor. His talk ended with his picturing a little beggar girl, whom he feigned to have visited that very day, though actually she had stopped at their house the previous week.

"Citizens, as I pondered today on the Finnish people's battle for their rights, the door opened cautiously, and a little roving beggar girl stood shyly on the threshold. You know those little ones, whom you see all too often. I knew what she wanted, but still I asked her what it was. She remained silent and timid. There she stood, her older sister's tattered shoes on her feet, her brother's ragged coat on her back, and her mother's kerchief on her head. After a long time, she managed to whisper fearfully: 'A little piece of bread... something for the poor.'

"Citizens! Ashamed, I filled her bag. My heart could not rest content with a piece of bread. I said to her: 'Today, the people of Finland have risen to defend their rights. But not just their own political rights as citizens, but your rights as well. You still have some distance to go along your bitter path, but travel it with a light heart, for it soon will end. Indeed it will.' Yes. My good listeners, you can well imagine her looking at me in wonder and going home to tell a tale of the 'uncle' who filled her bag but raved like a fool. How otherwise could she understand what had happened? But some day she will understand. For this strike will smash the bolts that keep us from curing the ills of which these little ragamuffins are the end product. With political freedom will come social reform. Then the look of pain in those timid eyes will no longer accuse us. Citizens! This dark November, we can see the sun of springtime rising in our country's skies."

Halme stopped, but was bitterly disappointed when the storm of applause he so confidently expected did not come. There was some applause, but it was weak and hesitant. With a sinking feeling, he coughed and made a perfunctory bow. The audience, he noticed, was looking back and forth from him to the gentry. Realizing that their presence was the cause of the uncertainty, he said, with a bow in the vicar's direction, "Yes indeed. All our people are united in this strike. I would wish the vicar to explain further."

The vicar, in turn, stepped behind the table and began to speak in his gentle preaching voice.

"My dear friends, who among us has not felt for our people, thus stripped of their rights. The strike is indeed nation-wide. All levels of society have joined in it. Public officials are on strike as well. But yet it is better for us here to await developments. A strike here would be of no benefit to anyone; we must lend our support in other ways. All parties are in agreement on the passage of electoral reform. But it must be done in an orderly and lawful manner. First of all, the Diet must have its legal rights restored, and it will then proceed to enact legislative restructuring. According to information I have received, there is hope that this will occur. Thus we have no cause to strike. We should wait for the restoration of law and order, and on that foundation, we can proceed with the work of reform which everyone knows to be inevitable."

The vicar went on to speak of the meaning of fellow-feeling and brotherly love, on the basis of which they should build the country, and concluded, "As Christians, we must pray to God for help in our trials. For only work done in His spirit will ever bear fruit."

With increasing astonishment, Halme listened to the vicar's speech. Slowly, the realization dawned that the vicar's purpose was to avert the strike, and his spirits sagged in despair. He could not even bring himself to join in the faint patter of applause that followed the vicar's speech. Now the audience was totally confused about all the ado over the strike.

Then Laurila stood up. Without asking for the floor, he began to speak, waving his cap in one hand and tossing his head.

"So. Could I ask one question? I mean, this kind of question — how do we support a strike if we don't go on strike ourselves. And then another thing. If I might ask. Since the gentlemen are now on strike too, how do they do it? I mean, will they go to work? Or how will they go on strike? What will they stop doing? In my opinion, a man can hardly stop working if he never has worked in his whole life. In my opinion, this is something I can't understand. If I might ask the high-and-mighty gentlemen. And could I ask the high-and-mighty gentlemen, when will there be lawful conditions with regard to tenants' contracts?

When will we get a law to keep tenants or other poor people from having to take to the road? If you would sort of answer this... If I might ask."

Antto made a bow or two before sitting down. Immediately afterwards, Otto's laugh could be heard in the room, followed by the tittering of a few others. His landlord, Töyry, emitted a small, dry laugh. Akseli voiced his approval of Antto's words, but only those nearest to him could hear it. When the laughter grew louder, the vicaress stood up and strode to the table.

"The question has been raised of what the so-called gentlemen will do in a strike. It is easily answered. They have stopped carrying out their duties and have placed themselves in the very forefront, pressing the people's demands. They are precisely the ones who have the most to lose: their jobs, their futures, their very freedom. Their strike truly furthers our cause. For what does the Russian oppressor care if we stop chopping our wood here? Very little. But he cannot be indifferent when the official machinery of an entire country comes to a standstill. A strike here is unnecessary, since it affects us alone. But there are those who would use this strike for other ends. They fan the flames of confusion and anarchy, seeking the means to endanger our country, and that is playing politics to their country's peril."

After the vicaress's speech, there was a troubled silence in the room. The people looked at Halme, waiting for him to reply, but not having regained his mental equilibrium, he was unable to take a stand in opposition to the gentry. For a moment, his mind flirted with the possibility of calling for a strike vote without them, but he was not flexible enough to make so sudden a change.

The silence, however, demanded some response. Its prolongation revealed its artificiality more and more. Halme coughed lightly a time or two, brushed his shirt front a couple of times, then rose and stepped stiffly back to the table.

"Citizens! My original intent was to have us join in the people's united battle, but to my surprise, I have encountered disagreement about what to do. As the person who summoned this meeting, I must therefore conclude that a decision to strike cannot be made. Let us adjourn this meeting, but let us not even think of abandoning the struggle. Let us follow developments closely. I'll make contact immediately with authoritative quarters, and call you to another meeting. Then we can decide what to do on the basis of new information. At any rate, I feel we are obliged to sing our national anthem in support of this battle."

Halme's look was accusing, his face a study in injured dignity. The parsonage couple looked at the floor, and the vicar's face turned red. The audience stood up and began to sing "... land... our native land..."

Halme had a good baritone, but on this occasion, it sounded very feeble. Valenti sang out loudly, his head cocked to one side and his voice a soulful tremolo. The older people did not know the song, and the young, who had learned it in school, were prevented by shyness from raising their voices. During the song, the full extent of the betrayal slowly dawned on Halme. Along with the realization came a belated anger and regret at his failure to speak out against the gentry and to demand a strike in spite of them. When the song was over, the crowd began to leave, clattering, whispering, and buzzing. The vicar stepped to Halme's side and began a good-natured explanation.

"We have come to the conclusion that a strike here would be fruitless, if not actually harmful, if you consider our food supply. But has Halme heard that Yrjö Mäkelin in Tampere has drawn up a proclamation calling for a new government and an assembly of the people?"

"I have heard."

A sober look on his face, Halme gazed off somewhere over the heads of some of the departing crowd and blinked his eyes. He continued, unable to suppress the bitterness in his voice.

"There they seem to be clear about the goals of the strike. They are not satisfied with a return to the old system of class representation, but are demanding something new as well... as I believe the situation demands. For what good is all this uproar if it doesn't result in something new... Ahem. It looks right now as if our country will have to be satisfied with the restoration of a few lost official positions."

The public school teacher rocked back and forth from heel to toe and said, "But a government cannot be established in the marketplace."

"As I see it, a strike is revolutionary by nature. Everybody accepts that idea. So I have read. This is no ordinary dispute, and therefore, a government can be established in the marketplace. The fact is that some people want to return to things as they were in 1899, that is, before the manifesto. But the working people are striving to go forward."

The vicaress had seen how heart-stricken Halme was. In a honey-sweet voice, she began to chirp, "Now Mr Halme is mistaken. They do want to go forward, but in a lawful way. The old Diet of the Estates naturally must have its rights restored, but only in order to pass a new election law and then disband."

"And what guarantee can the lady give that this hip-pocket legislature will make these reforms?"

"Why, we two radicals, Mr Halme and I, will guarantee it. We will call a new strike if electoral reform is not forthcoming."

But Halme's mood could no longer be alleviated by sweet-talk. His answer was surprisingly venomous. "My dear lady, I believe there would be only one radical to declare a strike, namely Mr Halme."

By then, they had moved with the crowd as far as the cloakroom, and people were listening to the exchange. They were thoroughly confused about the strike, a confusion revealed in Kankaanpää's question.

"How on earth do we strike now? We are on strike against the Czar and against the factory owners. If we are on strike against the Czar, why are they striking in the factories? The factories don't belong to the Czar. And if we are on strike against the factory owners, what sense is there in that? The factory owners aren't Czars."

"The owners are on strike against the Czar, and the workers are on strike against the factory owners. They just happen to be striking at the same time."

The last was Otto's comment, spoken in a deliberately loud voice.

The vicar thought it pertinent to reply. "No, the objectives of the strike are common and national. It is directed against oppression."

"It's just that there are so many kinds of oppressors."

That was Janne, trailing in his father's wake. He was leaning against the coat rack, looking at his fur cap and twirling it as if he were unsure of how to put it on. He wore a friendly smile and seemed to be brimful of goodwill.

The owner of Kylä-Pentti, in all his humility, felt it appropriate to state his opinion here in the entryway. "Really, no strikes here, I say. Farming is the sort of thing where strikes don't help, I say. The cows have to be milked anyway, I say. And fed... It's different out in the great world, I say."

Laurila was passing through the outer exit, but they could hear him roar out a parting shot: "No goddammit... Not when it hurts the pocketbooks of Finland 's masters."

The comment was followed by some equivocal laughter and a few troubled smiles on the faces of gentlemen. Halme was silent while putting on his coat, but said loudly as he departed, "As I said, we'll discuss the matter and reach a new decision."

Preeti Leppänen had a new pair of work-mittens. He put them on, jamming together the opposing slots between thumb and forefinger. "Yes... It's better to see how it goes then. It's in those big issues there. People like us sort of have to be leaning that way."

They disappeared into the darkness of the November night, returning home in small groups that ultimately scattered at the forks of roads and paths. There was discussion and argument. The young boys roared out their own opinions into the darkness:

"Let it all go to hell!"

"Hey, to hell, said Mandy Hailu."

"Down with Yrjö Koskinen and Jalmari Tanielson."

"Banzai, goddamn. Bash Russian Nikki in the snout."

At home in hut or cabin, wives asked their returning husbands, "What was it all about?"

"It was all so darn confusing. Halme and the parsonage masters had an argument. A lot of nonsense was talked. Nothing at all about the land question. But something sure must be going on out there. The gentlemen seem a little afraid. Who knows, maybe we'll get some relief from this misery yet."

Akseli walked as far as the Kivivuoris with Otto, Janne, and Oskar. He was disappointed. "You can't make anything of Halme's talk. He should have gone for a strike without the gentlemen. Why the hell did he drag them into it? If the strike was supposed to be about tenants' conditions, the preacher had no business there. Halme should know that by the fence in our swamp."

Otto was amused. "The strike won't start just like that. This situation may mean eviction for the tenants, and that forces many of them to stop and think. I've thought about things too. We'll soon be in the soup, my boy. As the tenant issue heats up, the landlords will start evictions to get rid of the whole problem. The more talk there is of land distribution, the harder the landlords will try to get rid of the tenants."

"They can't just do that. Where would they all go?"

Oskar looked at the situation from a practical point of view. "You think the landlords are that farsighted? What do they care where the tenants go? The roads of Finland are already swarming with beggars. Kankaanpää's rent is three kilos of wool per year. The baron just stopped accepting it because he no longer needs the wool. In its place, he slapped on five days of work per week. Expensive wool, that. They never give a thought to the matter. If they did, it wouldn't be like this."

"Goddamn, we've got to start doing something." Akseli was in a rage.

"Just go nicely to work tomorrow. And if we get the right to vote, we'll pull their hair a little. We'll even make the baron think a little before he starts ordering work-days. That goddamned scraggle-beard has been complaining that I don't take proper care of my place."

210

"He's not too far off the mark in that." Janne laughed, and Otto had to smile.

"What the devil business is it of his? But it's not because of that. It's the steward's tattling. When I was plowing the field, he came out and started to beat my horse, saying it wasn't moving fast enough. Just for the devil of it, I grabbed the shafts and started to pull as if my life depended on it. He let out some gawddamns, but I kept a straight face and went on pulling. That goddamn Swede-Finn is always hanging around. He lies to the baron and probably steals too."

They parted at the Kivivuoris' door. Akseli started for home in a state of disappointment. Excited by the strike rumors, he had imagined that reform would come at one stroke.

He was angry with Halme as well. "Goddamn... I have to start reading those books and newspapers myself."

He was beating a man who was already down. Halme was walking home with Valenti along the dark and muddy road. The boy was bubbling over with the urge to talk about the night's occurrences, but his master's silence frightened him. The only sounds were the shuffling of footsteps and the drawing of breath. It was difficult for the master's conceited and self-important mind to admit the possibility that he had played the fool. The story of the beggar girl entered his thoughts. They must have laughed. Halme nearly trembled. His mind groped in despair. His dreamy patriotic socialism experienced its first fissure. And from that cleavage there sprouted the seeds of bitterness. Two darknesses confronted each other, the November night and Halme's eyes.

At home he said little to Emma. She could feel that something painful had happened, but she was quiet, as was her wont. She tried to make small gestures of consolation, but on going to bed, Halme said in a fateful voice, "Tomorrow I will go and meet with Comrade Hellberg. We must consult with each other."

II

So there was no strike. Akseli went dutifully to his rent-work. Jussi was horrified at the mere idea of neglecting it. If the boy refused to go, then he would go himself.

"If a strike comes, you won't go to work then either."

"What will stop me?"

"It won't be right to go then."

"It's been right for me to work every day for over forty years, and it will

211

go on being right as long as I'm able to do anything."

Evenings, the boy found it impossible to stay at home. Even on weekday evenings young people gathered on the dark roads, and the wildest rumors circulated among them. Every time someone joined a group he always brought some news.

"Captain Kock has seized power in Helsinki. The Russians' ass-kissers have been thrown out of office. Our boys hold the whip-hand there."

"They've set up a republic in Oulu. The gendarmes have been led out of town."

"They're bringing in weapons by ship from abroad. First we'll get the vote, and then we'll divide the land, and then we'll head for St. Petersburg. We'll put the document in front of the Czar and tell him to sign or he's heard his last cock crow."

"What document?"

"Well, the people's law. Parliament reform law. And laws that will give the tenants their land and others land from the manors. The wages will be set higher and the working hours lower. We won't have to work at night."

Halme had given out no information. He had been to see Hellberg, and the two had held a long discussion. What had happened in Pentti's Corners had happened in the church village as well. The landowners and gentry had opposed a farm-workers' strike. Only Mellola's sawmill crew and the railroad workers were on strike.

Hellberg laughed bitterly. "It's easy to see that the bourgeoisie won't go all the way with us. Their demands are political and ours political and social, and that's where we part company."

"To my knowledge, the majority of the bourgeoisie are demanding reform of the assembly."

"Heh, heh. They are forced to. Who would dare to stand openly against it now? There are a lot of good intentions. But when this pocket-book legislature is restored, and the Cossacks are riding through the streets, we'll see if the times are ripe for such far-reaching reforms. Our bourgeoisie will always be waiting for a more suitable time. Remember that."

"What should we do then?"

"Kock and his guards should carry out the whole program."

"Well. Violence is still foreign to the working class."

Hellberg fixed his piercing eyes on Halme and said with a short laugh, "Listen, anything is acceptable if it puts you in power."

212

A long debate ensued, during which Hellberg was sometimes angry and sometimes covertly scornful of Halme's childishness. Halme defended himself in a calm and dignified manner, surprising Hellberg with the pertinence and scope of his citations from socialist literature.

"In my opinion, it is illogical to demand legislative reform and be ready at the same time to seize power with the help of Kock's guard."

"Humph! What the devil is this socialist movement coming to? In the church village, Kalle Silander is explaining that cooperatives will lead automatically to socialism, that if people establish cooperatives and buy from them, the bourgeoisie will die out all by themselves."

"Ahem. A very suitable tactic."

"Well, what are the people in your area doing?"

"Nothing definite. The old fears are still strong. The manor's workers are especially wary. But I think my small efforts have had some effect."

"Uncertainty among the people is the result of your own uncertainty. You should establish a workers' organization there and begin to take action based on a firm party program."

Halme's stiffness increased. He was offended by Hellberg's overbearing manner of speaking and even by his taking an occasional bite from the bread on the table as they spoke.

"I do plan to found a workers' association and to affiliate with the party. Then I will present the party's program to the group for its approval. Permit me to observe that I, with my feeble intellect, have detected a good deal of vagueness in the party program itself."

In the end they agreed that although a strike was not feasible, they should at least try to agitate in support of legislative reform. It was Hellberg who used the word "agitation;" Halme insisted on "enlightenment." A workers' association had to be established, if there was sufficient support for it.

Halme departed. After he had gone, Hellberg let out a dissatisfied growl. He knew that Russian soldiers were already marching toward Helsinki and that the strike would end with goals only half accomplished. "The gentlemen will reap the benefits. And what kind of workers' organization will it be with that damned "church-warden" at its head? But there isn't a better man available."

Halme was engaged in writing a speech. He planned to hold a meeting at the firehouse on Sunday. Valenti was going the rounds again, bringing the invitations. But there was a surprise in store for them. That evening the vicar brought the news to Halme. The Diet would be assembled to take up the matter of election reform. The February manifesto would be retracted. Thus, it had been decided to end the strike. The vicar was happy and said, "Well, Mr Halme. We won after all."

But Halme did not share his happiness. He asked for further information in a matter-of-fact voice and then said, "Judging from all this, you have won. But the workers' victory has been left to the mercy of shaky promises."

"But how can that be? The announcement clearly states that the Diet's task is to reform the system of representation."

"Master Vicar, you know as well as I that the consent of the Estates is required, and they are known for their reactionary tendencies."

The vicar assured him earnestly that the Estates could no longer prevent reform. "Tomorrow we are holding a patriotic rally at the town hall. By all means come. Spread the news to others."

"Whether I will take part in said celebration depends on circumstances."

Halme was saddened and embittered. At the celebration, he would be a nothing. How great it would have been if, working together, they had gone on strike here, and were now celebrating their victory.

And to make it even worse, the changed circumstances made his prepared speech worthless. It was no longer relevant.

The people did gather at the firehouse, and Halme explained matters to them.

"So. Citizens! Perhaps we should be happy, but there is still a bad taste in our mouths. The fulfillment of the working people's hopes has been left to an uncertain future. We expected the wall to crumble at one blow, but that did not happen, and therefore we must prepare to continue the fight. The time has come to establish a workers' association in our community. We can settle that later. But although our hopes are only partly realized, the restoration of our country's rights is such a great event that we shall stand and sing our national anthem."

After the song, Halme was besieged with the strangest questions imaginable, but having only the vague information from the vicar to go on, he had to leave them all unanswered. He promised to get in touch again with authoritative sources.

The authoritative source was Hellberg. On Monday afternoon, Halme strode toward the church village, energetically swinging his cane. The officers of the village workers' association were already gathered at Hellberg's. The organization had been formed only that fall, although socialist activity had developed even earlier as a result of Hellberg's efforts.

When Halme arrived, he found the group in a state of intense excitement; here they had more information, for Hellberg had a telephone. After greeting them, Halme said, "Well, the strike is now over..."

Hellberg responded by barking, "The gentlemen's strike is over, since they have won their demands. Our strike will go on."

"But aren't the trains running again? That's what I heard."

"They probably are. The gentlemen have confused everyone with their stories. But I just got word that at least the Red Guard in Helsinki has refused to stop."

"Doesn't the strike committee in Tampere know how matters stand?"

"They're getting the news piecemeal. But I'll try again."

Hellberg put through a call. After a long wait, he got a connection.

"Is Mäkelin there in person?... Well, Salin then? They are all in Helsinki... This is Hellberg. Is there any more information about the strike situation?"

They were asked to wait, and Hellberg went on speaking during the interim. "They've all gone to Helsinki, or rather, they haven't come back from there."

Then someone spoke on the line, and Hellberg's part of the dialogue gave the others some idea of its contents. He hung up, paced the floor glumly for a while, and then laughed bitterly.

"Well, boys. The strike is over for us too. The gentlemen have won a clear victory. The government will be made up of constitutionalists, that is, of the Finnish and Swedish bourgeoisie. They've stuck in someone named Kari from the socialists, but without the party's approval. In Helsinki, the university guard threatened to shoot the Red Guard when they were shutting down stores. No, God help us, boys. They won't even stop at shedding blood when it comes to suppressing the workers' demands."

Discussion and debate ensued. Halme and Silander opposed Hellberg's bitterly angry response. They maintained that universal suffrage would open up new possibilities.

"That's why we have to keep things stirred up. We have to wake up the sleepers and keep the morale high. When the Diet convenes, there has to be constant pressure on the bourgeoisie to see to it that the right to vote is granted. But there is one good thing about this. We know where the traducers are sitting. There's been a lot of talk about reform, but when it comes to action, out come the guns."

"They're meeting at the town hall. How about it, shall we go?"

Hellberg's eyes flashed. "Let them celebrate their victory by themselves. We'll celebrate ours at another time, and I don't think we'll hear them cheering then. They began to hate me when they saw people joining the association. But more will join, they'll see. And the longer they delay reforms, the more there will be."

From time to time, Hellberg resumed his pacing. He was no orator, but every now and then he had gusts of fervor, and could make his points with telling effect, but as if he were speaking to himself, oblivious of his listeners.

Hellberg had not been born in the parish, but had moved into it as a young man. His earlier life was known only from hearsay; he himself had never spoken of it directly. From his talk, it could be inferred that he had traveled widely doing construction work. When he first came to the parish, he had had a little money, and, having married, he spent it on building a house in the church village. He was known to have been born out of wedlock and to have been given his name by a preacher. These facts were ascertained only after his socialism had awakened attention in the parish. The money demanded an explanation, and it was discovered to have been a remnant of his mother's inheritance. She had been the daughter of an estate owner in a neighboring parish, his father a traveling woods-boss or log-drive foreman. His mother had been driven from home with the child, and the foreman had vanished.

Later, the girl, who had supported herself and her child in service, had been partly forgiven. She was allowed to die at home and they had had to give her a share of her inheritance. What remained of it was left to the boy at her death. The boy himself had to leave, which he did willingly, first having beaten his uncle for calling his mother a whore and himself a tramp.

And here he was pacing about now. He exuded a controlled but destructive strength, staring directly at the others with his piercing eyes, with none of the sensitivity that normally cushions the relationships among people.

He irritated Halme. From the very beginning Halme had not liked Hellberg. He hated the discussions with him. Halme's opinions were accorded no respect unless Hellberg happened to approve of them. Often, the only answer he got was Hellberg's snort of laughter or a twitch at the corners of his mouth. But nothing could discourage Halme. He knew what Kautsky had said and how Tainio had explained the matter in his writings.

On the other hand, it was even pleasant at times to sit here among the leaders of the working people and listen to the wheels clattering by on the road outside as others made their way to the hitching rail for their patriotic celebration at the town hall.

The town hall was packed to the rafters. Speeches were delivered and songs were sung. Every last notable wanted to be heard. The vicar was asked to say a short prayer and did so. The vicaress spoke too.

"The most crucial point in the coming legislative reform is the right of women to vote. Now that the Finnish people have fought to regain their freedom, women must be granted a share in that freedom. Women are this society's most oppressed class; they are a caste without any rights. Our socialists speak of social slavery, which indeed exists, but not as a general feature of society. In a social sense all men are free. Only the women are not. Now that all our strength is needed to guard the freedom we have won, it is time that women too be drawn into the fray."

The actual main speech was given by the schoolteacher in the church village. He was a "Young Finn" and thus a constitutionalist, and so his speech was jubilantly triumphant. He even stuck a few pins into the *Suometar* faction, for which he received good measure in kind from the town physician, who was an "Old Finn." Many of the speakers attacked the socialists, for they had heard of the melee at Stockmann's corner in Helsinki. In his talk, the teacher dealt with the issue.

"....The support of the workers in this fight has been most worthy, but some of the groups in their midst have decided to fish in muddy waters. Is this a time to fan the flames of class hatred, just when there is hope of universal suffrage? Fortunately, the majority of our workers are a peaceful and law-abiding group. Our country's interest is more important to them than class advantage. The country's leading classes are sympathetic to rational reform, hence there is no excuse for social unrest. The differences of opinion which arose at the time of the strike are best forgotten as we now go on to constructive work for the country's benefit."

After every speech, there was singing. It was already quite late when they all started for home in the grip of an elevated patriotic emotion.

The parsonage couple rode in a coach. Going up a hill, its carbide lamps illuminated a pair of feet, whose tempo was set by the rhythmical swinging of a cane. The light left his upper body in darkness, but from closer up, his full figure was revealed.

"Good evening. So you were there. We didn't see you."

"Good evening. Your observation about my absence was correct. I was not at the celebration."

"But why?"

"Certain other affairs kept me away."

"Please get on alongside the coachman. You can surely fit somehow."

"Thank you very much. But walking in the fresh night air will do me no harm."

217

"But there's always a chance to walk."

"Thank you all the same. Walking at night is always pleasant. It stirs one's philosophical inclinations, heh, heh."

The coldness in Halme's voice made the couple realize that their persuasions were futile, and they went off. As the coach drew away, they could see only the long legs again, rising and falling as Halme stepped along, raising his knees high with every stride. The last thing in sight was the ferrule of his cane which flashed with every swing until it too was lost in the darkness.

III

The workers' association was named "W. A. Endeavor."

Very few people attended the organizational meeting, the workers at the manor being especially wary of coming. Although Halme expounded at great length upon the meaning of democracy, and declared himself willing to sacrifice what little strength he had for the good of the organization as a regular member, he was of course elected chairman. Valenti was appointed secretary because Halme nominated him for the post.

"For obvious reasons crucial to the work itself, such as the chairman and secretary's sharing the same abode."

At first there was a shortage of directors. Antto Laurila was chosen because of his fulminating speeches, although Halme was privately opposed to the choice. Otto Kivivuori was nominated but declined at the first meeting. He was not held back by fear of the baron, as were others, but had other grounds for finding it hard to become a director. Surprisingly enough, Janne Kivivuori tried hard to persuade him to accept. The boy's enthusiasm for socialism seemed in strange contrast to his earlier attitudes. Be that as it may, the boy urged his father.

"Go on now. Just think about it. If we get the right to vote, then we'll need to get the people to the polls. If only for that reason, an organization is important."

"Why in the hell are you getting so steamed up?"

"Steamed up? I'm not getting steamed up. But if we get a majority, the tenant problem can be settled. We'll be through with that goddamned rent-work. Putting in those days is enough to get anybody worked up."

"Well, it's very few that you've put in except for those gift-days, or nights rather, in the maids' rooms. Tell me, is that Lydia's brat your work?"

"Certainly not. I never touched her. Someone else had the pleasure."

218

"I don't know about being a director. They're quick to put the cuffs on a man nowadays. They might up the rent-work, and a workers' organization won't be able to stop them."

"I'm not worried. Our family's never been too good at it anyway. But what do you say? Let's become socialists."

Anna opposed the move to the point of indignation, but Otto consented at last. His action had a further effect in that Kankaanpää and Mäkelä dared to go along now that Otto was with them, and so the board of directors was constituted. In practice it had little significance, for Halme generally ran things by himself.

Little by little, the membership grew. Although the people were hesitant and in part indifferent, they attended the meetings anyway. The success of the strike had given greater countenance to Halme's speeches and so new members one after the other showed up.

"Put my name down too. If you can wait until the next pay period for my dues."

"There is no hurry. And we don't consider the dues mandatory in themselves if it's difficult to pay them. We need people now; later we'll need money. Yes, we must work, and to the greatest possible effect. We can see that this country's upper classes will not lift a finger to improve our lot. We have to take our fate into our own hands."

"They laughed at him, but if anyone around here was stupid, it sure wasn't Halme."

Many of them were already saying that about Halme.

The prestige of Valenti's position as secretary almost made Henna and Preeti confused. They went out and bought a new dress for Aune. The girl was of confirmation age, and was showing the first signs of a fresh and vigorously developing womanhood. Although the development was yet incomplete, many an eye took note of it. A family cow began to seem possible now, and with Halme's help, the dream came true. The aid was masked as payment for Valenti's work. Halme sometimes gave such aid secretly; the resulting boost in self-esteem was as great a reward for him as the respect of others.

The meetings were held at the fire hall. Since it was in a sense the baron's property, Halme thought it fitting to ask his permission for its use. He knew that it annoyed the baron when people presented matters directly to him and not through his steward, but he also knew that this matter was none of the steward's concern, and so Halme dared to break with custom and intercept the

219

baron on the road.

The baron eyed him appraisingly and blurted out, "You socialist now?"

"Master Baron, I confess to holding socialistic ideas."

"Everything go to hell. Everyone vote. What one maid or one Leppänen know about politics. It go to ruin. Scarcity come. Hunger come. Everything mix up. Nobility won't agree."

Halme was surprised at this open proffer of discussion and accepted it gladly. "Master Baron, neither Leppänen nor any maid, but their authorized representatives will decide affairs of state. And the workers' association I have founded has as its fundamental purpose precisely to raise the level of enlightenment, to make people capable of participating in political affairs. I disagree on the effect reform will have on hunger and scarcity. I believe that social legislation will end those evils."

"I read everything. Swedish socialists same talk and writing. It mean no law. Revolution here in Finland. Valpas and others. If tenants get land, no bread. Now they till only when I much force make them do it. They slack and lazy. Forests gone. They get forests. Fell all trees, sell them, and no work while they have money. Mix-up. Land all ruin."

Halme found it difficult to wait for the baron to finish. He hardly had time to shape his words in proper literary form, for the baron had opened the door to a discussion of his most cherished ideas.

"The master baron has managed his manor so well that agricultural students come to study it. But what would it be like if it did not belong to the baron? The tenants' poor farming methods are the result of their not owning the land. They are forced to live with the constant threat of eviction. If they improve the condition of their tenancy, they get no payment for their work when they leave. We have a good example of that. The parsonage tenant carved a home out of a cold wilderness, and when it was finished, he lost a part of his best land. No man's spirit can survive such conditions."

The baron glanced toward the parsonage. For a second there was doubt in his expression, but then he spoke again.

"Those Finnish speakers talk election rights. Because language. But the tenants no better. When there is good man, no eviction. The lazy and the wood stealers wrangle. They away. The tenant who is good, not away, and children after him."

The baron stopped suddenly. He no doubt realized that he had been improperly critical of the masters of the parsonage. Starting to walk away, he said abruptly, "You permission fire hall. These conditions. No wrong uproar. No booze, no

220

fighting. No speeches from revolution, only from laws."

He was gone, cutting short the auspicious beginning. But when the news of the permission spread, his hired hands became bolder. The meetings were more frequent and it became a habit to "go to the hall." Akseli Koskela would always sit there, seldom expressing an opinion, but eager to listen. Jussi was afraid of what they might say at the parsonage about Akseli's going, but they said nothing. Just once, the vicar asked Akseli, "Does Akseli know if Halme intends to go on with the training of the fire department now that he has organized a workers' association?"

"He did say it would begin again in the spring."

"Is that so. Well, it's good that some thought is being given to putting out fires when igniting them has become so common."

What did he mean by that? Akseli pondered the question to himself. There had to be something nasty in it.

The association followed the proceedings of the Diet very closely when it took up the new election laws. At one of the meetings, Halme announced, "Comrades, the opposition has crumbled at last. The nobles have agreed to revise election procedures. Comrades, rise and sing 'Now forward our native sons.'"

They had rehearsed the song at their meetings, and so now its strains echoed throughout the firehouse at Pentti's Corners.

Now forward our native sons, you young and fearless band.

Whenever developments reached such a climactic point at their meetings, Otto would stand up and look gravely around the room. If he saw anyone who seemed to share his amusement, his eyes would move on, and only a slight tremor would tug at the corners of his mouth. He never took part in the singing, although he had a good voice. Antto Laurila beat time to the "Marseillaise" with his shoulders. Sing he could not. Akseli stood with his lips sealed, but his consciousness echoed the words emphatically:

Forward even unto death, the earth is drenched with blood.

Halme had written a short letter from the province to the *People's Journal* and received a letter back asking for more. It praised him a little and urged him to become the rural correspondent for the district. With that encouragement, Halme became the paper's representative and ordered it for himself, in addition to *The*

221

Worker. Others were satisfied with the *People's Journal*, but he needed to be acquainted with larger issues, and needed the chief organ for the movement. Halme often requested that *The Worker* be given free of charge to the poorest members and helped others pay for their subscriptions. Halme himself earned good money, for even the parish gentlemen were beginning to have their suits made by him. By nature a friend of fine dress, he followed the new fads closely and ordered sketches and patterns from the best tailors. In addition to his cane, a pair of glasses from the right-hand frame of which dangled a black ribbon had appeared among his accessories after the organization of the association. A secret dream burned in his breast. Would the party put him forth as a candidate? He tried to smother the dream, for it seemed an impossibility. Hellberg, on the other hand, was almost certain to be a candidate.

When the first copy of the *People's Journal* arrived at the Koskelas, the boys read it eagerly. Jussi's view of the excitement was what one might expect. Because Akseli had had enough left of his money to pay for the subscription, he had no real cause to grumble on that score, but he always managed to find reasons.

"Why weren't you so eager to read when you were in school? I wonder what kind of shenanigans those moneys are paying for? It's your own business where you throw your money around, but you could have found better places. They spend the day writing nonsense for the people and the evening drinking up the fools' money."

The boys did not bother to argue the question. Alma's attitude toward the paper was quite different, however. She was glad to read it when she had a bit of time.

Sometimes she had Aleksi read aloud. The boy read in an expressionless monotone, column after column, and the items were easily muddled. But even Father-Jussi heard in passing about world affairs. He looked contemptuous and indifferent, but occasionally a topic would catch his attention.

"...it is our opinion that the problems of the rural poor will be solved only by conclusive measures. The bourgeoisie's proposals for land acquisition by non-compulsory means and for the regulation of contracts are mere stopgaps with no meaning at all for rural people. They are the usual childish measures the bourgeoisie resort to whenever a social ill has reached an explosive point, and they are no longer able to take refuge in their customary assertion that the ill does not exist. When the need for land in the country is sorely felt, it should be clear that under a system of voluntary land redemption, prices will rise to

222

such levels that the tenants will be unable to redeem their lands. Not to mention the fact that the landowners' willingness to sell, even at exorbitant prices, is highly questionable. When thousands of tenants are threatened with eviction, when they cannot keep their lands even under the old contracts that bind them as slaves to the land, then any talk of the free acquisition of land is bloody mockery. There is only one solution: freedom for the tenants decreed by law, with prices for their land set by the government, and with the assurance of a loan-assistance program."

"Everybody has a lot to say on the subject. But that doesn't settle things."
"If you think that way, things will stay as they are. When you have your say at elections, it'll be a different story."
"There's voting enough for me right here."
Jussi went out angrily. Having to admit that the paper had things straight irritated him, and he believed that the truths in it were mingled with much he disapproved of.

When the paper included such passages as "...our preachers are very good at explaining to the poor how difficult it is for the rich to enter the kingdom of heaven while they are stealing a poor widow's cow...," it was too much even for Alma.

"They shouldn't be writing things like that. Now they are mocking God, even in the newspapers."

That gave Akseli the opportunity to declare: "But it hits the nail on the head. We feel it in our bones, don't we?"

That brought on a quarrel, with the usual result that the boy stormed out after his father.

The *People's Journal* also reported on the strike at Laukko, and when Töyry notified Laurila that he had to leave his tenancy the following spring, the news found Laurila well prepared in spirit. He declared that he would go nowhere, demanding that his tenancy contract be extended and put in writing. If not, he would go on strike.

The matter was discussed at a meeting of the directors of the workers' association. The angry Antto would heed no warnings and went on threatening to strike. Otto tried to explain to him that the situation was hopeless. "You have only a verbal contract with so many eviction clauses in it that you can be thrown out on almost any pretext. And a strike by one man alone is futile."

"One man alone? Others are sure to join. What's the point of this goddamned association if you can't get any help from it?"

The explanation that the manor crew could not strike against Töyry was of no help. Antto was completely inflamed. It was decided that the association would try to negotiate the matter. Otto warned Antto again not to bring the issue to a head. "We'll try to talk to him. If that doesn't help, you can go to court, but the idea of a strike is useless."

On Sunday, Otto and Halme met at the Laurilas', from where the three men would go together to the Töyrys. Ascending the Laurilas' steps, they could hear Antto bellowing: "You goddamned boy, stop teasing the idiot!"

The shout was mingled with insane howling. At that instant, the bake-room door flew open, and eleven-year-old Uuno burst through it. Antto was hot on his heels in pursuit, and charged roaring past the visitors, but the boy managed to skip lightly to safety. From the bake-room they could hear Aliina scolding, in a voice where anger and tears were blended. "My God, what a life! It isn't enough that one of them is crazy — the others are complete devils. Where in hell will I end up?"

Whenever Halme chanced to witness such shameless behavior, his own dignity increased measurably. He was embarrassed and tried to cover that fact by making small, throat-clearing noises. Otto, for his part, turned to watch the pursuit, and when he saw Antto stop, cursing and shaking his fist, he called out, "Let him go. You can't keep up with him."

Antto returned, grumbling. "I'll give it to him yet. That age, and he comes at me already. I'll beat the crap out of him."

They went inside, but what had happened made things awkward. Aliina seemed angry, even with the negotiators.

"It's useless to go shooting off your mouths there. We have to move and that's all there's to it. They're going to put up a store here for his brother, that pus-balls. Not long ago, he tried to mount me from behind when I was doing the wash in the sauna. I even told his old lady about it. He came at me like a bull, from the rear. But I told him I didn't need anything like him on my back."

"Stop your goddamned stories. He wouldn't have tried if he hadn't done it before." Antto was so furious that he ignored the visitors. The two began to quarrel.

"Kiss my ass... you bastard! I've never needed anything like that."

Halme stood unhappily rubbing the grip of his cane. He forced himself to start talking. "Perhaps it is useless to talk, but we have to try that approach. You have no rent in arrears? Is everything settled to date?"

"It is, and to boot... I've put in every last goddamned day. They can't deny it. And that crooked-face himself knows that I did better than him at every job. And every day was a full day."

A six-year-old girl was sitting on the floor. It was Elma. Her uncut hair fell over her face, and through a slot in it, she stared at the visitors from one eye. Otto laughed and said, "Is that girl hiding behind her hair?"

Aliina snatched the girl up from the floor and brushed her hair aside. A pretty, albeit dirty, face came into view.

"We don't have time to brush her hair from morning to night, as they do in some places."

It was an obviously spiteful reference to Anna Kivivuori's well-known pretensions to refinement for her daughter. Otto pretended not to notice.

"But it pays to brush the hair away from such a pretty face. At least when she gets old enough for boys to start looking at her."

And a miracle occurred; Aliina put the girl down on the bed, brushed her hair back, and snuffled in an almost gentle voice. "There's no way of knowing what kind of hell she'll wind up in — who will torment and use her."

On the last syllable her voice broke. She was barely able to swallow her sobs.

Halme hurried their departure. The situation was too agonizing.

IV

It was Sunday at the Töyrys. The farm was so large that the servants had their own quarters on the opposite side of the yard. A handsome stone barn, built by the previous master, had once been reckoned among the great wonders of the community. The main building was a long, timber structure painted in red ocher, with two porches.

In the living room, the mistress sat at the head of the table, intoning in her thin voice:

...Oh Lord, take my hand and lead me...

It was their custom to do a bit of hymn-singing at home on those Sundays when they missed the church service. The master of the house did not take part in the singing but sat listening in the rocker. He had just finished reading the

225

parish newspaper from cover to cover. A meeting of the bank directors announced in it occupied his thoughts as he listened to the hymn. He was somewhere between forty and fifty years of age, a tallish and sinewy man. Laurila referred to him as "crooked-face," and one of his narrow cheeks actually did seem more deeply sunken than the other.

When they heard the knock on the door, they were both startled. Such occurrences were rare, and the master of the house very nearly had to swallow before he was able to call out: "Come in."

The couple exchanged covert glances when they saw who had come.

"Sit down."

"Thank you. You've had the benches painted since I was here last."

"Well, a touch-up... To make them easier to wash. And Halme hasn't been working in homes for years."

"No, I haven't. I find it more pleasant to work at home."

"Why shouldn't it be, yes."

"Ah-Ahem. To take the bull by the horns, I'll explain our business. As you know, we've formed a workers' association in this community. Along with other duties, the association tries to act as an adjudicator in cases of labor disputes, especially where our members are involved. Since differences of opinion have arisen between you and Laurila, who belongs to our organization, we thought it fitting to ask for a discussion of the issues. Perhaps we can find some way of reaching an agreement, which would, I believe, be to the benefit of both parties."

Small red splotches appeared on the landlord's face, and his foot gave the rocker a controlled but agitated thrust.

"Well, the thing is this is not a case of disagreement. I have issued an eviction notice, which I certainly have the right to do. And since I never do anything on a whim, it's useless to discuss it further."

Antto moved, but Halme had specifically warned him not to enter into the discussion until he himself had tried persuasion.

"But is it absolutely necessary for you to do so? The store doesn't have to be exactly on that lot, does it? You have other land along the road, don't you? We understand, of course, that the store itself has to be as close as possible to the village, but there is room for both of you there."

His wife had already opened her mouth to say something, but she was slower than Töyry.

"Yes, there is room, but I have to give my brother land to cultivate as well. He means to keep a cow there for his own use, and he needs land for potatoes."

226

The landlord paused a moment, kicked the rocker into motion, and continued: "And to my knowledge, I'm dealing with my own uncontested property, so I don't understand... Whatever the case may be with the store... The racket they raise is impossible... I won't listen to those rows... If they behaved like human beings... But I've decided that I don't have to put up with abuse from tenants..."

"And I don't have to listen to those nasty laughs." His wife managed to put in her word too, and Halme's stipulations could no longer hold back Antto.

"Goddamn... I'll abuse you as long as you treat me that way. Who in God's name can listen to that everlasting whining. Sometimes my horse can't keep up with the farm's horses, sometimes I'm not doing a thing myself. His boy runs around the fields spying on me like an ass-fly. I've done my work, you know it, you haven't been able to keep up with me in anything, so keep your mouth shut. It's always been a rule that a man ask no more of another than of himself. If the landlord is in the field, the tenant only has to keep up with him. But I've left you behind many a time, so what in God's name do I still have to do for it to be enough."

The menace he had restrained by force was now beginning to boil over. The landlord's wife began to stretch her apron across her knees with jerky movements, and started in.

"Is it all right for people to come raving into another man's house now? Can a person no longer be at peace in his own home?"

Töyry stopped rocking. Pressing his elbows against the arms of the chair, he tried to speak in as controlled a voice as possible. "I've stated my position. I'm not going to fight with you any longer, but you're leaving in the spring. I'll do with my land as I see fit."

"You goddamn well won't. We'll go to court about that. My great-grandmother got the land as her portion and you know it. If we go to court, you know it'll come to me as inherited land. I've done the rent-work as gift-days according to the law."

Otto had sat silent all the while, looking from one speaker to another. Now he asked Töyry, "What is the legal status? Is it an inherited tenancy?"

"The status is that it was given to a daughter of this farm and to her husband. But in all discussions, it's been treated as a regular tenancy. If it had ever been given outright, papers would have been drawn up. I gave it to the Laurilas at my father's request. There were no proprietary rights; they were to have it for the payment of rent like any other tenant. Once the rent was lower because a daughter was involved, but it was later raised, and new clauses added to the

227

agreement, including one authorizing eviction for misbehavior. And another part of the oral agreement is that the tenant must leave if the landlord gives him six months' notice. So let's just go to court. And I tell you I won't have any association meddling with my affairs in court. I'm willing to listen to people talk, but outsiders have no business interfering in something that's only between my tenant and me. My word has always been good and it still is. You'll leave on the appointed day, and if you won't go peacefully, the brass buttons will come to clear out the place."

The landlord had become more and more heated as he spoke. His jaw quivered and his breathing accelerated, causing his voice to crack. His son Arvo, a boy of confirmation age, appeared at the kitchen door and looked uneasily into the main room.

Halme reversed the crossing of his legs.

"We do understand that we have no legal right to meddle in your affairs. But we have seen fit to act as mediators, as has been the custom among people in the past. This is clearly a long-standing dispute. Where it began is impossible to ascertain. We know that one word leads to another. But a possible solution comes to mind. Payment with work breeds awkwardness. You two don't seem to be able to work together. But what if we were to calculate the value of the work in money? The contacts that cause friction would be reduced to a minimum. This being the case, your "personal" relations would cease to be a factor. What do you think?"

"I stick to what I've said. I've given the eviction notice, and the matter ends there. I have the right to do as I please with my own property, don't I? I don't take orders from outsiders."

"Well, we didn't come here to give orders," said Otto. "But Laurila must have some kind of right to the place. If everybody did as he pleased, the world would be a bad place to live in."

Töyry's wife became furious. "When did Kivivuori become a juror? Kivivuori may find that he has trouble enough of his own without interfering in other people's affairs. How long can you go on stirring up the manor workmen. They may put a sudden stop to that."

Halme banged the floor with his cane. "Socialism has shown its strength in the recent great strike, and we haven't seen the end of it. We stir up nobody, but we strive in our organization to protect the interests of the poor, which are in obvious need of support. Laurila has the right to seek our aid since he is a member of the association; that is one of the tenets of socialism."

228

Töyry stood up. He could no longer control himself. "But I am not a member of that association. In this house, we know nothing of this disease of socialism. Things have now reached the point where you must either stop this talk or leave this house. You can come to visit us, but not to hold a trial here. If my word doesn't hold good in this house, then the world has become a strange place indeed. That's my last word."

Antto stepped to the table and began to dig out a wallet from his back pocket. He threw his coat-tail aside, and having succeeded in extricating the wallet, he dug out ten markkas from it and threw them down on the table.

"Let's clear the record now. There is the ten I owe you for the seed barley. There are visitors here so for once I have witnesses. Put it in your goddamn vest pocket so that you won't miss it at hell's gate. And here in the presence of these men, I say that I don't accept the eviction. And that I am going on strike. I want a written agreement, and if I don't get one, I won't come to work. Until then, I'm on strike."

"If you don't come to work, then by law, the eviction will occur before the appointed date. In any case, it will happen in the spring. And now it's my duty to show you the door to this house. There it is. You may use it."

Halme and Otto rose. Töyry's wife seemed almost afraid of Antto, and Arvo stepped into the room too. The younger boys peered through the doorway in fright. Halme turned at the door and said with all possible dignity, "It's useless to negotiate in such a heated frame of mind. We are leaving. But for the future I wish to inform you that the association will not remain a bystander in this matter. It will support its member in every way, and presumably even in this house there is some awareness that the disease of socialism does exist. I ask your pardon for the disturbance, which was not of our causing. Ahem. Our respect for your home is great, and we therefore expected a business-like discussion. Good day. Our activities in this matter will not end here."

Töyry's wife, who had been trying to restrain herself up to this point, now broke out into tears of rage and began to rail at them. "Do we have to start calling the police now since they come brawling into people's houses with big gangs. It's not enough that they fight among themselves...They go around stirring up peaceful people to wild extremes... But God will soon show his hand to His mockers..."

Otto smiled as benignly as if they were involved with the most pleasant matter in the world. "Dear lady, don't be upset. You can order Cossacks from the governor for the protection of God, country, and the law. They'll come running if you just send for them."

They left, with Antto trailing, still cursing and raging, even in the doorway. "That goddamn brass-balls is going to find out yet. The only way they'll put me out on the road is as a corpse. We'll meet force with force on the threshold. You'll see, you bastard. I've drudged for years to put money in your purse, and now you'll drive me out onto the highway... No, no by God... Talk won't help any longer... Now we have to take up arms... by God we do. But no good will come of this for him. Stuff your mouth with everything you can lay your hands on... He's as gluttonous as the devil but stays the same goddamned sunken-cheeked... Where the hell does he stuff it all...?"

On the return trip, Otto and Halme tried to calm Antto's rage. Antto continued to threaten a strike, and the two tried in vain to talk sense into him. No explanation had any effect. Antto would merely burst into angry insistence that he had the right to strike and had declared he would do so in the presence of witnesses.

In spite of everything, and with full recognition of the futility of their action, Otto and Halme still agreed to continue to support Antto.

V

Antto went on strike and was ordered to leave the tenancy at once. When he refused to obey, the bailiff arrived with an eviction order. The result was the same.

"Take us feet first. Kill the whole bunch of us on the floor, kids and all, but I'm not leaving here alive, that's for sure."

The bailiff threatened to have him evicted by force, but then Antto appealed to the courts.

The case was hopeless, but nevertheless the association decided to hire a lawyer for Antto. A fund was established for that purpose. People were so incensed that the necessary money was soon collected. Akseli no longer had any, and it was useless to ask his father. But since he was in a frenzy about the case, he swallowed his shame and asked Otto for a loan.

"I'll work for you when something comes up. Like that excavation. I have no other way of paying."

"Do you work at home for nothing at all?"

"Yes. Father won't give me money for anything like that. But if Laurila wins this case, then I'll take our case to court. We'll get that fence moved yet."

230

Otto looked askance at the boy. He understood his confusion and shame, but could not help saying, "You poor boy, you're really up against it. You do double work for nothing: for your father and for the parsonage."

The boy became even more rattled, and Otto let him off the hook by saying, "Well of course you can have the money. You can do something for me when a job comes up. But don't imagine such lawsuits will get your fence moved. Antto is sure to lose anyway."

"What good is the law then?"

"We will get to show clearly what a tenant's lot is. We'll make the court demonstrate, as part of its official business, that the talk of land slavery is absolute fact."

It was hard for Akseli to understand carrying out an action known in advance to be useless, but it was better than doing nothing. He gave the borrowed money to Halme, who thanked him in the name of the common cause.

"You have experienced the same injustice as Antto and understand what is happening. It occurs to me at this point that I should go and ask the parsonage masters for a small contribution to this fund."

And there emerged on Halme's face something rarely seen and unbefitting his gravity, a smile of mischief.

"Yes, and tell them it's small payment for what they themselves have done in the matter of their tenancy," said Akseli.

"Well, I don't know if it is advisable to give personal offense. It doesn't have to be said; the matter is self-evident."

Antto's case had really aroused the community. The Laurilas were not especially popular, but the issue touched all the people so closely that they took it up as their own. Even Preeti brought in two markkas for the fund, explaining at length that he didn't happen to have more on hand at the time. The tactful Halme accepted the gift and said, "The amount is not the point. The entire case has only symbolic meaning since it will end in defeat. Your gift is symbolic as well, and I thank you for it, valuing these two markkas more highly than many another gift."

Preeti chattered happily to people about it. "I gave too, although a man like me... but it's something... Like an ideal, sort of... Something foreign. I don't remember the word... my boy will be sure to know it since he's learning from the master and is sort of a helper and stand-in for him."

The case was threatening to become a major issue. Hellberg arranged for a lawyer through the party. This was not the first or only eviction in the parish, but it was the most striking in nature and, above all, it happened to come just before the elections.

Some of the influential landlords and gentlemen from the church village went to Töyry with the recommendation that he put off the eviction, at least until after the elections, but he would not listen to such talk. I've given my word, he repeated to everybody, and there he stuck. He had support as well, for the issue was becoming one of principle. A number of the landlords stood by Töyry's right to evict.

"If we bow to this kind of pressure, where will it end? Some fine day they'll say that they own the tenancies. And who would put up with a tenant like that Laurila? I certainly wouldn't take insults from my men."

When Halme appeared at the parsonage and asked to speak to the vicar, the couple were quick to surmise that his arrival had something to do with the eviction. They had a position all prepared and presented it to Halme.

"We don't approve of the eviction as such. We think it wrong. But we approve even less of its being used to stir up the people during an election. You can't turn an isolated case into a general issue."

How annoying such a self-taught tailor could be. How he would sit there, stroking his trim mustache with his sensitive fingertips. How he enjoyed parading his knowledge and learning, spouting his bookish phraseology. He wasn't as foul-mouthed as other partisans, but that oratorical defender of the fatherland had turned out to be a socialist agitator. His desire to shine had become lèse majesté.

"Perhaps we can discuss the case as a matter of principle. The master vicar has stated his point of view: 'an isolated case.' But we know that from a civil and judicial point of view, individual cases are not considered as isolated instances. Moreover, take such an extreme example as a murder committed in the course of a robbery. It is no less criminal for being, to everyone's good fortune, a rare occurrence. We would not, however, leave it untried, even though there were only one such case in a hundred years."

"But that has no relevance at all to this case. My point is that although these regrettable exceptions do occur, they are still exceptions, and that hatred against society should not be enkindled on such grounds, much less when new regulations offer the possibility of resolving the tenant issue legally."

"Consider the imminent evictions in Laukko. Such evictions will soon be occurring frequently throughout the country. Nor is Laurila's the only case around here. These are not isolated cases. I thought you might support our cause with a small contribution."

The vicar felt some discomfort. But the realization that Halme's visit was a deliberate provocation helped to steady his resolve. His wife, always more quick-witted, settled the question adroitly. With a friendly smile, she said, "We would do so without hesitation if your point of departure were different. As soon as you stop dragging the association into the matter, I will lend my support. But you cannot bring socialism into it. Justice is too great a concept to be used as a political tool. Let's establish an organization for the support of Laurila, say, on a non-partisan basis, and we'll join. Not otherwise. We will not contribute to a socialist campaign fund."

She shook her finger at Halme in mock anger. "What would Mr Halme say if I came to ask his help for my party?"

The vicar smiled in relief. Ellen knew how to handle people. Halme, a little less assured, said, "As soon as the lady's party acts as defender of the poor, I will even become a member. Gladly."

"But it is already doing so. Its program includes the acquisition of land by the landless, but by voluntary means. We admit that tenants do have rights, but so do the landowners."

"Ahem. The right to evict, at least."

A long argument followed, with Ellen presenting her refutations so lightly that a pleasant atmosphere prevailed. Money Halme did not get. Nor had he expected to, but he had enjoyed the discussion.

After his departure, they found much to criticize. He had deliberately made allusions to the Koskela question. That could hardly be compared to the Töyry case. After all, Koskela had not been evicted.

"That Akseli is the root of all evil in this case. His father has come to understand, but the boy has become more and more sullen at work. Socialism has made him rabid. Actually, I no longer have regrets about the entire affair. Any injustice involved in it is slight when compared to the boy's insubordination. And as it turns out, it didn't help us a whole lot. Things are still not too good."

"But they would be even worse without the land. And what harm did it do them? They are still eating, still living as they did before. Only their work has been eased. There's no reason for them to get involved in the Töyry business. They've been left completely at peace on their place. But there's another cause for Akseli's socialism; it's just in his nature."

"That's part of it, I'm sure. It can't be his upbringing. It must be hard on old Koskela. He is a man of order and discipline. But everybody has problems.

Our Ilmari's behavior has begun to worry me."

"Well, he's at a difficult age. And I can't consider it wrong if he attends demonstrations against officials who tend to be lawless. He is wild, but he has a sense of justice. He's even getting better at his studies."

"Well, perhaps he'll settle down. Everything is just so unpleasant. Everyone is sowing hate and dissension when they should be supporting one another. I was very sympathetic to socialism at first. In many cases, an honest person has to admit its truth. But they have made it a weapon of anger, and as a preacher, I must deny it my sympathies. The whole business has gotten into questionable hands. It's no longer constructive, but anarchistic."

"Are you still mulling that over? It's all been clear to me for a long time now... Emma... Emmaaa... Will Emma please set the table."

"Goddamn, I told the judge too that I would never leave this place alive. And I asked the high court to tell me what the law is for. Why not just say you're allowed to steal land and let it go at that. I said goddamn honored high court, I said, I don't understand sections and clauses, but I've done my rent-work. And I said it again when they came to the section about disobedience, the cause of the eviction. I said I won't bow down to old man Töyry. I'll do my work but I won't crawl, I said. And that goddamn lawyer started shooting off his mouth to me in that side room, saying I spoke out of turn. That I should have behaved myself, to put the plaintiff in a poorer light. But I told that goddamn pantywaist there would be no wriggling and squirming here. He told me I was impossible too, but let him go drink piss. All kinds they send to help you."

Yes. Antto had lost his case outright. In addition, he would have been fined for contempt of court but the judge had considered him not responsible for his actions with regard to his speech. The judge also knew that he had rendered an unjust decision. But it had been according to the law.

Fiery meetings were held at the fire hall, with one recommendation following another. Akseli took the floor for the first time and kept insisting: "Let's go and stand on Laurila's porch so the police will have to drive us off by force."

But Halme vetoed any notion of a violent demonstration and presented his own program. They would gather on the day of the eviction, but no illegal action would be permitted. A flag for the association would be made in advance of the day, and they would carry it and sing revolutionary songs.

Many of them grumbled that songs would do no good, but with Otto's help, Halme put down the advocates of more drastic measures. On the question of

234

legality, he suggested that Janne Kivivuori use association funds to obtain legal texts and study the most pertinent sections.

"It is good to be informed on such matters, but I don't have the time to study them myself. Since you're a sharp-witted boy, it's just the job for you."

Surprisingly enough, Janne bought the books and began to study them diligently. Otto was dumbfounded. What bug had bitten his son?

"Check the marriage code carefully now, so that at least you'll be able to seduce in compliance with the laws of Finland."

The young man was quickly up on many matters. He soon explained to Halme that it was permissible to organize a demonstration provided that it in no way interfered with officers in performance of their duties. Demonstrators must be careful not to shout anything relevant to the issue involved. They could sing all they wanted, but they could not enter the yard. They were to keep their distance, so that in a pinch, they could claim to have had nothing to do with the eviction. The wisest thing would be to stay within the manor's boundaries and not go onto Töyry's property at all. They must also keep off the highway. A suitable site for their purposes was a hill very close to the Laurilas.

In order to be completely prepared, they went over the ground in advance. Their young legal expert drew a map for them to follow. Laurila, meanwhile, had refused to look for new housing or to give any thought to leaving. Nevertheless, the association arranged that he be lodged temporarily in Kankaanpää's empty "grandpa's cabin," and that his livestock be housed in several tenants' barns. Akseli even got Jussi to agree to taking the lambs. Jussi condemned banners and processions to the depths of hell, but he could not deny his aid to an evicted tenant. Janne even devised the strategy of not providing the aid in advance, but of letting everything go to the farthest possible extreme. They would gather the livestock only after it had been driven from the barn. The same with the children. "And the lunatic is to be taken on a separate sled. If it can be worked out, we should even let him escape for a while."

Halme looked at the boy somewhat askance. What a schemer! Otto approved the proceedings.

"You'll go far with that kind of trickery, my boy. Read those law books a little more and even the devil will be ashamed of you."

"Uh-huh... You'll make a good partner for me."

Halme was trying to reserve a place in the association for Janne so that the boy would not take a notion to choose his own, but Janne was not working purposefully toward any goal. Life carried him along with its own impetus, although getting the law books may have been a decisive push. In any event, forty years later a worthy old man strolled by the market now standing on the Laurila site. And a group of men out front said to each other:

"Town Councilor Kivivuori has come to visit his home grounds."

"Ya-ah, a real goddamned mother-pol. The things they pick for the legislature with workers' votes."

But that was still far in the future. Now they were setting the scene for the eviction drama. Further startling news had arrived. The bailiff, hearing rumors of their activity, and wishing to be prepared for any eventuality, had sent for ten mounted policemen to carry out the decree.

"Better and better. Better and better."

They awaited the day of the eviction. At the meetings, as well as individually, they went over their course of action. Halme kept emphasizing the importance of discipline and organization.

"First of all, for the honor and prestige of the organization, and secondly, because undisciplined behavior may cause trouble for the association, even its dissolution. As you know, being chairman, I bear the responsibility, and I am ready at any time to go to prison for a good cause. But with the election work, we can't afford an interruption now."

About this time, people in the village started to call Akseli Koskela a "hard-core socialist." The loss of the swamp had indeed set the young man in motion, and his momentum soon began to seem out of proportion to its cause. In the Laurila affair, he was living his own situation. The loss of the swamp did not embitter him in the same way as it did his father, who saw daily before his eyes his lost property, a field which grew crops for another's benefit. The boy resented the wrongness, the injustice of the matter. Before long it had developed for him into a generalized land question, over which he was continually seething. While waiting for the Laurila eviction, he could not endure staying at home. Most often he went to the Kivivuoris, so often, in fact, that he was ashamed of himself. Otto might tease him about girl friends, or rather, about the lack of them, but otherwise the atmosphere there was completely relaxed and pleasant. His father's back problem often made things strained and oppressive at home, making him want to leave.

As a skilled workman, Otto had been given the task of making the flagstaff for the association. Halme himself was to make the flag. One night when Akseli was on a visit to the Kivivuoris, Otto was whittling on the pole. "I'm making a staff, you see. We'll soon be charging the oppressor under the flag of Emma

236

Halme's red underskirt."

Akseli, who was literal-minded, regarded the Kivivuori brand of socialism with some suspicion. Janne was getting ready to head for the village. He seemed quite willing to talk socialism and near-obscenities in the same breath. But it didn't pay to argue. Father and son would have been a match for someone much more glib than he was.

"Come along with me," said Janne. "We'll go and pay a visit to the maids."

"What'll I do there?"

"Nothing special. We'll play pairs."

The men laughed, but Otto's eye happened to light on his daughter in passing. "Akseli must be waiting for that girl of ours. Her blouse is starting to fill out a little."

Fifteen-year-old Elina blushed to the roots of her hair. Her voice nearly caught in a sob as she said, "Father is just ter...ri...ble."

The situation was made worse when Oskar bawled out, "Look at the blush on her face."

Akseli gave a highly forced laugh. He was embarrassed that they teased the girl, using him in the process. Now the poor thing was even more embarrassed. She tossed her head angrily and left the room.

Anna scolded Otto. She understood the girl's embarrassment, knew that it was profound and serious. Her father had touched a sore spot. The girl was blossoming into a woman, and the change was now at its crucial phase, causing confusion and restlessness.

The girl did not show herself for the rest of the evening. She went into the inner room, where they heard a door slam when she went somewhere. Akseli had already forgotten the incident by the time he was leaving, but he ran into Elina in the entry. By the light of a storm lantern burning on an overturned bucket, he saw her recoil in renewed embarrassment, plunge into confused and panicky motion, and slip through the door in flight.

The boy was completely baffled. "What was all that about? She could hardly have taken Otto seriously. She's still just a kid."

But for the first time it set him to thinking about her in a different way. "She is a little bit calf-like. But she's going to be a pretty girl. She looks like Oskar and her mother. And she has such terribly thin hands."

And then he scowled angrily at his own thoughts.

I wonder if I'll get to carry the flag.

VI

The eviction day happened to fall on a weekend, when many of the tenants had already completed their rent-work. The manor crew was nervous about missing work, but Halme appealed to them to risk something too, and very few were absent.

They gathered at the firehouse. Akseli was indeed made flag-bearer. There was even a small honorary ceremony:

"Akseli Koskela. I give into your hands the beautiful flag of our association. Carry it high today in honor of our first battle."

Akseli took the flag, and Halme launched into a complacent exposition of its design. It was naturally red, with a green wreath enclosing an emblem embroidered in gold letters: "W. A. ENDEAVOR."

There had been further consultation with Antto. Having learned from Janne that Antto would be imprisoned if he refused to obey the police, Halme had gone again to explain things to Antto and to advise him to leave when ordered to do so. Janne indeed was of the opinion that it would be better to let the police use force. It would give a cutting edge to the affair. And a jail sentence of a few months was not such a heavy burden.

Halme could not endure the weight of such deeds on his conscience and even reproached Janne for his lack of consideration. "You are willing to sacrifice an innocent family to stir up feelings during an election. We won't carry things that far."

But Antto's position settled the question: "I'll fight on the threshold, as I said."

Halme was horrified when Antto stuck to his course of action. He looked nervously at the axe standing near the door.

There was nothing to do now but wait for the inevitable. The nervousness of the men was reflected in their faces. Shouldn't they start already? What songs would they sing?

Then Elias Kankaanpää came running from the turnoff where he was on guard.

"A gentleman is coming from the village on a sleigh. He's coming this way, not along Töyry's road."

A livery horse was indeed approaching them. A gentlemanly-looking young man was sitting in the back of the sleigh.

"Good day. I would like to see Comrade Halme."

"He is inside... Halme..."

"Halme, come here. Hey, go tell him."

Halme came out. The gentleman greeted him and introduced himself.

"I am from the *People's Journal*. Comrade Hellberg suggested I speak to you. I intend to write an article on the eviction and the demonstration. May I march with your group at the start? Then I'll go to the eviction site."

The reporter's presence raised their spirits. With him there, it seemed they got support from some larger and more powerful quarter. Halme welcomed the man and could not at the moment have asked for more from life. He even had a camera.

"Welcome. May I express my pleasure that the party has not forgotten us in our lonely struggle."

And then on a more personal level:

"I was expecting Comrade Hellberg to be with us. But apparently, since he is a candidate, he does not expose himself to danger. Well, I have to lead the fight alone then. I have no such position to protect."

So it goes. There in Tampere, they seem to know nothing of Halme's existence when it came to picking their candidates.

The reporter said the police would be coming soon. There were ten mounted policemen plus the bailiff and two constables in a sleigh. At that moment, Elias, who had returned from his post, brought new information.

"They're coming... on Mäenpää's Hill. Horsemen and two sleighs. Darn nice horses."

"Line up in back of the flag. Akseli, march in front at a slow pace. Small boys and women to the rear. If anything happens, don't panic. And above all, no shouting."

The reporter shouted his contribution. "If they start to disperse the group, don't be afraid. They'll ride toward you at first, but then they'll start to force you back with the flanks of their horses. They won't ride you down. So don't worry."

Victor Kivioja stood in the group and blustered, "Goddamn, we should have come on horses. I would have jumped on my racer's back. They're not the only ones with horses, goddamn."

"Comrades! Forward in the cause of justice and truth."

Akseli started forward nervously, trying to get the flag to wave, but there wasn't enough wind.

They turned at Töyry's juncture, which the police had already passed by. This road also led to the parsonage, and from it turned the actual road to the

Töyry house, along which Laurila's tenancy lay.

At Halme's prompting, they started to sing softly. The tension grew and grew. They had never experienced anything like this before. Fear began to gnaw at their hearts, and so the song grew stronger as they sought reassurance in it:

Arise ye slaves to work's oppression...

At a bend in the road, Wolf-Kustaa appeared with a frozen fish-trap on his back.

"Join the ranks, Kustaa. Come along."

"Go on yourselves, damnit. Just go ahead... They'll slice all your heads off with sabers."

Because of the song, they could not hear clearly what Kustaa was muttering, but they heard enough to know it wasn't good, and so there were a few shouts:

"What's he mumbling about? Is he too good to march with workers?"

"Yes I am. Screech with your necks stretched out, you bastards! The world will swallow up your sounds and the fields your crap."

There was more yelling and cursing as Kustaa passed the tail end of the group and went off angrily with his fish-trap.

The reporter ran quickly ahead of the group and set up his camera. Halme stepped abreast of Akseli beneath the flag, and several of the others in the front row tried to crowd forward. The act was repeated at least twice.

Now they could see the Laurilas' place and the people in the yard. The procession turned from the road in the prearranged manner, plowing through the snow toward the small hill that had been chosen as the site of the demonstration. From it they could see clearly into the Laurila yard. When the singing marchers appeared on the scene, there was movement in the yard. The bailiff approached, accompanied by a constable. Halme cut off the singing and told the group that he would do all the talking.

Walking quickly in their direction, the bailiff asked while still some distance off, "What is the meaning of this crowd? And by whose permission has it assembled?"

Halme took a few steps toward the bailiff, raised his hat in greeting, and said in a voice that carried very clearly, "Master Bailiff, the intention of this group is to bear witness to the destruction of one of its comrade's homes. And it is assembled under the right granted by law to every Finnish citizen."

"The law also requires notification of the gathering, but I received no such

240

notification."

"Master Bailiff, this is not an official occasion. People have made it a practice to gather at Whitsun bonfires, for example, and there has been singing on such occasions, but they have not been considered illegal."

"This is no bonfire. This is obviously a demonstration."

The bailiff studied the group for a while and came to a decision.

"I give you solemn warning not to interfere in any way with the actions of the officers. I order you not to come any nearer to the place of eviction. Otherwise, you will answer for the consequences."

"Master Bailiff, we will not harass the officers. We are only demonstrating our opposition to the general state of affairs which permits such occurrences."

The bailiff continued to eye the group doubtfully. Every one tried to look sober and matter-of-fact. Any sign of mockery might have affected the bailiff's decision, but since he saw none, he departed, saying, "I warn you once more. You will be held responsible for the slightest disturbance and will be charged with hindering officials in the performance of their duty."

The bailiff returned to the yard. The Laurila family had remained indoors, and the police awaited only the arrival of Töyry, for the landlord had to be on the scene when the official order to leave was given. The reporter followed the bailiff into the yard, and the bailiff asked, "What are you doing here?"

"I am a newspaperman. Here is my card. This is a public act of eviction."

"All right. You stay out of the way too. Of course you intend to write an account derogatory to the officials."

"The editor-in-chief will answer for its legality, as the bailiff must know."

The bailiff shouted to the police, "I wish to remind the constables of the behavior befitting an officer of the law in the performance of his duty."

At that moment, Töyry drove into the yard. His wife was with him, for she had not been able to overcome her curiosity, even though the occasion was an unpleasant one. But she remained seated in the sleigh.

The bailiff spoke in a low voice to the officer commanding the mounted police, who ordered his men to take up a position opposite the steps, facing in the direction of the demonstrators. Töyry greeted the bailiff. He was gloomy and nervous-looking, but nevertheless he spoke in a decisive voice.

"So-o. Let's go on in."

The Laurila family were sitting in the main room. The boys and Aliina were in the chimney corner, but Antto himself sat on a long bench near the table. The bailiff greeted him but the only response was Antto's sullen gaze, fastened on his boots.

The bailiff took out a paper and read the eviction verdict. Then he turned toward Töyry. "Does the master wish the verdict to be executed?"

"I have given my word and I stick to it."

"Anton Kustaa Laurila, I advise you and your family to leave this building, and to take all your movables and your cattle with you from this property. Referring to the terms of the eviction verdict handed down by the court, I inform you that if you do not leave voluntarily, I am to avail myself of police action to carry out the verdict."

"Kill me right here. Kill the whole family, kids and all. But I won't go nowhere from my home. That's my last word."

"Laurila, for the sake of clarity I am informing you that insofar as I must carry out the eviction by force, there will be the added charge of resisting an officer."

Aliina began to laugh, a hysterical and spiteful laugh, in the background of which tears awaited their turn. "Well then, we do have a home somewhere. Better to be in jail than on the road."

Red-faced and uneasy, Töyry said to Antto, "Listen now, Antto. I'll give you one last opportunity. If you promise now to take everything away within three days, I'll wait that long. You can surely find a place to live around here if you just try."

"Goddamn, not in three years. You know, you goddamned thief, that I won't leave my home except in pieces."

"Well, don't then. If a man won't pay attention to words, there's nothing left but to let the law go to work. There still is law in this land, no matter how much you shout."

The bailiff knew it was useless to talk, but for the sake of the reporter, he said, "I ask you to inform me where we can take your goods and cattle. Otherwise, they will be left outside."

"I have no place to go. Cart them out onto the roads of Finland. A poor man can still live on that common ground, as long as he gets nicely out of the way when a gentleman comes along."

"Raitamo and Saari. Get some tools and remove the doors and windows. The fireplace also has to be wrecked so that it can no longer be used. Tell two of the mounted policemen to carry the stuff outside. And woman, get the children dressed. I warn you not to make trouble."

"Let them freeze! What the hell will they do in this kind of world? Let's all

242

go to hell together...."

Aliina burst into tears, took Elma into her lap, buried her face in the child's back, and sat swaying back and forth. The policemen came back with the tools. They too were beginning to look troubled, mostly because of Aliina's weeping. Töyry attempted to leave, saying he was no longer needed, but the bailiff, who was also getting annoyed, said angrily, "You are to stay here. It's your job to wreck things — they are your responsibility. The police will follow your instructions in the matter."

It had been decided to wreck the cabin so that Laurila could not return to it, and the bailiff felt that Töyry should be on hand to give permission to smash things.

One after another, the windows were torn loose, and cold air flowed into the room. So were the doors, and now, from off on the hill, the sound of the demonstrators' singing could be heard in the room.

...where our flag waves... our country's glory is secure...

The mounted police began to carry out the household goods. There wasn't much to carry. When they began to empty out the bake-room, the madman began to bellow and jerk at his chains, which were long enough so that he could lie down on a platform near the wall. The wretch even had a name — Antti. He was a horrible sight with his filthy beard and hair. On his forehead, just next to the "madman's wrinkles," was a huge strawberry mark. Rags were wrapped around his wrists so that the chains would not chafe him.

As the police carried out the crocks and kneading-troughs, the lunatic stamped his feet, clanked his chains, and laughed. Apparently he wanted to join them. During pauses in his laughter, they could hear confused, mumbled words: "Aaa... a... ntti. Dough... dough..."

One of the mounted policemen asked the bailiff what they should do with him.

"He is to be released and dressed. Since they haven't found lodging, he is to be taken to the poorhouse."

"But don't you need a permit for that?"

"We can't turn him loose. In this case, permission is unnecessary because they themselves are not caring for him... But what an assignment!"

The whole time, Antto sat on the bench without saying a word. Gritting his teeth, he tried to smile scornfully. Aliina wept continually with the girl on her lap. The boys had retreated behind her. Finally none of the furnishings was left but for Aliina's chair and the bench on which Antto was sitting.

"Laurila, get up from that bench. It is to be taken out."

"You must understand that it stays under my ass."

"For the last time, get up."

"Kill me, goddamn it."

"Constables. Lead this man out. Put a hat on his head and take him outside."

A policeman took a hat and tried to put it on Antto's head. The latter swept it to the floor, and the fun began. The police seized Antto, but he rose and began to tear himself free.

"Goddamn Jesus... I'm on my way to jail now... God help us... we're going to hell, the whole gang of us."

Elma screamed horribly. Aliina joined in the cursing. The police lost their composure and pulled and jerked at Antto to get him out. Although they were two strong men, they were flung about on his arms so that the door frames rattled.

"Get handcuffs and a rope from the sleigh. We can't hold him when he's loose."

One of the policemen brought the handcuffs and rope, and Antto was bound. Töyry's wife began to weep and wail in the sleigh, and her husband paced feverishly back and forth in the yard repeating from time to time: "I told you, you can't resist the law... And I gave my word..."

Antto went on cursing and bellowing, unable to do more, now that his hands were cuffed and his feet tied.

The demonstrators had only a fragmentary view of the scene through the mounted policemen, and some of them began to shout in the midst of the singing.

"What's going on? They're not killing him, are they? Are they clubbing him?"

The women began to take fright, and a few of them started to sob. Akseli looked on, gritting his teeth. He turned toward the group, offered the flag to Halme, and said, "No, God help us... I can't just look on... I'm going, no matter what happens."

"In your place... Stay in your place... Remember what you promised..."

Otto also stepped to Akseli's side and said, angrily shaking his head, "Boy, boy, boy... Use your head."

"Goddamn... They're beating up on people..."

Now the women began to cry out, sobbing, "At least go and talk to them, Halme... It's awful... Good God, what are they doing?"

Halme was beginning to fear the group would get out of control. His voice trembled with agitation and shock as he turned to face them, arms outspread, and shouted, "For God's sake, comrades... Keep quiet... If you don't it will be horrible... Some of our group are little more than children, and you plan to defy mounted policemen... Let's sing... Comrades, do you hear... 'Now forward our native sons...'"

Once more the group began to purge its mind with the "Marseillaise", but Halme continued to follow the events from the corner of his eye.

During the course of the song, he spoke once more to Akseli. "You're upsetting people. I order you once more to obey."

"Who can bear to watch that..."

"You have to... Remember that no good will come of such behavior. There are children in back of us... little boys..."

Halme's pleas calmed Akseli down, and then a wonder occurred. Emphatically, although fearfully out of tune, Akseli began to sing: "...unsheathe the avenging sword... confront the tyrant's horde..."

The drama in the yard continued. Antto had been hoisted onto the policemen's sleigh and kept up a constant clamor.

"Lay me low, goddamn... Throw the kids onto the pile. Get the mad boy too... Kill the whole bunch of us."

The cows were let out first. The barn and the stables were completely emptied, and the animals, stupefied and bellowing, began to blunder this way and that. There was a bull in the group, too. After staring blindly for a few minutes, he emitted a wild bellow and began to gallop so furiously around the field that he raised a small snowstorm. Soon the lambs stood bleating out in the cold as well.

Now they were finally able to get Antto's bench out. But the chair that held Aliina was still there. No fight developed over it, for she rose voluntarily, and, wrapping a quilt around Elma, started for the door, with the boys following. Weeping, she emerged into the yard, but when she saw Töyry's wife sitting and wailing in the sleigh, she put the girl down and rushed toward her.

"Goddamn... You watch too... watch them driving the kids out into the cold... Laugh, goddamn... laugh... You've had your way... I'd scratch your eyes out, but you're such a miserable... dried fish... nose-in-the-air... Your ass looks like two penny crusts wrapped up together. But I'll show you my own so you can see..."

And Aliina snatched up her skirt, showed her rear, and raged, weeping, "There it is for you. Look at it... It even has two holes... Look at whichever you like."

At first the woman covered her face with her hands, but then she began to shout hysterically as she pointed with her finger, "Dirty... dirty... Look at how dirty... look..."

Shame had driven her from her senses. Realizing her state, her husband ran to the sleigh, turned it onto the highway, put the reins into her hands, and told her to drive home. Then he returned and said to the bailiff, "This is too much... Are indecent acts now allowed during an official action?"

But Aliina had already crossed the barrier of restraint on human actions. She turned her rear and exposed it to the bailiff as well. He was at a loss for a second, but then he shouted, "Reporter... Now you can get a picture. Come and take it."

The newspaperman had been taking notes all this time with a smile on his face. He did not however, photograph Aliina, but said to the bailiff, "An interesting sight... Aren't you ashamed?"

"Don't interfere with the performance of my duty. Otherwise, you can leave. I also demand the photographic plates for inspection."

Aliina ended her show and snatched Elma, who was crying at the top of her lungs, up into her arms. Holding the girl, she threw herself at the bailiff.

"Goddamned saber-bandit... Haven't you got anything else to do than drive children out into the snow? Shame on you, you brass-buttoned dummy from hell."

"Woman... Clean up your language."

But Aliina, weeping, kept trying to attack him, so he ordered a pair of policemen to restrain her. The boys, who up to this point had stood quietly to one side, were enraged when they saw the policemen seize their mother's arms. Ice-chunks, wood-chips, and even horse-droppings began to shower down on the police. One of them started toward the boys, who plunged into flight. As they ran, Uuno shouted, hissing and sobbing, "...F—, f—, f—... Goddamn devils... Shit, shit, shit..."

The cows, the lambs, the ram, and the bull continued their lunging about. There was yelling and brawling, there was battling, thrashing, and bellowing. They brought Antti into the melee, wrapped in Antto's sheepskin coat. He guffawed and bellowed and began to clank his chains, excited by what he was seeing.

"Take him onto the sleigh."

Then Aliina let out a horrifying scream. She tore herself loose from the policeman's grasp and tried to get to the mad boy. At that moment, Laurila's bull rushed to the spot, snorting and tossing his hindquarters. The policeman leading Antti turned instinctively toward the bull and loosed his grip for a second. The madman bellowed with joy and went running after the animal. His greatest

246

joy during the summer was to watch the animals as they moved around the yard. He could see them from his window and would show his enthusiasm by bellowing. Now, with his chain dragging along the ground, he ran wildly after the bull. The slow-moving policeman was unable to keep up with him as he followed the animal with unbelievable speed. He had tossed the sheepskin coat aside, and ran in a tow smock only, his hair flying, shouting joyfully to the bull, who galloped ahead of him, tossing his rear and bellowing in a manner much like that of his pursuer. With the howling, cursing, and weeping were mingled the heated commands of the bailiff as he ordered the mounted policemen to seize the fugitive. And above all this, there resounded from the hill nearby the strains of the melody of the "Internationale" carried at times to a piercingly high range by the women's voices.

> *Starvation always hovers o'er us,*
> *like vultures circling round the dead,*
> *But we will drive the foe before us,*
> *and find a brighter day ahead.*

All this was too much for the bailiff's composure. "Lieutenant Grönberg, disperse that screeching mob. Ask them first to go peacefully, but if they don't obey, then use force. But only as much as necessary."

"Horsemen. Easy trot forward!"

One of the horsemen was still chasing after the madman, but the other nine began their trot toward the group, past the well and across a small field, beyond which they were singing.

"The Cossacks are coming..."

That caused a slight movement, and the women became frightened. Halme knew, however, that the men would not ride into the group without a preliminary command to disperse, and shouted to the people to stay calmly in their places.

The lieutenant did indeed stop his horse some thirty meters from them and shouted in his poor Finnish:

"Group, disperse at once. Each one to go home in peace. If you don't this command obey, then the riders into the group."

"Let them come... They won't kill us... Let the women go farther off."

It was a severe test for Halme. He knew well enough that it was best to leave, but he did not wish to do so without some word of rebuttal. He took a couple of steps forward and answered the lieutenant, "Officer, sir, the group is peaceful

247

and organized and is causing the officials no trouble."

The lieutenant took his words as a refusal. He too was uneasy and nervous. "Forward. You men know what to do."

When the horsemen began to advance, some of the women screamed. A number of those in the rear began to run toward the road, but those in front stood their ground. Akseli pressed the flagpole to his breast, wrapped his arms around it, and turned his side to an oncoming rider. Halme, his face pale, stood rooted to the spot. He felt that for some reason, the horsemen would stop, that somehow it all was unreal. His mind groped for some quick decision, but could find none. He had expected to leave in peace and dignity after a discussion, but the officer's hasty decision had changed everything. He realized that departure was inevitable, and furthermore, he was personally timid when confronted with bodily force. He stood as if stricken: fear bade him to go, but the thought of a shameful flight awakened his pride. He actually had his mouth open to give the command to scatter when he saw that Akseli, who was foremost, was already being pushed back by the leading rider. He took a deep breath, closed his eyes, and simultaneously turned his side to the approaching horsemen. He could not leave when he saw his flag-bearer standing firm. A horse was already snorting immediately in front of him when he heard Janne's shout:

"The national anthem, boys... Lets sing for the Russians' lackeys..."

Halme opened his eyes. The horse's muzzle was right in front of him. As if galvanized by Janne's shout, he began:

Oh Finland, our dear native land...

The mounted police were already pressing against the group. The trained horses sidestepped neatly, mincing along, seeming almost to guard against stepping on people's toes. The group had joined in the song. The ones farthest to the rear had actually withdrawn to the road, but they kept up the singing there. Some of the women were crying out: "Jesus save us... They're trampling them... Come away..."

...With plow, with sword, with might of thought...
our fathers waged their wars...

The commander of the police tried to shout the order for dispersal above the singing, but his words had no effect.

248

Your flowery earth will bloom again...

The song became confused as the voices of those in front changed to gasping for breath as they strained against the horses.

...You kindle in our hearts the flame of love,
your hope and joy shine on us from above...

Victor Kivioja grabbed a horse by the corners of its mouth. "You've got a nice gelding there. Sell him to me. I'll give you seventy-five... Step down from the saddle. Vic will count out the bills in your hand."

"Let go... let go at once..."

The policeman raised his riding whip, and a puff of dust burst from Victor's coat. At the same time, a snowball thrown from behind the group by Elias Kankaanpää sailed overhead and struck the commanding officer on the shoulder. He lashed out too. When Halme felt the light blow on his shoulder, all his fear vanished. The reality was far less terrible than his earlier imaginings, but the blow succeeded in precipitating a decision to retreat. He felt now as if he had won a moral victory, and in a voice that shook, he shouted: "Comrades! To the road... Akseli, take the flag... take the flag to the road... they're flogging us."

Gritting his teeth, puffing and blowing, Akseli was straining against the side of a mount that was pushing him back step by step. He felt a hand clutch his shoulder and heard Otto's voice: "Take the flag to the road... the others will follow."

"We're not going, goddamn."

"Go right now... This won't do any good... The group will soon be broken up anyway..."

The boy started off with the flag, and at Halme's urging, the others followed. The little boys made faces at the police and shouted insults. Halme trudged to the road and ordered the boys to be quiet. The commander of the police had the good sense to give the group time to reorganize and ordered his men to stay on the hill. He himself trotted to the road where Halme stood.

"You leader?"

"I have the honor to enjoy that trust from my comrades."

Halme spoke in a voice still trembling with outrage, and stood affectedly upright, looking the commander directly in the eye.

"You take group away quick. You can go with flag if good."

"We will leave following our flag, but I wish to protest the behavior of the police. Today, for the first time, I have seen the free people of Finland struck with a whip."

"You not struck. Just brushed a little. Police follow orders. You resist police. I recommend you get summons for resisting police."

"We will answer it. Comrades! Let us march back to the fire hall. We must get horses and find shelter from the freezing cold for this unfortunate family."

The procession departed and to show its feelings, loudly struck up the "Internationale."

After they were sure the group had gone, the police returned to the yard. Antti had already been captured and was bound on the sled with Antto. Aliina sat on a bed in the yard and wept. The boys peeped out from around the corner of the barn.

Antto was threatening to kill Töyry, whereupon the landlord said to the bailiff, "That kind of talk during official actions is too much. He must be arrested. We don't know what he might do."

"He will be taken for a judicial hearing, but after that he must be freed, under condition, of course, that he cease his threats."

The bailiff demanded the photographic plates from the reporter, but was told it was impossible. The negatives might be spoiled. To support his denial, the reporter appealed to the laws controlling the press, to which the editor-in-chief must answer. He was allowed to keep the pictures, especially since he had been unable to photograph the dispersal of the group.

Then they left. Aliina and the children remained in the yard. Antti bounced up and down on the sleigh, happily shouting out a jumble of words: "Antti... Antti... Horsey... moo... mooo... ihahahahahahaha..."

Töyry had had time to leave before the men of the association came to gather up the livestock and the belongings. The cows gave themselves up meekly to capture, but the bull was the cause of much running and cursing. The family was taken to the Kankaanpääs along with the milk cows. The other cattle and the sheep were taken to other tenants.

The last loads were driven away in the darkness of evening. Silence reigned around the gray cabin. A rising storm drove snow in through the open door and the window apertures. Little by little it covered the tracks left by the trampling in the field and yard.

CHAPTER EIGHT

I

There was a lot of talk. Töyry stayed at home for a long time. People said someone had threatened to drop his pants and whip him. They discussed the affair at the parsonage too, on farms, estates, and at the manor as well. "The whole thing was organized by the workers' association. The truly guilty ones are that agitator and his helpers. Laurila would have consented to leave peacefully if he hadn't been encouraged to resist. No one can defend Töyry's actions, although he certainly has the right to evict a troublesome tenant. It wasn't wise, though, to do it so abruptly, and so close to election time. But we can see now what all this agitation leads to. Laurila should be absolved of guilt and the association brought to trial. Didn't they even send for a correspondent from a socialist paper just for the occasion? One has to pity the simple-minded family, whose misfortune has been exploited so callously to whip up emotions for the election. So much for their vaunted humanitarianism."

One can imagine what the tenants and hired hands were saying. Bitterness was beginning to develop into hatred. The whipping had assumed monstrous proportions. It didn't matter that many of them had been disciplined with the rod until they were almost full-grown. These few light lashes took on truly philosophical dimensions. "They beat us like slaves."

Halme elevated his gaze above the others' and declared, placing one hand on his shoulder, "The blow did not strike here..." Then, pressing the other hand to his heart, "...But here."

There were some, however, who did not take the matter with such profound seriousness: Otto Kivivuori and his sons, and Victor Kivioja. Victor merely went on bragging that he had offered the man the "seventy-five." Otto hadn't been

251

whipped either. The blows had fallen only on Halme, Victor, and Oskar Kivivuori.

There were mixed opinions about the edition of the *People's Journal* that carried the eviction story with a banner headline and pictures. The latter were actually quite obscure, but they were examined with great interest.

"There I am... Whose head is that over there? The bugger didn't take a picture of Aliina mooning."

The story also became known throughout the entire parish. Even the workers joked about it, so that Halme felt obliged to say, in a slightly offended tone of voice, "You might expect the unfortunate woman to be driven out of her senses with grief. However, I do not consider her action an appropriate one. The display of the part of the body in question is not among the tenets of socialism. In truth, it has been practiced for hundreds of years as a means for one woman to shame another, but it is at the same time an indication of the uncouthness that still prevails among our people. I beg you to forget the matter. It is not to our advantage, nor is it kind to that poor unfortunate."

His words could hardly be expected to divest such a fascinating tale of its interest, and Halme learned, to his dismay, one of the age-old truths, that humor is the greatest foe of idealism.

Akseli had to suffer the most because of the pictures. In one of them, he was seen leading the procession with his banner. The caption underneath read: "Proudly waves the banner of socialism, borne by the steely arms of a young worker-hero."

His father looked at the pictures and grumbled, "Some heroism. Carrying a thing like that. What good did it do? They were thrown out anyway. And if there are more such pictures of you in the papers, we'll be thrown out too."

Alma looked at the picture and could only say devoutly, "But you're so handsome in it, no matter what. Your head is so high that... You really ought to go and have your picture taken in the village as a souvenir of your younger days."

The text of the report itself added to Akseli's embarrassment.

"As if by common accord, the workers of the area had come together, incensed by this unprecedented deed of violence. With the flag of their association in the van, the small band of people started off toward the site of the eviction, singing patriotic and workers' songs. The procession was led by the chairman of the local association, Comrade Halme, a man who is always on the scene whenever the interests of this country or the working class are threatened. Fearless and

252

unflinching, he has fought against the oppressor. Fearlessly too, he has placed himself in the forefront of the long-suffering workers' aspirations. There he marched, firm and erect, behind him the workers' organization, whose growth he had nurtured. The beautiful banner was carried by a young worker, a sturdy and proud youngster, just the right type to carry a workers' flag. A fearless, proud, and dedicated fighter...

"By violence they dragged out the tenant, who had cleared the land in the sweat of his brow and slaved on it over the years for his hardhearted landlord. Proudly he refused to leave his home and scornfully he hurled these words at the police: 'My home is my castle, and you will destroy it only over my dead body.' It was heartbreaking to witness the tears of the children. Two boys upwards of ten years of age held on to their mother's skirts and watched in somber silence, as if asking in their frightened children's hearts: 'Why are they destroying our home?' A little girl on her mother's arm could do nothing but weep. Torn from her warm bed, all she knew was that her mother was in tears and that her father had been dragged handcuffed into a sleigh. What pain must have dwelt in this child's heart. But the most shocking was still to come. There was in the family a mentally defective boy whom they had tried to care for lovingly in all their misery. It was true that he had to be kept in chains, since the parish poor relief had done nothing for him. This boy escaped from the police, and now there was acted out a drama that compels us to thought. The family's cattle had been driven from the barn, and when the half-wit noticed it, he tried to capture the bull. What thoughts this must evoke! The landlord and his supporters, this country's power structure, drive an unhappy family and its few cattle out into the snow, and a pitiful half-wit, whom fate has robbed of so much, has still been endowed with more humanity than his savage dispossessors. This poor wretch's first thought is to drive the cattle back to the barn, for he cannot comprehend a social system that would drive them out. His imagination cannot conceive of anything so contrary to nature. No. He thinks the cattle have escaped and tries to catch the bull. What a scene! More sense of justice in the heart of a half-wit than in the landlord and their police.

"The landlord's wife had arrived on the scene in a handsome church sleigh, and the unnatural creature laughed as she witnessed the destruction of the tenancy. According to the people of the locality, she is uncommonly cruel to her servants and a fit mate for her husband, this hardhearted dispossessor, this church-board member, this bank-director, this town-councilman, this whip of the *Suometar* faction, who thus distinguishes himself in the conduct of 'his country's affairs,' as do the rest of Finland's masters and money-bosses. But the tenant's wife, child on her arm, steps over to the sleigh and says: 'Laugh, laugh, as you look at children being thrown out into the snow. Go and present a program on the women's question to the women's organization in the village. Go and tell them of your heroic actions against helpless children.' And proudly, with cold contempt, the worker's wife turns her back on the landlady...

"The policemen ride toward the demonstrators. All this time, the strains of the "Internationale" have been echoing from the hill. The group of workers watches the manhandling of their comrade, helpless to do anything more than send their song to the cold heavens of Finland although they realize there is no God there, at least not one of a kind to hear their pain. God is on the side of the landlords, so says the vicar of the congregation, he too a *Suometar*. But steadfastly the group awaits the police, their heads held nobly high. Suddenly the strains of our national anthem ring out strongly.

"The workers greet the policemen sent to guard the dispossessors with our national anthem. Think of it! This is not a tale from the time of the Ilkka rebellion more than 300 years ago or the uprising of the German peasants. No. This is happening in the Grand Duchy of Finland at the start of the year 1907. These embittered tenants and workers carry no clubs or staves; they belong to the organized workers' movement. They stand in back of their flag, singing their country's song, looking directly and fearlessly at the whips of the approaching Cossacks and the foaming muzzles of their horses. Some of the women scream, but the stentorian voice of Comrade Halme quiets them. The horses begin to trample the front row. The song grows fainter as the people struggle under the beasts. At the same time, the whips begin to whistle through the air. Well, that's nothing new. We've seen it on the streets of our beloved capital city. But there it was horsemen from a foreign country that were flogging our people. Here the whips were wielded in the interest of our home-grown oppressors. 'Such blows leave no external scars. For they strike not the body, but the heart.' Thus spoke Comrade Halme. One need say no more.

"But what do the Cossacks encounter! A heroic and steely wall of workers that will not crumble. The raging floggers lash out blindly, but only upon Comrade Halme's calm command do the workers withdraw to the road and take up a position behind their flag. Singing, the demonstrators leave the site, not fleeing, but going for their horses, poor wretched nags worn out from overwork in the fields of the landlords, to carry the unfortunate family and its possessions to shelter from the snowbank where they had been cast by this society of exploiters.

"To eliminate any possibility of error, let us again remind our readers that the site of this occurrence is the Grand Duchy of Finland in January of the year 1907. Apparently this is a dress rehearsal for the evictions just getting under way at Laukko. Well, there is a kind of difference between the *Suometar*-skinflint-landlords and the Swedish-bloodsucker-evictor barons. They speak a different language. The baron at Laukko needs a translator when he drives his tenants out onto the highway. This landlord doesn't, for he is closer to the people.

Finland, dearest land of them all
A country so wondrous and fair,
Every isle, cape, and valley breathes forth a call,
For my home to be built there.

"What the devil is he writing about?"

"Well. He can't go into depth about every detail, but in general a most effective presentation. Of course, there are a few inaccuracies. Among others, the importance of my organizational work. Well, perhaps my small efforts have not been without results. I have been thinking that perhaps we shouldn't expend our best resources on the legislative effort. In our current phase, fieldwork is more important. It's right that Comrade Hellberg be a candidate. Despite his wide knowledge and his ability, he is not exactly suitable for fieldwork, particularly because of his rigid personality."

But the noble, fearless, and dedicated worker-warrior was angry. When Otto taunted him once or twice about his steely forearms, and Aku hinted in the same vein at home, Akseli stormed angrily, "Well, it's not my fault if they write that stuff."

Victor Kivioja was indignant at the phrase about the wretched nags worn out from overwork in the landlords' fields.

"Let that newspaper gentleman bring his horse here for comparison, if he has one. I guarantee you that Liinu will show him her heels, and then some, in the first hundred meters. Let him write about tenants' affairs, but not a word about horses. He probably couldn't hitch one up without help."

For the most part, however, the demonstrators were satisfied, especially the ones who were visible in the pictures. Even a half of Preeti's head could be seen, and that picture was cut out and pasted to his wall with boiled potato glue.

Halme received a summons to the manor. No cause was stated, but it could only have to do with the demonstration. He dressed with special care, even waxing his mustache. When he set out for the manor, had a stranger been told that he was an official of the Senate on vacation, it would have provoked no denial.

Halme's cane swung rapidly and there was a slight rasp in his throat. Going to the manor was not as easy as it might seem outwardly. Despite his sojourn in Tampere and his present eminence, he felt the secret uneasiness that typically beset an underling if for any reason he was compelled to traverse the tree-lined walk to the main building. The tenant or hired hand would feel himself alone and exposed in this world which seemed so imposingly haughty to him. Halme had at least spoken with the baron about fire-department matters at the same coffee-table, and when he called for further moral support on his command of statecraft, he was calm and composed, at least outwardly.

The hall-like entry was dark and still. A maidservant whom he knew came to greet him. In the atmosphere of the manor, she seemed a stranger. She said little, and that little was almost whispered. Behind a door could be heard the soft whining of a dog, who scented a visitor, but knew that barking was forbidden.

The study was large. There were bookshelves, weapons, and the inevitable moose antlers around the walls. The ancestral portraits were in the hall, however. The old major's portrait was there, a wretchedly botched affair, done by some wandering portrait painter of the day. Everything was as it should be.

Halme waited in the study until the sound of rapid, heavy footsteps signaled the baron's approach.

"Good day."

"Good day, good day. Chair. There. That one."

They sat down. The baron's full beard was already gray, but he carried his head impressively up and back, a position which had become natural to him during a lifetime. His life had really been colorless and unvarying. He had spent it entirely on the manor, leaving it only for brief excursions, never so much as going away to school, but receiving his few rudiments of book-learning from

256

a tutor at home. As a young man, he had behaved in a manner unusual for one of his rank. Massive in build and powerful, he would sometimes shock the hired hands by displaying his strength. He might spend a day mowing, and since he excelled at it, mowing competitions became a point of special interest to him. What Finnish he knew, he had learned from hired hands, who had slyly taught him obscenities as a child, obscenities which he repeated at home with no idea of their meaning.

He had spent his manhood running the manor. His marriage was childless, and a nephew would be his heir. He was happy to have the young man stay away from the manor during his own lifetime, for one master at a time was enough. Great physical strength and an energetic spirit had made the baron a petty tyrant, who never took advice. His orders were brief and irreversible. It was quite programmatic. When he had issued an order, he did not back down from it, though he might sense it to be wrong and even injurious to himself. It can well be imagined that he had great respect for Alexander III and despised Nicholas II, even before the latter had begun his russification program.

The memory of his grandfather also affected him. The man had actually been a soldier in the Finnish War of 1808–1809, and the people had named him "Finland's War-Major." The baron had never seen his grandfather, but had heard all the more about him. The people had feared and hated him, for as a landlord, he acted like a soldier: he cursed and stormed and even resorted to flogging. In the baron's imagination, he was a paragon among men, straight, severe, and right-minded. Reading the *Tales of Ensign Stål* had given birth to that conception. Runeberg had not, of course, written about his grandfather, but the grandson conceived of him in the poet's terms: "A noble mind and a tender heart, and blood boiling with ardor."

The Ensign was actually the basis for much that went into the shaping of the baron's ideals. It was truly lamentable that Runeberg's tales were not universally applicable. Where was "Matti, the soldier," who was as upright and straight as the baron himself; Matti, who could be cursed and commanded, but who got a drink for his manhood. Today's Mattis were made of some stubborn gray pulp, which yielded to force, all right, but grudgingly. They wasted the forest, loafed at work, intentionally let their cattle stray onto manor land, and were as sullen as the devil. Now and then a type of Matti would appear who said: "I kick; I'm afraid I kick like a stallion." That type of Matti could quickly

257

pack up his belongings and be on his way.

And that tailor? From the beginning, when they had come into contact because of the schoolhouse and the fire hall, the baron had felt a degree of contempt for Halme. There were many causes for it. First, the desiccation and ineffectuality of his physique. And then his behavior and his dress, both unsuitable for one of his class. But worst of all was that schoolmasterly preciseness. The baron, a down-to-earth land and dairyman, placed little credence in scholarship at best, but in that tailor, it was manifested in the most infuriating way possible. Furthermore, he had been involved in an action that foreshadowed the end of the world. His men had been absent from work without permission and had been brawling with the police. And that tailor was responsible. The baron looked at Halme for a few moments from his round, prominent eyes, as if measuring his strength against this scarecrow of a man. But without effect. The visitor had regained his composure after an initial nervousness and could no longer be shaken. If the baron had been annoyed earlier, now he positively began to boil with silent fury. A man of that rank had never before returned his glance in that fashion. Actually, the man was not a tenant of his, but still...

"You take men to quarrel with police."

"Master Baron, the police created the disturbance, not the peaceable demonstrators. As to the cause of the demonstration, it was the eviction. Therefore, in my opinion, anyone with the most rudimentary sense of justice knows we did no wrong."

Halme deliberately used the Finnish title for baron in addressing him, a practice he had planned on the way. The baron raised his voice.

"That not my affair. Töyry's affair. And not my affair that you go there I'm not judge with that matter. My business is this: my men absent from work without permission. That my business. You taken them, so talk with you. Other thing is: you keep fire hall like one socialist house. It made on account of fire, not on account of socialism. I said that live according to law, you can meet, but you uproars and brawls. I no longer fire department affairs with you. You out. I my own fire department and coachman captain."

"Master Baron, taking into account that the building is on your lot, and that the building was built from your timber, with the necessary moneys provided by you, I must acknowledge your authority over it. Nevertheless, we have some kind of right to meet there since the building was put up with volunteer labor,

258

and many of the men who worked on it were members of the workers' association."

"Volunteers. You bill me every man's work. Price no matter. I pay. All out. And I say. Not one time more my men away from work on roads singing and with flag. Then those men out of cabins and huts. You understand. You leader, so warning to you. You take responsibility these people. If you take away work, then I speak up. Remember word."

The higher the baron's voice rose, the more calmly and respectfully Halme responded. He appealed to the right of free assembly, but the baron argued that the right of his men to be absent from work was not one of its provisions. There he was indubitably correct. Halme steered the discussion to the area of general principle. The baron simply refused to admit the existence of a tenant or land question. A good tenant had nothing to worry about, and lazy rioters and wasters of wood could be sent on their way without further ado. Shorter hours simply meant more time for misbehaving, drinking, and card-playing. In their debate, Halme's knowledge sparkled, putting the baron's home tutor to shame. The baron, you see, was confronted with a question about which he knew nothing. He had no grasp of the theory of socialism, for the newspapers from which all his information came had nothing to say on the subject. Halme himself did not fully understand it, but in a dispute with the baron, that was hardly necessary. He did at least have some grasp of such matters, for during those years, under the auspices of the socialists, much of the literature that dealt with social issues had been translated and glossed. Halme was continually ordering all such books and reading other literature as well. The baron read only trade publications on agriculture and dairying. His philosophy remained on the level of the lead editorials in his Swedish-language newspapers. Now that Halme had managed to engage in discussion with an illustrious gentleman, how titillating it was for him to rattle off all those names: Spencer, Saint-Simon, Comte, Marx, Kautsky, Bebel, Ingersoll, and — preceded by a slight cough — Tolstoi.

"As the great Leo Tolstoi says..."

"Those fool books I read. Why always angry land question? Give away his farm. Peasants drink it up right away, so no more land question for Tolstoi. All one. Tolstoi not do my men's work when they run around with songs. Clear matter."

Toward the end, the discussion grew louder and louder. In the baron's speech, there began to occur with increasing frequency a word that seems agreeable

259

to even the most hardened partisans of the Swedish language on certain occasions: "Gawddamn, gawddamn."

Then the door opened revealing the baroness's uneasy countenance. "Magnus..."

The baron turned toward his wife. After a wordless communication, in which only their eyes spoke, the baron uttered a single word underscored with impatience and intimidation: "Leave."

His wife vanished, but the discussion became more restrained. That was no indication of agreement, however, and in leaving, Halme said, his face red with indignation, "Master Baron, despite our long hours of work, we still do have time to meet, if only at night. In regard to the firehouse and the fire department, your wishes will be observed. I hereby resign from the auxiliary and consider the whole organization to be dissolved as such. I am also sure that those firemen who belong to the workers' association will no longer take part in the training. We will probably find a suitable place to meet until we can make other arrangements. I apologize for disagreeing with the master baron's opinions. Goodbye."

While the maidservant was handing him his hat and cane, Halme, totally unaware of her existence, said not a word. His mind was seething. The baron had offended him, not by the substance of his speech, but by his personal attitude toward him. On the return trip, his agitation gradually subsided. A proud man was journeying home. The prime minister was returning from one last attempt to reach an accord with a stubborn ruler before casting his lot with the revolutionaries.

"Why is Halme lording it on a week-day?"

"Look at his cane fly."

The bystanders along the road received not a single glance. At home, there was silence for a time. Only as they were about to sit down to dinner did Valenti dare ask if the baron had perhaps been angry.

"It looks as if the battle is intensifying. He is mustering all his strength against the association, and his powers are formidable, considering the subservience of his tenants. I must take all that into account. For the time being, we must yield, until the new legislature convenes and we get legislation to protect people from this kind of pressure. Yes. It is once more apparent that God has struck them blind, that his settled intent is their destruction. There is only one possible weapon against ruthlessness, a reply in kind. The battle grows grimmer all along the line. Peaceful reform has become a dream, and that one-time dream of mine lies on a litter."

Sitting down to the table, Halme proclaimed: "*Alea jacta est.*" Valenti committed the phrase to memory for later use with the gang of boys. It was frustrating not to dare ask its meaning. During the meal, he tried to carry on a discussion, partly to divert attention from the quantity of meat he was eating. At Halme's, where they lived rather well, you were allowed to eat unsparingly, but the hunger he had known as a child had given the boy an insatiable appetite for meat and butter. He ate like a rabbit, chewing rapidly, his eyes flicking from one dish to another, as if greedy to hasten them to his mouth.

"Was there perhaps, some mention in the master's letter of Edward Salin's coming here to talk?"

"It hasn't been decided yet. Yrjö Mäkelin is another possibility. Hellberg insists that someone important speak at one of the meetings. The plan is to hold one such big event in every community. Now the only question is where we can hold it. Actually, we have local people who are qualified to speak, but it's important to have someone new."

"That's true. The schoolteacher said that the master is a first-rate speaker. Mäkelin and Salin can hardy have anything to teach him in that respect."

The boy's fork was on its way to the meat dish, but the master's eye happened to fall on it. It changed direction and speared a potato.

II

As in the past, they rode up front on the sleigh when they hauled firewood, manure, or gravel. As in the past, their eyes followed the rhythmical swaying of the horse's flanks. But their thoughts had acquired much in the way of new content. New concepts, new perspectives were flourishing under the old fur caps. That "workers' thing" had brought new events in its wake. The baron had dismissed those with "workers" tendencies from the fire department. Some big shot named Eetu Salin was coming soon to give a speech. Antto Laurila had been sent to jail. The demonstration had also produced summonses. Those named were Halme, Otto and Janne Kivivuori, Akseli Koskela, Victor Kivioja, and Kankaanpää. It was

261

said that only the worst offenders would be held responsible. Halme explained that the anger provoked by the large-scale evictions at Laukko had made the masters cautious.

At first the summons caused a fright at the Koskelas. Jussi and Alma simply could not understand the nature of the matter. Law and the courts were a source of terror to them, and they were horrified to think that their son would wind up in court, perhaps in jail. Akseli himself was not too concerned, and his parents calmed down somewhat after Otto visited them and explained that it was not a matter of an actual crime. The whole thing was the result of hasty action by the police, and a verdict of dismissal was the obvious outcome.

"Why in hell would they put peaceful people in jail for that kind of reason? We would have left if they had given us time."

Nevertheless, they were still uneasy. What would they say about it at the parsonage? The question was soon answered. The vicar asked Akseli, "Well, has Akseli received a summons about the matter?"

"Ya-ah, the summons came."

The boy's eyes were averted as he muttered his answer. The vicar bristled and said, "I don't think much will come of it. But it was foolish to take part in a futile demonstration."

"Ye-ah. It seems that way. They go right on throwing out the tenants at Laukko. And the horsewhips are whistling there, too."

"They are probably exaggerating because the elections are near. Not that the baron at Laukko isn't to be condemned, but he has the law on his side. What that means is that the law should be changed, not resisted. The tenants' question will come under regulation in due time. People in the *Suometar* organization have become aware of it."

Controlling himself with great effort, the boy looked at the ground. Finally, he was able to manage a tone of indifference, "Ya-ah...It's time for that, all right."

The vicar left the stable where the discussion had occurred, sensing in the boy's answer a coldness and bitterness that would never thaw. This time it depressed him more than it had before. The Laurila episode, and, even more, the evictions at Laukko, had brought the Koskela matter to his consciousness again, after he had succeeded in getting rid of it. But in another sense, the events eased his burden. Compared to them, the Koskela thing was a trifle, and he again took refuge in that thought.

262

"They are completely at peace on their tenancy. Their lives have not been disturbed in the least. Where would that boy get his strength, for example, if he lived in want? Others use a pry-pole to dump a load of clay, but he just grabs the side of the sledge and lifts. Could a hungry man do that? No. They have plenty of everything. They don't really need that swamp. They're bitter about it only out of greed. That's what it is. Have I evicted them? No. I've even been friendly, although that boy's rudeness is approaching a point that no one would tolerate except me."

The vicar was walking along the path toward the shore. He looked out at the lake, and the February day seemed so cheerfully bright that his mind turned away from troublesome things.

"Spring is already in the air. You can feel it. This is what Aho meant when he wrote about the spring of spring... But how do they manage to cross over that place with the current? Isn't it too dangerous? Look, Wolf-Kustaa is sitting on that island point again. I wonder if it's the best spot for fishing. What about his confirmation? But how can I force him... How everything sparkles... how everything sparkles..."

Antto had been freed after the hearing. Afraid that he might resort to violence, Halme and Otto went to speak to him. Jail had calmed him down to some extent, but he growled menacingly that things weren't over yet. The others assured him that the matter would be remedied in time, but warned him against brawling. He would only wind up in jail and lose his martyr's role.

"You will have your rights restored, but you mustn't ruin things. You're too hot-tempered to go and give Töyry a thrashing. Worse might come of it. I have to admit that, even though I'm a man of peace, I wouldn't consider a little punishment out of line. But only the kind that fathers administer to their children, heh, heh..."

Although Antto would promise nothing, they assumed that he understood the state of affairs. Yet he was not to be relied upon. Halme even found lodging for the family. There were empty rooms at Kylä-Pentti, and the landlord agreed to let him have them.

"People have to have a roof over their heads, I say. Land I can't give him, I say. Except for a potato patch. And a hayfield for one cow."

The cattle, therefore, had to be sold. Antto kept his horse, for he planned to start working in the woods during the winter as a driver. He would have to buy some hay, of course.

The trial was held very shortly. The people attended en masse and were provided with abundant subject matter for talk. Antto was given six months in the house of correction for resisting the police. But Aliina's case proved difficult. The writer who drew up the charges had to sweat before he could come up with the appropriate language for her mooning, language fit for legal texts and the ears of civilized people.

"...as it appears from the testimony of the constables at the scene, the defendant, Aliina Maria Laurila, is charged with turning her sitting part in the direction of the bailiff supervising the eviction and uncovering the aforementioned part of her anatomy, so that at the moment specified it was not curtained by any article of clothing, thus acting with the clear intent of casting shame and discredit on the proceedings. Furthermore, she is charged with calling the bailiff such demeaning names as cutthroat, brass-button dummy, etc., and with using profanity in addressing the bailiff."

Aliina's sentence was a fine of thirty markkas. And when she gave her own uninhibited account of the incident, the judge kept his eyes firmly fixed on the desktop to keep from bursting into laughter.

Halme made a statement on behalf of all the demonstrators. It was a long speech replete with "general considerations," and he concluded it by saying gravely, "...although we admit to no illegal actions, whatever punishment the High Court, ignoring that fact, wishes to visit upon us, I will take upon myself. Since my comrades have honored me with their trust and chosen me as their leader, the responsibility for decisions is mine, even though democracy prevails in our organization. It is in the moral sense that I alone assume full responsibility. And the Almighty knows that at this moment, it is an easy burden for me to bear. Would that everyone in this room could leave with as clear a conscience as mine."

Halme was fined thirty markkas, and the others twenty, except for Victor Kivioja, who was assessed twenty-five. The extra five was for taking hold of the horse's mouth, which was deemed to have represented active resistance.

The sentences were light, because the police were forced to admit that no clear command to disperse had been given. They had also heard the shout: "The Cossacks are coming," but the culprit remained anonymous. While that issue was being discussed, Janne Kivivuori gazed innocently out the window. The

264

editor of the *People's Journal* was also fined in that connection. He had used the word "Cossack" to refer to Finnish mounted policemen, with the intent to demean.

When he heard his sentence, Victor Kivioja dug his wallet from his pocket and threw two twenty-markka bills onto the judge's desk. "Take it out of that. Victor is the kind of man who backs up what he shouts."

It was explained to him that official procedures required payment to be made to the bailiff.

"That's okay. I carry that much in my pocket when I go to take a piss."

"Watch your language here. That kind of talk is fit for a flophouse, not a court of law."

"Master Judge, I beg your pardon. I'm weak on school language, but I'll pay for that too, if you want."

"Get out!"

"Sure, I'll go."

Halme thought the sentence levied on him too light. He would gladly have gone to prison for a couple of months. Stolypin's reign of terror in Russia had cast an aura of heroism over revolutionaries, and while there, across the border, man after man was thrusting his neck into the hangman's noose, here the fine he was paying was merely the price for making a measly suit of clothes.

"You got the same as Aliina."

Otto had to remind him of that. Halme coughed dryly.

"What do you think, Aliina? Was it too much? Thirty markkas for the whole show."

"Those gentlemen know the going rate, all right. They've priced so many whores. They're just getting a little of their own back from my ass when they've spent so much on others."

"You should have said that to the judge."

"I didn't think of it. I wouldn't be at all ashamed to. But we're in for it now."

It was all said harshly, without a trace of a smile as Aliina sat stony-faced in the sleigh.

But she could not hold out. Suddenly she grabbed her kerchief by one corner, drew it over her face, and began to sob. "What'll I pay it with? The old man is going to jail... I'll be alone with the kids."

She went on weeping for a long time, even though they assured her that they would all pay her fine and that the family would be cared for as long as Antto was in jail. Gradually, her weeping subsided and the harsh expression returned to her face. Those with her had stopped joking.

A chill prevailed on the journey home.

Money was needed again. Akseli did not ask his father for it but simply said it would cost twenty markkas.

Jussi muttered and mumbled and grunted and grumbled to himself. He went back to the inner room and returned with twenty-five markkas.

"You can keep the five for yourself."

Akseli experienced a sense of confusion and amazement. He had been anticipating a long sermon about the waste of money. Now it seemed as if the extra five were some kind of sign of approval. With a rare gentleness in his voice, he said, "I wouldn't have needed that."

Jussi sat down on the bench and stared at the floor.

"I don't know. I'll be leaving this to you soon enough... It's getting to look that way. I can't handle it any more. And now the tenants are all involved in quarrels... First to the hill and then to jail... And I'm not much good at work any longer... Useless trouble-making... Hmh... I thought I might be able to buy this while I was living... But it looks like we'll soon have to leave too. That's the way things seem to be going."

It was the first time Akseli had heard anything of the sort. Jussi had never spoken seriously of leaving the place to him. On the contrary, he had always had the impression that his father would cling to it tooth and nail. So he couldn't really take what he had heard seriously, and merely said on a note of finality: "The work will get done here, even if the place is in your name."

III

As it turned out, Jussi's despondency was temporary. When Akseli asked for the horse to drive Salin from the village, Jussi grumbled irately again.

"What kind of chauffeuring is this? We're not running a boarding house. All kinds of travelers climbing aboard to be fed and ferried all the time. They just sing away. The whole world is going to live by singing. In my time, only choir leaders lived by singing."

266

"I only need a horse. I'll use the Kivivuoris' church-sleigh."

"Hah. Is he such a grand gentleman that he can't ride in an ordinary sleigh?"

"He's not a gentleman. He's a shoemaker."

"Hmm. So... Does he really make shoes?"

"I don't know if he does now... But he used to, anyway."

Jussi was slightly more favorably inclined when he heard that Salin was a shoemaker. That was something more tangible and useful than all that singing and parading.

Halme had asked Akseli to get Salin from the church village, where he had spoken the previous night. Victor Kivioja had offered to drive him, but Halme did not consider him a suitable driver. Their visitor would get a bad impression. He raised such a ruckus with his horses.

Having driven into Hellberg's yard, Akseli noticed that he had been observed from a window and so he did not go inside. He was also a little shy. Despite his being a shoemaker, Salin was one of the bigwigs among the workers, actually the founder of the whole movement.

Soon men began to pour out. Not being acquainted with all the leaders among the church village workers, Akseli could not at first tell which one of the group was Salin. Hellberg and Silander he knew. But the visitor's identity was soon evident from the way the others behaved and spoke. Down the steps clambered a large, slightly stooped and bony man, not the least bit aristocratic in appearance. A round Pori fur cap was perched askew on his head. Underneath it was a man who wore a quite ordinary coarse wool coat and felt boots on his feet. Everyone was bidding him goodbye and thanking him. Hellberg was to accompany Salin, and the others escorted the two to the sleigh. Akseli greeted them by raising his cap and turning the sled-rug aside. He was the object of the close scrutiny of two slightly bloodshot and hung-over eyes and heard a hoarse voice say: "Uhuh... uhuh... So you're the driver? Well, what else but into the horsey's sled then... The sled, I say... But you've got a goddamn small sled, boy... You must not have known that such a rack of bones would be coming."

The hoarse and familiar chatter had its effect on Akseli. His shyness vanished, and he said, relieved, "They didn't give me any measurements... But there's not much room to stretch out in these sleds."

"I guess so... Yes... Well, goodbye then... Let's go... That's all there is to it. My woman won't wear silks or my kids have toast in their mouths if I don't get a move on. Just paint the country red... yes, yes... huh, huh, huh."

Hellberg had received word in advance that strong drinks were not to be offered to Salin, for they were his weakness. But Salin had had his own supply of liquor and was groaning from its aftereffects. The meeting had not been ruined, for Salin had done his drinking after it was over and behind closed doors. He had now run out of liquor. The fanatical Hellberg frowned on his behavior but had not wanted to play nursemaid to his visitor.

During the early part of the journey, Salin sat meditating, or at least, he sat silent. More than likely he was dozing rather than thinking. Suddenly, he awakened and asked Akseli, "Whose boy are you?"

"Koskela's."

"Uhuh... So you're Koskela's boy."

To judge by Salin's voice, he must have known Koskela well, for he spoke as if everything had been made clear, although he could hardly have been any the wiser for Akseli's words. "So Koskela's boy... Hired hand or tenant?"

"I'm a tenant's son."

Hellberg helped out by adding, "This parish's parsonage tenant."

"I see... Then you're a preacher's tenant, no less... They're the worst devils. Tell me boy, what do you think about the tenant question and the workers' movement?"

"Well, shouldn't the tenants be freed?"

"But how?"

"Through intervention by the state."

"With payment or without? As owners or renters?"

"As owners, of course. We're no better off if we become tenants of the state. And there should be payment according to law, but only for the land itself for those who started from scratch, as we did."

"Is that so? Well, when you own the land, will you still vote for the socialists as property owners?"

"Yaah... Of course... Otherwise they would take it back again."

"No they wouldn't. Mhmm... a knotty problem. You won't vote for me any longer once you get the land for your own."

Then Salin turned to Hellberg. "You heard him. They have only one aspiration, to be free. They are temporary allies, nothing more. In essence, we are working against socialism when we advocate their freedom."

268

"Let them be tenants of the state under terms set by law."

"Hmh... Freed from their landlords but bound to the state they will be just as discontented. And the landlords, once they have lost them, will be ready to free them from the state as well, so the two will join forces against us. Well... So what... Down with land-slavery, profit who will... Yes, yes... Does the young man have a girl friend?"

"I haven't... had time for it..."

"Had time? At your age? Listen, they're nice, those girls. No girl friend? Is that so... Koskela's boy... Uhuh... As soon as I find a really pretty girl, I'll be your matchmaker. Valpas is such a devil that he won't let a woman so much as set foot in his house... hah, hah... He rails at me for drinking... Well, he has cause... he has cause... What are you mumbling about? When I was in jail for lèse majesté, I thought I would never touch a drop when I was free... They say God sees merit even in trying..."

"Well... heh, heh... as advocates of prohibition and temperance, we should stick to such resolutions." The accusation in Hellberg's voice was crystal-clear, although he tried to cover it with a forced laugh.

Salin emitted a resounding belch. "Ya-ah... I don't deny it... I don't deny it... Were you in the demonstration, young man?"

"I was."

"Yaah... is that so."

They lapsed into silence once more. Akseli was confused. Wasn't freedom for the tenants a clear issue? What had he been asking about? And these leaders didn't seem to be exactly what he had pictured.

A man of the people could not conceive of his ideals as questions of tactics.

Then they reached the village. Faces appeared in the windows, and people even ran out onto the steps at some of the cottages.

When the horse turned into Halme's yard, the tailor himself came out with Valenti at his heels. Salin rose from the sleigh and stood upright, ready to assume command. He was probably trying to mask a slightly guilty conscience with such behavior. Since the hangover would show anyway.

"As chairman of our community's association, I am empowered to bid you welcome, Comrade Salin, on behalf of the association. Most sincerely welcome."

"Mhmmm... Thank you... thank you, Halme... So... Well, how are you, how are you? We made it, even if it was windy. Who is this, then?"

"My secretary... or rather... the association's secretary."

"Yaah so...You look like a poet. At least by your hair... Something like Kurikka... Well then... Let's go in."

Halme looked at the visitor doubtfully. Neither the fur cap, nor the felt boots, nor the hoarse chatter seemed to him appropriate for a great leader of the workers. But something powerful still breathed out from the man. Even his look had a quality that was frank, honest, and sincere.

Akseli went to take the church-sleigh back to the Kivivuoris. On the way, first one and then another ran out of their cabins.

"What's he like?"

"What did he say? Did he say anything about the tenants' question?"

"He did talk, all right... He's like that... A pretty big man..."

"You ran into some of the men from the manor... They were hauling manure... He waved like this..."

"He waved, all right."

They questioned him at the Kivivuoris too, and Akseli told them his impression of the man. He took the church-sleigh to the shed and hitched the horse to his own. Elina was on the way from the well with a bucket of water on the sled and stopped at the barn. After the time that Otto had made fun of her and Akseli, she had avoided him. Now she greeted him casually and began to lift the bucket from the sled. Akseli went over to her, removed her hands from the grips on the bucket, and said,

"Let me do it."

She blushed again, but smiled as she said, "I could have done it."

"It would have been left there."

He picked up the bucket, doing his best to conceal any sign of effort and set it gently on the ground, supporting it to the very end to avoid the appearance of having had to drop it. A hint of mischief flickered in the girl's eyes. Ladling water from the bucket, she said, "Well, you did that easily, didn't you. But it's no wonder, since your arms are made of steel."

Now it was Akseli's turn to flush, but with annoyance, almost anger. If the reporter responsible had been at the scene, Akseli would probably have struck him. "Stop grinning."

"I'm not... But it was right there in the paper."

"There are a lot of other things in it too."

270

The girl went into the barn, embarrassed, but with the irritating smile still on her face. Akseli watched her go. He noticed that her thick blond hair was no longer loose, but wound in braids around her head. It was an attractive sight.

A mixture of disturbing emotions made the boy leap quickly onto the sleigh and start off. One hand on the reins and the other in his pocket, he urged the horse into a run. Although the sleigh swayed and jolted, he kept his balance firmly by means of alternating the pressure on heel and toe. His lips essayed a whistle of sorts.

IV

That whole evening, a holiday mood enveloped the life of the community. Salin was at the Halmes. "He's even had important dealings with gentlemen," mused the people, who found more cause than usual to pass by the Halmes', but who were careful to conceal their interest. They found little to see. Emma went back and forth to storehouse or cellar, carrying a butter plate or something else. Once Valenti dashed to the storehouse and came rushing back, carrying a loaf of coffee bread wrapped in a dish towel under one arm.

They had not succeeded in finding another meeting place, so they would be forced to squeeze into the Halmes' home. If all the rooms, even the hallways, were pressed into service, then perhaps everyone could be accommodated, thought Halme. People in the other rooms could hear the speech through the doorways.

In the evening twilight, people began to congregate. They stayed out in the yard, not yet daring to go in. They wore their best clothing if they had any such. Not all of them did. There was happy talk. A party mood held sway; the entire event was viewed as a party.

"So you've come to the party too."

"I thought I'd come and see the real leader of the Reds."

"Old Big-Manu couldn't do anything about it, even if he didn't give us the firehouse. We're having the party anyway."

The baron had recently acquired this nickname. The tenants were frightened by his threat to evict anyone who missed work for political reasons, but they cursed him in secret and often. By this time, there was a crowd in the yard, and since no one had the audacity to step inside, Halme came out to the porch.

271

"Step inside and to the rear. There is room enough for everyone. We'll fill up the main room first."

Those entering first, however, would have stayed in the doorway had not those following pushed them forward. The main room, which doubled as Halme's workroom, was quite spacious. More people could fit into the parlor adjoining and into the kitchen. The inner and outer hallways could hold a number of them, and the rest could listen from outside. Fortunately, it was hardly cold at all.

Loud voices could be heard from the parlor. The luminaries were hidden away there for the time being. More and more people squeezed in. Little boys were perched on the attic stairs like cockerels on a roost. The sound of a hubbub arose on the porch:

"What's going on out there?"

"Wolf-Kustaa is coming."

"The hell he is."

"He is too. With his fishing coat on."

It was indeed Kustaa. He took up a position leaning against the door frame, looking at no one. Otto came in from the yard and said casually to him, "Is Kustaa coming to join up?"

"Join yourself, goddamn."

The answer would surely have caused a quarrel if the people had not been inhibited by Salin's presence behind the door. Halme entered from the parlor and said, "The directors will sit together here in front. We have to keep this bench clear for our visitors."

Then he went back into the parlor. The people strained to see the visitor through the doorway. The notables entered the living room, Halme in the lead, followed by Hellberg and then by Salin. Valenti brought up the rear, wearing a new suit he had made for himself with the assistance of Halme. Two fingers of one hand were thrust into a pocket of his vest, his neck was craned forward, and his face wore an expression of intense concern, as if he bore a heavy load of responsibility in the affair.

People in the rear pushed forward to get a better view of the guest, while those in front countered by trying to draw away from him. Halme said, in a voice that all could hear, "Listen, Eetu, sit down at the head of this table."

He was using the familiar form of address!

Then Halme turned toward the audience. "Comrades. Let me present our

272

famous guest. You all know Comrade Hellberg already. And you all know something about our guest. He is one of the founders of the workers' movement, a renowned speaker, and a man who has done much to awaken our people. Comrade Edward Salin, once more I bid you welcome on behalf of all of us."

Salin had time only to grunt out, "Good evening..."

And the applause began. On the porch outside, people turned to one another. "What did he say? Did you hear? What did he say?"

"He said good evening. Goddamn it, stop yelling... Clap your hands."

Salin raised his hand and the clapping ceased.

"Comrades. Thank you for the reception, but we're not here to applaud one man. Let's sing instead. Join me. 'Arise, ye slaves to work's oppression...'"

Those in the rear were the first to join in the song; those in front took the longest to work up the courage. For want of space, they stood almost button-to-button, their eyes fastened on each other's lapels, for they would have found it difficult to look into one another's eyes while singing.

The song did serve to relax them, and when it was over, there was whispering, and necks were craned to see better over the shoulders of others. Salin greeted the directors before Halme began his welcoming speech. His zeal led him to make it a long one, for didn't Salin need to be shown how they could do battle here? But the audience was restless. Salin was the main attraction here. He was surrounded by the mysterious aura of a public man, which makes people forget that he too leads a quite ordinary life. They had already heard Halme, and besides, he had too often measured the members of this audience for the size of their trousers, his mouth full of straight-pins.

Eetu sat facing the audience during Halme's speech. Sometimes his eyes met another's, and then a slight smile appeared on his face. An occasional young woman with a pretty face was the recipient of a wink, but a very fatherly one, suitable for a man close to middle age like Salin. By such means, he soon established a friendly rapport with the audience, and their respectful shyness continued to evaporate. When Halme's rising tones told him the speech would soon be over, his expression changed to a grave and serious one, as if he were following the talk. In fact, he was hardly listening to it at all.

"...we have the pleasure tonight to hear about socialism from the lips of the man who first made it known in this land. The movement that preceded him was no true workers' movement. It was the bosses' effort to tame the poor of

273

Finland and to blunt the edge of their uprising. I well remember those days some years back when, from my observation post here on the sidelines, I had come to a clear understanding of the inevitability of social reform. I could see that in the great world there were men who had attained a mature awareness of the same fact. You were one of those men, Eetu, and I now have the personal pleasure to thank you for the spiritual support that your many books and newspaper articles have afforded me in my solitary battle. You, Eetu, have had the honor of being in the spearhead of the fight, and be assured that here tonight you are the object of the warmest respect."

"...Listen to him lay it on... Eetu doesn't often get to hear that kind of praise..."

Salin's shouted comment made Halme clear his throat a couple of times, but the audience was delighted by the interruption. With an approving laugh, Halme continued.

"Apparently you have been too much among the enemy, where you do not hear your praises sung. But here you are among friends who respect and admire you. Indeed. Here you see many young faces. By my own feelings I can guess at yours. We old men, solitary veterans at the start, can read the future in these many eyes that flash with youth and spirit. The seed that we have sown, I in my remote forest cabin, and you in your great sphere, has borne good fruit. But let my flute be silent tonight, let it give way to your great clarion of war that has shocked into life the long dormant heart of the Finnish poor."

It was Hellberg's turn to speak next. He was the candidate for the legislature and thus was required to appear. He was no great speaker, but the redeeming feature of his talk was that it dealt with straightforward issues: freedom for the tenants, regulation of working hours, and social legislation. At the close of his speech, he declared that possibilities for the future legislature were nil. At that point Salin raised his head. He was on the verge of shouting an interruption several times, but restrained himself.

After Hellberg's talk, Halme announced that there would be a short intermission.

"The smokers will be able to satisfy their damnable craving, which I assume to be urgent."

Many left, but others crowded around the celebrities to see and hear better. Halme introduced a few of them to Salin.

"Here is our young lawyer. The son of one of our directors."

For once in his life, Janne was ill at ease.

274

"So. Are you a law student?"

"No... I study the books a little."

"I have assigned him the task of reviewing the law of Finland, for I feel that such knowledge will benefit our organization."

"So you're well read in the texts... But you're not a Pharisee as well?"

"Something like that," said Otto. "He doesn't study how to abide by the law, but how to get around it."

Salin burst into laughter and said, "Right... I predict that you'll go far, my boy, if you continue in that vein. That's exactly the way this country is governed."

"But how does conformity to law jibe with revolution?" asked Hellberg. "You argued last night that the revolution had to be directed into lawful channels."

"I did not argue that it should be so in all respects. I argued that if the proletariat had full power to draft the laws, then they would be bound by those laws. In those circumstances, they would at least have the security that comes from a position of power. Current legislation is not morally binding on us. If we had full power to make the laws, that would be another matter. That's what I said, and don't confuse the issue."

"Yes, yes, but what does full power mean? If we are in a minority in a legislature, then the laws will not be for the benefit of the working class. Do we still have to obey them?"

"Hell, yes. Otherwise, we would have dictatorship again."

"Marx takes that for granted."

"Hmph. Marx doesn't prescribe anything; he merely predicts. And he assumes a situation just like this, where the workers can have no effect on legislation."

A dispute arose in which Halme took sides against Hellberg. The latter began to lose his temper, and the audience listened curiously as the leaders argued. They did not understand, but it was entertaining to hear great issues discussed. Victor Kivioja was standing in the entrance when Salin's voice was heard above the hubbub, saying, "...I don't take absolute stands... Circumstances, of course... But I will say one thing. Those puppy preachers strut too much."

Victor slapped the back of one hand with the palm of the other and said, "Goddamn, that's telling them... puppy preachers... that's putting them in their places."

Akseli too heard the words "puppy preachers" and they won his instant concurrence. He knew all too well that they were worthless. They could see

it here. Now Preeti came pushing through the crowd toward the higher-ups.
"Move a little... I've got something for the boy..."

He forced his way through the throng to Valenti's side. The boy sat near the leaders listening to the discussion, wanting but not daring to take part in it. His father said, half aloud, "If you could come home tomorrow... There is something..."

The boy blinked rapidly a couple of times and said, "I'll come."

Then he turned away, a flicker of annoyance on his face. Food remnants gleamed on his father's breast, his coat sleeves were frayed, and one elbow sported a patch held in place with stitches one inch long. But his father showed no signs of leaving. As if his message were incomplete, he repeated, "You'll come in the evening then."

And he added, to Halme, "Got something to say to the boy... If he would drop in at home tomorrow."

The master coughed disapprovingly but said nothing. Salin glanced at Preeti, but his glance slid over him, stopping on Hellberg, and he continued his briefly interrupted statements. "...a change in attitudes... The weak and lowly are to be raised. They will be appreciated from now on, and be placed in the seat of the proud and mighty. That is socialism... "The weak cannot govern... Socialism implies strength, and strength it must have if it intends to govern."

Since Preeti apparently did not intend to leave, Halme hissed, "Go away, it's crowded here..."

Preeti left meekly, unaware of the seething resentment in Halme's voice. He returned to the entry, joining Henna, who whispered, "What did he say? Did he speak to you at all?"

"Nothing special... Just that socialism."

There were a few grinning faces in the crowd around them, but Preeti, in his innocence, was oblivious of them all. Akseli too was leaning against the wall in the background. Halme had urged him to come forward, but he was reluctant to do so precisely because he had met Salin. "They'll soon think I'm pushing myself in there just because I was his driver."

Nearby, Oskar was fooling around with Aune Leppänen. She was giggling and whispering, "...you are such a..."

Oskar looked around to see that no one was watching and pawed at Aune again. Akseli was uncertain what the whispering was about, but nonetheless it attracted his attention. Then Halme rose and asked the people to return to their places. The

276

argument between Hellberg and Salin could still be heard above the murmuring, but they too fell silent when the movement settled down, and Halme spoke.

"Well, dear comrades. The best for the last. Now the great Salin will speak. But first the secretary of the association will recite a poem of his own composition. It probably comes as a surprise to all of you that he practices such an art, but so it is. So there thrives, here in the spiritual fields of our remote community, a shoot that we hope to see grow into a great tree some day."

It was no surprise to them that Valenti wrote poems, but it was indeed a surprise that he should recite one of them before an audience. Would he have the nerve?

Indeed he did, and he showed not a trace of shyness. Quite the contrary. Not the least bit flustered, he stepped to the table, thrust one hand into a vest pocket, let the other hand fall to the table-top, closed his eyes, and drew back his head.

Next, he tilted it slightly upward, opened his eyes, and began:

Freedom, beacon strong and dear,
You kindle our hearts with your melody clear.
You sing of people's power waking,
Of harsh oppression's cruel chains breaking.

O Freedom, thou light of the morning sun,
Night and darkness away doth run.
Reaction sinks down to earth in disgrace.
New life steps forth the light to face.

O Freedom, thou strength of the poor,
Like spring floods you rush and you roar,
Bring joy to the poor through these years,
And dry the weary sufferer's tears.

They all clapped when they saw that the men of note did so. Valenti nodded and bowed. His bow was stinted, not out of a poet's pride, but because of the eminence of the occasion. Then he returned to his seat, and having learned from Halme, he kept his face an absolute blank. Hellberg chewed at his lip and looked at the floor. Salin stood up and grunted, "Yee-es... Good boy... That's the way... mmhmmm, mmhmmm..."

277

His gaze, however, was focused off in the distance. But now he stepped up to the speaker's place, and Halme led the applause, which might have gone on indefinitely had not Salin himself put a stop to it.

"Freedom, as the young poet said just now, has truly cast the first rays of its dawn over this gray landscape. But only through breaks in the clouds, like an enticing gleam to a traveler in the dark. After the bright days of the great strike, the shadow of reaction is falling over us again. The night of Finland's political life has seen no lasting dawn. But something remains. A universal, equal, secret suffrage. And that is something great. That offers us possibilities."

The people listened without breathing a sound. The words fell into the silence with strength and precision. Their effect did not rise from the speaker's fame alone; they had behind them the weight of a powerful personality.

At first the speech treated general issues, but then it began to impinge more directly on the listeners' lives. Akseli was watching Salin and listening closely. The speaker's long hands had begun to gesture with increasing vigor. Then Akseli started and looked down at the floor when he heard the speaker say, "....There is among you a man, who by grinding toil has wrung a homestead from a raw wilderness. When he was finished, they took away the best part of it. And who was the man who did it? A man whose mission in life is to see that others abstain from such deeds. A man who represents, or should represent, justice and truth among mankind."

Akseli saw many glances turning in his direction, and he continued to look at the floor in increasing embarrassment. He shouldn't have talked about that. Everybody was looking...

But his distress diminished as Salin continued.

"...Another man refused to leave his homestead, which he and his father had tilled. The mounted police of the Finnish government threw him and his family out into the snow. The man is no longer in our midst. He sits in prison, guilty of the crime of refusing to leave his home. When you, his comrades, demonstrated on his behalf, you wound up in a court of law.

"Just read our bourgeois writings. Finland is a progressive land. Here dwells a free people, whose democracy dates back hundreds of years. We have never been bound to the land as serfs. The level of education is high: everyone knows how to read and write. Indeed. What is it that you write? Contracts that bind you as slaves to the land. And what is it that the hired hands and the men who

278

work for their board write? They have no reason to write anything. Well. You've been taught to tell time in the public school but you don't have a watch. And you don't really need one. Daybreak tells you when it's time to go to work, and only darkness puts an end to your work at night. But you are also taught Topelius's stories and Runeberg's poems. And what they teach is noblesse-morality, the gentlemen's conception of themselves, sprung from their own brains. And a part of that conception is the notion that the simple, steadfast people look up to them humbly and respectfully. Humble the people have been, out of compulsion, but any notion that they have ever honored their masters is pure falsehood."

Suddenly Salin raised his hand. He seemed to have forgotten where he was and to whom he was speaking. He brought his fist crashing down savagely on the table, and the speech took its own course.

"Who would honor such men? They send their sons into the Russian army to serve the enemies of this country. Goddamnit, has this country ever been more bitterly shamed!"

From the entry, there came the sound of a few titters, but Salin seemed not to have noticed.

"....They themselves run through the woods with guns on their backs following a pack of baying hounds. The baron of Laukko is destroying two hundred tenancies because they shouted "Down, down with him." And the devils can't even pronounce the words that infuriate them. And our *Suometars* and our Young Finland masters are doing the same thing. Is there an iota of patriotism to be found in such men? No, I say, in pure Finnish. Our manor lads spend their time skating along the hallways of the winter palace, bowing and scraping before the Czar, who is not only the head of the most reactionary government in the world, but who is otherwise totally worthless as well. No sooner does he give his word than he breaks it. And he likes champagne. That's where your labor is swallowed up, in the liquor stores and among the prostitutes of St. Petersburg."

Suddenly Salin's voice faltered. For a moment he fumbled for a new starting point, and then he began again, as if hurling himself upon the subject by force.

"Your own cup is certainly never full, but the dog's cup is. When you can no longer work, you die a miserable death in the corner of some rotting hut, but oh my dear, the lady's poor little lap-dog is sick. Let's call three veterinarians. 'Children, you must pray that poor little Mopsy will recover. You must ask it in your bedtime prayers.' What can I say? O you ancestral mothers, shapers

279

of our Finnish tongue, you created a rich language, but its words cannot be stretched to cover all cases. But come to my aid, you liberator of our forefathers, you goddamned devil of devils..."

Halme sat stiffly, adjusting his coat lapels from time to time, and casting severe and sometimes troubled glances at the tittering audience. But then the demonstration of approval began. People were clapping wildly; some even stamped on the floor. Salin recovered his composure, stood silent, smiled a little, and then went on more mildly.

"Well, there was a little too much of our souls' enemy in that, but you yourselves know how it rankles when you think about it. But I forgot to mention another of our words, a useful one. It is the line, the red line. Don't forget it. And remember not to let one vote go to waste. You must awaken your neighbors too. Speak, workers of Finland, after thousands of years of silence. Hurl your demands into the insolent faces of those insolent bullies. Remember that much will be demanded of you. For you fight on two fronts, against your own oppressor and a foreign one, who will soon find one another, like Pilate and Caiaphas when they see a common enemy before them. Take this country's fate into your own hands. Raise it high overhead, and raise yourselves even higher, for those others have forgotten, now that they have their own positions back. Rise, red flag, over these gray huts, from which nothing has been heard before but a feeble whining to a harsh God, who must either be a bourgeois God or else be blind and deaf.

"Comrades. Let the hearts under your rags beat to the rhythm of a new age."

Salin ended, wiping the sweat from his brow. Now even those outside stamped and shouted, although they hadn't been able to follow too much of the speech.

Akseli banged his palms together. In truth, his soul could not follow Salin's changing emotional states, but their power affected him. As the storm of applause continued, he heard underneath it Aune's whisper from nearby, "Stop tickling... do you hear..."

He glanced aside. Oskar had his arm around Aune's back, and from underneath one arm, his fingers were toying with the side of her breast. Akseli realized that Oskar was using the noise of the applause to his advantage. "That devil is pawing it..."

Aune hissed and blushed. Akseli turned his eyes forward again and saw Halme shaking hands with Salin. He must be thanking him. Then he became interested in Oskar's activities again.

280

At last the noise quieted enough for Halme's words to be heard above it. "We have now had proof that your reputation as a speaker is not an empty one. Eetu, you are Finland's own son, a true tribune of the people."

From the side, Akseli heard Oskar say, "Listen, wait for me where the path turns off to the spring... but not where we can be seen."

The people began to crowd toward Salin. He grunted and said:

"Well... I don't know... better ones have been given..."

Wolf-Kustaa had been silent the whole time. Bushy eyebrows raised, he had stood there without taking part in the applause. When the people flocked forward, he muttered, "Eat him up now... Pat his ass too..."

"What's Kustaa mumbling about?"

"What business is it of yours?"

"Go inside with your talk. Don't stand out here on the porch mumbling to yourself. If you have something against the man, go and tell him. He'll shut you up soon enough."

"Nobody tells me who to vote for. I might not vote at all."

"Then beat it. You're not wanted in the workers' gang, if you're going to suck up to the big shots."

"Kiss my ass. I'm going... Vote all you goddamn please."

Kustaa started off, but to the accompaniment of muttered threats. Halme, noticing that something was going on, signaled to Otto, who went out to the porch. Seeing what was up, he demanded silence.

"No, goddamn, he should be taught a lesson...The nerve... acting like that at a workers' party."

"Ya-ah... But don't start trouble over something like that. Finland may be a free country now, but we still don't mouth off whenever we please."

"Well, that's the way things are now."

"Hell, now don't start a row with Kustaa."

Otto had to subdue the fervor that Salin had kindled, and succeeded in calming the men down. Preeti spoke up to help him, authorized by his status as the poet's father.

"Aw, he's not worth the bother... But these days, us workers won't stand for anything."

Henna was whispering to those around her, "He thanked him, he thanked him, yes... I heard it. He thanked our son..."

281

Salin raised his hand and said, "And the Marseillaise to end the meeting... 'Now forward...'"

Again they sang. Here and there the toe of a boot beat time on the floor. As if in compensation for their earlier shyness, they all sang out freely, at full volume. Subconsciously, they were aware that their mood would wilt on the return journey and in the loneliness of their homes, so they gave out with all their might. They had been brought eye to eye with great affairs. The presence of Salin had accomplished this. "He's been abroad studying socialism, and he even knows foreign languages. He's a shoemaker's son and a shoemaker himself. By God, a common man can do as much as any gentleman. 'Forward unto the death...'"

Then they took their leave, but lingeringly. They noted that the directors remained at Halme's. "But why did the Kivivuori boy stay too? He's not a member of the directors, is he? It must be on account of Otto."

In the parlor a coffee table was prepared by Emma. The directors were staying to have coffee with the guest and to make election plans. Janne was not there under Otto's wing, however, but at Salin's request. They sat down at the table, cracking jokes. Salin spread his hands.

"But Emma. You've really done yourself proud... Really... 'Let's sing with a hey and a ho... And enjoy what the forests grow...'"

Emma laughed with quiet pleasure. They talked with enthusiasm, but said little about the election. Most of the talk was of the recent meeting. After a time, Salin began to tire. His glance wandered here and there, and his speech grew listless. Now and then he glanced at Janne, and finally he said, "Listen boy, if you're studying law, I have a book with me that explains the fundamentals of legislation very well. Let's go and get it."

Salin's travel gear was in the entry, and Janne followed him out. Salin picked up a book and said in a low voice as he leafed through it, "Listen... I'd like a little drink. Couldn't you get hold of a little bit somewhere?"

Janne considered all the possibilities. "I can't get any right now... Except from so far away that it wouldn't be here until morning."

Salin gave a short groan and said, "Well...It doesn't matter... Don't bother. It's not all that important... But don't mention it to anybody... They are so churchy about such things. But then... they're right..."

Salin's groan had betrayed his disappointment. They returned to the parlor,

282

where he began to talk earnestly about the book he had given Janne. The boy kept a straight face, but continued to study Salin's behavior covertly. He observed the conduct of the others as well, and a suspicion began to take root in his mind that there was not necessarily anything remarkable underlying even the greatest affairs. Sharp-witted, he soon realized that the participants in the discussion were driven by the most familiar of motives. The argument about the course of revolution had been revived. Hellberg was growing angry again, but Janne noticed that it was not ideas which annoyed him as much as Salin's devastating humorous thrusts. "He is tormented by the thought of Salin's power and reputation."

As he sat there, a number of ideas began to assume a vague shape in his mind. "People in this world are apt to do anything. Salin whispers in secret like a little boy about that business of the liquor. Hellberg really has a one-track mind. Father is trying to be more witty than usual. It looks as if one man can make his way in this world as well as another."

A liberating sense of his own possibilities was born there, along with a self-awareness.

The bright moon lighted their way home on that March night. Akseli walked alone. Ahead of and behind him, he could hear people talking:

"That part about the watches was good."

"And those dogs, and the guns..."

"But does he curse like that when he talks in the city?"

"Why shouldn't he curse? That business really calls for a few goddamns."

"But he's a goddamn powerful old man, isn't he? Those gentlemen are in for it when someone like that lets fly."

Akseli was approaching the turn into what they called the spring path. Curiosity about Osku's doings began to blend in with the mood of the meeting. He had an impulse to hide and see what would happen, but he was ashamed too. The spring path, however, was a shortcut for him, which gave him a kind of justification for turning off onto it. Had he been with her before? Aune was seventeen... She'd had the looks for a long time.

Another path turned off the one he was on. It was really just a ski track, broken by the footprints of a couple of passersby. Men out looking for shaft wood, probably. There was no reason for turning onto it, but he did so anyway.

283

He followed it for a short distance, then stopped and stood in the shadows, waiting.

Then they came. He could hear a faint murmuring and giggling. "That devil of an Osku." He was tramping along beside her in the snow, his hand around her waist.

"Stop it now... I'm not that kind of a girl."

"Of course not... You're a different kind..."

"I'm getting snow in my foot-wrappings... They're going to buy me shoes if Valenti maybe gets to be a newspaper correspondent."

"You don't say... Is he going to..."

"He may... Tee-hee... You're such a thing..."

The voices faded to a murmur again, and Akseli went plowing homeward along the ski trail. It looped around and the footing was poor, but he couldn't go back to the spring path. He'd had to go and take a shortcut.... The image of Aune's slack prettiness obtruded into his mind. Osku is younger than I am, and he plucks her off just like that. Like Janne too. He must be getting it from her... She's as soft as butter... Does he really mean to? It can't be... He's too much of a clown.

Akseli continued along the ski trail, then stopped and stood listening in the breathless stillness of the woods on a winter night. Then it occurred to him to wonder why the devil he was wallowing around on this ski trail.

He let out an angry groan. "A grown man... out here..."

And grim-faced, he resumed his homeward trudging. "He really had it right about contracts. They're the only reason for us to know how to write... These are Big-Manu's woods... I'll break a branch just to spite the bastard... He'll soon insist that kids be beaten with sods to spare his woods..."

V

The *Suometar* party held its election meeting at the firehouse.

The speaker, who was from Helsinki, was put up at the parsonage. Akseli wound up as his driver too and had to get him from the station. He was a lawyer, a friend of the vicaress's brothers. He asked Akseli about his home life in a friendly way, but steered clear of political questions. Was Akseli a hunter?

Weren't there a lot of rabbits around here?

Sometimes, he would be silent for a long time. Once he touched on election matters sufficiently to ask if his driver had been to hear Salin.

"I was there."

"Ah-hah."

Nothing more came of it. In the parsonage yard, they vied in complimenting each other. There were handshakes and even embraces.

"It's been a long time... You haven't aged... I told them we positively must have you... You have a nice parsonage... You'll be getting a letter from the children... They wrote especially... Doing very well..."

The audience at the fire hall was quite small. Only three of the farms were represented, and very few of the workers from them had showed up. There were people from the neighboring communities to add to the number.

When Halme walked down the aisle between the benches, many eyes followed him with barely concealed curiosity.

The vicaress rushed up to him at once. "Mr Halme... Welcome. Come and sit up front here."

She was graced with Halme's finest bow. "Thank you very much. But people might misunderstand."

"Ohooh... You're such a well-known socialist that no one could be in doubt about your position. Here is our speaker... Surely as good as Mr. Salin. He's not quite as good at cursing, I'm afraid... Salin apparently called on the devil to help him. How was that now? Did he really?"

"Ahem. A rhetorical device. He complained of the inadequacy of language to describe some of the flaws in our society."

"But our speaker will not only describe them; he will present remedies for them. You'll soon hear. And of a kind that are feasible."

Halme proceeded to the front bench and greeted the speaker respectfully, exchanging a few casual words with him. There was whispering along the benches:

"Those judges' ranks are strange. An assistant judge is higher than a judge."

"They say he doesn't actually preside at trials.... He's some kind of bank official, although he has the title of judge."

The schoolteacher handled the opening ceremonies. He introduced the speaker, who rose and bowed in acknowledgment of the applause. Then they sang the national anthem, with Halme joining in. After the song, the vicar said a "few words."

He stood silent for a moment with his head bowed, trying, as was his custom, to pray for life in his words. His gesture affected the audience, some of whom bowed their heads slightly, stopping the flow of thought prompted by the occasion and experiencing a brief gap in their consciousness.

The vicar began. "My dear friends. The Finnish people have gained the right to express its will regarding general issues. With that purpose in mind, we have gathered here tonight. Different parties, with differing programs and differing goals, have joined battle in this election. So be it. But remember that we are first Christians, secondly Finns, and then only thirdly are we members of a political party. Great issues should be resolved in harmony, in that spirit which Our Lord Jesus Christ bequeathed to us as our heritage. But dissension has begun to develop among us. The desire for advantage, for personal victory, a spirit of bitterness — these are gaining control. Therefore, we must return continually to that fount which is the source of all lasting goodness. Let God's will be the guiding star of future political activity. Then we can be sure its fruits will be lasting. I offer this brief reminder so that you won't forget. May God bless our endeavors and may we be worthy of his blessing."

There was restrained applause, for they were aware that clapping was not really proper after hearing God's word, even though it had been unofficial.

The *Suometar* party lacked a poet of its own, but Hollo's daughter, a student in the upper grades of a girls' school in the city, recited a poem. She was a niece of Töyry, whose wife swelled with pride at her relative's performance.

> *In the wilderness of Saarijärvi,*
> *on a frosty plot lived Paavo,*
> *Busily he hoed and weeded on his land.*
> *But he placed his hope of a harvest in his God.*
> ---
> *"Mix our bread one-half with pine-bark,*
> *frost has killed our neighbor's planting."*

During the applause for the poem, the speaker whispered to the vicar, "Which would be better? Should I use the word 'plowman' or 'farmer'? I wouldn't

286

want to exclude anyone by my choice of words. Are there any tenants or farm workers in the audience?"

"I don't see any tenants, at least none that I know. There are a few hired hands and maids. 'Plowman' is bound to be better."

The gentleman walked to the table, adjusted his tie, and began. "My dear listeners! He hoed and weeded his land diligently, but he placed his hopes for a harvest in his God. Our young reciter has illustrated for us, by way of this stanza from Runeberg, the essence of the Finnish plowman's life and being. He has brought this beautiful, but frost-prone land, under cultivation through centuries of toil, but he has also bowed his head humbly before the highest, leaving the harvest to God's will. In this picture of the plowman, we see the very best that resides in the Finnish people. Believing in work, believing in the land, but humble and attentive to his God, we see him before us, our Finnish plowman.

"The question of greatest importance, after that of our political rights, is the land question. Our socialists have made of it an issue to inflame the passions, but they have no true desire to resolve it. The *Suometar* party, on the other hand, has made it a central part of its program. It advocates land for the landless, and raising the tenants' standard of living by means of legislation and resettlement on government land. The chief aim of the socialists is to sow dissension between the landowners and the farmers who till rented lands. They will not succeed, for the same things benefit both landlord and tenant. When those flaws which do exist have been remedied through legislation, there will no longer be a land question in this country. But those who strive to find fault and tear down rather than to build up will have, within the week, the Finnish farmers' answer to their efforts. It will be a harsh judgment upon those who, under the guise of social idealism, are trying to destroy society. Does anyone deny that there is room for improvement in our system? No, we of the *Suometar* party are the first to admit it, and the first to seek that improvement. But ours are truly practicable means. It is easy to tear down, but who will take the responsibility for building up? We have done so. By means of patient and intelligent effort, we have already accomplished much, and will accomplish even more. And hasn't there always been in this country a warm sympathy for the disadvantaged? The frost has killed our neighbor's planting. So spoke the thriving Finnish farmer of his less fortunate neighbor. The Finnish farmer has always been generous to those in need. It has been an unwritten law in this land that an honest man can always get a night's lodging, and that a beggar never leaves empty-handed. Is not the tradition of the working bee vigorously alive? What is that but mutual aid lent to one another by neighbors? Haven't men in this country always rushed to put out a neighbor's fire? Helping and supporting each other, tenant and landlord have tilled their fields. A few contrary examples cannot destroy this truth. The particular cannot negate the general.

"For they are joined by a love of the land. A love of this bleak turf. And now with the birth of a Finnish-speaking educated class and bureaucracy, this most bitter cause of friction will disappear. The fight between the gentleman and the man of the soil will vanish. Officials who have risen from among the people will be one with the people. For they will have a common goal, this country's prosperity and success. For the land, this dear turf, this sacred bosom baptized as ours by our fathers' sweat and blood, this is what binds us all together. Through it we are united, brother to brother and sister to sister. This battleground of heroes and grave of the valiant, this land, whose every square meter has been washed with the blood of the brave, so sacred is this land that one cannot conceive of its giving rise to any dispute. What was our forefathers' question when they spilled their blood on its surface? They asked nothing. 'God protect our land' were the last words they whispered to its breast. Did the lad from Pori who had the honor and good fortune to offer his breast to the bullets on the field of Lapua — did he ask whose piece of land he did it for? Did the foot-soldier from Savo ask at Oravainen whose land he shed his blood on? Did the halberdier at Lutzen ask what German owned the land on which he fell? He did not ask, he only knew that far to the north was a land for whose sake he must strike and die. One land, a united land. Therefore, that land can give birth only to brotherhood, never to strife and discord."

Halme had sat listening all this time, his face a blank. As the speaker searched for a new starting point among his papers, there was a slight pause, and Halme stood up.

"I beg your pardon for troubling you. I realize that it is bad manners to interrupt a speaker, but a higher sanction compels me to remind the speaker that we in this community have experienced the ardent love the landowners feel for their land. Not to mention the Baron of Laukko's love for his. It is a pity that a tenant is not granted the joy of loving his land, for if he chances

288

to do so, the consequence may be six months in the house of correction. True, sweat and blood have watered this land, but our honorable speaker has forgotten a third fluid. I am referring to tears. Again I ask a thousand pardons."

Halme's cheek was twitching slightly as he walked up the aisle and out the door. At first there was silence in the room, then an indignant murmur, and finally words of outrage. But the speaker merely said, "Too bad the man left. I would gladly have discussed the matter with him, for dialogue is precisely what we hope for. But you can read his opinions in *The Worker* any day of the week. Pure socialism. As for what he hinted at, my only comment is that the Baron of Laukko is not a member of the *Suometar* party. He represents the old Swedish aristocracy, to whom this people have never meant anything."

Then the speaker returned to his prepared text. It was not really his, but had been written for him. As a banker from Helsinki, he felt ill-informed about rural issues and had therefore sought the help of an expert in drafting his speech.

After the anthem, the vicar thanked the speaker, who proceeded to shake hands with a few of the landlords and their wives. Halme's behavior gave rise to a good deal of talk:

"The nerve of that man... Interrupting a judge's speech..."

"And after she even welcomed him... She should have known what to expect after that melee with the police..."

"He's really gotten peculiar... You wouldn't have guessed it when he used to gawk around here as a little boy. If Pentti's landlady hadn't sent him to learn a trade, the wretch wouldn't have a crust of bread to put in his mouth."

"How long will the gentlemen of the church village continue to have him make their suits and pay him good money to buy those books."

"He even plans to get a telephone... to get his socialism by wire. He's been heard to say that he has to facilitate access to influential circles for the association. That's the way he talks... 'facilitate access' and 'influential circles...' Where in the world did he pick up that outlandish jargon?"

Töyry took no part in the discussion. Halme's innuendoes had struck home, and he could not bring himself to talk. But his wife did.

"That he had to go and talk like that, and in such a nice spot... He was the one who egged the Laurilas on. He was behind it. And if they keep on stirring up the poor this way, where will it end? We've never turned away a single beggar empty-handed. We've always given him his morsel, as the judge said.

289

But if this keeps up, it won't pay to go on feeding anyone out of kindness. Soon they won't ask, they'll just take."

Among the gentlemen the matter was not taken so seriously. At some meetings, opponents had been challenged to debate. They were vexed only by Halme's leaving before the speaker had a chance to refute him.

"He's not a bad debater. Actually he's quite sharp. He was making a good point. But God Almighty, how tiresome he is when he starts to speak at length. He drags in everything he has ever read. That hodgepodge of reading makes him comic."

"But what can come of their election efforts? There are so many like him among their candidates. They have no educated people except for the so-called November socialists, young gentlemen who have failed in their own class, and with complete lack of principle, have joined the socialists just to attract attention."

"There's no need to worry. They will elect no one, except for a few of their bellwethers. The people don't trust them."

"They'll do about as well as the Swedish speakers. I believe we'll get about a hundred and fifty seats. The country people are waking up."

The most important people had been invited to the parsonage after the meeting. There they condemned the village's Young Finns, the Swedish baron, and Halme's socialists roundly for their all-around uselessness.

A late supper was served in the visitor's honor. The vicaress had many personal matters to discuss with him. She was highly curious about the latest gossip from the capital. The landowners, however, were ill at ease, and tried clumsily to observe good table manners. The vicar noticed and tactfully eased their awkwardness by playing the bumpkin.

"This is good... You must be hungry by now... Have some, have some. It's there to be eaten."

"Well, ha, ha... But about those working hours. I guess anyone can give long speeches about them... In the summer, though, you have to tell the time by the sun in farm work... If those socialists have their way, this country will soon run out of bread."

"That Koskela boy has been frisking around at the association doings. The vicar needs to watch out for him. He's so pigheaded that if he ever becomes a tenant, there's bound to be trouble. His father keeps him in line now, but

290

who knows what he'll be like when he gets older."

"Well, I can't dictate opinions. I think he'll settle down as he grows older. He's still young. In any case, not many are his match as a worker... So tough that..."

"Uhuh... That's true... But he's been grumbling to people about that swamp." The vicar was upset and focused his attention on cutting the meat. Through the years, he had overcome his tendency to blush when caught off guard, but now the meat seemed to require all his concentration before a piece would come loose.

"So I've heard... It's too bad... Too bad... But I had to abide by the congregation's wishes... And I must say they didn't lose much. They have plenty of land. They got it almost for nothing... Just by lowering the rapids a little... All they had to do was dig ditches through the swamp... and under no circumstances should the boy talk... His father understands... But my dear... We need milk!"

Töyry had been silent for the better part of the evening, but now he said tautly, "Don't landlords have any rights left here? I'm going to start demanding more land from the manor. If justice goes by a man's demands, I'm going to demand plenty. Those representatives have to be careful not to mess up the laws. There would be plenty of demanding in this world if things could be had for the asking."

The visitor assured them that landowners' rights would not be trampled on. The intent was only to legislate uniformity in the status of tenants. There had to be an end to arbitrariness on either side. Freeing the tenants was out of the question. A fund should be established, with the help of which they could redeem their lands, but the entire transaction was to be voluntary. No compulsion would be mandated.

"That's a different story... If a man wants to sell his land, let him sell it."

The visitor spoke mostly with the vicaress. From time to time, names came up: Mechelin, Danielson, Castrén... "Is that what he said? Is his eyesight really that poor? As for the Russians, I would go farther than the party. From the very beginning, I have been opposed to the conciliation line... You don't say... Are his parents agreeable? Really, the Esplanade is a dangerous place... There they often trade glances for the first time..."

As the guests were leaving, the judge once more thanked them all.

"We can rest easy while we wait for the election returns. We just have to get everyone to vote. It's important to emphasize the significance of the election to your servants. Our success lies in the hands of the patriotic country people."

"Ya-ah... We'll all try our best..."

The servants began to clear away the dishes. The vicaress was dissatisfied with their performance.

"You must understand that country people don't always know how to behave. You ought to serve them in the most fitting way, and not create embarrassment by getting confused... Our guest will be leaving early, so Emma will see to it that we can offer him a light breakfast at eight."

Then she went into the parlor, where the vicar and his guest had withdrawn. On the threshold, her look of annoyance changed to a sweetly enthusiastic smile. Their guest was speaking.

"True-blue people... That Töyry seems to be an upright man. He knows what he wants. A true type of Finnish farmer. He's not pushy, but he says what he has to say like a man."

"He is... He evicted his tenant... But that was an impossible situation. The man was a brawler and a constant threat to him."

"It's clear that there are limits to anyone's toleration."

"But when will you be promoted to dean of the parish?"

"Not for a long time. I'm not ambitious."

"But promotions are given for merit, not ambition."

"Well, they should be. At any rate, I'm happy. I've begun to feel at home with the congregation."

"But when the election is over, I'll take that Halme to task. It will be fun to hear him explain away their defeat."

Leaving the firehouse, Halme had trouble controlling his excitement. At the very core of his being throbbed a surging jubilation. Everything had gone better than he could have hoped. The speaker had given him the opening.

Halme forgot that he hadn't really come up with the words on the spur of the moment. Having a good idea of what the visitor would say, he had planned his interpolation in advance, had even phrased it in part. Obviously the speaker would bring in patriotism, and he'd had a good response in readiness... But those tears. They did clinch the point.

292

The excitement subsided gradually to an elevated and solemn sense of self-congratulation. No doubt he would succeed as a legislator. He would be there too. By the next election he would surely be well enough known to be noticed.

The feeling of success always had a direct effect on Halme's physical appearance. Alone and in the dark, he could feel his posture grow more erect and his narrow chest expand. Literally, even his body felt pleasure.

Still Ilkka's deeds live on,
who can say for how long,
in the hearts of the people...

VI

Jussi Koskela had bought a colt. It was a cheaper way to get a horse than to buy one full-grown. Now the colt had to be trained. Even Alma came out to the porch to watch when he was hitched up for the first time. Jussi brought him out of the stable, but as soon as the collar bow touched his back, he began to leap and prance. Finally, he broke loose. Jussi caught hold of the reins, but fell and was dragged along behind the horse.

"Lord Jesus bless us! Boys, run... Help your father... He'll get hurt..."

Even the usually calm Alma panicked when she saw Jussi tumbling after the horse. Akseli caught the horse by the bridle at the corners of his mouth and pressed the bit to his lower jaw. The frenzied horse stopped, but tried to rear up again. Jussi clambered to his feet and limped to the boy's side.

"A real spitfire of a horse... Never seen anything like it... But don't crush him like that... You'll break his jaw."

"How else will I hold him?"

"He'll stand without it."

"He didn't... You can feel that in your bones..."

Jussi clamped his lips shut tightly. "I'm still man enough to hold one horse..."

"Well, there he is."

Jussi caught the horse by the corners of its mouth and patted it soothingly."Steady now, steady. You're Poku, that's right. Come on, Poku... steady now."

293

The colt came snorting and prancing to the sleigh, but as soon as the collar touched his back again, the scene was repeated. Jussi was able to hold him in place, but he kicked and pranced so that the shafts rattled. Jussi was getting upset. Aku had to turn his face away to hide a smile. Akseli tried with the collar again, but the horse slipped out from under it.

"Press his head against your chest and hold him there. Squeeze him with the bit."

"How can I hold him? He's like crazy... Never seen anything like it... I was thinking... It's in his blood..."

"This is getting us nowhere..." Akseli was angry.

"Well, come on and hold him yourself then, if you think you can do better..."

Akseli grabbed the horse at the corners of his mouth and forced him into the shafts.

"Now boys... Lift up the collar bow... Aku, you go to the other side."

Alma shouted from the steps, "Father, come away from there... You'll get hurt... Let the boys try."

Jussi puffed and snorted angrily, hoping that the boys would fail to get the colt into the collar. But when it once more settled upon the animal's back and the colt began to thrash around, Akseli forced its head into his chest. The colt kicked and jumped, but he stayed between the shafts, and finally the collar was in place.

"God...damn. This horse is going to stay in those shafts... Now buckle the breast-band... Aleksi, get the reins ready and hand them to me..."

They managed to close the breast-band, and though the earth resounded and the shafts clashed, the colt was hitched up. Akseli snatched the reins and leaped onto the sleigh at the same instant as the horse bolted. It was a wild ride, and the sleigh was soon out of sight.

Jussi grunted and grumbled, "What can I do with my sore back? And besides, if you're going to ruin a horse's mouth... Let him keep the balky creature... Let him drive it. They're two of a kind... Not one bit of difference..."

But in the middle of his carping, the father in him said worriedly, "As long as nothing happens... He might run into something..."

Alma understood the source of his anger. But there was a smile crinkling the corners of her eyes and delight and pride in her voice when she spoke. "But they're both so handsome... And that boy can more than hold his own..."

294

"Hmph. He should, at that age... But if he had a back like this."

"Just let go... You don't need to worry any more."

"Ha, ha... not worry... The world's problems aren't over just because one horse got harnessed."

Jussi went by Alma into the living room, eyes fixed on the floor. She followed and found him pacing back and forth, grunting, with a look of pain on his face.

"Does it hurt?"

"Of course... with something like that..."

Jussi kept looking at the floor, avoiding her eyes at all costs, and she tactfully dropped the whole subject.

For three kilometers, Poku ran blindly, ignoring all of Akseli's efforts to restrain him. The boy kept pulling on the reins until his arms were completely numb and nerveless. Then he let them go slack.

"Well, run as far as you like. You'll stop some day."

They went through the village, and people turned to look. The boy took quiet but intense pleasure in the wild ride. Snow thrown up from the horse's hoofs made a blizzard before his eyes, and the sleigh swung wide on turns. Finally, the horse began to steam and pant. He was beaten.

The trip home was much more subdued. His father and brother were waiting in the yard. Jussi did not come to unhitch the horse, but when Akseli was about to take the animal directly into the barn, Jussi said, "A horse that's been pushed to the limit can't be left just like that. Walk him a little."

The boy did as he was told. Jussi's mood lifted. Just how would things go if he wasn't around to see to them. Appeased, he went to check the horse, feeling its muscles and patting it.

"You can train him... I don't want to, with my sore back... But he has some disposition... I thought so already when I bought him... He's of tough stock."

They were hauling manure. Aleksi drove Vilppu and Akseli Poku. Their father and Aku made the loads and chopped fir sprigs onto the manure pile during the intervals. Poku still lunged ahead so hard that corners and gateposts were in danger, but no accidents occurred. When Akseli turned a corner, Jussi's hand still rose as if to grasp the reins, but he never completed the gesture. He always drew back his hand and maintained an approving silence.

"We probably need a third pile to a strip because they're longer. Or will there be enough? What do you think?"

295

Akseli looked appraisingly at the strip. He thought the manure would suffice, but the unfamiliar humility in his father's voice kept him from expressing a definite opinion.

"I couldn't say. But let's try three... We can always add more later when we get more. Even haul it in the summer with the wagon."

Twelve-year-old Aku was still in school, but he had a holiday. Alma had said something about his being free during the vacation, but Jussi would not hear of it.

"We're not going to teach them to be loiterers. Up on the pile, that's all there is to it."

Aku showed signs of a sense of humor, a rare phenomenon at the Koskelas'. He could laugh in secret at his father's outbursts and would sometimes taunt his older brother into threatening growls. There were times when he had to take to flight. He got along better with Aleksi. The middle brother, now of confirmation age, was quiet and serious. He was of a slighter build than the others. Aku sometimes lied to him intentionally and would go to ridiculous extremes before his innocent and serious older brother would look at him reproachfully and say, "You are lying."

He lagged behind as they drove, for Vilppu was almost twenty years old. He should really have been destroyed, but they didn't have the heart. He still could pull, but load after load, Akseli outdistanced him with Poku.

"You're already four loads behind," said Aku.

Aleksi pondered soberly. He took no offense, but began counting to see if the number was actually right.

"So I am... four loads."

His father never scolded Aleksi, for he never found a reason to.

The boys took a short break every now and then, but their father went to the sprig log and hacked away while they rested. During one of the pauses, Akseli looked out at the swamp and asked, "Are they planning to put in oats on the parsonage side?"

Jussi looked toward the swamp. The fence that ran along the drainage ditch no longer galled him as bitterly as it once had, but even now his brush hook snapped more sharply into the log at the sight of it. His answer was an unintelligible snarl: "... know... or care... do what they want."

"Halme is talking about getting a retroactive law through the legislature that would nullify earlier evictions... It would have to apply to us. From the year 1902 on, I believe. Some law went into effect then."

"Hmh... Don't you believe anything like that."

"It's not a matter of believing if we get the representatives... You go and vote too."

Before Jussi had time to answer, Victor Kivioja drove into the yard.

"Hello Jussi... What kind of a creature was pulling your boy's sleigh the other day? Let me see the colt... Let's make a deal... I saw him go by myself... Trade him or sell him."

Jussi looked at Akseli and said, "I won't sell. I've promised him to the boy... Ask him."

"Well, boy. Make your first deal. Show me the colt."

Akseli looked at his father for a moment. Did his promise mean outright ownership? He had understood only that he was to drive it. Sure now that his father was serious, he answered Victor's request, almost arrogant in his joy: "It's all right to look... And we can make a deal, but it'll take a nice wad of Finnish bills."

"Hah, boy... Let this old man take a look..."

Victor examined the horse, looking for defects. Akseli stood by, smiling smugly.

"Take two," said Victor. "Shake on the deal."

"We're not talking Finnish animal fairy tales. We're bargaining about a horse, not a horseshoe."

"Hah... Listen to the boy talk... I'll give you another ten and not a penny more."

"It's not going for anything under three-and- a-half. And I don't know. I'm not sure. He's the kind of colt I'm not letting go for any money. Money is made from silver and paper in Helsinki, but good horses are heaven's gift."

His father was watching the boy covertly. He saw the manly superiority in his attitude to Victor and liked it. He had always been repelled by Victor's bluster. And for the first time, Jussi clearly understood that the boy was beginning to be a man. He spoke to Victor as to his equal. Akseli's words drove Victor so wild that he began to flail about with his hands and to shout that the price was insane.

And of course it was, for Akseli would not, in fact, have given Poku up.

297

The horse was his own, and money would have been no compensation for the feeling he had in straightening out the mane of the restless and spirited animal.

Realizing that the horse was not for sale, Victor began to talk of other things He was planning to vote. Halme had been to the gentlemen's election meeting and had said something to them. Akseli knew what it was, and told him what Halme had said. Victor got excited: "Goddamn... You don't say... He told them that... Is it really true? ...He said six months... By God, that socialism is fun..."

Jussi muttered into his beard as he watched Victor's fit of glee. But when Vic asked him if he was going to vote, he made an inarticulate sound, more like refusal than assent. The subject was quickly dropped, for except when the talk was of horses, Victor never stuck to any one subject for any length of time. After he had left, Akseli said, in a mild and propitiatory voice, "You go and vote too, along with Mother. We'll get some help from it, even if it isn't much."

Jussi took another limb and began to chop at it furiously. "They keep telling you to draw lines on those papers. What good is that?"

Akseli explained once more. He tried to speak in as matter-of-fact a voice as possible, even though he was irritated by his father's opposition. Not that Jussi was so stupid as not to understand the significance of an election but he despised from the bottom of his heart everything that he lumped together under the designation of "parades." He did not believe that the socialists would be represented strongly enough to matter. There was one final complication, of no little weight.

"And I won't be able to. How do I know where to draw those lines? Let people who don't have anything better to do go and vote. And what will they say at the parsonage?"

"How will they know who you voted for? That's why it's a secret ballot. And Halme will be there on the election board. He'll tell you what to do. You just draw a line in Hellberg's square."

"I won't vote for anyone like that. If they haven't got a better man, then let it go."

"What's wrong with Hellberg?"

"Hmph... he has his faults... And what's that tower he built on the station-master's villa?"

298

Turned away from his father, Aku began to pitch manure rapidly onto the sleigh. Even Akseli felt like laughing but restrained himself, afraid that his father would lose his temper.

"The station-master ordered it. That isn't Hellberg's fault. And there will be other men. It doesn't matter, as long as you vote for socialists."

His father, however, had realized the weakness of his recent argument, and began to storm and hack more peevishly. Akseli gave up for the time being.

After a while, he returned to the subject, and this time his talk got results. Jussi's resistance began to crumble when the boy pictured all the things the legislature might be able to do.

"Just think. If we could limit the working day to ten hours, that alone would cut down on the rent-work. And a law to end compulsory work in addition to rent-work. A tenant wouldn't have to be on call during busy seasons. And if we can just get enough representatives, some day we can get a law allowing tenants to buy their land."

Yes, yes. That was all fine and dandy, but would such pinch-noses ever get anything done. The boy had risen so much in stature, however, that Jussi listened. He had to take the boy's opinions more seriously now.

But it was a lot to swallow. On the eve of the election, Jussi finally did agree to go. But Akseli made a last-minute mistake: he offered to act as his guide and tutor.

"When did you ever see anybody lead me?"

He was not going to be led around like that by the boy. However, he did go after all, but only as it was getting dark and in a sullen state of mind. Alma's mind was made up along with his, and she went as well.

Halme greeted them with the utmost courtesy. He knew Jussi's attitude, and seeing Akseli's father finally appear at the school, he considered it another victory for socialism. He advised the two of them what to do, and Hellberg got two more votes. Jussi voted for him too.

"Well, well, Jussi. You've exercised your right to share in government."

"... Um... hmm... don't know..."

Jussi hurried home, not stopping to chat with Halme, for the schoolteacher and a couple of landlords were also members of the election board. Jussi felt as if he had committed a crime, and only wanted to escape to his home, to his own world, away from the fringes of this suspect world of "parades."

He had managed the voting without difficulty, and that was a relief. The election board had its troubles with Henna Leppänen, however. She had finally offered the pen to Halme. "You draw it... It doesn't matter... There anywhere..."

At last that vote too was cast, and when the newspaper headlines read: "Great Victory for Socialists—Eighty Representatives," the vicar's wife could say, "Is it any wonder? With all that agitation? They should have replaced the financial requirement for suffrage with a cultural one. Women like that Leppänen make a mockery of suffrage."

The vicar was thoughtful.

"It's surprising... It's surprising... It's dangerous too... Too much power without any experience. They must be celebrating now."

Akseli was unloading firewood in front of the parsonage woodshed. The vicar was outdoors. He walked about, scented the air, and then went over to Akseli, greeting him, "Good day. Those are nice birch blocks."

The boy went on working as he returned the greeting perfunctorily. The vicar kept up a forced conversation about the thaw that would soon be upon them. To complete the hauling before it arrived, he was asking Akseli to work extra days with pay. The boy agreed to do so without complaint, for the burden of extra days was not as bad during the winter, when there was not as much to do at home. Finally the vicar asked, "Well, what does Akseli think of the election results?"

The boy fitted a block into the pile. "What should I... They must have counted the votes correctly."

The vicar laughed. He found it difficult to talk about the matter, and so he tried to be playful.

"I'm sure they did. But did people think correctly when they voted? You won this time, but wait until the next election, when we get our ranks organized. You've had extraordinary success. You got everyone moving. We don't have the kind of political organization you have."

"It's not the organization, it's the large number of workers. And there is so much poverty..."

The vicar had spoken in the tone of voice used in joking among friends, but the boy's face had remained serious. Now the vicar's attitude changed. Roused to resentment by the curt reply, he said dryly, "Exactly so. That's true. But fanning hatreds doesn't improve conditions; it can only make them worse.

We should achieve an intelligent mutual understanding in order to correct what is wrong. I, at least, don't oppose reforms which are clearly necessary. But the center of gravity in human affairs does not lie there. We already have a truly socialist doctrine proclaimed, if we would only hear it. Changing conditions won't help unless people themselves change."

Akseli began flinging blocks onto the pile. A troubled silence prevailed until the boy, his words interspersed in the feverish rhythm of his work, replied, "Yes... people to change, sure... Why bother to vote then... But they must have counted them right... I don't know... I had nothing to do with it... I didn't draw the lines or put in the dots."

The vicar put his hands behind his back, looked at the sky before leaving, and said, "Of course not. Akseli will go on driving for the rest of the week then."

The vicar left. Bile rose and swelled in his heart. On the porch, he beat his shoes to clean the snow from them, stamping his feet, nearly raging. "They must be celebrating. It will be difficult to feel sympathy for them after this... They're becoming impossible. It isn't just because he's a tenant—he ought to act like a human being too... How poorly they bind these brooms...This one too is falling apart."

The load was soon emptied. Block after block flew up to the pile. Sweat dripped from under Akseli's fur cap. "He knows all about centers of gravity. Let him lift something on his goddamn back for once. Then he'll know something about centers of gravity."

CHAPTER NINE

I

He has reached the age of twenty. He is wearing a slightly worn suit and new boots. He is even wearing a hat; the days of the visored cap are over. He has his own horse, and his father has finally agreed to the purchase of an old but usable church wagon. And there are eighty socialists in the legislature.

In addition to all this, it is Pentecost, and his next younger brother is being confirmed. No wonder he pats the horse as he hitches it to the wagon. When he drives up to the hitching rail at the church, Poku's neck will arch as he tightens the reins. The pressure from the bit will force open his mouth, and his front feet will carve out longer strides in the air than they will actually measure as they hit the ground. It shows what he would do if he were given free rein.

Father and Aukusti would stay at home, but Mother would go with them.

Pentecost morning of 1907 at Koskela is one of those light and happy occasions that occur in every life. The livestock are already out of doors. The barn and stable doors are open. Despite the early hour, the sun has warmed the steps sufficiently for his father to come out barefoot. He is checking to see that the horse's feed-bag is not on the wagon. "Just so he doesn't filch any oats to take along. The boy tries to feed that horse as if it were something special."

But there was no feed-bag on the wagon. It was true that Akseli grabbed an extra handful for the horse now and then. He didn't exactly steal it, but he did it on the sly to avoid his father's nagging.

"Don't drive like a fool now."

Akseli did not answer. Father had agreed to the wagon, and even gave him spending money now and then. He was no longer so quick to boss him at work,

302

but was often heard to grumble, "I have to see to everything. They tug and pull, all right, but how would things go if there was no one to check up on them."

Jussi was particularly apt to talk that way after something had occurred in which he was forced to admit his inferiority. He had also unconsciously slipped into doing the lighter work: he made trips to the mill, chopped the sprigs, and set up the shocks in the grain fields. Not by arrangement; it just happened that way.

The boy might lend a hand in loading sacks for the mill. Jussi would first lift the sacks onto some kind of elevation, then carefully begin to shift them to his ailing back. Akseli would come and grab them from him. "...no use... with that... I'll throw them..."

And throw them he did. He would take a sack in both hands, raise it to his chest, and heave it onto the wagon from the threshold.

"Don't break the sacks now."

"They won't break... Are you taking these too?"

The remainder of the sacks flew onto the wagon in the same way. The boy's movements suggested some kind of enjoyment in the work. The lift was secretly explosive but apparently controlled, with enough strength conserved to make a clean toss to the wagon.

It was after such an occurrence that Jussi would start grumbling. Now he had to say something from the steps so that the boy wouldn't think he had a free hand on the trip to church. But there was also a note of kindly concern in Jussi's voice. "Isn't that belly-band too loose?"

"Could be... He plays such devil's tricks. He swells when you're tightening it and then it's left loose."

Aleksi came out. He wore Akseli's old confirmation suit and was shyly pleased with it. His movements were a little different than usual; they were somehow stiffer and more solemn.

Then their mother came waddling along, holding her skirts up as she came down the steps, a hymnal wrapped in a handkerchief held in one hand.

"That rose bush is getting old... I should ask Anna how to cut it back... Feed the piggies at one o'clock... How can I ever get up into that wagon?"

In spite of the bad years and the troubles they had sustained, Alma still looked blooming and healthy, but added weight on her short frame had made her look quite portly. Her foot could not quite reach the wagon step, and Akseli helped her to mount. He felt awkward doing it. Since he had been a little boy, he had never touched his mother, unless by accident. This helping smacked too much of closeness, of familiarity, if not actually of some highfalutin fondling. So his proffered help was brisk, and his mother's feet still trailed along behind as she landed on the wagon seat.

"Oh, Lord... My book is falling..."

Aleksi got onto the back seat, and when Poku sensed that the wagon was nearly loaded, he began to toss his head and paw the ground. Aukusti came out to the steps to watch their departure.

Akseli put one foot on the step. As the other left the ground, Poku started off. He took a few uncertain, pawing steps before settling into a spirited trot. Springs rocking, they were on their way. They were traveling the Koskela road, well cleared and sanded, with the muddy spots marked by gravel piles hauled in during the winter, ready to spread when necessary.

Alma held on to the seat with one hand. She blinked her brown eyes as they passed through the alternating patches of bright sunshine and shade from the roadside spruces.

The lake sparkled. They passed by the parsonage on its shore, where some of the servants were moving about in the yard. They passed the fork of the road to Töyrys', where disordered piles of boards and timber could be seen, the dismantled remains of what had until recently been the Laurila place. By the roadside were some new timbers as well. Construction of the store was to begin at once.

They also passed other travelers. Prettily, without urging, as if sensing his owner's wishes, Poku quickened his pace as they went by. Akseli needed only to hold the reins lightly.

Approaching the village, they could see the parsonage coach ahead of them.

"Well, Poku..."

The trot accelerated. In passing, Akseli merely nodded. He could not raise his hat, for he was holding the reins in both hands. Alma's greeting was limited to raising her rump slightly from the seat, a gesture which went completely unnoticed. How could she do more, with a lunatic driving like that?

Ani and Ilmari were also in the parsonage coach. Ilmari was being confirmed. He had gone to school in Helsinki, but arrangements had been made for his father to confirm him in his home parish.

A childish pleasure rippled in Akseli's cheeks. He tightened, then loosened the reins. That was enough for Poku. The horse arched his neck, and after a couple of faltering gallops, he found his best and speediest trot. His feet drummed an incessant, exultant tattoo on the road. Alma could not see a thing. The wind of their movement brought tears to her eyes and blinded her completely.

"Slow down now... God save us..."

But they kept on until the parsonage coach was sure to be far behind them. Then only did the boy begin to rein in the horse. As the animal walked up a hill, Akseli leaned over the front of the wagon to give him a couple of approving slaps. "Poku knows what the gentlemen have coming to them."

For her part, his mother complained mildly both about the ride and about passing the gentry like that. It was improper. They should have stayed behind.

"If you can, you do," said Akseli.

Driving up to the hitching rail, they did not attract nearly as much attention as Akseli had imagined they would. So many spirited colts showed up there on Sunday mornings that not one of them stood out.

But Akseli spent a long time adjusting Poku's harness and straightening his mane before leaving him.

Pentecost and confirmation had brought a larger crowd than usual to the church. Landowners drove up in their red- or yellow-wheeled church wagons, drawn by placid, well-fed horses. Up front sat the master and mistress and in back the boy or girl who was to be confirmed. The underprivileged came on foot, trying as much as possible to lose themselves in the crowd, for what had they to show?

Aleksi Koskela stood by the side of his mother and brother, gazing soberly around him.

He was a little nervous. How would he manage with that drink?

The master and mistress of Yllö arrived with their son. They were on foot, for their house was only a stone's throw away. A lane through the people opened before them as if by command. Uolevi Yllö was also being confirmed. Passing by Aleksi, he winked and whispered, "Hi there."

Aleksi nodded in answer, hiding his delight. His mother and brother had seen the crown prince of the church village greet him. Only in passing, and in church-village style, but still... Uolevi had been the kingpin in the class because of his family's prominence. He was further admired for daring to play little pranks, the more so because his father was one of the mighty.

Arvo Töyry arrived with his parents. He too was being confirmed.

Then the Kivivuoris' small brown horse drove up, pulling an equally small church wagon behind him. Elina and Anna were on the front seat. Osku was driving from the rear, where Otto clung to a precarious perch, his knees drawn up to his chin for lack of space, and his rump projecting in a peculiarly funny way.

Oskar tied the horse to the hitching rail, and Otto said loudly, "Give the halter more slack so that he can steal hay from his neighbors."

The remark made his wife and daughter draw to one side quickly. Anna's face wore its dolefully reverent church expression, which it never lost, even though she kept tugging at Elina's dress secretively and otherwise checking her over. Noticing the Koskelas, they came over to them, Anna's expression becoming ever more devout.

Although they were familiar acquaintances and saw each other often, they now shook hands. It was an intuitive gesture, a manifestation of the mood engendered by the churchyard and their Sunday dress. At first only Anna and Alma shook hands, but that demanded a general handshaking, and so they pressed and they squeezed, criss-cross and back and forth. And strange to behold, Akseli took Elina by the hand and said, "Well, let's shake a paw then, once we've begun."

The girl smiled happily. But the handclasp wrought an unconscious change in the boy's attitude toward her. It was the first time he had shaken her hand. Earlier he had said only meaningless words to the girl, the kind one uses to a friend's little sister, really paying no attention to her at all. Now he was also struck by her failure to curtsy. She merely nodded, as to an equal. It was a new kind of attitude, and therefore a bit confusing, but it made him see her in a new light. Now and then, he studied her with an oblique glance. Almost frightened, he realized she was a woman, a very pretty woman.

The girl was at a stage where femininity was molding her being. It was an early phase, but the signs were there. Her limbs were still thin and calf-like, but her waist and hips already revealed the woman. The top of her black confirmation dress, adorned with silk embroidery, was already filling out.

At the moment, an inner glow radiated from her. The excitement of confirmation and the dizzying possibilities of life which the ritual opened up before her brought on the glow. But they made her restless and uneasy as well.

The gravity of confirmation was not exactly in harmony with the spontaneous joy of life she felt, and the result was a continually changing play of expression on her face. Her eyes shone and her lips kept shaping themselves into an indefinite smile, but when she looked at her mother and Alma, her face took on a sober expression, in harmony with theirs. But only for a second, as if a light cloud had passed overhead on a bright sunny day.

Her mother's careful upbringing had not been without effect. Having lost her hold over the boys, Anna had concentrated on the girl with an almost pathological intensity. She had watched over Elina like a jewel, to prevent her from taking the slightest corruption from the atmosphere at Kivivuori, where the "asses" and "goddamns" filled the air like flies. She had succeeded. The girl was entirely free of the attitudes that characterized her father and brothers.

She tried to hide her pleasure in her confirmation dress, on which so much time and money had been sacrificed, but she had to show off her watch when Alma noticed the thin gold chain around her neck.

Was that why Anna had gone to Tampere?

"Is it really gold?"

"No. The chain is, but the watch is silver. It's just gold-plated."

Elina drew the watch forth from the neck of her dress. Akseli held it in his hand too, and felt its warmth. He could not keep from thinking that the warmth had come from between the girl's breasts. He handed the watch back quickly, disturbed by his own thoughts.

He remembered how embarrassed the girl had been by her father's teasing last winter. Now such a reaction would have pleased him, if he hadn't come to the realization that the girl's state of mind had nothing to do with him. He had been only the ostensible cause of her inner confusion. She showed no trace of it now, but smiled happily as she looked at him.

But then his thoughts took another turn. People might easily notice his interest. So he began to talk nonsense with Otto and Oskar in an abnormally loud voice.

The people standing around on the church grounds began to crowd in through the door in a thickening stream. From the graveyard came the sound of hymn-singing. Someone was being buried there. The bells tolled, sending their sound over the landscape, and on this clear summer day, dwellers in outlying villages could hear their distant ring. Old folks could read their message, be it a death knell or a summons to worship.

307

The confirmation class entered first, for they were to be seated in the first row. Elias Kankaanpää arrived at the very last minute. He too had to be confirmed, although the vicar had repeatedly threatened not to do so.

"Not to mention your total lack of knowledge or ability, you desecrate an important matter with your very expression."

When Elina took her place with a classmate, Anna whispered something in her ear, of which the others could catch only a few words: "...that... you be prepared.... ready..."

Simultaneously she gave one last tug at her daughter's dress.

Elina's face took on a sober expression and she bowed her head for a moment. But as she approached the church door with her classmate, her sobriety vanished, and the joyous glow of life lighted up her features. The two girls walked abreast, each one glancing first at her own dress and then at her partner's. Both seemed pleased with the sight. Elias and Aleksi were the next in line. Aleksi was solemn and confused, and gave a forced laugh when Elias said, "I'll grip the chalice with my teeth and tilt it so much I'll get a good drink."

The vicar's confirmation sermon was more solemn and moving than usual. His own son was in the group, and in writing the sermon, he had committed to paper his own hopes and fears for the boy's future. The couple had wanted him confirmed in his home-parish church. There was in it something that appealed to them: his own father as confessor, and he, the son of this spiritual shepherd, here to be confirmed together with other young people of their congregation.

Most of the time, the vicar preached in a gentle and devout voice, as a means of appealing to his listeners. But routine sermons had dulled the meaning of the words, and his mind was no longer on them. Devotion was becoming more and more a matter of the larynx, enkindled in the vocal cords. This time, however, he spoke with the full weight of his soul.

"My dear young people. The joys and perils of life await you. Life, the tester of man, the scales where each one of us is weighed, can more easily lead us wrong than right. But if you take as your guide the spirit of this sacred moment, your life will be blessed. Whatever fate may have in store for you, you cannot find the way without God's help. Side by side, you kneel to receive mankind's greatest

308

God, and to your country's good fortune and success."

The boys and girls received the communion separately, as the space before the altar was too limited to fit them all together. Rehearsals had been held in advance, but little mix-ups developed. Aleksi's place was between Ilmari and Arvo Töyry. Ilmari prodded him slyly in the ribs, and the expression on his face seemed to say: relax! Aleksi had already begun to work at the parsonage the preceding summer and had come in contact with Ilmari, who was on vacation. Under other circumstances, he would have been pleased by such a familiar gesture from a gentleman's son, but now his anxiety did not permit it. There was no thought of sin on his mind, nor had he ever been guilty of any very extraordinary sin. He knew, of course, that all life was sinful, but he was not able to see that as his fault.

His mind was concentrated completely on one single thing: he must not be clumsy. The thin communion wafer stuck to his palate, which was dry because of his anxiety, and the wine dribbled from the corners of his mouth when the assistant pastor, who was serving it, withdrew the goblet too quickly from his lips. Surreptitiously he licked his lips clean, hoping their bowed heads had prevented others from noticing.

With a sigh of relief, he began to look around, curious to see if Elias would carry out his threat. Nothing of the sort happened, but the serious expression on Elias's face was novel and amusing.

Then he turned his attention to the altar painting, which he had never seen so close up. It seemed strangely crude. The cracking surface of the paint gleamed in the light, and the highlighted face of Jesus was expressionless and cold.

Akseli was sitting on one of the benches. He too was nervous that his brother might blunder. As the girls were being lined up in their places, he was able to look undisturbed at Elina. She did not look so extraordinary among the others, but when she took the communion, there was a world of unconscious charm in the inclination of her head. It made the boy's thoughts run freely: "...good-looking... soon... her watch between her breasts..."

Next to him, Anna was pressing her head into the back of the pew before them, drying her tears with a handkerchief. A vaguely worded prayer was running through her mind.

"...Take my hand... on the road of life. Keep me pure... lilies of the field... Jesus take my hand... through life."

309

Anna was thinking of the girl's sexual purity precisely because the chief significance of confirmation, as the people understood it, was to make a girl marriageable. The young also had a vague idea that it gave them the right to keep company as men and women. A dim picture of her daughter with a man flashed through Anna's mind. Otto's head was turned to one side, for he had never learned to tolerate Anna's weeping in church, although she did it nearly every time she was there. He wanted to go outside, to get out of this numbing sitting position. The need to smoke was also plaguing him.

During the closing hymn, people were already disappearing unnoticed through the door. As they jostled their way out, a common feeling of relief possessed them. Having to sit for hours and sustain the appropriate mood had begun to weigh on them, so they began immediately to chatter and to light up their pipes. They met and chatted with acquaintances for a while, until it was time to attend to errands at the apothecary or the tanner's, at the store through the "inside" door, or something like that. Some of them bought "church coffee bread" from the baker.

The bell in the belfry was tolling, but the people heard it only on the periphery of their minds, which were now settling back into their everyday mood on the way home.

As they rode home, Akseli reined in Poku so as not to outdistance Kivivuoris' brown, which was following them. He shouted his remarks to Oskar, but every time his head turned, he looked at Elina, where she sat on the front seat. They were talking about Poku, which pleased Akseli.

"He is that, all right... Father didn't know it when he bought him... He couldn't tell anything about him as a colt."

"Hey, Aleksi... Are you going to visit the maids tonight?" Osku yelled in the middle of everything.

"Where would you go if I did?"

Aleksi was pleased, thinking he'd gotten off a clever retort, although he realized it only after the words were out. Osku made no response, but looked at his sister for a second and said, "Or come over and see our girl. She's ready now, body and soul."

That brought a muttered complaint from Anna, an angry slap at her brother's face from Elina, and a forced laugh from Akseli. Aleksi said nothing, but merely smiled. Osku began to slap at Elina's bottom with the end of the reins through

310

the lattice-work of the seat back.

"Don't... you'll get my dress dirty."

"What are you doing?"

"I'm teaching my sister to be afraid for her ass. So that she'll be touchy about it."

Dead serious, Elina slammed her palm into Oskar's face so hard there was a loud smack, but he merely jerked his head back and laughed. Anna threatened to do the same, but subsided into weak complaints. They could hear her in the Koskela wagon.

"You act like the worst tramps in the world... Is this any time to talk like that? My heart is in my mouth when I have to be in public with you... I never know what might happen..."

Otto sat silent, his rump hanging far out over the back end of the wagon. He smiled to himself as he twirled a cigarette from one corner of his mouth to the other, acting as if he were happy to let the boys have a go at it.

Akseli laughed, but in a forced and exaggerated way. The remark seemed nasty to him. It was too coarse for the way he was beginning to feel about Elina.

Even Alma drew her features into a disapproving scowl, but a strong impulse to laughter threatened to overcome her. She gasped out, "But really... that talk... where have they learned it all..." And her body shook with concealed laughter.

She was afraid, with good reason, of hurting Anna if she laughed. Anna sat with her mouth pursed, not saying a word the rest of the way. Only at the turnoff did she break her sullen silence to mumble a restrained farewell. Elina had already forgotten the whole thing. She waved her hand gaily at the Koskelas. Akseli's eyes remained fixed on the retreating wagon until it disappeared around a bend.

II

The gentlemen continued having their suits made by Halme. He had work up to his ears. From the people in the community, he earned little, especially since he had to be philanthropic now and then and sell to them at a reduced

311

price. It was the gentlemen's suits that brought in the money. Not only could he charge high prices for them; he had to. The gentlemen were glad to pay up, for it was the price that gave status to the suit. Customers came from all over the parish. Some gentlemen suggested that it would be worth his while to move to the city and establish a tailor shop, but Halme rejected the idea.

In a city he would have been one among many; here he was the only one, and he knew that his importance lay in his closely following the fashions of the city. When a gentleman paid for his suit, Halme spoke of other things. He named the price with a slight cough, his eyes averted, and if possible, he had the customer leave the payment on the table. He did not like to accept money from another's hand. There was something unworthy and degrading about handling it.

The village telephone cooperative agreed to let him have a telephone. There was some opposition to it at the meeting. "He only needs it to get instructions on stirring up the workers." Others, however, argued that he could not be refused on such grounds, and the permission was granted. His line was even strung on the parsonage poles, which prompted the vicar's wife to observe venomously that Halme could now see how liberal the *Suometars* were, since they permitted a line by means of which they were reviled to be strung on their own poles.

"Heh, heh... I must admit this to be a demonstration of a certain impartiality. And since the manor's lines are on the same poles, it's appropriate that they should carry the people's voice too. Hmm. Just think. The three chief facets of Finnish society on the same pole. The constitutional party is missing, though, which is perhaps appropriate, considering its defeat at the polls."

"If we could only remember those shared poles," said the vicar. "The lines may be separate but the poles are one... One should think of that."

Feeling that he owed them thanks, Halme agreed that the vicar had the right idea, and when he had departed, cane in hand, the vicar said to his wife, "As a person, he's not objectionable. If we could only let the ideas do battle while the men remain at peace."

"When his wires are in place, the man will renew the battle. His conceit is so annoying. I've never ever seen a man so convinced of his own excellence. If you were to say something to his face as rudely as possible, he would bow without the flicker of an eyelid and launch into a formal exposition."

That summer, Halme's telephone went into service. At first he kept making

312

constant calls to Silander, who had taken Hellberg's place as leader of the village workers' organization. Hellberg was busy with his duties as a representative in Helsinki, but he still kept the reins of the parish in his grasp. Silander was only a fill-in. Halme's frequent and pointless calls were beginning to annoy him, but they gradually ceased, and the calls he did get were more businesslike.

A notice also appeared in the parish newspaper:

I wish to notify my customers that I have procured a telephone and that they can reach me by means of it to inquire about their work or for other such reasons. By name, or Pentti's Corners, two rings.

Respectfully,
A. Halme
Master Tailor

Whenever he had the chance, Valenti rushed to answer the ring of the telephone, but he was not allowed to say anything more. He had to call for the master. The trill of the bell always cut sharply through the day's routine. No matter what kind of rag they were patching, what kind of trivia they were discussing, the shrill note changed the atmosphere completely. Halme rose, set his work down, and went into the parlor. His appearance changed, his carriage grew more erect, and with careful, deliberate movements, he took down the earphone and said, "Halloo. Halloo... Halme residence."

People could see him through the parlor doorway, standing by the telephone, receiver to his ear, the fingers of one hand in his vest pocket. Some even penetrated into the parlor to read the inscription on the side of the marvel: "Ericson. Stockholm."

Even after he returned to his work, the mood lingered with Halme for a while. If a customer was on hand and asked about a call, he most often received only a vague response. The curious were granted only a fragmentary glimpse of the large and significant world.

At one of the meetings, Halme considered the time ripe to present the bold idea that "our community needs a workers' hall, even if it is to be a modest one. Without a place to meet, we cannot get down to work with full effectiveness..."

He had been promised a loan from the savings bank in advance. In that instance, too, the masters had been at loggerheads. Should they grant a loan for the furtherance of socialism? But money has no odor. His own house would be sufficient security when mortgaged.

The question of a lot was more difficult. They did not even consider asking Töyry or the manor. The owner of Kylä-Pentti agreed to rent them a lot for thirty years, but adamantly refused to sell. He had a worthless pine slope alongside his farm, but he would not sell the land.

"It's a matter of principle, I say... But you can stay there all right.. But no bad living ..."

Offended, Halme totally rejected such a possibility, explaining that it was the association that would put an end to bad living among the young. The master was sympathetic. He had nothing against the association, but he feared his peers.

Volunteers were needed then. The labor would cost nothing. The wood was purchased as standing timber, which made it cheap.

During the winter, Akseli hauled timber from the woods with Poku. His father fretted and fumed, going on and on, trying to be sarcastic, but always succumbing to his sizzling temper.

"That's a great way to educate people. One work project after another. First a school, then a firehouse, and now a workers' hall... If they would put all that effort into building houses for people, the poor devils wouldn't have to freeze. But what does Halme care about people as long as the association lives high. How does that debt work now? Some day they'll come and take your horse. And you haven't got anything else."

"They won't take Poku... They'll take Halme's house if we can't afford to pay."

"Ha, ha..."

Mornings, Akseli would go to pick up the Kivivuoris. Otto and Janne worked felling trees; Oskar trimmed the limbs and helped Akseli load them. Akseli did not always enter the house those mornings, but preferred to wait outside. He had stopped visiting the Kivivuoris so frequently. Elina was developing before his eyes into a frightening and dazzling creature, difficult to look at calmly and speak to naturally.

The girl treated him in a friendly fashion, somewhat like one of her brothers. She sometimes joined in the friendly game of poking fun at his seriousness and single-mindedness.

One morning Anna called to Akseli from inside the house.

"They're not ready yet."

Indeed they weren't, for at nine o'clock in the morning, the Kivivuoris were teaching their daughter to dance. Osku was leading her, and her father was trolling away, sitting on the bedside, mittens on his hands and fur cap on his head. They had been planning to leave when they saw Akseli coming, but Osku had burst out in the midst of everything, "Hey girl... A couple of spins..."

Elina first objected but then agreed. In the middle of her chores, she brushed her apron, tidied her hair instinctively, and so the two began. She was a little shy of her father, but her face glowed with concealed enthusiasm. With a cavalier gesture, Oskar put his arm around her waist. "Hey old man. Let 'er rip."

Otto sat on the bedside and began tapping his foot on the floor.

> *Your memory, old Viapori,*
> *is ever dear to me,*
> *Although you did unto her death*
> *my one and only love*
> *...tralalala tralaIa...*

At the head of the table, Janne sat watching with a gently mocking smile on his face. The sight of his father singing in cap and mittens made him want to laugh, but he refrained from sarcasm this time. He had written a petition for Kankaanpää requesting a reduction of town fees for him. People were beginning to request such services of him.

"Since you read those law books."

The legal texts were of no help in such matters, but he had run across the forms for such petitions in his other reading. After the first request, one followed on the heels of another, until he had gained a kind of reputation as a penman. Even Halme used him when the association needed to draft official documents.

When Akseli stepped inside, Otto merely nodded and went on chanting. Embarrassed, Elina tried to stop, but her brother dragged her along.

Akseli sat down on the doorway bench. Leaning his elbows on his knees and swinging his mittens on one hand, he tried to smile with amused condescension. Here he was, engaged in important business, on his way to haul

315

timber for a workers' hall. The men should be leaving from here as well, but they had started dancing. Well, for them it's appropriate behavior; one need only smile and keep the matter in perspective. Osku has some childish habits, and Elina is barely seventeen, so it suits her. She's just a silly girl.

Underneath the condescending smile, a vague, oppressive jealousy was sprouting. "She's learning to dance. They'll be having evening socials at the workers' hall when it's finished. She's sure to go there." His own feet had never taken a single dance step.

As a little boy, he had sometimes sat on this same bench. Out of shame he had hidden his rag of a hat behind his back. Now his hat was beginning to bother him again, not because it was ragged, but because it was new, his Sunday hat. His mother had wondered why he was wearing it when he left. "I just happened to pick it up. It won't be ruined."

He was also wearing his best felt boots, with stocking tops and pompons. At the moment, these little refinements seemed shameful and embarrassing.

Auntie came in with the trash pail and frowned reprovingly at their play. But then she started to watch, and Akseli saw the furrows disappear from her brow, to be replaced by a look of pleasure. The sight of her children dancing delighted her.

The boy was finding it increasingly difficult to smile. A small, bitter resentment toward Anna began to rise in his mind. So much for her piety.

The expression on her face showed how obviously proud she was of her daughter. She was probably imagining great things for her.

The thought increased his spite. Otto, too, seemed repellently childish. Did he have nothing better to do than sing for those clowns?

He kept the scornful smile on his face, but his eyes followed the dance with a quite different expression. "Even if she's wearing stocking feet, they look trim and neat on her. She spins gracefully, though she doesn't exactly know how yet." But the main thing was her face. A light inner excitement made her cheeks glow and her eyes sparkle.

Otto ended his song. Oskar spun Elina around, shoved her away by the shoulders and said, "Pity the poor man who has to haul you around. He'll sweat for it. You'll never learn."

"Don't expect so much from her right at the start... She's going to be better than you are."

316

It was Anna, almost indignant, coming to the defense of Elina.

"It's some job. She's like a goat. Whichever way you lead her, she goes the opposite."

Elina straightened her clothing and looked at her skirt, apparently satisfied with her performance. Otto rose and asked for a beer.

"I had to sing my throat dry for those imps. The vicar's wife may carry on about the lot of women, but we fathers have a lot on our hands. First you have the trouble of making the kids, and then you have to feed and clothe them, and then you have to turn musician when they start to dance."

"You learn too, Akseli," said Oskar.

"Huh... no, nothing will come of that."

"Why not? I'll teach you... Take a few turns with the girl."

Even the very thought made Akseli stiffen. He dared not look in Elina's direction. His smile faded, and there was an unexpected manly severity in his voice when he spoke, "Shouldn't we be going to work on the hall? We can dance when the ballroom is ready."

Akseli's stern tone of voice reminded Anna that she had forgotten her usual role and she said in a tone of reprimand, "Spoken like a man... The rest of you fooling around like that... Elina and I have to burn icy wood because no one even sees to that."

The bitterness Akseli had just felt toward her vanished from his mind, and he was enormously pleased by her praise. But Osku seized his mother by the shoulders, glared at her, and said, "Woman, shut your mouth or..."

He put his fingers to her neck and pretended to squeeze.

"Get out of here..." Anna seized a dish-cloth and slapped at him in pretended anger, but broke into a smile. She sensed the covert caress in her son's touch.

Then they were on their way. The Kivivuori men were the first and Akseli the last to go. Auntie was behind the fireplace, and Elina went over to a dim mirror on the wall. The boy had a chance to look at her as he was leaving. She was arranging her hair, which had been tousled in the dance. An oppressive melancholy gripped him. The girl was looking at herself in the mirror and was completely alone in a world of her own, a world full of promise in which there was no place for him.

When they had settled themselves laboriously on the double-decked timber sleds, each one holding on to whatever he could grasp, Akseli set Poku in motion with a jerk of the reins.

"Did you read in the *People's Journal* about the land-rent law? The sons-of-bitches have blocked it... in some committee. Why do they have committees?"

"How did they block it?"

"I don't understand... They just put it last on the program... in the hope it won't be decided this session either. By God, if they vote it down, or play us false with the Czar, there's nothing to do but grab an ax."

To Otto, who was hanging on to the rear of the sled in an awkward position, the rent law did not seem so crucial. He had his hands full staying on the sled, and said disparagingly, "The rent law isn't all that important. If money-rental goes into effect, it changes things. We'll be able to work wherever we want."

"Yes, and there will be so many clauses in it that the landlords will always find a loophole."

They were discussing the land-rent law that was up before the legislature, a law to regulate tenants' conditions and to prohibit arbitrary evictions. It had been hashed over at the previous session of the legislature and left unfinished. The socialists were demanding more than the bourgeoisie would approve, and the controversy dragged on.

There had just been a large meeting of the tenants with Halme as their spokesman. They had been highly angry at the delay, especially since they considered the law itself to be inadequate and unworkable. Today, Akseli was in a worse temper than usual, and the brothers grew tired of his bitter railing.

Other men were already in the woods, and their mood changed when they arrived. Halme was there, although he did nothing. Emma, on the other hand, frequently served the workers coffee and sandwiches. Halme's earnings did little to enrich him, for he put all his liquid assets into the association.

"Maybe you young people will give me a piece of bread when I can no longer work. I have no heirs, so I don't have to heap up money for them."

Halme tapped a timber with his cane and said, "The association is my child. I would die happy in some corner if I could just see it great and flourishing."

Ten years ago Otto would have said loudly enough for everyone to hear what he now said softly to Janne:

"There seems to be more than one way to make a baby. I like the old way better."

Janne's lips stretched into the semblance of a smile. The old man's line didn't

318

seem worth a laugh.

All the rest of the men had to contribute to every imaginable kind of collection, but what they gave was little compared to Halme's donations. It was known that he was even supporting Aliina Laurila. Things had gone badly for Antto. His sentence had been doubled for assaulting a guard, whom he had struck on the head with a metal tray when the man had reprimanded him. The result was another six months. They were all waiting anxiously to see if he could get through the final weeks of his imprisonment honorably.

Halme sometimes tried to help with the logging. If Akseli was lifting a heavy pine log onto the bunks, Halme would rush to his side. "Wait... don't hurry... I'll help a little."

He would thrust his cane under the log and lift so gingerly there was no fear of its breaking. "Just adding my straw to the soup, heh, heh."

Concealing his amusement to avoid hurting Halme, Akseli grunted his approval. He was aware of the tailor's growing fondness for him. It was to be expected, for Akseli's sober pragmatism was pleasing to Halme. When the boy was older, he would sit on the board of directors. He was still too young to be sufficiently respected by the older people.

He was accorded a certain type of esteem, however. He toiled in earnest at the volunteer labor. If a heavy lift was facing them, the boy did not hesitate, but took hold. When they hit a really big log, someone might ask, "Who can lift this by himself?"

Akseli did so willingly. He averted his eyes modestly when one of the older men would say, "There's some of the old-time stuff in that frame."

That was the reason they repeated another remark only behind his back: "How did he manage to sneak enough food from Jussi to get so damned strong?"

During the breaks, he sat with Osku on a tree trunk, and the two of them talked in low voices about Aune Leppänen. Akseli knew that Oskar's walk home with her that winter night had not been the last, but Osku hid his exploits so adroitly that no one could be sure of anything. Even to Akseli he spoke only in laughingly veiled hints, which made the other all the more curious. The hints made Akseli look often at Aune and even awakened some fantasies in him, but he was unable to make even the most cautious approach to the girl. He laughed at Oskar's talk in pretended comprehension, speaking more coarsely himself at such times, to show that he was no novice. "I'm sure you're getting it from

319

her."

"Not really... Just squeezing her a little to pass the time."

Osku's smile revealed that he was lying, which Akseli already knew.

"Don't talk, boy. She must really be something."

Osku characterized Aune with a sharp but obscene comparison, which brought a guffaw from Akseli. But it was somehow repellent that a brother of Elina should say such things, especially one who looked so much like her. He needed only to look at Osku's face to recall hers, and such boorish talk didn't fit that context at all. It seemed nasty and annoying, and Akseli rose from the tree trunk. "Well...Let's get going again."

III

The logs for the workers' hall were ready on the lot, awaiting the springtime and the broadax. Some of the logs were driven to the mill to be sawed into lumber. Others were taken to the planer to be made into shingles. The work fell mainly onto the tenants' shoulders, for the hired hands and boarders did not have the time.

The baron had been heard to say that the rent-work must be too easy, since the men and horses had time for such hauling. They swear and they loaf at rent-work, but when they haul timber to the mill in their straggling caravans, they laugh and they shout, they run from one sleigh to another, they even stop to wrestle in the middle of the road, and then run to catch up with their sleighs.

He said all this to the schoolmaster, whom he happened to meet on the road, and the teacher agreed that the people had completely lost their joy in work. Earlier it had been man's sole honor, but with the constant spread of socialism, it had been stamped as a curse. And the teacher told how he had explained to his pupils the Russian threat of a new era of oppression.

"When I asked them what this meant to the Finnish people, one of the boys answered in all seriousness, 'More rent-work.' To such an extreme have they succeeded in distorting even the children's world view. And there is a real danger. Stolypin is more dangerous than Bobrikoff because he is equally ruthless but smarter."

"Well. That legislative reform... Fruit same as tree. Person sow one wind, he reap one storm. When bow to people, is under their rule. They don't know thanks you. They just get more bold. My program: Don't do good with people, do right."

The teacher caught the innuendo about the Finnish movement's support of legislative reform and began to defend it. "Their success is temporary. The middle-class parties were unable to see the danger and fought among themselves. They should have fought the election battle against the socialists, not against each other. They will correct that mistake in the next election. Furthermore, there is no real danger, because even if the socialists, with the support of some liberals, put through some of their insane demands, they will still need the approval of the Czar-Archduke. And we must admit that many of the measures they demand should be put into effect soon."

"Not one demand. Honorable man live in this country. He not come into need with anything. Only lazy hoboes have need by own fault."

The baron departed, furiously swinging his cane. The land-rental law would go through, and then they would do what they pleased. That shit-landlord of Kylä-Pentti had given them a lot to build on. His old father wouldn't have done it. He had been a real farmer. The baron forgot that the behavior of the "Czar" had always infuriated him. Now, from a distance, he even seemed exemplary. The baron stormed by the Kivivuori place and recalled that its occupant was a director of the workers' association and a slack tenant to boot. The steward complained of his poor maintenance of the place and his mouthing off at work. Now it chanced that Elina was pulling the water-sled with a load of sprigs from the loft on the opposite side of the road. To show her instinctive fear and respect when she saw the baron, she quickly pushed the sled into the snow, and she herself slipped completely off the road. Looking at the ground, not daring to raise her eyes, she curtsied deeply. The old man's irritation softened a little. The pretty young girl's humble curtsy caused him to drop the idea of stopping in and putting hand-irons on the socialist. He nodded, unable to withhold the smile of approval that lighted his eyes.

Elina had saved her father for the time being.

Otto's position was increasingly insecure. It was true that he was a careless tenant and that his outspokenness aroused a spirit of opposition among the workers. But most of all, he was personally infuriating. And when his being a director of the association was added to all that, only a small spark was needed to light the fire.

But if the land-rental law went through, it would be too late to evict him.

And then they dreamed up a celebration for Antto Laurila's return from prison.

Antto had managed to control himself, had avoided further quarrels, and was allowed to return home. They arranged a true homecoming celebration. Halme spoke, and Antto glared at the floor as he listened. Aliina burst into tears, and thirteen-year-old Arvi and twelve-year-old Uuno turned their heads peevishly from their weeping mother. Elma, who was in her eighth year, regarded the people from under her brows with her lively, shrewd, and somewhat brazen eyes.

"...dry your tears, Aliina. It's over now. And you, Antto. Remember that your grievous sufferings are a sacrifice for a brighter future. Welcome to our midst once again. On behalf of the Finnish working class, I welcome you on your return from the road to Golgotha."

They drank the homecoming coffee, and even though they were at Halme's, Antto was soon tipsy. They kept passing the bottle out on the porch and around the corner of the house, despite Halme's coughs and the disapproving glances he threw at the participants when he noticed.

"...goddamn... that hook-nose kept quacking away... it was too much. He treated me like some kind of eyesore. I had a metal tray in my hand, and I thought, even if hell opens up, I'm going to let him have it. I brought that goddamned tray crashing down so hard the hook-nose's knees gave way... 'Prisoner Anton Laurila,' said the warden. 'You are guilty of assaulting a guard.' 'Master Warden, you're right,' I said. 'The worst is bound to happen when you persecute an innocent man...' 'You are uncontrollable and dangerous,' he said. 'Nobody needs to be afraid of me,' I said, 'as long as they act like human beings,' I said. 'You'll be put in chains,' he said. 'Go ahead, goddamn,' I said. So on with the leg-irons, goddamn genuine government shackles... I counted the links. There were eleven. I sat there... I was chained to the wall. They kept me there a month. I thought about the boy, it would be better for him to die. I was there a month... He'll have a whole lifetime... That's how they treat them in the poorhouse too... But when I saw old hook-nose at the grating, I would start to sing, 'Kill the ugly old sheriff of Kauhava, and I'll marry his pretty widow...'"

Antto took Elma up into his lap. Shy of him and perhaps a little afraid, she tried to draw away.

"I missed you... sometimes... I thought of you, little girl, sometimes."

322

Antto's jaw trembled. The drink, the talk, and the homecoming had been too much for him, and he said,

"I thought of father's little girl. But I didn't have... In the evening I would lean against that wall, and I would get so goddamn lonely.... Goddamn, I thought, that girl won't bring her father his boots from the fireplace hook... Don't be afraid... Father is home... go to your mother... I like the little ones... the very little ones..."

Antto wiped his eyes and went back to the story of his experiences. In the end, he had to be led home.

A day or two later, he met Töyry on the road. Spreading his arms, Antto growled, "Now, you brassballs, we're on the common road. Now let's try it... You skull-face... Even beggars aren't evicted from this lot, you know."

The landlord stepped to the side. Not out of fear, for he would have been able to put up a good fight. They were of the same age, and Töyry's sinewy body would have been a match for Antto's shambling strength. But governed by a sense of proprietary dignity, he skirted the road along the woods, walking steadily with his head held high. It would have been a shame to start brawling with Antto on the highway, and since he felt no fear, he did not consider the retreat a loss of honor.

His decision was fortunate in another sense as well, for Antto found compensation in it.

"Goddamn it, when I yelled out, the old man took off so fast his balls dropped off."

Antto's account was soon known to be a lie, for there had been a witness to the incident. But there were no further quarrels.

With the approach of spring, they began to hew the timbers for the workers' hall. Antto was there and talked about how "I said, goddamn..." Gradually, his experiences as a prisoner faded, and he became his old self. He fought with Aliina and thrashed the boys.

Janne Kivivuori was no longer with the working party. He had taken on his first masonry contract on a job near the village. Because of the distance, he stayed overnight, boarding at the Silanders. Silander was trying to drum up a cooperative store for the village and had good hopes of getting one. Actually, it would be only a branch outlet, as there was no possibility of a separate store. And after a short time, rumors went round the village that Silander's daughter's body and

323

soul were now in great danger.

The story was hardly a sensation, for Janne had sported with the girls since the age of sixteen. Gossip had it that he had even fathered a baby born to a girl in a neighboring community.

When they asked Janne at home about his relations with the Silander girl, he pressed the point of his upper lip down on his lower, with the familiar smile that suggested everything and denied everything. There was hope in one quarter that the rumor would prove true. Silander was a respected villager. "He even has some land. And if he gets that store, he's sure to be some kind of manager."

It was Anna who indulged in such calculations. And hadn't Sanni even worked at the Telephone Exchange. She's sort of better than the average person.

Otto made a scurrilous remark and did not probe further into the matter. Damn. He would have to work on the fireplaces at the hall by himself. Osku could do the rent-work for the time being. He would take Akseli Koskela as his hod carrier.

"Where will he find the time?"

"In between the rent-work. Jussi and the younger boys can take care of the work at home."

"What's come over him? He never stops in any more."

"He swings a broadax every free evening. That boy is completely wrapped up in the workers' movement."

"A little too much. There's something about him I don't like. He used to be so quiet and serious, but now he raves about the tenants' cause and his eyes start to burn."

Akseli was indeed hard at work with the broadax. He had to learn how to use it at first, but soon grew accustomed to the work. There were a number of beginners on the job, and Otto had to keep a sharp eye on them to avoid wasting timber. Victor Kivioja had ruined one log. It was narrower on one edge than the other.

"What the hell kind of wedge are you making there?"

Vic looked and took note of the disaster. "Look at that. How did that happen? I was going like hell on the log and wasn't watching. But Vic will pay... It won't be on the association's neck... You pay for what you break."

"Well, it won't go to waste. We can use it on the roof."

New and strange words had begun to appear in Halme's speech. He was reading certain pamphlets and was thought to have joined a sect, but soon everyone

324

calmed down. His socialism did not seem to be affected.

One night Akseli was seated at the Halmes. Work had ceased because of darkness, and he had stopped off on his way home.

Aune Leppänen was sitting there. She had come for Preeti's trousers, which Halme had patched.

Aune had been given a bag of caramels at the opening of the market. Töyry's brother had given them to each first-time customer. Seldom having had any, she gobbled them down greedily, but still she had the generosity to offer some to the others.

Halme was discussing the new ideas he had become acquainted with. "I read a pamphlet by Madame Blavatsky, which I ordered by chance without knowing its contents. I sought out more of the same kind of literature and found in it support for many of my own ideas. Our spirits are really distinct astral beings, which dwell in our physical bodies, but which can separate from them before we actually die. Death, as I view it, is only an incident during which our astral being leaves our bodies."

Akseli listened, frowning. It was all incomprehensible to him, but he felt a profound respect for all wisdom. To him Halme's talk was a higher version of socialism, one he did not understand.

Valenti drummed on the tabletop with his fingertips and said, "True. Spirit is the highest manifestation of life. A poem, for example, can be the attempt of the spirit to free itself from the body's chains."

He rose and paced back and forth with his hands behind his back. Then he stopped, raised his hands, and began.

What public man is he, who looms upon the sands,
Gazing far abroad o'er land and sea?
With menace on his lip and flashing eye he stands,
A fiercely blazing sword grasped in his sturdy hand,
Some warrior-hero he must surely be.

Valenti's head bobbed up and down to the rhythm of the verse, and at the conclusion he brought his hands down in a sweeping arc. Aune's jaws stopped chewing during the recitation, but now began to work again. Halme looked askance at the boy, who had begun to take words from Halme's mouth and to explain things with an air of tolerant superiority.

Akseli sat quietly. He had nothing to say about such matters. Aune listened absent-mindedly, sucking on her caramels and now and then unobtrusively scratching her back against the chair. She had begun to work summers at the manor and was buying clothing for herself. She even had on a coat. It was unbuttoned, and from underneath, a black skirt and a red blouse were visible. The blouse was missing a button, and a piece of her chemise showed through the opening. Akseli could plainly see how filthy it was, for his eyes were eagerly scanning those parts. Oskar's remarks came to his mind, and their tenor was much in line with his present interest.

Having tired of the discussion between her brother and his master, which was growing more and more incomprehensible to her, Aune was getting ready to leave. With a sudden access of confidence, Akseli came to a decision. He would go along with her. Valenti had just said something Halme considered superficial, and the latter said, sighing as if tired of listening to some old familiar thing he had experienced long ago, "Well... Many a wise man before us has reasoned from cause to cause. Such is man. Our dust inhabits this Tellus-Planet, but our astral being strives toward unknown worlds. Uhuh. You're planning to leave. Could you bring the lime from the store, Akseli? Otto plans to get the mortar ready. He says it has to cure for a couple of days."

"Yes, I've already arranged it with him."

"Is that so. Well, thanks again."

Aune left first. Akseli took his broadax from the entry and hurried after the girl, who was walking lazily, waiting for him to catch up, scratching her side under cover of darkness. It had already been itching in the house, but there she had been ashamed to scratch it.

Akseli fell in beside her, and she offered him the last of her candies. He thanked her, trying to get a conversation going, but without success. The road was muddy. The early spring evening was cloudy and dark. The trunks of the trees were dimly visible against the paler sky, which despite the clouds, was illuminated by the glow of a spring moon. The black surface of the road, now bare of snow, wound into the darkness, its course revealed by muddy puddles in the ruts and hollows, which dimly reflected the glow from the sky.

Akseli concentrated on sucking the candy. The silence demanded conversation, but he could think of nothing to say. Soon they would reach the junction where

326

he would have to turn off, unless...

"I would take you all the way home, but I'm afraid Oskar would find out."

"Aah, haa, haa... The way you talk."

Aune had come alive. In the last note of her laughter, ending on an indrawn breath, was an intimation that she had some idea of the boy's intentions and a hint that she approved. She raised her head, and her voice had in it a note of affected refinement and sobriety when she said, "I don't like Oskar. I like a different kind of man."

"What kind?"

"A different kind... Someone more serious... Oskar is sort of wild."

"Come on. You like Osku, all right."

"No. Really and truly. I don't like him at all. I've changed a little too."

Although the rough-hewn Akseli's intuition was none too keen, it dawned on him that the only problem now was one of initiative. The knowledge made him swallow hard.

"If you don't tell Osku, I'll go with you. I even have an ax, so I'm ready for anything."

"Ha, ha... Why would you need an ax? You're such a..."

The girl had forgotten her recent gravity and begun to titter again. The boy stepped nearer and put his hand on her waist. She moved slightly, but let it stay there. The touch made him inhale sharply. He sensed her nearness, her slightly slack body with its smell of stale sweat and dirt. Something within him resisted. It was all strange and unmanly and thus repulsive. This kind of behavior had always shamed him, even as a bystander. But the contact heightened his excitement, and his hand tightened its grip.

"Don't... You're such a thing... tee-hee..."

"What am I... Nothing much."

"Don't talk... Everybody knows you."

They reached the Leppänens' yard. The house was dark.

"I have to go."

"Don't go yet. There's time."

"It's a little cold."

"Let's go into the sauna to get warm."

"It isn't warm... and I don't..."

"Come on now..."

327

Akseli began to tug at the girl, who resisted, squirming. The air in the small, sooty shack was dank and raw, smelling strongly of cold smoke, rotting leaves from bath-whisks, and home-made soap. They sat down on a bench. Through a small window, one pane of which had been stuffed with some kind of sack, a little of the night light shone in. Akseli set his broadax down in the doorway. A silence ensued, which threatened to destroy his initiative. He was at a loss, but Aune began tra-la-la-ing some tune in a low voice.

He found her somewhat loose and wet lips, with the taste of caramel candy still on them. Only at the third kiss did they respond, and then only lazily. And just as lazily came those old words, whispered so many times in so many dark corners, "Keep away from there... That isn't why I came here. You're just terrible."

As he dragged the girl half forcibly down onto the bench, Akseli knew that her resistance was only pretense. He wrestled with her unsteadily and clumsily, afraid the wretched, shaky bench might collapse. This retiring twenty-year-old son of a Puritan family had not the slightest idea of the arrangement of feminine clothing. But in the year 1908, in Finnish country districts, it was a very simple matter. Beneath the skirt and underskirt, there was nothing.

"Don't... so high... it's cold..."

"Put your father's pants under you..."

Afterwards, as they sat on the bench, the girl kept trying to kiss him, much more warmly now. The boy, in turn, responded limply and loosely.

He wanted to leave, but could hardly go so soon. The girl hummed to herself between caresses, and the boy could see her eyes gazing off dreamily through the dark window. It was troublesome and annoying, but he felt forced to respond more actively to her endearments.

"Are you going to the Salmi dance on Saturday."

"I don't know how to dance."

"But come anyway."

"I'm not going there."

"Oh... Not with me... You go to such places with that Kivivuori girlfriend of yours."

The boy started. His words came out haltingly, "I... with her... what are you..."

His thoughts raced. She's noticed... Then everybody knows.

He was mistaken. Aune knew nothing. The name of Elina had come up naturally. She had not only attracted the attention of the boys, but of the girls as well. Pretty and well-mannered, she was developing into a competitor and so had come into Aune's mind without premeditation or implied meaning. But Akseli was uneasy.

"What would I...? She's still a brat."

"No she's not... She's seventeen..."

"'What do I have to do with her?"

"I was just thinking. Since you go over there."

"I just go to see the boys."

"You're all chasing her."

From her tone of voice, Akseli realized that the girl knew nothing and felt a wave of relief. He started to talk about Elina, although the mention of her name was difficult under the circumstances. Then he said, "We won't go to the dance... We'll arrange to meet when we can... I can't say when I'll be free evenings because of the work parties... But I'll let you know when I am."

With this vague promise, he was able to smooth things over. Now he could leave. He took the broadax from the doorway and looked out carefully. No one was there.

"Bye then... See you."

"So long..."

Aune went in. The boy quickened his stride. His scattered, restless thoughts weighed the event. It had been a disappointment. What had been a source of excitement for years was now diffused in the pettiness of reality. On the other hand, he had a sense of satisfaction. An underlying, worrisome feeling of helplessness was gone. But his manhood had been achieved through an unmanly trick, and he was ashamed. Mockingly, his own words came back to him, his clumsy, cooing words. Ugh... My God.

Passing the market, he was able to escape into thoughts of the storekeeper. He's moved from near the station, where he was some kind of agent.

He caught the smell of kerosene in the barrels near the hitching rail. Then the market was left behind, and with it the thoughts it had evoked. His previous musings, no longer as oppressive, returned.

He grunted and shifted the ungodly big broadax to his other shoulder.

The next morning Akseli awoke with an unusually troubled mind. It lasted for some time, until last night's events grew clearer in his mind, explaining the cause of his mood. He rose quickly, trying to think of other things, and hurriedly got ready for work in order to get away from his mother and father. Alma asked casually, "Where were you so late?"

"I stopped at Halme's house."

He was loathe to think of his mother in any connection with the affair. She must not know, under any circumstances. Mother and Aune. From his mother there radiated everything that made him despise what had happened yesterday. As she set the bowl of gruel before him, the boy looked fixedly at the floor. Only when she had turned away, did the boy begin to eat.

He felt as if her eyes had seen everything from some hiding place.

By evening, he was able to smile to himself as he thought about it. His work had gone well. Nor did his mother's eyes any longer seem to know his secrets. At times he paced the floor and even hummed off-key. He was free and happy, taking part with unusual complaisance in the family matters that came up for discussion. In his opinion, they would make it through the spring rush now upon them with extraordinary ease.

"No big deal. There's nothing to it if we push ourselves a little."

By the third evening, he was planning another attempt. The sense of aversion had vanished completely, and he now imagined Aune to be tempting and alluring. Thinking of her, he even laughed arrogantly. He had been childish. He thrust his hands into his pockets, striving for a relaxed pose, and thought, "No danger there. Grass doesn't grow on the highway."

At work on the hall, he gave Mäkelä advice on notching the corners. When the opportunity presented itself — and there were plenty of them at the site — he dropped a few man-of-the-world observations about women. He warned Elias Kankaanpää about having shouted harassing comments at Jussi on the road. The community's display of amusement at his father's blunt eccentricity had always been a sore spot with him, and it was time now to show that while there was room for fun, it had its limits. Jussi had been on his way home from the flour mill, sitting squatted on his sacks. Elias ambled toward him, and after Jussi passed by, he shouted, "Has the doctor ordered Jussi Koskela to sit?"

330

Jussi puzzled over the words for a minute but could find no meaning in them. This much he knew, they must be somehow mocking, and he growled angrily, "Keep your mouth shut, you goddamned crooked face. Just keep walking."

Jussi seldom swore, but the incident irritated him so much that he was still muttering about it at home. "He's such a good-for-nothing ...But what do you expect... Like his father... All he does is lap up booze..."

Akseli sought an opportunity to be alone with Elias. "I'll tell you nicely to stop your shouting. I don't mind joking, see, but leave the old man alone. If you feel like shouting, shout at me. I mean, I can answer you like an equal. Look, he's a sick old man. It's no trick to yell at somebody like that. So if you have something on your mind, tell me about it."

Elias was frightened and tried to explain that he'd meant no harm. Akseli's shoulders were thrown back slightly as he said on leaving, "There is freedom of speech in Finland, but you have to answer for your words. I won't say any more, but if I hear anything like this again, then things will get tough. Don't bear a grudge; the matter is over now."

Later he felt a little ashamed, for Elias was younger and weaker than he was, but at any rate he had spoken "man-to-man" for the first time.

New meetings with Aune were easy to arrange, but the long hours of daylight made them difficult to conceal. Aune would not stoop to obvious efforts at concealment and took offense. "If I'm not good enough to be seen with you by daylight, then let's call it quits."

A word or two would dispel her displeasure, but the boy was nonetheless ashamed of the shifts he was put to for secrecy. Crouching in the willow thicket behind the Leppänens' sauna, and watching Preeti plod through the yard, he shrank with shame.

Then he began to worry about the loose-mouthed girl's dropping careless hints. Sometimes she looked at him meaningfully in the presence of others, and such omens made him feel that the visits must stop.

His conscience began to gnaw at him when the girl sang sentimental songs and talked of love when they were together. Once she even said in a reverent tone of voice, "This is really something... I never thought when we were in school that we would be a pair."

"Mmm... well..."

In such a situation, he worked to turn Aune's mind into other channels until he heard her uninhibited cackle: "...ah, ha... You should have been a musician, with those fingers... Don't... I'm so awfully ticklish... Don't... eek..."

In talking to Osku one day, Akseli learned to his astonishment that the two of them were taking turns with Aune. The disclosure eased his conscience, and he carefully concealed the urge to smile, oblivious of the fact that Oskar, who knew the whole story, was doing the same. Oskar always made him think of Elina, whom he had not seen for a long time, for the work parties had kept him from visiting the Kivivuoris, and Anna would hardly allow her daughter to stand around in the group that had begun to gather in the evenings at the construction site. She had somehow faded from his mind, until one day toward summer when he went to the Kivivuoris' and saw her. That was enough to revive his old interest, no longer wavering and uncertain, but astonishingly strong and more painful. For she was now fully mature, a shapely blond girl whose beauty had once been her mother's. Her neat and careful dress added a touch of refinement to her country beauty. At the same time as his love flared up anew, Akseli began to despair of his own chances. The girl seemed unattainable. She even washed her hands before meals, and they said she had underclothes with lace on them. They had been seen hanging on the clothesline.

Elina spoke to him in a friendly way, but her remarks were plainly indifferent and inadvertent. He felt a rankling jealousy of her joy in life and the happiness that radiated from it. He sat in his old place on the doorway bench and watched her come and go with her pots and dishes, looking as if some secret joy had set her dancing.

It was even difficult to maintain his composure. Having known her for such a long time made it necessary for him to act in an ordinary, everyday sort of way, which was not easy for one in his state of mind. There was so much to be sorted out in his thoughts and imaginings. Aune... All that sank into insignificance. The image of Elina rose and grew in its place. It rose, and soared, and seemed to reach unattainable heights. "Why? She is a human being too. There's nothing so remarkable about her, even if Auntie tries to make her into, to imagine her as some... some..."

But whether or not Elina was an ordinary person, he could not conceive of her as one. The manly experience he had acquired with Aune was of no help to him now. With the aid of the lace underthings, Akseli tried to drag her down, closer to himself. "Lace doesn't make her any better; she's the same underneath

332

as anyone." But coarse thoughts were of no avail; he could see nothing ordinary or ugly in her. Everything about her seemed different from other people. The smile in her blue eyes, the twitch like her father's at the corners of her lips, the shape of her body and the lightness of her step — it was all equally exciting.

He did not go to meet Aune as they had planned. And how common the Koskela place seemed now. Who were they anyway? Out-and-out bumpkins. The Kivivuori place changed its character completely in his mind. It rose to a higher plane than their own.

"Something really should be done to these benches. They haven't been touched except for a little planing on the seats."

"Plane away, if they're not good enough. I haven't gotten any splinters in my rear yet, but the plane is in the storeroom if your hide can't take it."

Jussi was offended, but Alma was pleased when the boy really did get the plane and smooth off the benches.

In the boy's opinion, the main building was deteriorating. "It wouldn't be too much to stain the logs with red ocher, or at least to paint the window-frames white."

"Heh, heh, heh. Let's fix the roof first, and then paint the walls. Decorations are nice to look at, but they don't make a place any better to live in."

"Is that so? Well, paint is for protection as well as for looks. I was just thinking that it's about time to protect the walls before they rot away completely."

"Be thankful there's a roof over your head. I haven't got the money for all that."

When Akseli looked at the boundary fence in the swamp, and saw the parsonage hay field spreading out beyond it, his old anger awoke, stronger than ever. The place had been mutilated by the seizure. Its size was no longer a subject of talk in the community.

"Goddamned preacher. Why the devil did a man like that marry such a fine lady when he can't support her without feeding off others. If he'd found himself an equal, he could have done with less. What's this place worth now? There's one like it on every hillside."

Oskar seemed to be attracting a lot of new friends. One young man after another stopped by to ask for him, and if he wasn't at home, the inquirer seemed in no hurry to seek him further. A budding atmosphere of courtship, obvious, even

333

if clandestine, surrounded Elina. Anna was resentful of it. Like every mother, she had wedded her daughter in her imagination when the first signs of womanhood appeared, and like every mother, she had pictured the groom as someone better than those available. She had no specific complaint, but it seemed downright offensive to have those hired hands' and tenants' sons try to please Elina with their witticisms. Such suitors she regarded with dissatisfaction, almost with anger. When Elina said she would like to go and watch the building of the workers' hall, there was something akin to wonder in her mother's voice.

"Why would you go there? What can you be thinking of? Really. I thought you had a better opinion of yourself."

And so they bought lace-point underthings for the girl, and other stuff of the sort, nor did the envy of the neighborhood wives disturb Anna in the least. Out of malice, Otto sometimes contrasted her religiosity with her pretensions for Elina, but Anna merely sighed, "Well, I haven't found a place in the Bible forbidding a person to be neat."

"No, but there's no passage that commands us to sew lace on the borders of bloomers."

"You might pay more attention to God's word on more important things. Should I let my child slop around any old way?"

Otto too had noticed the more frequent visits of the young men. After one of them had left, Elina, sensing his interest, would glow and sparkle with happiness. Her father would eye her closely, a smile on his face, but there was good-natured mockery in the smile. In the grip of the new-born pleasure, Elina smiled and moved lightly about, but then she noticed her father's smile and stopped her humming. His glance continued to follow her closely, and finally she grew flustered and stormed angrily, "What are you staring at?"

"Well, I guess I have to look at something."

Her father's look and smile told the girl that he had seen right into her soul, and she left the room. For a long time, she remained in the inner room, which had become hers that spring after Janne's departure for the village. Oskar too had slept there, but he was evicted and the room given to Elina. It was even furnished for her.

"Mother is setting a net to catch a big fish for the girl," said Otto.

But when Elina's departure left him sitting alone, a brooding look came into his eyes. The old chatterbox felt pain in his heart. The feeling he experienced

334

was somehow akin to the one he'd had on first discovering the existence of menstrual bindings his mother had hidden.

"Well, she'll lose hers with a bang."

Then he thought about the rumors about Janne's courting of the Silander girl. "That boy is going from bed to bed like the grim reaper with his scythe."

The thoughtful look disappeared from his eyes and was replaced by a pleased, nearly proud smile. Elina entered the room again and left, and the sober expression

reappeared. Scowling, he said to himself:, "Hell, every last bastard doesn't have to come buzzing around here."

But they kept on coming. Akseli too stopped in after a short time. He had contrived a new pose and spoke in the same style as Oskar, but with him it was artless and clumsy. It was particularly offensive to Elina, and she showed her displeasure. Then Akseli turned curt and stiff and would not linger. But he came again, nor could he hide the changed reason for his coming. The others were still unaware of it, but Otto was taking note of his behavior and making astute guesses at the state of affairs. Once they were all standing in the yard as Akseli started for home. The path to the gate made a small loop, but the boy went straight across the yard to the fence, took a few bounding steps to gather speed, placed one hand on the top rail, and vaulted over lightly. It was an overt demonstration, although only Otto understood its purpose. Even on the road, the boy's stride was springy, supple, and strong, as if he were demonstrating the excellence of his body.

At first the thought was distasteful to Otto. He simply knew the boy too well. On the other hand, he had always liked Akseli in his own way, and once used to the idea, he would like to have seen Elina notice the boy's state of mind. But she didn't, because Akseli deliberately concealed it beneath a gruff attitude. Anna was oblivious to it all, being incapable of even imagining such a possibility. Furthermore, Janne was providing them with a new focus of interest. He had not returned home, but had taken another contract near the church village. At about this time, people who went to the church village began bringing news of his close relationship with the Silander girl. When the subject was discussed, Anna would incline her head devoutly and sigh, "Well, if it were only true. That would be one less worry."

Anna's approval was the result of Silander's respectable position. Anna found

335

the girl quite acceptable as a daughter-in-law even though she had seen her only occasionally and then at a distance. But her father was a saddler, he owned his own house, and had an income large enough to merit a vote in township affairs. Silander belonged to that class of alert artisans who first awakened to a social consciousness in the rural areas of Finland. He was a director of the village workers' organization, although socialism to him meant primarily the "cooperative ideal." Anna was no judge of socialism, but Silander had even been a summoner's witness at one time. His daughter had only attended public school, but she had studied independently under her father's tutelage and had learned enough Swedish to qualify for a job at the Telephone Exchange. Anna asked Otto, who knew church village affairs and people better than she did, "Hasn't she even worked at the Central Exchange?"

"I think so. At least she was a clerk in Järvelin's store for a while. She has to be a somebody because she wears a hat."

When Janne visited at home, they questioned him curiously, but he only smiled. The veil of secrecy was lifted very simply one Sunday when Janne and Sanni Silander appeared at the Kivivuoris. They arrived on bicycles, which attracted notice in the community. Janne was on Silander's bicycle, which he had learned to ride.

When they were seen approaching from the window, Anna quickly dusted off a spot or two and ordered Otto to put on his shoes.

"The hell I will."

"You will right now. You're not going to sit there in your bare feet. Hurry up."

Barefoot, Otto greeted the arrivals, the more prosaically for Anna's agitated fluttering.

"Hello, Janne!" she said. "Why didn't you tell us? Sit down. Over here. Please."

Sanni was a little awkward and stiff. She was surprised to learn that Janne had told them nothing about their engagement here at home. The rings were a source of astonishment to the family. Anna's honey-sweet compliance soon dissolved the girl's stiffness. Anna wept a little as she congratulated them. Elina radiated a young girl's sympathy toward lovers.

Whispering and bustling about, they made coffee and planned frying the crêpes. Behind the stove, Anna and Elina conferred about eggs, butter and sugar. Elina had to run to borrow something from Emma Halme.

Otto sat on the bedside, studying his future daughter-in-law, who sensed the scrutiny and was upset by it. The smiling gaze from under those dark brows was difficult for anyone to endure calmly. There was something essentially baring and stripping about it, and to the girl, brought here for display, it was doubly disturbing. Finally he began to question her, and she was able to overcome her embarrassment.

"When is the wedding?"

"As soon as..."

"Uhuh. Well, it happens all the time."

Sanni denied Otto's innuendo, which was not actually true. Janne took no part in the discussion. He sat or moved about, putting in a few words during lulls in the conversation. His fiancée followed his movements with her eyes, which shone with boundless admiration and love. But when she noticed that his collar was awry, her small mouth puckered, and she corrected the fault immediately. At the same instant, a sharp, almost hard, glint appeared in her eyes. Beside the substantial Janne she seemed small. Otto said later that her eyes were the color of swallow-shit. Her brown hair was carefully gathered into a tight knot. Her whole person gave the impression of dryness, and her behavior was purposefully formal. Her position at the Telephone Exchange could be heard in her carefully articulated words.

Otto wondered what had attracted Janne to her and was baffled. It seemed strange that he could stand the starchy formality of her behavior. Janne did smile at some of her worst displays, but he let her go on talking.

"I had to resign my position at the Exchange after Mother's death to take care of the house for Father. I did enjoy the profession. We will take over the ground floor, and Father will move into my apartment."

There were actually two attic rooms in the Silander house which had been hers, but she was pleased to refer to them as an "apartment."

"Father is completely helpless. He would surely starve to death if he were left alone, and we must therefore keep him in our home. He is blind to everything but those social problems. Now he will finally get that cooperative branch in the church village, and it will only add to his worries, for the management of it will surely fall on his shoulders. He says that Janne can share his duties and help him. Janne just has to start studying Swedish. It is indispensable if he is considering broader social spheres of endeavor."

At the end of her speech, Sanni's small mouth tightened a fraction, and her hand checked her knot of hair carefully. Had Otto laughed, it would have been in heartfelt sympathy. The girl's naive sense of self-importance left her utterly defenseless.

They drank the coffee and ate the crêpes. The young couple left, and the family gathered in the yard to see them off and to look at the bicycles. Janne fastened his trouser legs with clothespins to keep them from accidentally catching in the chain. Starting off, he threw his long leg over the saddle. Sanni adjusted her skirt over her knee with one hand. Some of the people had gathered to watch from a respectful distance.

"Kivivuoris' boy came to visit with his fiancée and with a real bicycle. It can't be his own."

Anna was struck blind with admiration for her future daughter-in-law. Otto kept silent about his opinion. Osku defined the paragon in his own terms.

"So that's what you think," said Anna. "At least Janne has gotten some sense, thank God. I'd like to see what you'll bring in."

"She'll at least be a little warmer. Hell, nobody's going to be tugging at my shirt collar. Hello, Mr. Stonemason Kivivuori, how's your coat sitting today?"

"I thank God with all my heart. Many a night I've lain awake, not knowing where each one..."

Anna burst into tears and said, in unintentional parody of Biblical phrasing: "...he has... he has found a bridal bed... the warmth of a hearth..."

"...Hah... In my opinion there's precious little warmth in that girl. In that bridal bed, she'll be killing bedbugs on the wall and talking about Papa's cooperative while Janne is stroking her."

Annoyed by his mother's attitude, Oskar spoke more grossly than he had intended. But it was Elina who was the most angry. She exploded into a nearly unbelievable fit of rage, jerking Oskar by the hair and almost weeping in her fury.

"Always... everything... filthy..."

Oskar had devised a defense against the attacks his sister sometimes launched at him. He needed only to jab his forked fingers toward her breasts to make her give way. He did so now. Elina, loosing her hold and drawing her hands back to shield her breasts, beat a frightened retreat.

"You are so disgusting. I'll tell everybody what you're like... Nobody likes you... Nothing... always... filthy...

Elina was truly angry. She withdrew to her room, still indignant. Her brother's

338

engagement had inspired in her seventeen-year-old heart a dreamy adoration of his fiancée and of the love between the two. And then one of her brothers had proceeded to trample that love into the mire. But as usual, she could not stay angry, especially with Oskar. This time it ended with his sticking his head through the doorway and saying in a saccharine-sweet voice, "Chick, chick, chick, chick, chick..."

Elina reached for something to throw and found a matchbox, which struck the door, for Oskar had already withdrawn his head. Then it appeared again: "Yuk, yuk, yuk..."

She could hear Osku's footsteps going out, and she forgave him, smiling in spite of her anger. Then she recalled the hints she had heard, that Oskar met secretly with Aune Leppänen. They said that Aune...

A look of fright appeared on her face. The thought upset her, but the imaginings that followed upon it were worse. In her solitude, she was overwhelmed by confusion. She was ashamed for Oskar, but instinctively she was also ashamed of the excitement the thoughts kindled in her. Then her imagination shifted to Janne and Sanni. She felt a completely groundless affection for the girl, whom she had known for only a couple of hours, and her brother rose high in her esteem.

The summer Sunday had reached the evening hours. The light took on a soft reddish glow, which cast a veil of delicacy and detachment over the landscape outside the chamber window. Elina's mood responded to the environment. Her fantasies of love disengaged themselves from Janne and Sanni and began to revolve around herself. Her imagination pieced together the picture of a boy whose hair was dark and perhaps a little curly, and whose eyes had in them something grave, but smiling as well. He stood there in front of her but made no move to touch her. She felt a surge of warmth run from deep in her breast through her arms.

A fist banged on the door. "Hey. Go help your mother with the milking and stop lying around."

Elina started, but recognizing Oskar's voice, she sank back into her reverie for a moment. Then, like an automaton, she began to change her clothing, feeling rather than seeing the things she picked up from their usual places. She stepped outdoors and went quietly to the cattle-pen, like a sleepwalker.

Janne and Sanni came often to the Kivivuoris. Sanni was happy to bicycle along the roads with her sweetheart, for her imagination, with the prompting of her love, so heightened Janne's genuine good looks in her eyes that she had good reason to show him off to others. Now that Sanni was aware of Anna's approval, the couple sometimes came on weekday evenings. If Akseli were there, he would feel left out. He was unable to take much part in the conversation, and when he did, his remarks were commonplace and disparaging.

After Sanni and Janne had left, he would say smiling, "So Janne got hooked. I wouldn't have believed it."

Luckily for him, he did not see Elina's expression. It was not just disapproving; there was pure venom in it. The girl was truly in love with love. Often, she took Sanni into her room and questioned her with naive candor: "How did you meet? What did you think then? Did you know immediately that Janne was the man for you?"

The proper Sanni was softened by her frankness, and humored the younger and more inexperienced girl's moods.

"Not immediately. Halme telephoned my father and said that a young man needed a room in the village because he was coming there to do masonry work. At first he talked politics all night with my father. But once he looked into my eyes, and I had a feeling."

Then Sanni began to giggle quite improperly, "But he, hee, hee... Once he hee, hee, hee..."

She put her hand before her pretty little mouth as if to keep from talking. "Hee hee... He took my unmentionables from the clothesline and tried to raise them on the flagpole... hee hee..."

Sanni did not notice the shadow that crossed Elina's face. Nor did she continue the story of the campaign over the unmentionables waged beneath the flagpole, or what had ensued after many evenings of growing intimacy and a vow of marriage.

"Once he took my hand and I knew that it was love."

The shadow disappeared from Elina face. She began to examine Sanni's ring, and in drawing it from her finger, held her hand in a kind of caress. Here in the room she dared to ask, "Speak a little bit of Swedish."

"*Du är en mycket vacker flicka.*"

"What does that mean?"

"That you're a very pretty girl."

Elina's body moved in little jerks of laughter, and she smoothed her skirt. "Ha, ha, ha... Don't talk... And my hair is so terrible..."

340

Akseli was jealous of Sanni. He saw the effect she had on Elina, which he felt was drawing her farther and farther from him. To counter her Sunday daydreaming, he would become more emphatically down-to-earth and would at last succeed in making her angry. Sometimes, she looked at him in loathing and made a scathing remark. He would stiffen and act the roughneck even more. He took an increasingly bitter or disparagingly mocking attitude to things. Because of Janne and Sanni, love was often the subject of discussion, and Akseli willingly sang a refrain in Otto and Oskar's mocking chorus.

He watched as Auntie waited on Janne's fiancée, addressing her with sickening sweetness. An Exchange miss, indeed. And Elina was of the same cloth. "Aren't there any cake recipes to be had? Couldn't we get some new cookie cutters from somewhere? Hah, hah. It's still the same old dough. How in God's name could Janne, a grown man, go so far wrong? But that's the way it is when your brain suddenly stops working."

He had placed all his hopes in politics and the success of the tenants' cause. But in that sphere it was the same old thing, even if the socialists had the eighty representatives.

"Goddamn, life in this country isn't worth living. That solid prop of independence, Jonas Castrén, is battling the tenants' law, and every single other workers' law in the assembly. It would be better to head west. This whole country is such a dung-heap that a grown man can't stand to live in it."

Once he met Aune on the road and went with her. He really hoped they would be seen, but no one happened to come along. At first she was angry about the past, but she soon thawed. She had little chance to show her resentment, all her efforts in that direction being swept aside like so many dried twigs. Her laughter was embarrassed, but she offered only token resistance to his unusual demands, going so far as to undress herself, although she had previously resisted even his efforts to do so. He forced her into strained and humiliating positions, and once she said reluctantly, "I won't... not this way... not used to..."

"...stay there..."

It sounded like a command to a horse. There was something intentional in the boy's coarseness, as if he deliberately and knowingly wanted to be crude. Nor did he pay much attention to Aune as she dressed herself, still embarrassed at the peculiarity of it all. As they parted, he agreed to another meeting, with no intention of being there unless the mood should strike him.

341

A few days later he went to the Kivivuoris, his mind filled with bitterness and scorn for the Telephone Exchange and the Swedish language.

He was left sitting alone with Elina on a stone in the yard. Oskar, who had been the third person present, had left, and the atmosphere immediately became strained. Elina began to talk about Janne and Sanni's wedding, which was to be the opening event at the workers' hall.

"It's nice that it will open with a wedding."

"Yeah. The beginning of a thirty-years'-war."

"It doesn't have to be a war. You're just like Osku. You never think of anything nice. Nothing but indecencies. I don't like you at all."

The boy looked first at the ground and then directly into the girl's eyes. His slightly Mongolian cheeks, burned brown by the sun, hardened. His jaw was clenched, and his bitter words came through tight lips. "Well. I can't do anything about that. I can't turn myself into something extraordinary. Just one of your plain, ordinary men."

Elina's hurt face quivered. His appearance, his direct, harsh, and pained look frightened her. Hurt, she began a hopelessly confused explanation. "I... didn't mean.... like that... but that... You always talk that way... That's all I..."

"Don't bother... Look, no point in trying to be what I'm not."

Now the girl was almost crying. She knew that for some reason Akseli was deeply and severely hurt. She hadn't intended her words to do that. She tried to explain again, but the boy, realizing he too had done something without meaning to, said in an affectedly belittling tone, "Well, what of it... We are what we are. Time to go and see Alma Koskela."

In spite of his behavior, Elina could see that the boy was hurt. She felt bad the whole evening. She would like to have explained things, but the boy stayed away for a week. During that time, the incident came often to her mind, and her contrition made her look with especial favor on Akseli. "He's not like that, even if he does talk that way."

And she decided to be especially friendly from then on.

Nor could the boy stay away. He came again, as if nothing had happened. Elina was quite friendly, and Akseli was consequently more self-controlled. Sometimes he noticed a serious and apologetic expression on the girl's face, and he felt soothed by it. When he left, the girl came out to the yard with him, and looking in slight confusion at the earth, said, "Are you doing the floor there yet?"

"Yes... You can dance then."

"Noo-nobody will ask me..."

The boy vaulted over the fence again, even though the gate was open.

V

Otto was plowing fallow land. It was hot, and his small bay horses were sweating profusely. He himself was in the same condition. A handkerchief was tied around his brow, but even that was too much. His hair was wet and the back of his shirt was soaked.

At the end of the row, he sat down on the plow. On other strips, Mäkelä, Kankaanpää, and other manor workmen were plowing. They too stopped for a break, but it was short-lived. On the road, a horseman could be seen approaching. The men rose to resume their plowing. Only Otto remained sitting. The horseman was the steward. As he drew nearer, Otto took off the handkerchief and began to mop his brow. He drew his hand along it and made as if to cast a handful of sweat to the ground.

Despite his being born a lordly Swede, the steward spoke a little better Finnish than his master. He was one of the men the landlords on Finnish manors had imported from Sweden to try out new agricultural methods.

The steward stopped his horse. Glaring angrily at Otto, he said, "One man is sitting. The other men are plowing."

"They're so far behind they have to work through the breaks."

The steward could see by the strips that it was Otto rather who was behind.

"Get up and start plowing again."

"I have to let the horses catch their breath."

"I said, start plowing."

"And I said to let them breathe a little. It's too hot. They're heaving. The steward's horse is sweating too. The rye will really dry out."

The steward could no longer be deceived. He knew Otto too well. Through the years he had grown to hate this tenant, who was so slippery you could never catch him.

"Which do you want? To go now or to go altogether?"

Otto knew from experience that the situation was critical. He yielded, but

343

he got up slowly and went to straighten the horses' mane and hames, dawdling over the tasks an unnecessarily long time. Taking hold of the plow handles, he pretended to see something wrong with the harnesses and went back to them again. The steward waited impatiently until Otto was finally in motion. He stayed a while at the start of the furrow, then rode after Otto and, drawing alongside him, began to lash the horses with his riding whip.

"Let's see if they'll move. They're all the same. Man and horses. Just as lazy."

Otto looked to one side. His cheek was twitching, but the smile remained on his face.

"Ya-ah. Looks as if they've been reading the *People's Journal* too."

"It's time you stopped shooting off your mouth. Don't you understand what you are?"

"If I didn't, this should have taught me."

"You haven't heard the end of this."

The steward hit the horses a parting shot as stand-ins for Otto and rode off.

A couple of days later, Otto received an order to speak to the baron. He did not want to evict a long-time tenant, whose forebears had occupied Kivivuori for three generations, but that tenant must be humbled. If he refused to bow, then let him go.

Otto did not get to go to the manor. Out walking one day, the baron passed by Kivivuori, and in his impatience, decided to stop in.

They saw him coming and guessed his errand.

"Uhuh. Manu's coming. It's goodbye for us."

"Let him throw us out. But no begging for mercy."

Janne was at home too. Frightened, Anna demanded that they go to greet the baron, but the two men had already reached a decision between them. The issue had really been pretty well resolved in advance. If the baron started a row, they would answer in kind. They would leave the tenancy and begin masonry and construction work as contractors. Unwilling to leave Kivivuori, Anna and Elina opposed the idea. Nor did Otto want to leave, but Janne had been urging him to do so, and he'd had just about enough. "Good day."

"Good day."

Anna and Elina curtsied fearfully, but the Kivivuori men deliberately remained seated as they spoke. Otto had his cap on as well.

"Sit down," said Otto.

344

"You sit... You talk with steward against manor. You poor day-work. Nothing. You know I not hear such talks. I give land and buildings where you are. My cup now boiling over. If no change, one more year there and another man. Decent men and do work, not push others be lazy and do bad with manor work. I warning to you. Know it the last."

Otto hesitated a moment. Anna's frightened eyes looked pleadingly at him, but the decision had been made.

"Master Baron, day-work is mostly contract-work. How fast you do it doesn't matter as long as you finish the contract. As to my talking, would you get that book, boy. Doesn't it say something in it about every Finn's right to free speech?"

Janne located the book quickly, but did not even have time to open it when the Baron went on.

"I not want your books. I want your day-work. And I want you take care of tenancy. Now you care of nothing. You all time do masonry work with other people and workers' hall. You no farmer. Your rye all green. Manor's rye already ripe."

"Well, God knows where it's needed most."

Otto spoke off-handedly and with a straight face, but the boys' smile made the baron sense the provocative nature of the remark. He groped for words, but rage blocked his access to the language, and he instinctively reverted to an attitude that was already going out of style.

"Up in front of me... Up... When I am my feet on. You too. Hat off your head. You are inside... Aren't people manners your manners? Like hooligans. Not good... This not good.. Your face grin. You up. Now summer. One year. Mark up this day, that day next year you away."

Janne had laid his book down and was twirling a match-box in his hands.

"Master Baron, you don't seem to know what a hooligan is. In our circles we've always used the word about people who barge into other men's houses and start yelling."

The baron tried to collect his thoughts, but Oskar was quicker.

"And further. A threshold is a place one never crosses without permission. At least, not in order to start a fight. And the people who live this side of it have always decided what good behavior is."

Both Anna and Elina were weeping. The situation had become worse than they could have imagined. The men, as a matter of fact, had nothing more to

345

lose once they had been ordered to rise, so each one for his part heaped all the fuel he could on the fire. The baron made a heated gesture, but controlled himself and bowed toward the women.

"I ask pardon. Good women. I ask pardon my anger. I forget place."

Then he went, saying from the door, "You who father. You said too much... Too much... More can't be."

He made another deep bow to the women, but did not look at the men.

Otto looked at the boys. Anna and Elina were weeping, their hands over their eyes: "We have to leave our home... Where will we go from here..."

"Stop your moaning. We can surely keep a roof over one family's heads."

The women didn't doubt it, but the thought of leaving their traditional home and way of life so suddenly was a shock. Even Otto's face was rigid, but Oskar said, "If he were younger, we would have thrown him out the window with the frame draped around his neck."

"That's the second time my horses have been whipped. Let it go, to hell with it. We'll build a house in the village and do construction work. We'll have enough to build one when we sell our things."

Thus Otto consoled himself, although leaving Kivivuori was not easy for him. Anna wailed at them between fits of sobbing, accusing father and sons of behaving badly and of not caring about losing their home. Elina went to her room and wept there. For the whole day, an atmosphere of gloom prevailed in the house. Father and sons went about sullen and touchy. By evening, however, they were beginning to be themselves again. Their natural dispositions prevailed, and when Akseli came to visit, he found them playing cards. The first words he heard were Oskar's shout: "Hey, goddamnit old man, you're cheating!"

Akseli's first concern was how far the Kivivuoris intended to move. Then, seeing the signs of weeping on Elina's sorrowful face, he felt a deep tenderness and pity for her. On the girl's account, his temper began to seethe again over the old tenants' question, more strongly than ever. That he was at the same time pleading his own cause was evident. Couldn't Elina see how angry he was for their sake, especially for hers? But it was comic to hear Elina make her first political statement, words that sounded weird on her lips: "Those bourgeoisie are terrible... They beat horses and drive people out of their homes."

It came out so childishly that everyone had to laugh.

But when she burst into an uncontrollable fit of weeping, they stopped laughing.

346

How Akseli yearned to go to her and offer words of sympathy.

Soon, he had the chance. By now she was becoming reconciled to the thought of leaving, but still the tears welled up in her eyes when Akseli said, "You'll still come to see your neighbors after you've gone?"

"Of course... But it's been... This is terrible."

"Don't feel bad... You would have to leave some day anyway."

Elina could feel a solicitude, if not an outright tenderness, beneath his awkward words, and a wave of gratitude flooded her mind. Suddenly the boy seemed thoroughly likable. Her mood, softened by her resort to tears, intensified her gratitude and fellow-feeling. Ashamed of having wept, she smiled, and at that instant, there was something so appealing about her that Akseli made a small gesture toward taking her in his arms. He cut it short, but Elina dimly sensed its meaning. She started and drew back hastily.

For the first time, she saw Akseli in another light. The idea shocked her to the very core. At times she doubted that she had interpreted the gesture rightly; it all seemed so impossible. How could a boy she knew so well be a... be a... a something. But the more she thought about it, the more possible it seemed. She began more and more to see the pleasing traits in Akseli, soon even finding some that weren't there. Her restlessly wandering need to love had found an object and was groping, still uncertainly, toward it.

Her moods were otherwise receptive to the feeling. She needed a counterbalance to her desolation at leaving her home. Because she had known Akseli since childhood, the boy was as familiar and ordinary as could be, but little alterations began to appear in the picture. A certain manly movement of his head, a particular expression, now seemed extraordinarily pleasing.

Harvest days were approaching, and an idea had occurred to Otto. A new foreman had lately arrived at the manor, a young bull of a man. He was hated from the very start, for he made the tenants' lot harder by being himself a hard worker. Cutting the rye was the worst of the jobs, and the tenants' anger took the odd turn of humbling the foreman by besting him at it. Otto was too old to compete, but Akseli had shown himself an exceptional mower at the parsonage. Let the boy try.

Even though he felt the whole thing to be a bit childish, Otto resolved on this last bit of mischief.

Akseli was doubtful. He did not believe himself a match for the man.

347

"You can do it. He's strong, but he's clumsy and simple-minded. We'll fix it so that you'll mow, Elina and Oskar will bind, and I'll stack."

Otto had taken note of Akseli's displays of strength in Elina's presence, where he would cross his arms over his chest to expand his biceps, or make heavy lifts easily with one hand. Otto repeated from time to time, "Elina can come and bind."

"Well, maybe I'll try then, but don't say anything if I lose."

The boy planned his tactics in advance. "I have to tease him at first by hanging back, and when he gets rattled, go all out."

When Akseli appeared in the manor fields on the first day of the rye harvest, the others looked at him wonderingly. "What is the parsonage tenant doing here?" Otto's explanation made them suspect that something was up. "I'm afraid they won't stop at whipping the horses, so I paid the boy to do my share. Then he'll be the one to get whipped. I'll just stay quietly in back and build the shocks."

Elina had begun doing some of Kivivuori's women's day-work at the manor that summer, where the young men paid court to her. Now they looked sourly at Akseli, who was wearing a white shirt with the sleeves rolled up to expose his strong brown arms.

The foreman, who knew that he was the object of hatred, was off to one side sharpening his scythe. The manor crew and the tenants made common cause in their anger on these harvest days, for the work of the foreman determined the day's rigor. The morning sun burned through the haze, promising a hot day. A barrel of beer on large wheels had been driven to the edge of the field. When they left for work that morning, they'd had the traditional drink of hard liquor outside the bunkhouse. In past years, the baron had always been present at the ceremony, but the custom had been abandoned of late. The baron knew that the people were beginning to hate him. Certainly he had been hated by many before this, but now it was programmatic, general, and consensual. Behind it were the strains of the "Marseillaise" and the "Internationale."

The foreman began to parcel out the strips. He took the first and assigned the second to a manor workman, but Otto slipped onto the end of it and said, "Can't give this to him. It's the Kivivuori strip."

"What's the difference? They're all the same."

"Not at all. There's a rock pile here that saves a few strokes."

There actually was a pile of rocks on the strip, but it was of no consequence. The foreman yielded, since it all sounded so much like Otto's typical behavior.

He couldn't start checking on everything.

"Well, take it then."

Akseli stole a glance at the foreman. If he hadn't known every last trick in mowing, he would have given up then and there. The man really did resemble a bull. Only externally, of course. Otherwise he was known to be simple and well-meaning, if not actually childish. He must surely have been upset by the hatred he sensed.

The early hours passed uneventfully. The first swath meant little, and he and Akseli reached the end of it more or less together. They whetted their scythes and drank the beer. Their shirts were already steaming. The back of Akseli's Sunday shirt was wringing wet, a sign that he was well warmed up.

Nervousness about the trial facing him so possessed his mind that he could not freely indulge the mood of happiness caused by Elina's nearness. It was pleasing to think that the girl was at work, helping to pay the rent for the tenancy. It brought her somehow closer to his level.

They started again. Otto looked up at the sky. "It's going to be a hot day. We'll see if I can keep up when that boy really gets down to work. He's like that. He just came over to show us how it's done."

The foreman's chief desire in life was to excel in competition, and he began casting glances at Akseli. Halfway down the swath, he noticed that Akseli was drawing dangerously close and soon was ahead by a stroke. The foreman bore down, and the boy dropped back enough for it to be noticeable. As they drew near the end of the swath, the same thing happened again, and the first signs of tension appeared. The foreman bore down again, but this time Akseli contrarily eased up. He looked absent-mindedly at the horizon, letting the foreman finish first.

"Is that boy so shameless he'll try to beat a grown man?" Otto's tone was one of outright condemnation, and the covert laughter of the crew was like water on hot sauna stones. Oskar did most of the binding, trying to spare Elina, whose hands were stinging and whose back was aching. He stood up and looked around. "Well, who else could compete with him here?"

The rest at the end of this swath was cut short as the foreman hurried to start in again. There was a faint murmur of talk.

"Big Manu is coming..."

Indeed he was. He took a drink of the beer for the sake of custom and then

349

began to watch the mowers. He always felt an urge to grab a scythe himself when he saw how it hissed through the grass, but that time was over for him. He also knew the truth of the old adage: "It's fun to watch, but hell to work."

He likewise knew that the real competition would begin toward the end of the harvest, for everyone was still sparing himself. There was absolute quiet when he was present. Nobody said a word, and only when he was gone did the conversation revive.

"Even Magnus Gabriel was here to take a look."

"Yaa. He came to see if barley beer will pass through his men."

"Taking a peek to see that Finnish agriculture is advancing."

"The trail-blazer has to see to it that his tenants are blazing trails through the rye fields. The future of Finland won't happen if he doesn't keep an eye on it."

Everyone tried to be more spiteful than the last.

It happened that lunch time coincided with their reaching the end of the first strips. Halfway down a swath, Akseli again took the lead. He didn't want to strain yet, but it was tempting to think of going to lunch a winner. The foreman took up the challenge, and although both of them tried to seem outwardly unhurried, the amplitude of their strokes increased and their blades bit more deeply. The rhythm of their movements remained constant. Akseli curbed his nervousness and fell into his best rhythm. They mowed obliquely across the strip to the end and walked back to begin another swath, with no apparent sign of haste. Sometimes they stopped to gaze around a bit, but once into a swath, they speeded up again. The foreman was clearly falling behind, and at the end of his strip, there was a badly matted and tangled patch of grain, which retarded his mowing, but did not quite account for the ground he had lost. Akseli finished first and stood wiping his brow.

"Well, you're through already. I didn't notice because those others are so far behind." Otto pretended to have noticed only then that Akseli had come to the end of the strip. Now the crew began to understand why the parsonage tenant was here, and looked slyly at the foreman. He was still not badly upset, for one strip did not decide the contest, and in addition, he had the matted grain to serve as some sort of excuse. There was still a long way to go; only the day after tomorrow would show who would endure.

But the competition had been brought out into the open by this means. No one could have any doubt about it, and the sympathies of those embittered sneerers were on Akseli's side.

350

Many of the manor crew went home for lunch, but the tenants had brought their food with them. Those whose strips were unfinished tried to catch up during the lunch hour, for all had to mow the same number of strips no matter how long it took. If the strips differed in length, that too was taken into account. Here they were regular, and the division was clear. The last of the tenants' strips to be finished was the Kankaanpääs' and that too was a familiar story.

Akseli was on "house rations" and so ate with the Kivivuoris. It was pleasant to take his lunch from Elina's hand, but difficult to eat it. He was ravenous, but could not bring himself to wolf down the food in her presence. Something which emanated from her demanded that he control himself. He bit off a piece with his front teeth, not a big one, and chewed on it, being careful not to smack his lips or to make gulping noises when he swallowed. Otto's everyday coarseness was totally offensive to him. Otto went so far as to take up the subject of eating.

"Don't eat your belly full... You might even break for little snacks. And don't drink much of that beer, even if you're thirsty. You lose your strength when you sweat."

"Eat your belly full." How could one even think of such a word as "belly" now.

Since the time that Akseli had noticed the girl looking at him with warmth and approval, his pretense of coarseness had vanished completely. Now even harmless profanity seemed too much in her presence. Had he been able to analyze his own state of mind, he would have found it different from before. His mind was thoroughly cleansed, and he experienced states of feeling he would earlier have considered shameful and childish. To experience them, he needed no more than to meet her eyes and see in them the slightest spark of approval. Of late, he had seen it often. His altered behavior had changed hers as well. From time to time, she remembered his hurt expression on that day, and then she was always especially friendly to him. Unwittingly, she thought of the day often. And sometimes she felt outright tenderness when she saw his clumsy attempts at refinement and realized that they were all for her sake.

In the morning, Akseli was startled to see Aune Leppänen appear in the grain field. She was with the manor crew, however, and no embarrassing situation developed. But when she returned from lunch a little early and joined their group, it looked like trouble. Luckily, Oskar started to talk to the girl, and Akseli stepped back to sharpen his scythe.

As he rubbed the whetstone back and forth, he decided that he must break off with Aune once and for all. A slight fear began to weigh on his mind: what if Elina were to find out.

Elina soon drew away from the others. She could not stand her brother's prattle, with its open references to things she had heard hinted at. In her company, Aune tried to act with a refined sobriety, but Oskar's stories soon reduced her to her old cackling. She wore her Sunday best to work, or to put it another way, her work clothes on Sunday, for as soon as she got her hands on a garment, she wore it. She always had on her best.

Elina stood alone for a while, then walked over to Akseli.

"Is it sharp now?"

"Like a razor."

"Are you planning to beat the foreman?"

"If I can."

"I think it's completely crazy. Why is everybody sneering at him?"

"Because he's so dim-witted. He tries to please Manu by working the tenants so hard they spit blood before they're through."

"But you're only making it worse."

"Yaa... But you don't understand...We sweat a little more blood, but we cut that devil's throat at the same time."

"I think the foreman is nice..."

"He may be... But he's Manu's catspaw and has to be crushed, whether he's nice or not."

"But the baron hasn't done anything to you."

"Not to me... But he has to you."

The words slipped out almost without his noticing, and he began quickly to change the subject.

It was too late. The tone of his voice had an extraordinary effect on the girl in her impressionable frame of mind. Trying to cover her confusion, she said, laughing, "Are you mowing for me?"

"For you."

Elina went to her father's side. Akseli was left alone. For the first time he felt as if something momentous lay ahead of him.

Good God. It started at once. Akseli took the lead on his strip, but he soon realized that the question was no longer one of speed, but of endurance. He could

352

take the lead whenever he pleased, but what would it be like tomorrow and the next day?

The third day was half over. The atmosphere was tense. If the foreman were to retain his honor, he had to win all of the remaining strips. He had already lost so many that that alone could save him. They had mowed three strips in the morning, and Akseli had won on two of them. He had lost the third, but it had been a convoluted and difficult one. The foreman had gotten poor strips as well, but not enough of them to mask his defeat.

The baron came to the field from time to time. They were always silent in his presence, but when he was gone, they burst into malicious chatter at the foreman's expense. For that reason, the struggle was not exactly a fair one. Akseli had the moral support of the group, besides which the foreman saw that the baron was following Akseli's mowing more and more.

The baron was standing right on the Kivivuori strip. He would not deign to look at the family, but spoke to Akseli, "You mow parsonage too?"

"Yaah."

The baron nodded approvingly. Then he looked at the foreman and frowned. The manor was losing.

They were mowing the last strip. The others had been left behind, some by as much as an entire strip, even though they had worked by moonlight. Akseli's senses were buzzing from weakness. Sometimes his ears rang and he felt as if his surroundings were completely unreal. He had to come in first on this last strip, otherwise the victory would be an inconclusive one. But at times he felt as if he would stop on the spot. His arms and shoulders were afire. After three days of turning with the swing of the scythe, his hips almost creaked.

In those three days he had lost so much weight that it showed in his face. There were black circles under his eyes and the corners of his mouth were stretched tight. Even Elina's smile could not cause them to relax.

As late as that morning, it had been pleasant to hear Oskar talking behind him. "Mowers are in a class by themselves; the rest are men's shadows... You see all kinds of European windbags hanging on to a scythe handle, but that doesn't prove anything..."

Otto had driven Akseli on for these three days. If the foreman seemed to be gaining too big a lead, his voice could be heard. "I wouldn't have believed the boy had it in him... Hey girls, I'll be his matchmaker..."

"You've got a girl to marry off yourself..."

"No match... No match... But I would send her off with a slap on the rear if he would have her."

And Akseli increased the tempo.

But now even Otto's praise seemed offensive. He shut out all distractions from his consciousness. A full half-strip remained, and the foreman was behind, but Akseli was on his last legs. He had to exert all his willpower to control his movements and maintain a good rhythm. He knew that defeat for the foreman was the result of panic. The bull had not nearly exhausted his strength but did not know how to use it. The binders were even beginning to complain that he was cutting a poor swath in his flailing around.

And in spite of the baron's presence on the field to witness the end of the battle, the crew had begun to throw out sly innuendoes. They irritated Akseli; he could no longer be prodded by them. It didn't even matter whether Elina was behind him or not. Eyes stinging with sweat, he stared ahead. The hissing blade cutting through the straw shone as a complete blur before his eyes. He could no longer see clearly. His numbed and buzzing consciousness repeated constantly: "Have to win this strip... mustn't push too hard... Mustn't panic..."

Soon it was clear to everyone that unless the boy quit completely, he would win this last strip as well. The remarks now grew louder and more clearly suggestive, and the baron too became aware of the crew's attitude.

"Marttila... Now manor honor... Parsonage boy ahead. Too many strips his... You this last row."

But the foreman had fought his fight. The crew's antipathy had robbed him of the relaxed and loose approach which is the first prerequisite for victory. He answered the baron's words in an almost quavering mumble, "I... wasn't competing... trying to do my work..."

The baron felt no pity for the stricken man. His exasperation was made complete by the knowledge that behind it all was that cashiered tenant, who was setting up shocks with an artless smile on his face. Contemptuously, he turned his back on the foreman.

" Not good."

The crew was no more considerate than the baron. Kankaanpää was just completing a strip, but for him as for the others who had been left behind, there

354

were additional strips waiting along the border of the field. Elias was taking turns mowing with his father, and he now rushed to complete the strip as if he were the first to finish. Then, in the midst of it all, he ran to get a drink of beer, taking his scythe with him and whetting it as he went. Returning, he continued running and whetting the scythe, but in addition he opened his fly and began to pass water, regardless of the women.

"Things are really getting tough... That Akseli is going to win if we don't hurry up."

The baron's back was to him, but the crew's tittering caused him to turn. By this time, Elias had closed his buttons, but the laughter and the evasive glances made the baron suspicious. Elias continued to run and whet his scythe. Reaching his strip, he began wildly to mow. "That foreman doesn't worry me, but Akseli is catching up."

The baron's eyes were rolling. "What, what... What the boy doing?"

Those nearest him pressed on with their work, and the baron, damning them all, let the matter drop. Akseli took his last strokes and stood leaning on his scythe. He wanted to throw himself on the ground, but had to act casual. The baron walked up to him.

"Good boy... Gawddamn good boy. I want good men. You leave parsonage and come be my man. I place for you."

From his dull and sluggish eyes, Akseli looked at the baron. By rights, he should have let him have a piece of his mind, but he was unable to, and said wearily, "I can't move... There's no one else to do the rent-work."

"You only? No father, no brothers?"

"I have, but my father is sick and my brothers are too young."

"If you one time want, you by me... For you, always place open."

The foreman was finishing his strip and listening to the exchange. He had done all he could for his landlord, but did not rate even a glance.

Otto put up the final shock of rye and said, as if to himself, "He's quite a boy... He hasn't read the *People's Journal* and he's not spoiled yet. The others have even taught their horses to read up on socialism."

"You there — What you say?"

"Just talking to myself."

"You bad-mouth. You every word something nasty. You go from work. No more come."

355

"Not even for rent-work?"

"No. You this year with no rent, until year's notice full. No rent-work. I no want you at work. And nobody from your family. That my word. Go away."

"The master will remember what's been said then. You've all heard it. I live on the tenancy for a year without rent. If you change your mind, I'll do the rent-work from then on, but no make-up work."

"My word no need witness. This boy good boy, you shit. Go away."

But the baron left first. When he was at a distance, the others all began to chatter, sharing in Otto's glory. Not many men had spoken to the baron like that. And the foreman was again bespattered with words. He picked up his shirt from a thicket and muttered, "I can get a roof over my head... I don't need... I can get a place if I want... I have enough... A roof... over my head."

But the slaves to work's oppression went on mocking. Exhausted, completely spent, finishing the last strokes of their allotted work with nerveless hands, but enjoying their revenge with the last bit of energy in their exhausted souls. "Finland's gentry" had profited again, but had also been struck a blow. Under the mustaches dripping with beer and sweat grinned a pair of scornful lips.

The victor drank his beer, holding the dipper in both hands. Now that the effort had ceased, weariness began to weigh him down with its full force. His hands shook nervelessly and his legs balked at raising his body from its kneeling position.

They were silent on their way home. To Otto, the episode already seemed childish and he no longer wanted to dwell on it. Osku was worn out, for he had had to do most of Elina's work. As for her, she dragged along dully. They approached the turnoff where they would part, and Akseli waited for even a little glance from Elina. She did look at him, but her face was a total blank. The indifference of complete exhaustion showed in her eyes, and at that moment she looked ordinary and commonplace to Akseli. She was not as pretty as before: the lively expressiveness was gone from her face and eyes. Weariness had killed it.

In parting, Otto said, "We'll settle up later. You'll get your share." Oskar said nothing, and Elina departed in silence.

But Akseli did not have in his soul enough energy to be depressed. Scythe on his shoulder, he inched toward home. At the "Beggar's Spruce," he was forced to sit down. Then he turned onto his side and with circles of different colors dancing before his eyes, he threw up the barley beer.

CHAPTER TEN

I

T he whole community was in a ferment. There were trips to be made to the city, and clothing was being readied. A big wedding was in the offing. The workers' hall had been completed, and Janne Kivivuori was to be married there to the Silander girl.

An argument was going on at the Koskelas. Jussi would not agree to having a suit made, although Akseli had forced him to get a hat.

"You're not going in that old top hat. If you do, I'm staying home."

Lately, Akseli had begun to take marked care of his appearance. He bathed regularly and shaved often. Once or twice, Alma was confounded when he helped her with the cleaning. His younger brothers were frequent targets of comments about their slovenliness. "And couldn't we have rugs woven for the main room floor?"

His mother got a new dress for the wedding, but the boy's efforts were wasted on his father. Say what he would, the crotchety, fuming old man stubbornly held his own. Whether Akseli suggested, demanded, or ordered, the response was mumbled mockery or sarcasm: "Orders, orders. Save your breath and pretty up yourself."

There was another argument about the wedding gift. Alma had fine linen ready to be made into the kind of sheets that were kept in drawers and never used at the Koskelas, but the boys considered them unsuitable as a gift. They had their way, and a sparkling smoked-glass vase was purchased in the city. Its low cost was something of a surprise. The price-tag, of course, had to be destroyed.

After the mowing competition, Akseli had gone to the Kivivuoris. He had

357

been paid there, after first refusing, but he received not a word of praise. Elina did not value his efforts at all, but rather pitied the foreman and expressed sympathy for him. But otherwise Akseli received an abundance of pretty smiles and kind words.

For many days, wedding preparations had been under way at the workers' hall and at the Kivivuoris. Emma Halme was the chief cook, and Anna did her best to help out. Contrary to custom, and mainly for practical reasons, the bridegroom's family was running the wedding. It was to be the opening event at the workers' hall.

"They are both children of trustees of the workers' association," said Halme.

Akseli came to the hall a little apart from his father and mother and his two brothers. Although he could not admit it even to himself, he was ashamed of his father.

The log walls of the new building were unpainted. The surroundings had been cleaned up, but everything still seemed raw. Nevertheless, the first tops from cigarette packs gleamed among the tussocks. However, there were still no empty bottles, no candy wrappers, no rain-faded women's garters, and no strange paper wrappers, with the picture of a nude woman and a few words printed in French on them. Later on that kind of rubbish would indeed appear around the dreadful-looking fire halls, youth-club halls, workers' halls, and community halls that the idealistic, organizing Finns had erected across the length and breadth of their land by means of volunteer labor to mark their journey.

Akseli mingled with the crowd without trying in any way to get close to the Kivivuoris. He saw Osku bustling around, carrying a woman's coat over his arm. Osku was forced to keep company with the Silander relatives, and so he was unable to spend his time chatting with Akseli.

Then there were whispers: "The vicar is coming...let him through."

The vicar passed through the crowd, nodding to right and to left. His smile was friendly but awkward. He clearly understood the political overtones of the wedding. It had fallen upon him to perform the first ceremony at the workers' hall, and he was troubled by the thought that he had been chosen with some purpose in mind. On the other hand, he took a slightly malicious pleasure in the thought that even here, they found it necessary to begin with God's word. With exceptional courtesy, Otto and Anna led him to a seat in the rear. In a situation like this, even Otto showed himself capable of polite behavior.

The musicians, an accordionist and a fiddler, were getting themselves ready when a whispering began: "They're coming... get away from the door... hey, move aside..."

The couple appeared in the doorway, and the musicians began to play. Many of Janne's friends were curious to see his expression. What would he look like? But there was no faulting his behavior. His face was serious, and he looked straight ahead, leading Sanni, who leaned on his arm and blushed in confusion as she walked forward. Bathed, shaved, dressed in a new suit, Janne looked especially handsome, and many of the women whispered as the wedding took place that she was not as good-looking as he was.

"He's such a good-looking boy, but he's so devious."

The ceremony followed. The vicar stood, book in hand, making slight throat-clearing noises before he began. Before the face of God and in the presence of these witnesses, Janne was then asked if he wished to take this woman, Alexandra Mathilda Silander, as his wife. "I do," Janne answered, and his father thought to himself: "For once in his life, he had to give a straight answer."

Anna looked on with a pious expression. Then, little by little, her face began to twitch, and she had to resort to a handkerchief. Her mother's weeping caused Elina to weep too, but she did not dry her tears.

The entire time, Akseli watched Elina and not the wedding couple. Once again she seemed distant and unattainable. There she stood, among the Silander people.

The vicar then delivered a speech. They were a loving couple, who were to establish their future on a rock of mutual love and honor. Some of the boys' mouths went slightly askew. They could not forget Janne in his usual mode. But he himself stood there like a candlestick, his mind probably as impassive as his face.

The vicar congratulated the pair, and the others followed suit. Silander patted his daughter's cheek and shook Janne's hand, saying a little ceremoniously, "I wish you happiness. You have taken my only child, but I give her to you willingly."

The man of ideals had waxed poetic.

Because of her tears, Anna could say nothing. She hugged her daughter-in-law, a form of behavior not completely unknown but highly unusual among country people. But when it came to her son, a hug would have been too much, and

359

difficult as well because of their difference in height. In his case, Anna contented herself with a handshake, after which she drew back, dried her tears, whispered something to Elina, then gazed blinking at the edge of the roof, her expression changing suddenly to one of commonplace sobriety.

What Otto said by way of congratulations no one could hear, but the bride's face spoke volumes, and people wished they could have heard.

After Osku, it was Elina's turn. A few strange young men, Silander's relatives most likely, were standing near Akseli. He could hear one of them click his tongue against his palate and say, "Oh my... If I could get that one into a bottle alive."

"I'll hit her up as soon as the dancing starts."

"She's really pretty."

Akseli drew back. He was dejected, for the boys had a church-village air about them.

In turn he went to offer his congratulations, casually, his face devoid of expression. Then he withdrew by himself, back into the crowd. Even his father went forward, making a half-successful effort to smile, nodding over and over again as he shook hands.

The boy turned his head away.

When everyone had wished the young couple good luck, Halme stepped up to them.

"Sanni and Janne. Before we avail ourselves of the refreshments provided by the women, which we all know, always lower a person's spiritual level, I would like, as a friend and a kind of civic uncle, to say a few words to you.

"The bare, moss-chinked walls of this building surround us here. The marks of the ax can still be seen on its timbers. But with what love, with what enthusiasm, with what pure idealism were those axes wielded. Yes indeed. Sanni and Janne. Until this moment this was merely a building, but now it is something more. It has been initiated into use by this first function, and even a person as old as I am can find pleasure in the fact that this first function was a wedding. A wedding is a union. Eternal and inseparable, and as such, most highly suitable to this building, which is and will be the symbol of the union of all of us. Indeed, Sanni and Janne, I have just referred to the blows of the ax. When you begin to build your life together, do it with the same love and purity of mind with which this building was erected.

"Remember that marriage is a union not only of the dust of the earth, but

360

a union in the highest realm of the spirit as well. Your auras have come together, and on that level, your astral beings were joined before your earthly thoughts knew anything about it."

"Here comes the higher socialism," someone whispered in the background, and another hissed impatiently: "There go his few words... damn... he's just getting his second wind..."

"Sanni and Janne. The workers' hall is the proper place for your wedding. Socialism is, so to speak, another witness at your wedding. Without it, I might not have asked my friend Kalle if he could give you, Janne, a place to stay. I am sure that the worldview you share has helped your auras to meet. But remember that an ideal is beset by many dangers. Defilement always threatens its pure and bright aura. We are bound to live on this Tellus planet, but we are nonetheless bound to a better and cleaner life by means of the spirit. Man's road is a long one, and there is still much of the meat-eater in us, but little by little, the pure ideal of socialism will refine us to that perfect form, of which great seers have had momentary glimpses.

"Sanni and Janne. Life's rose garden awaits you with its flowers and its thorns. Go now then. Lead the new generation to the place we dream of, but have not been privileged to see."

Janne bowed, and Sanni curtsied prettily. Halme returned to his place on the rear bench, cleared his throat of excess ceremonialism, and said in the same breath, "Well now, it must be the women's turn."

Then he twisted his neck to ease his tight collar and turned to Silander, who was sitting beside him. "So... and as for the cooperative ideal..."

The vicar was served coffee. Approaching Halme, he praised the fine speech, and Halme laughed to show that he took the praise to be a form of courtesy. The married couple were now facing the most severe trial of the day: they had to sit like statues at one end of the hall with everyone staring at them while the servers came and went, red-cheeked and whispering, that typical whispering, without which no affair of any kind can take place.

Then the punch and snack trays were passed around. Elina carried one of them, and Akseli could see the church-village boys he had just observed rushing to be served from her tray.

"Thank you, miss. Me first... Don't serve him. He's a little silly..."

"Ooh my... Could I have that heart? I mean the one on the tray... I don't dare hope for more than that."

"Didn't you notice me, miss? Those two are taking from everybody. They're going to carry things home in their pockets."

Akseli tossed his head back. "Now they're calling her 'miss'..."

But the worst of all was to see the sparkling smile that Elina turned in the boys' direction. Akseli was unaware that she turned the same smile on everyone of that age. For the older people, her smile was more restrained and more respectful.

Akseli avoided Elina and took his drink from Emma Halme.

The coffee tables were arranged along the wall. Father Jussi was seen to indulge, since it was free. Otherwise, he sat gruff and alone, his whole being proclaiming to the world that he had no cause to be here.

The musicians sounded their first strains for the dancing.

After a few preliminary trills, the wedding waltz began. Janne rose, took Sanni's arm, and they were off. The swift tempo of the old-fashioned waltz set the wedding pair to spinning furiously, their extended hand pumping the rhythm in the customary way.

The first of the young men to have drunk too much tapped the floor with his toe and hummed to himself, "I know a blue-eyed beauty, rose-cheeked, with lips of red..."

The wedding waltz was succeeded by the family waltz, in which Osku danced with the bride, and some cousin of Sanni's with Elina. Osku was considered a good dancer, for he sometimes added a few extra spins to the waltz, or made the turns so wide that the couple really flew. He did not hold his arm straight out as the others did, but bent his elbow at a neat angle, holding the girl's hand close to his ear.

Elina was a little unsure of her dancing, especially as she was exposed to the gaze of the entire wedding crowd. Confused, and flushed with joy, she tried to follow her partner, who, having observed Osku's special talents, put into play his complete church-villager's routine.

Then the din of public dancing began. The wedding disintegrated into a unique and noisy mixture of music, the buzz of talk, the clatter of dishes, and the tumult of coming and going.

As proper etiquette demanded, the parson had left before the dancing began. Before his departure, he had exchanged a few words with the men of substance

362

seated on the rear bench, men like Halme and Silander. They had spoken of the workers' hall, and the vicar expressed his appreciation of Halme's plans for holding socials there. Nodding, he kept on repeating:

"Good recreation... just so... good recreation."

Yet the discussion was stiff and inhibited. Gone were the days of the fire-department ideal. They no longer looked each other freely in the eye as they spoke of such things, and both sides were well aware that they spoke only for the sake of conversation. Their friendly and courteous tone was only a concession to the occasion and to the demands of propriety.

After the vicar had left, bystanders could hear a heated discussion from the rear benches:

"...what the hell good is it when the Senate is in their hands. And as soon as there is a crisis, the legislature will be disbanded... Yes, that's right. Well, at least we get to talk about things, if nothing else... But when you think that the ministry of industry and commerce is prepared to take the question of working hours all the way to St. Petersburg. When he was here, Hellberg said they were planning to do it, that they're absolutely shameless. They talk about 'the fatherland,' but when it comes to putting down the workers' demands, the Czar and the Russians are fine with them... The worst part of it is that the voters will get tired when they lose faith in Parliament... They're trying all their tricks... but if it's made retroactive, even Otto won't have to go, the old evictions will be invalid. Paasikivi's proposals too... but that Jonas Castrén is a real devil. And the Swedish landlords, of course, but there's no point in expecting anything else from them... It's the same with municipal laws. They will be killed in the Senate... they keep up a whispering campaign. Yaah. Let's have a snack now so that the women won't start to worry, since they've gone to the trouble of making them."

The discussion among the men of substance grew increasingly animated, for they kept stepping outside in groups of two or three from time to time. Both because he was a visitor and because of his position, Silander was a central figure among them. The church-village workers' association was considered more prestigious than that of Pentti's Corners, and he was its chairman while Hellberg was off attending to his legislative duties.

From time to time they would gaze at the dancers and comment on "youth" and "people of that age." Valenti Leppänen sat with the group, taking part in the discussion whenever he was permitted to do so. Silander said to him in passing, "Doesn't the secretary intend to dance? The others of your age are all out there."

Laughing, Valenti refused. He did not dance, nor did he seem interested in girls. He did not avoid them, but his relationship with them was somehow sexless. In addition, he was in a subdued state of mind this evening, for the *People's Journal* had rejected a poem he had submitted.

Aune, however, was kept busy dancing. The drunks, especially, were her constant partners, for even strangers sensed the promising, half-indifferent looseness in her. Henna was pleased with her popularity. She kept whispering enthusiastically to the women nearby, "They're dancing with my girl... she has on her new blouse... she's so popular... so popular... look, look, look..."

Akseli stood idly in the doorway. One of his acquaintances would make a commonplace remark, to which he would give an equally commonplace answer. For the first time in his life, he regretted not having learned to dance. He could see that Elina was as if intoxicated with the bustle of the wedding and the dancing, and although he tried at first to be indifferent to the fact, he did not succeed for long. When Elina was free of her serving chores, she was engaged for every dance. Her new relatives from the church village treated her as their private property, and if a boy from the neighborhood managed a rare turn with her, it was by accident. Having recovered from her paralyzing shyness, Elina enjoyed the attention she was attracting. She was no queen of the ball, that place being pre-empted by a niece of Silander's from Tampere, an elegant city girl, whom only a few acquaintances had the courage to approach, along with Osku, who was quick to strike up an acquaintance. But the girl from Tampere was no longer seventeen, nor sweetly enthusiastic, nor did she laugh gratefully at every facetious remark. Elina was, and did just that. She did not have time even to wonder if it was right and proper that some of her partners smelled of liquor. Only when one of them pawed her buttocks in an odd way and asked her to go for a walk did she reject the suggestion in a fright. The boy passed the matter off in a natural way, and the succeeding dancer dispelled the last trace of the incident from her memory. Once she saw Akseli's face in the surrounding crowd, and a troubled look crossed her own. Her mood was confused for a minute, but she soon returned to her earlier state.

Akseli went outside. He was angry at himself over the state of mind he was in, angry at being jealous of the tide of enthusiasm that had swept Elina away from him. From him? Had she ever been his? Hadn't he leaped to a completely wrong conclusion because of a few friendly words? What did they mean? Nothing at all. Didn't Elina laugh in an even more friendly way with her dance partners? And dance all too close to them?

The boy thrust his hands into his pockets and thought to himself, "Well, what of it. Who wouldn't drive such a nice filly?"

He walked alone in the yard until Osku came out. "Where have you been?"

"Oh, I've been inside, all right."

"Come to the outhouse."

Oskar had offered him drinks on other occasions, but he had never experienced real intoxication. He took a couple of drinks now. He really felt like drinking, but he was restrained by the presence of his mother and father. After Osku, Elias Kankaanpää was the next to invite him, and the invitations did not stop there. Others came to contribute to his rising glow.

"Have a drink, goddamnit, Koskela. You're a real man through and through. I knew when you turned it on that the foreman had had it. You did what goddamn well had to be done... I've always got a drink for a man like you... I couldn't... Even though I've cut a few grain-stalks myself... Have another... Look, summer is short in Finland. Isn't it goddamn nice out under the blue sky... Goddamn moon is rising... Have another. No, I'm going, there's a helluva good-looking piece of skin in there."

His profferer would hitch up his trousers, set his face in the proper expression for entry, and go whistling off to the building.

The liquor went quickly to his head. Akseli walked into the woods. He could hear voices from here and there. The drunks traveled in small groups to their bottles hidden in the woods and forgot themselves there, talking to one another.

"Goddamn it, boys. I never thought for a minute that he would get away with it. One of these days, old man Töyry will have to measure out a piece of land for me again. Antto is the kind of man to show what hole the chicken pisses through if he doesn't get satisfaction."

"Listen, Laurila... Don't worry. You can be sure that there'll be a showdown one of these days. Listen, by God, the Finnish worker won't be put off with words forever. We're slaves by fate, but not by nature, and one of these days the masters of Finland will find that out. Aatu Halme has stopped eating meat, but as smart a man as he is, nibbling on twigs won't bring about a socialist state... That's just the way it is."

They shouted to Akseli to join the group. He did so, and was greeted with an extraordinarily noisy and friendly reception. The humiliation of the foreman had suddenly made him a favorite.

"Aksu is one of us. And the best kind of man, goddamn. Here's my hand Akseli. And you can bet it's a friend's hand."

Akseli had to shake a number of hands and take a number of drinks. But the company did not suit him for long. He started to walk along a trail through the woods. A pair of girls who were strangers came toward him, giving him that furtive, inquiring look to see what was on his mind.

"Why are you running around pissing in the woods?" That's what was on his mind.

"Some mighty big talkers around here."

He could hear the words in back of him, accompanied by affectedly mocking laughter. He started back for the building, and with an attitude caught from the group he had been with most recently, he thought, "The dancing shoes are really flying now. Let 'em fly... But they'd stop soon enough if I told them *stoi*."

By the time he reached the yard, however, that attitude was completely dissipated. He would not be a brawler even if he deliberately set out to be one. He remained standing in the doorway among the other half-drunken men.

A large oil lamp had been lighted in the hall. The windows were open, but the air was still fetid with tobacco smoke, the smell of sweat, and of congested humanity. Gouges from the shoes of the dancers gleamed on the floor, over which Otto was scattering wax made from chipped candlesticks.

There were more drunks around now. Victor Kivioja danced with his small, thin wife, dragging her almost by force out onto the floor.

"There was a time about twenty years ago that nobody was a match for Vic in this business. But I'm going to go and see Silander now."

Otto had made a few trips outside with Silander, and the cooperative ideal had been discussed from a number of perspectives.

"It's capitalism's own weapon. Take the distribution of goods into our own hands and we'll always be able to sell more cheaply since we need to make only enough to cover our costs. And when you take into account that the people will buy from us for idealistic reasons, then some day the exploiters will have to close up their shops one after another. That's all we'll need. That's revolution enough."

366

Otto had dragged Jussi to the rear bench, and Victor was seated next to him. In his enthusiasm, Victor suddenly grabbed Jussi by the sleeve and said, "Listen to what he's saying. He knows about selling. He's a real man, by golly."

Half angrily, Jussi tore his arm loose. He wanted to go home, but courtesy demanded that he stay a little longer. They brought around snacks, and Otto urged him to have some. Jussi studied the multi-colored offerings doubtfully, but did take one finally. Halme was also slow in choosing one.

"Don't you have a cheese sandwich? I've given up meat on principle."

"It's meat that keeps you going."

"Not at all. At birth, man is not a meat-eater. His straying from the true path is, in my opinion, sufficient to account for his bestiality. I feel that my whole being has grown lighter, and my spiritual part much purer."

Surreptitiously, they laughed at him.

Then a ruckus arose at the food table. It was Elias Kankaanpää who was causing the row. The young man was experiencing his first real drunk and had been making the serving maids laugh until he went completely off. He began having odd fits. His head would rock with laughter, he would snort like a horse through his lips, and make abrupt hand motions. Then he speared a herring with his fork, raised it level with his eyes, and began to speak, his head wobbling from side to side.

"Hi there... Greetings from the Atlantic Ocean... Isn't that so? I know who you are... You've traveled the western shores and you're not just a doggone manure hauler like everyone around here... You are food for human beings. I'll tell your history... Norwegians catch you and sell you to the fine folk in Finland, who eat you and give your head and tail to the poor... Can you sing... Let's sing together. Workers, plowmen, everyone... Labor's hungry masses... But not so hungry that I'd eat you... go away..."

Suddenly he snatched up a chair and began an oddly lurching dance with it. "My dearest friend... Our hearts were joined in Astrakhan... in the folds of astrakhan..."

The bystanders laughed, but then Elias put down the chair and grabbed one of the girls by the arm. "Let's go out there to the surface of Tellus... It's moonlight..."

The girl pulled away angrily, but Elias laughed and took up a pitcher of buttermilk from the table. "I'll dump this goddamn thing over my head."

367

Simultaneously he raised the pitcher on high, spilling liquid from the half-full mug all over himself. Noticing his idiotic antics, his father came over to him. "Get out of here..."

"What do you know, old man? Hi there."

Oskar, who had been assigned the task of keeping order, came up to them. Elias reached for another pitcher, but Oskar grabbed his hand. Kankaanpää told him to take the boy out, and Oskar began to lead him away. Suddenly, the boy spread his legs and said, "What's holding us up... My toenails must need trimming..."

"Come on now, Elias."

Oskar was reluctant to use force, if only because Elias' was buttermilk from head to foot, and Oskar's suit would have gotten smeared. When the boy kept on resisting him, he gestured for help to Akseli, who was standing nearby. Akseli, with a gravity of demeanor resulting from his drunkenness, had already drawn near, and now he took hold of Elias' arm, with an expression that was a warning to go peacefully, since he would have to go in any event. The older Kankaanpää urged them on, telling them to give the boy a beating when they got him outside.

When nothing else would do, they hoisted the boy onto their shoulders, taking pains to avoid smearing themselves with the buttermilk. Delighted, the boy clapped his hands and shouted, "More men... Come on, you goddamned lightweights..."

There were a few angry whispers, but most of the people were laughing, since the matter involved no danger. The two tried to carry Elias out, but in the entry, he grabbed onto the door frame, shouting, "We are arriving at the French border. Are your passports in order?"

Outdoors, they calmed Elias down. He was in such a condition that he consented without further resistance to go to sleep in Mäkelä's sauna nearby. On the return trip, Akseli got a couple more drinks from Osku, and, cleaning the curds from their clothing, the two returned to the building. Another ruckus had developed there. Wolf-Kustaa had appeared out back and knelt down beside a stone. Placing an object on it and nodding toward the building, he had mumbled some incomprehensible jargon, occasionally hitting the palm of one hand with the side of the other. Then he disappeared mysteriously into the woods. When they approached the rock to see what he had done, they found on it a stick of kindling wood with single crossing strands of gray and red yarn laid over it.

Kustaa had put a curse on the workers' hall. It was an easy assumption to make, since he had lately begun to play the role of sorcerer. He had placed a tarred snake on Mäenpää's hill, which was known for its snakes. They laughed at the curse on the workers' hall, but some of them were heard to say, with drunken gravity, "But still this devil's work shouldn't be left here... It's aimed at the workers."

The incident was soon forgotten amid all the hubbub. The drinks Akseli had gotten from Osku had raised his level of intoxication, and he entered once more, leaning against the door frame. Jussi and Alma were getting ready to leave with the other boys, and she said as they went by, "Father is tired... We're going now. You won't be long, will you?"

"I'll come soon."

Alma looked at the boy a little doubtfully, but she was not able to tell if he was drunk or not.

The departure of his parents made Akseli feel more free. He thrust himself forward and spoke louder, which nevertheless went unnoticed, for there were plenty of men shouting in the doorway. He went to visit the wedding couple, drawing an irate look from Sanni. Men were constantly stopping to whisper a word to Janne, at which a hard, watchful look would appear in Sanni's eyes. She did not let Janne out of her sight for a minute, and she assumed that Akseli's approach had something to do with liquor.

"Well, how are things with the newly-wed husband?"

"I'm beginning to feel the change little by little."

"Ya-ah. Now if you get a horse, you'll have enough to ride on. You've already got a wife and a bicycle."

The quip was not of Akseli's invention, but he felt he had to use it now. Sanni did not conceal her resentment, and the boy left the couple and went back to the doorway.

Then Elina spotted him as she danced by. She kept looking at him over her shoulder, and when the dance was over, came up to speak to him. "Where have you been? Have you had anything?"

"Have I had anything. I have, I have. I've had plenty."

Elina realized from his words and his glassy eyes that he was drunk. Her smile faded, and she said uncertainly, "I meant sandwiches... Since I didn't see you."

"Don't worry about it. You've seen me so many times that there's no reason

369

for you to look at me again. I've even had sandwiches. Everything's okay and in good order."

Elina departed. At first she was offended, but she found it hard to shrug off the incident. Was Akseli angry about something, and if so, about what? Her unhappiness affected her so much that her dance partner could no longer get a smile from her. She replied to comments absent-mindedly. The recent encounter with Akseli troubled her: there was something puzzling about it. Gradually, she came to the realization that there had been a kind of accusation in his behavior, an accusation she felt to be justified. At the end of the number, she went to the doorway, but Akseli was no longer anywhere to be seen.

For the rest of the evening, she was in a confused state of mind. At times, she was restless and upset by Akseli's disappearance, but at other times, she felt passionately happy. What she had guessed at earlier now seemed a certainty. And some instinct assured her that he was not gone forever. Then she smiled and laughed again, without her partner's being aware that she had not, as a matter of fact, even heard what he had been saying.

II

On the following day, Akseli was digging a ditch. His own words from the night before rang in his ears. "You've seen me so many times before..."

Then he would drive the shovel furiously downward, and mutter half aloud as his heel drove it into the earth, "Darned childish man. Whining like a... Letting people know his feelings..."

He kept on digging without a break, working at an almost frenzied pace. His body rejoiced in the effort, and a bath of perspiration cleansed both body and soul. Hour by hour, the dross was purged from them. A jubilant sense of strength and manhood gave wings to his work. He became almost defiantly arrogant, placing his right hand higher up on the handle of the shovel, making the lift heavier, but also showing off the strength of the digger. His bodily movements were impressively resilient. His hair hung down from the side opposite the usual one, but it seemed completely in place there. The sounds of his work were interspersed with an attempt at song: "...We toil for Finland's good... everyone to the war of work... there... goddamn... it's as sure as a poor man's death..."

370

He could not completely forget the events of the wedding. He had certainly made a complete ass of himself. He could not go to the Kivivuoris now, although he knew in his heart he would go there before long. He met Osku in the village and pleaded the pressure of work when asked why he had not visited them. Hope and humiliation gnawed at his mind. Sometimes he would put the question to himself directly: "Why the devil am I circling like a cat around a dish of hot porridge?"

He did find an answer to the question, but it was none too clear. There were many things to restrain him. One of them was too great a familiarity with the family. His close acquaintance with the Kivivuoris since childhood weighed upon him. The whole atmosphere of the household worried him when he thought of revealing the matter. On the one hand, there were the jibes of Otto and the boys, and on the other hand, there was Anna and her special status. He was plainly not aware of the fundamental reason for his hesitation — the fear of a decision. His state of mind, his imaginings prior to the wedding were now a prey to uncertainty. He had seen at the wedding how quickly his assurance could collapse.

Later that fall, Elina was often seen walking the roads of the neighborhood, but always alone and at a reasonable hour. Her route approached nearer and nearer to the parsonage and to the Koskela road juncture. That she could hardly turn into, for it had one clear destination: the Koskela place.

Inevitably, the two met.

"Hello."

"Hello, hello."

"What's new?"

"Nothing much."

"Where are you going?"

"Oh, nowhere. It's just nice to walk."

Their conversation was utterly inconsequential. They took turns in plucking a straw from the earth, chewing on it for a time, and throwing it away. Now and then, they shifted their weight from one foot to another. Not a word was said about what was most crucial in the encounter, but when they parted, a wedding was a foregone conclusion.

Janne's marriage kept being the subject of discussion at the Kivivuoris. They had heard various reports about it. Janne had celebrated a couple of times with his father-in-law, but the third celebration ended when Sanni, without saying a word, smashed the bottle and glasses to fragments. Janne had to spend the night on the second floor, for the bedroom door remained closed. The Exchange miss had otherwise taken matters firmly into her own hands. Janne had a habit of stopping to lean against his bicycle, in conversation with a group of men on the road to the village. If the hour grew too late, Sanni would appear on the road and announce in a conventionally cordial, but sufficiently expressive voice: "Your hot chocolate is getting cold. Come and drink it."

More and more often, Janne was seen bicycling around "on business," always wearing a tie knotted around his neck by his wife. The villagers were beginning to say, "Kivivuori's on the move," when they would earlier have said: "Silander's son-in-law is riding his bicycle."

Janne's "business" had to do with the workers' association and the affairs of the cooperative, into which Silander had immediately drawn him.

"He's even learning Swedish," said Anna.

Akseli laughed at Janne's having succumbed in this way to petticoat rule, but then he said in a sober and matter-of-fact way, "Janne really is the type for that kind of business. All he needed was a strict wife."

Recently, Akseli had taken to speaking of marriage with unusual respect. There was no further mention of the thirty-years'-war. Even Anna's eyes opened to see what was happening. The turn of affairs caused Anna to begin to suggest to Otto that Elina be sent to a folk high school.

"As far as I know, they don't take in pupils at this time of year."

"But she could take some kind of course. They have them in some places. We should be thinking of a better life for her."

"This is no time for anything of the sort. We may even have to move."

A gleam of hope was dawning for the Kivivuoris in the matter of the eviction. A strengthening of the rental laws was anticipated, and if it came about, there would be no eviction, for the law's provisions would be retroactive. The passage of rent reforms had been delayed for so long that the socialists had put through a provision that evictions carried out during the delay would be nullified. For that reason, Otto had made no preparations for moving.

Because of the uncertain state of affairs, he rejected all of Anna's suggestions about courses, and she was forced to go directly to the heart of the matter.

"Haven't you noticed anything?"

"I've noticed all kinds of things."

"I mean about Elina."

"What about her? There she is. She's healthy and she eats well."

"I am serious. Akseli comes here because of her. And in her inexperience, she likes him, I think."

Otto stole a glance at his wife and guessed her thoughts. "Maybe she does. I like him too."

Anna began to explain. "But Elina is too young. It's only a young girl's interest in a man who is available, who is closest to her. When she sees other men, elsewhere, then there will be trouble."

"This has been brewing for a long time, and I don't think it's a bad thing."

"But Elina can't get married yet."

"And I'm not marrying her off. I haven't interfered in the matter and I'm not going to. Let things evolve as they please."

In the end, Anna had to admit that she felt Akseli was not quite good enough for Elina, and that brought on a quarrel.

"It's your own fault. You've kept the girl in diapers. But luckily, she hasn't turned out to be what you've tried to make of her. Try to think more sensibly. Where the hell will you find other men here besides hired hands and tenants? She can't marry into a farm no matter how refined she may be. And if you'd stop your silly coddling, you yourself know you'd have to go a long way to find a better man."

The discussion ended there for the time being, but underneath her fears, Anna kept on hoping. She began to feel a secret antipathy toward Akseli, which increased as she grew more sure of Elina's love for him. Not that there was anything wrong with him, but... But her old dreams were suffering severe blows. In the end, she decided to resort to a final desperate measure: she took up the question in private with Elina.

They were cleaning the living room, each humming a tune of her own, the mother a hymn and the daughter a waltz. Anna began with distant hints, which gradually focused on Akseli's visits. Elina answered just as vaguely, until her mother asked, "What do you think of Akseli?"

"What should I... You can see for yourself the kind of person he is."

"It just seemed to me that some people might think..."

373

"Think what?"

"Just anything... they are so quick to gossip..."

Then Elina understood. Her mother looked at her and saw everything. Elina could not even answer, she was so upset by her mother's innuendo. After a pause, Anna said, "I didn't mean... but it's good to think about it... It's a serious thing..."

"I haven't been thinking anything... what are you... I can't tell him to leave."

Her mother could see how difficult it was for Elina and dropped the subject. The knowledge she now had was definite enough. Left alone, she could not hold back her tears of vexation. She had nurtured and cherished the girl in a dream of a better world, not out of a desire for status alone. She had hoped for something spiritually better, a compensation for the drabness of her own life, from which she herself had not emerged unscathed. And now the dream was sinking into a wayside tenant's holding in the woods, into the most commonplace of surroundings a person could imagine. Controlling her tears, Anna chastised Akseli in her mind.

For many days, a strange mood prevailed in the family. They all avoided any mention of Akseli. Osku had heard a hint of the matter, and had approved, after an initial feeling of disappointment. He did not feel that his sister was too good for Akseli, but it was not easy for him to accept the notion that such a thoroughly familiar companion should be sleeping in the same bed as his sister.

Mood and emotion were ripe for the event. It needed only Akseli's initiative, and that was slow in coming. Anna began slowly to give in to the inevitable, and Otto did all he could to clear the way for the boy.

"Folk high school be damned! They put on folk dresses and go down to the lake shore in the evening and sing up into the sky: 'Oh Finland, you are most dear to me,' and something about '... echo, song, on Aura's shores.'

Although the matter was a foregone conclusion, the final decision was still delayed. Everyone knew what would happen, but the event required its own rhythm for fulfillment. Everything had to reach full ripeness before the word opened the locks. The two young people knew each other's feelings, but something in them was incomplete. Then it happened during Shrovetide. They were sledding at the Kivivuoris with some of the other young people from the village. At first, they were using the water-sled, but Akseli, carried away, went to get the big sleigh from in front of the barn. It held a number of people, and Elina wound

374

up in Akseli's lap, not at all by chance. The boy could feel her body quiver in his arms, as if she were frightened by his touch, but then she pressed herself against him so obviously that he responded by holding her more tightly in his arms. The courtship was consummated.

The two were left alone when Oskar departed for the village with the others, saying as he left, "You take the sleigh back, since you brought it out."

Akseli started to pull it, and Elina said, "It's heavy. I'll push."

"Get into the sleigh."

"You're not strong enough."

"I could pull a sparrow like you no matter what..."

He settled the girl into the sleigh and began to pull, struggling silently uphill, trying to make it look easy. They stopped in front of the barn. Elina remained seated on the edge of the sleigh, and Akseli sat down beside her. The evening air was still and heavy. From farther off, they could hear the unintelligible shouts of the recently departed group. They could hear the horses crunching their food in the barn, stopping every now and then as if listening for something, but resuming their chewing when they heard nothing. The warm air was laden with the smell of the hay and of the barn. The familiar shape of the house loomed dark against the snow and the sky. The age-old ball atop the hop-pole was covered with snow. There was no light in the windows.

Akseli picked up a stick and began to poke holes in the snow's crust with it. Elina settled her dress around her legs.

"You've got such damned pretty boots."

"Stop it."

"But what a small foot you must have to fit into them."

The feet disappeared beneath the skirt, although there was nothing in them to be ashamed of.

"But you're pretty small yourself, too."

"I'm not..."

Elina straightened up.

"You're just the height of a crutch. Look at this."

The boy raised his arm and stretched it out over her head. Then he let it fall over her shoulders. The girl leaned into his arms, but kept her hands against her own body, as if she were ashamed to put her arms around the boy. A grunt of sorts escaped Akseli, in which the girl's name could be distinguished.

375

Elina caught her breath. Then she rose up in alarm, as if something had frightened her. Akseli stood up too.

"Will you come tomorrow at seven... say to Töyry's corner?"

"I'll come... Now I..."

Elina started for the porch, but returned and kissed him and said with a sob, "I'll come... I'll be sure to come... but I'm going... I have to go now."

She started off again, but stopped for a moment, then ran quickly to the porch and opened the door. Then she came back to the bottom step and whispered, "Good night."

Finally she disappeared indoors, as if in flight.

Akseli stood near the sleigh, half dazed. When Elina returned to say goodnight, he raised his arms, but dropped them limply when she disappeared. He was unable to answer.

Only after some time had passed did he rouse himself, utter a low sound, and set off quickly for home.

Elina darted into her room. She took off her short coat and threw it onto the floor. She was aiming at a chair, but missed. Then she sat down on the bed, sobbing and smiling in the darkness. She got up, paced back and forth, lifted her hair, and looked into the dark mirror.

As she undressed, she had trouble getting her slip over her head, for it kept getting badly tangled. Once under the covers, she lay for a short time with her eyes open, holding her breath. There she burst into a laughter mingled with sobs.

She was still awake when her father went to the stable for the morning chores, and it was only in the morning hours that weariness forced her into a restless sleep.

Shadowy evenings. Long walks, leaning into each other. Passionate embraces as they parted in the dark porch at the Kivivuoris. When the matter had to be expressed in words, Akseli said, "Since I have such a one-track mind, I'm absolutely serious about this."

It was the only way he could say it. Elina, who was no longer ashamed of her emotions, merely whispered, "I know that..."

No more specific plans were made. Akseli thought vaguely that his father might give up the tenancy now. But it didn't matter that much... What did such things amount to now?

"What are they saying at your house?"

"Nothing."

As a matter of fact, they did not talk about the matter at the Kivivuoris. One night, in her sleeplessness, Anna went quietly into her daughter's bedroom. The moon was shining as she looked silently at the pretty head of the sleeper. Tears rose to her eyes, and, clasping her hands, she began to whisper a prayer: "Jesus Christ... If it must be, then... Bless... I'm not... I only want... Not out of the sin of pride. Lord Jesus bless... If it... I only want what is good... but if you see this as good... then Lord Jesus Christ bless..."

Then she went quietly from the room. Her disordered braid hung down the back of her nightgown, still thick, pretty, and blond. On her feet were Otto's felt boots. Going through the entry, she was drying her tears devoutly when she slipped on the packed and icy snow on its floor. She staggered and hissed angrily, "I have to chop that too... They do nothing... And he's been sitting there all these nights... chasing after her... And is she already so hungry for a man at her age?"

Anna clambered over the sleeping Otto to get into bed behind him. Angrily she jerked at the covers to get some for herself; Otto tended to wrap them all around himself. Anna had a small fit of anger at her husband too. There was something taunting and annoying even in his peaceful slumber. As if it were breathing forth that same imperturbability of his, from which everything in the world rebounded... Absolutely everything. Nothing could dent it.

Then Anna sighed and whispered a prayer on behalf of that love which she found so hard to accept.

Nothing could remain a secret for long, and one day Otto, his brow furrowed, asked Elina, "Where are you running around every evening, young lady?"

"Just around."

"Around where? I'm a man who doesn't like night-prowling."

"Well, you must know."

"How would I know?"

Next Sunday, Akseli came to the Kivivuoris during the day, for Elina had explained to him that they could no longer get by without speaking of the matter. But Otto feigned ignorance, and talked of the most distant things imaginable. Then he set out for the stable, and Akseli disappeared in his wake.

Otto was in a stall, mixing a bucket of chopped straw. Akseli regarded him

377

for a time and said, "I've got something to talk about."

"Oh, I see... You always have to talk about things you have to talk about. Things are what people talk about."

"It's the thing about me and Elina."

The stick Otto was using to stir rattled against the side of the bucket. A horse, snapping at the feed, drew an angry growl.

"Is that so? What kind of thing is that? What kind of business do you two have?"

Akseli laughed, embarrassed. "Well, you must know."

"How should I know your business... Hell, am I supposed to know everything from half a word."

"We've been thinking a little..."

The boy raised his head. He was completely red-faced, but the words came out with surprising sharpness: "I'm going to marry Elina."

Akseli was so thoroughly disconcerted that his only recourse was to an air of forceful sternness. He knew that Otto, aware of how difficult all this was for him, was purposely teasing him. Barely able to breathe, he listened as Otto fiddled with the straw.

"I see... Well... Stop shifting around there... or I'll... Uhuh... Is that so. You're going to marry... Really marry... All hot to get married... Quite a boy at marrying... But I was pretty good at that too. She turned eighteen only last week as you well know."

"That's why I asked..."

"Uhuh... Yes... There's always someone there to marry them as long as you make them first. Feed them and clothe them... It's not such an easy matter as you might think... But I'll give her to you, all right... You can have her, but what are you going to pay?"

Akseli laughed in relief. "What are you asking?"

"Would a bottle of whiskey be too much?"

There was still Anna to deal with, but Otto took care of that himself. Tossing his fur cap onto the bed, he said, "The boy is buying our girl from us... I promised her to him for a bottle of whiskey... What does Mother think about it?"

Anna's anger was drowned in her tears, which could be interpreted as a sign of being moved, which she was in fact, partly.

They sat and talked, but about other things. Elina did not so much as come near Akseli, but the air was filled with a veiled happiness. It was there even

378

in the aroma of Anna's coffee. Osku gave them his blessing as well. He slapped Elina's rear with an open palm and said, "Uhuh... In a year, our girl will be walking with her ass on her arm."

Osku was treated to a tongue-lashing, while Akseli tried to cover his embarrassment with a laugh.

III

The early spring days began and ended like poems, brightly sparkling and translucent.

Their quality remained constant, even if one was driving manure from the parsonage dung heap, or milking cows in the Kivivuoris' low, dark barn, where slop-water squished underfoot. Such things did not exist. Sometimes one brushed against them lightly, but they soon gave way and disappeared. Fate had begun laying on happiness with a trowel. The rent laws were strengthened retroactively, and the baron had to rescind the Kivivuori eviction. If a tenant so desired, he could pay his rent in money, the amount to be set by a special rent commission in case of a dispute. Thus, a tenant could not be driven out by arbitrarily high rents. The law would be in effect only until 1916, but there was a vague hope that the number of socialist representatives would increase and that the law could be continued, although its opponents had indeed openly threatened what they would do to it.

There was a real celebration at the workers' hall in honor of the law. There, for the first time, Akseli appeared openly in the company of Elina. As happy as he was about the political developments, they were mere additions to his bliss. During Halme's speech, he held Elina's hand surreptitiously, and listened, not to the content of the talk, but to the turns of phrase he had found amusing on earlier occasions. At each one of them, he would signal Elina with a squeeze of his hand, and she would show her understanding by replying in kind. But there was no malice in their fun.

Under these circumstances, they were able to decide the question of the Koskela inheritance quite simply. Jussi announced that he would leave the tenancy to Akseli. When he made the declaration at the parsonage, both the vicar and his wife were present. The vicar said, "Yes, yes. He is your oldest boy. Of course

379

we'll continue the agreement. Even the law confirms that. An agreement can't be changed until 1916."

The couple exchanged meaningful glances from time to time, and the woman said, "Of course, we can't decide which son should get Koskela's rights, but wouldn't Akseli be able to find outside work more easily since he's the oldest? Shouldn't you be thinking of the younger boys' future... It just occurred to me. But that must be contrary to your plans."

"Yes, it may well be that way, all right. But the boy has done the rent-work for years now. It wouldn't be right to take it away from him now."

"Yes, yes. It's Koskela's affair, not ours."

Control of the tenancy would be in Akseli's hands within a year. He considered working to pay the rent more advantageous to himself. For a farmer like him, there was little opportunity to earn money in the area, so that a money rental was of no benefit. And, most important, there could no longer be excessive demands for compulsory work. Of course, it could be requested, but he had the privilege of refusing should he not have the time. So many things seemed to be going well.

The parsonage couple spoke to each other in private.

"It will be interesting to see if he changes, now that he has the law to back up his insolence. They say he's keeping company with the Kivivuori girl. Poor thing."

"One day in passing I heard him saying to the other men: 'The gentry must really be stewing now,' and then he went on in a provoking tone of voice: 'when anything goes and even beggars can get drunk.'"

"Yes, spoken like a true tramp. He's lived up to the formal requirements, but if he violates them, we'll see what happens in 1916."

Akseli was behaving extraordinarily well these days. Not only was he not bold and bitter; he was even quite friendly and courteous. He seemed to have forgotten his socialism, and when the point was made at the workers' association, Antto, to whom the retroactive law did not apply, burst out more angrily than ever. "His socialism has disappeared under the Kivivuori girl's nightgown."

Halme was indignant. "Ahem. Let's grant love its due season. I will gladly give him a holiday from his ideals now that the two of them are living life's highest moments. In my view, this type of love rises to a higher spiritual sphere and leads to marriage. Treating the question in spiritual terms, I would say that the aura of

380

their love is especially bright. I am pleased to see young people facing life's responsibilities together, and I would not wish to attach too much significance to lifting the skirts of the garment you just mentioned."

He followed his words with a couple of slight coughs, and Antto glowered at the ground, for he was still somewhat restrained by Halme's prestige. Nevertheless, he muttered to himself on his way home, "Hmph... damn it. If he stopped eating grass, he might have some business under those skirts himself... By God! The others are getting their holdings back, but not me... Yeah, yeah... Damn it, so it goes... When will this world rip open..."

Meanwhile, people were saying to Töyry: "It's as if we got him out in time through God's guidance. Now you wouldn't be able to get rid of him."

It seemed the law had been passed especially for Otto Kivivuori's benefit. The eviction had been rescinded, and he could earn a lot of money doing masonry and construction work, now that money rental was permitted. Since the baron could do nothing else in his anger, he announced that he would not accept payment in work from Otto. "I don't look you on estate fields."

"Don't waste your anger. I'll pay you in money. And since rent-work is a thing of the past, shouldn't we let bygones be bygones."

"Hell, I remember you. You big man now with law. Eviction in force 1916 when law gone."

"There will be a socialist majority then, and the law will be kept in force."

"Pay steward rent and not come my eyes before. Go away, not good."

It was a dazzlingly bright Palm Sunday, and the sun sparkled on the surface of the already gradually melting snow. Akseli was on his way to meet Elina, who was making her first official visit to the Koskelas. She had been there before, but this was different. On previous visits, she had been calm and casually friendly, but now she was shy and smiling in confusion.

She was most timid about Jussi. They had talked so much at home about how he would take things. But Elina bubbled over with pleasure when Jussi gave out with some sort of heart-felt mumbling in greeting her and said, "Is the girl looking for a place to set up her spinning wheel?"

Giving up the tenancy was not easy for Jussi, but he fought his battle alone, without a hint to anyone else. He could not keep it up without Akseli, and Jussi realized that when Akseli was married, he would still be in the same position as before. Either he would be given the tenancy or he would leave.

He had nothing against Elina. He knew that in spite of a few affectations, which he attributed to Anna's influence, the girl took care of the cows at home.

For her part, Alma would have welcomed even a worse daughter-in-law. For Jussi's sake, she was ready to give her immediate consent. Everything went smoothly, and if there were any rough spots, they were passed over in silence, either consigned to oblivion or postponed to a more propitious time.

The parlor had been heated for this express purpose. It smelled of new linen and of fumes from a cold stove suddenly heated. The sun shone through the six-paned windows, casting bright splashes of color across the throw rugs, which plainly showed that very few steps had trod their surface. Elina sat with a constant, involuntary smile on her face. When she was asked a question that had anything to do with getting married, she merely looked at Akseli and kept on smiling. Let him answer.

All other questions she answered humbly and shyly, but she herself did not initiate any conversation. The boys sat on the bed, side by side. The presence of a young girl at the Koskelas' was a rare occurrence. Even they sensed that there would be a change in their lives, and they were happy about it. Aleksi, who was seventeen, kept coughing into his hand and shifting his feet. He did not know if he should yet adopt the stance of a man. Thirteen-year-old Aku kept hiding behind his brother's back, looking out at Elina and flashing an occasional smile. Sometimes a small fracas broke out between the two brothers on the bed. Aku was pinching Aleksi.

The prospective groom sat on a chair, occasionally hitching at his trouser legs above the knees and smiling his introverted smile. His demeanor seemed to say: "If anyone has anything to say, let him say it now."

Carefully and guardedly, Alma explained that they would be putting up a new building.

"It's not that I'm afraid of you. It's just that we don't go for these shared households. We'll get along better that way."

Elina was startled, but she quickly realized that there was no animosity in Alma's words. The sunshine increased.

There followed the return trip along the Koskela road. At times they walked hand-in-hand, then arm-in-arm, or shoving gently at each other. Each tried to make the other stagger off the path into the snow. The game did not seem at all childish to

382

Akseli. His former curt stiffness had disappeared. Even as a small boy he had not experienced such a relaxed and easy feeling.

As they approached the village and began to meet people, they drew away from each other. Most of the people they met smiled at them in a friendly and happy way, or at least so it seemed. They could see an occasional head behind the half-curtain of a cabin. Some of the occupants had a nasty comment to make. In his passage through life, Otto had dropped a few remarks here and there, and their memory evoked such comments:

"That schemer really has foresight... He favored the boy, even gave him contract work sometimes. He was already counting Jussi's money in his mind. He sent his girl there... And he wasn't even evicted. What incredible luck the man has."

They did not know Jussi at all. When he made the first hint at surrendering the tenancy, Jussi spoke right out, "Whatever money there is, it's mine. And you'll pay your brothers for their share."

The young couple did not talk about such things. The landscape of the future glowed with the hues of morning.

Unbeknownst to the people in the community, they made an engagement trip to Tampere. It took place later on in the spring, when the timbers for the "grandpa's cabin" had been hauled out of the woods during the last of the winter sledding. Elina was the leader of the expedition, for she had been to Tampere earlier with her mother. Akseli rode on a train for the first time in his life, and tried to act as if it were nothing new.

In the city, they were only two young people from the country, who were somewhat at a loss in trying to find the jeweler from whom all their fellow parishioners were used to purchasing their engagement rings. Abashedly, they accepted the jeweler's congratulations. When Akseli detected a touch of smiling mockery at their rusticity in the looks of the other shop people, he jerked his head erect. The shopkeeper had to avert his gaze from the angry look in the boy's narrowed eyes.

"Damned crane... if we had been somewhere else, I would have grabbed his pipes to find out what kind of sound comes out."

He said it to Elina in the street to keep her from thinking that he could not respond in his own way to the harassments of these pantywaists. Elina paid no attention. It didn't matter.

They made some other purchases, and the first words of complaint the pair exchanged in their lives concerned a bottle of liquor. As was the case with many others.

"You're not going to take it to him. Mother will be angry."

"But that's the payment for you."

"You know that was only talk. You're not going to."

"I'm not going back without a bottle."

Elina yielded. The breach was healed within a couple of blocks. They bought sausage and unleavened bread and ate it secretively in some dark corner.

On the way home, they sat huddled in a corner of the coach. At the station, they had whispered to one another: "Shall we wear them?"

"Sure, as far as I'm concerned... As I said, I keep my word. No need to hide it."

The rings were thick and weighed many grams and it was important that they say 18 carats. "It isn't a Jewish shop, but they'll pull the wool over your eyes fast enough."

As the train advanced, their sense of insignificance decreased. Poku was waiting at the station, having been kept in the yard of an acquaintance for the day, and fed and watered there. As they approached Pentti's Corners, they were once again the center of the universe.

Anna had the chance to vent her spleen in a few disgruntled words which followed upon the appearance of the whiskey bottle. She was still not completely reconciled to her son-in-law. Later that evening, she said privately to Elina, "See to it that the bottles don't start showing up too often."

"He brought it for father."

"Well... I don't know that it makes any difference whose throat the sin goes down."

"Very little has gone down his throat."

Anna said no more, for there was something dark, almost forbidding, in the girl's eyes, and she realized that her daughter was gone. Irrevocably.

IV

The wedding was postponed until the following summer. There were many reasons why it was considered better to do so, and Anna was particularly insistent upon the delay.

384

"You can't go there and sleep on a bare bed."

Elina's wedding had come upon her before Anna had had time even to think about preparing her daughter for it. She had no stores of linens or other essentials laid up. Things were no better off with Akseli. He was a completely penniless man. His mother and father would take all the household furnishings and utensils into the house they would share with the boys, and he and Elina would have to start from scratch. At Alma's insistence, Jussi gave him a hundred markkas to set up house, and the boy took it, but with great reluctance. His father also negotiated the transfer of the boy's share of the property, asking full value for everything. He did so not out of greed, but to guarantee an equal share to everyone. Akseli understood everything, but he had a sizable debt to burden him even before he had begun. The boys did say that they would not ask for money until Akseli himself felt able to pay it.

Building the "grandpa's cabin" cost Jussi money, so he was unable to help Akseli. They even had to buy the timber, for the parsonage would not agree to take possession of the new property. It was to belong to Jussi and to be the subject of a separate agreement. It was to be the lifelong dwelling of Jussi and Alma, regardless of the tenancy contract. Thus they would not have to leave if there were an eviction from the tenancy.

As payment for the tenancy, Akseli had to take on himself the care of his mother and father. The stipulated provisions were indeed small, but they would nevertheless be an added strain. When there was talk of a written agreement, Akseli said somewhat stiffly, "Go ahead and make one, if my word isn't good enough."

None was made. Generally, there were no problems with the arrangements, considering they were Finns living in Finland. In return for their scant provisions, Jussi and Alma promised to help with the work on the tenancy.

"As long as we can be of any help. I can help out in the barn, but your father is fit only for light work."

So Akseli, a man already in debt with but a hundred markkas in his pocket, became the head of the Koskela household. And he was a bridegroom, with no other household furnishings than the benches nailed to the walls of the main room and bake-room. In addition, there were the spoon shelf and the ax brackets nailed to the same walls. A spoon he did not have, but an ax he did.

But he had a bride whom he still revered after getting to know her fully, revered, with a certain sense of his own inferiority to her. His feelings were not the same as before, when Elina's external attractions had been their object. Although his stock of ideas included no such concept as 'inner worth,' he felt himself to be coarse and clumsy when confronted with the girl's tenderness and purity. At the time, he felt that too much had been granted him.

After almost a half year of passionate courtship, his bride was still untouched. He had made one or two attempts, but they had frightened Elina so much that he had desisted, ashamed and troubled. The ghost of Anna still kept a close watch at the head of the bed in the Kivivuori inner room.

Fearfully, the mother watched the young people's comings and goings. She found it hard to take up the subject with Elina, but after a great deal of hesitation, she did.

"We have to have some of the spinning done in the village. We're never going to be ready in time. We should put it off again, but I suppose you can't wait."

"That's true. Since we've already decided on next summer."

"We have to try. Your engagement is long enough. It must be hard to wait. But... people have waited longer. It's just that there are risks. All sorts of things happen nowadays. You have to remember that marriage was instituted by God and that you must enter into it pure."

Anna studied the expression on Elina's face, and although it reflected a profound embarrassment, she was sure that nothing had happened. Having begun, she kept dropping warning hints, beating around the bush, saying how terrible it would be if the date announced for the wedding had to be moved ahead. Her hints brought Elina very nearly to the boiling point. Her eighteen-year-old body could not endure the constant presence and the caresses of a man without being aroused. In addition, she was further inflamed by her mother's attitude. Unless Akseli had felt the respect for her sensitivity that he did, what happened on a summer Sunday morning would surely have happened earlier. Anna had gone to church, and Otto had gone there to ferry her, his way of describing his church-going. Oskar went along on the same trip to visit Janne.

Barefoot and bareheaded, Akseli went to move Poku's tether. He was to visit the Kivivuoris that afternoon. But the pasture lay some distance in their direction, and the boy set out through the woods in the grip of a sudden, passionate yearning to be with Elina. His bride was somewhat shocked by the appearance of her groom, barefoot, secretive, glancing in all directions.

It was cool in the inner room at the Kivivuoris. They were lying in silence on

386

Elina's bed. Flies could be heard buzzing outside the open window. The goat let out an occasional bleat. The summer Sunday flooded in through the window.

Elina was preoccupied.

She would look at the ceiling, move a little distance away from Akseli and then cling to him passionately. Akseli realized that there was something exceptional in her behavior. But when he tried to show his understanding by reciprocating, Elina retreated to the wall like a cat whose tail had been stepped on, her hands thrust out defensively.

"No... not yet..."

"But why not?"

"I'm afraid."

"Of what?"

"Because we're not married."

The boy was silent for a time. Swallowing his natural impulses, he said, "If that's what you want... I'm sure... If it's important. I really can't think that it's wrong... But I won't force you..."

"I don't want to... it's nicer..."

Then the girl came back from the wall, and in a minute or two, the whole routine began over again. And she retreated again in exactly the same way.

The third time around, she did not retreat. She lay looking at the ceiling wide-eyed, as if she were concentrating on enduring something as ghastly as possible.

A small fit of weeping after the fact was smothered in the boy's shoulder. They exchanged a few words, but then left the matter alone. From time to time, they went to scrounge a salt-meat sandwich from the entry cupboard and then returned to lie down. At length Elina rose, straightened her dress, and looked at herself in the mirror. But she could not endure her gaze.

Then she returned to the bed. Lying on Akseli's arm, she suddenly began to embrace him passionately. When he looked at her, she hid her face in his shoulder, but soon raised it, and with a completely red face, emitted little bursts of laughter.

Now she began to repeat senseless terms of endearment into the boy's ear. Finally body and soul had found each other.

Then, for the first time, they spoke seriously of the ordinary things the future would bring. Akseli was quite candid about how hard their life would be at first.

"There's no hurry with the boys. I won't have to pay them yet. But Aleksi will have to work for us at least a part of the summer, and we'll have to pay him. And there's the food for Mother and Father... The fact is that I don't have a penny to my name. Father won't give me any money."

Elina listened seriously, but only because Akseli was speaking seriously. In themselves, such things could not cause her any apprehension, for she was unable to think them through completely. The discussion ended when Akseli said, "There will be a lot of hauling to do in Hollo's woods next winter. We'll make those logs fly with Poku whenever we don't have rent-work to do."

There was confidence in the boy's challenge.

Then Elina started. "Good God, they're coming and I haven't even started the fire for coffee." Akseli got up from the bed and looked down at his bare feet with a faint smile, "I have to go before they get here."

"Why?"

"I can't... like this... I'm going to get my hat and shoes."

They parted in the entry, Elina going into the living room and Akseli out the door. As he was leaving, he suddenly felt a pair of arms around his shoulders. He was turned around and received such a deluge of hugs and kisses that he could only stand there blinking stupidly, unable to respond to the unexpected caresses. Elina went to the inner door, but turned around again in the doorway. Akseli did the same at the outer door, and they stood there for a time, looking at each other. Elina's cheeks were red. She had the same half-confused smile in her eyes as she had had a short while back on the bed, and she was afflicted with the same short outbursts of laughter. The boy mocked her once or twice:

"He hee. He hee..."

Then they parted.

As Akseli emerged into the yard, he could hear the clinking of a tether chain from around the corner of the building. The goat appeared and stopped in his tracks, looking at the boy as if he had come out of curiosity to see who was carrying on in such a fashion. Then he let out a small bleating noise.

A jaunty grin appeared on the boy's face. He searched for something to pick up, found a small peg, and threw it at the goat. "Darned pointy-beard... bleating away like that..."

The goat merely looked at the peg that had landed near him and followed the boy as far as the length of his chain would permit. Then he remained watching, his head cocked to one side, bleating, as if in possession of some special knowledge.

"Keep your mouth shut, you goat."

Laughing, the boy glanced at his bare feet, looked down the road in either direction, and having crossed it, disappeared into the woods.

Summer was at its best. Although the work-days were long and hard, the young couple stole a little time to meet on weekday evenings. Even during the springtime, before their engagement, Elina had drawn away from Akseli to the opposite side of the road when they met someone. But now she did the contrary. She pressed closer to the boy's shoulder and greeted the oncomers from its secure refuge.

Akseli usually met her near the market, whence they would set off for some place or other, usually the lake. Akseli was no longer concerned about others, so he waited for her there, leaning against the hitching rail. Of the old Laurila place, only the storehouse was left. The other buildings had been destroyed, and in their place stood the market, its timbered walls stained in red ocher and its doors and window frames painted yellow. Outside was the hitching rail, out of which rabbits had already gnawed large chunks. Oil barrels nearby gave off an odor, which mingled with the smell of horse piss and rotting herring.

Some evenings the storekeeper might step outside and greet him in a playfully friendly fashion, letting fall some innuendo or other. In appearance, he was completely different from his brother. People said he took after his father, who even in his old age had a tendency to pat a maid's behind, if it happened to be nicely protruding as she went about her work. The result of such patting was their third brother, Wolf-Kustaa, of whose existence the legitimate brothers feigned ignorance.

It seemed strange to see a high-and-mighty Töyry currying favor with his shanty customers.

"What will it be? Have a candy... To sweeten your mouth..."

The slightly overweight creature was a strange combination of farmer and retail merchant, but it was well known that underneath his slightly inane benevolence was the same hardness and taut greed that his brother displayed openly on the surface.

Akseli responded to the merchant's greeting in a slightly aloof manner. He did not care for the rough-and-ready innuendo.

"Yaah... heh, heh... So Akseli's waiting for his bride... Ahah... ahah... heh, heh... You have to warm them up a little even on week nights... That's the way it is when these young girls get broken in to it, heh, heh... They have to get it all the time. So. But don't you need some good wheat flour? I have some American..."

"We don't need any."

389

Akseli spoke stiffly. Not wanting to show his feelings, he controlled his anger, which had been provoked by the aspersions on Elina.

Without further words, the merchant went indoors. The Koskelas were not good customers. After his back pains, the market was Jussi's greatest grief. "Children run around there, mouths smeared with lickoricks, even if they don't know where their next piece of bread is coming from."

Licorice represented for Jussi all the evils the market had brought into the community, although he had never mastered the pronunciation of that hated black and sticky stuff.

Elina arrived and Akseli waved and went to meet her. At first glance, he could see that there was something odd in her behavior. She did not look into his eyes except for panicky glimpses, and he was sure that she had been crying.

"What's wrong?"

"Nothing... Nothing's wrong with me... Let's go..."

Somewhat at a loss, Akseli stopped asking questions and they headed toward the lake. Ani and Ilmari came toward them along the road. The young people from the parsonage were also out for an evening stroll. Ilmari was now an upperclassman, and a small degree of formality had entered into his relationship with Akseli. This summer, the latter had stopped using the familiar pronoun. Ilmari still used it on occasion, but more often he spoke vaguely, avoiding the personal pronoun. In some respects, he was no longer the wild and restless "parsonage puppy," his familiar childhood nickname. Restless he still was, however. He was ill at ease in the country, and it showed in his perpetual roaming around the area. Out of curiosity, he had forced himself on Wolf-Kustaa as a fishing companion, but had had such a deluge of curses showered upon him that he was unable to repeat half of them as he laughingly related the incident to his parents. Externally he reminded people of his mother, with the difference that her features had assumed a manly cast in him.

Ani was a fourteen-year-old miss. Her skirt was still so short that her stockinged legs were visible below it. A large straw hat hung on the back of her head, held in place by a ribbon tied into a bow under her chin.

Both of them had already congratulated Akseli at the parsonage, but now they were seeing the two of them together for the first time, and they repeated their congratulations. Ilmari studied Elina carefully and there was still a flash of the impulsive parsonage puppy in him when he nodded to Akseli with an approving wink. Ani curtsied and said with extraordinarily careful and correct enunciation, "I congratulate you and wish you all happiness."

Akseli could see that even the congratulations wrung only a forced smile from Elina. As they went on their way, he made a remark about the young people from the parsonage, but got only a listless response.

"Now tell me what's wrong with you."

"There's nothing wrong with me."

But when they were seated on the little old rock ledge that still radiated the day's warmth in the cool of the evening, Akseli said sternly, "There is something wrong... Has anything happened... Have you heard something about Janne... or..."

Elina's shoulders began to shake, her head sank into her hands, and her words came brokenly between her sobs. "Is it true... that... you... you have... been... Aune's... Aune's... sweetheart?"

There it came. The secretly dreaded blow which had troubled his thoughts from time to time. At first he said as if he were thunderstruck, "Sweetheart? Who's been saying such things?"

"Aune... herself... said... that... that... she could have had... you, if she had wanted to... Everybody is lying... You and Oskar... But people have been hinting to me... and Aino Mäkelä... told me. Tell me if it's true?"

Akseli looked toward the lake, his face frozen. He drew in his breath heavily, about to say something, but Elina looked at him through her tears and burst out suddenly, "I know... it's true... you don't have to... you don't have to."

Akseli drew the girl into his arms, but he was met by slashing nails, unintelligible accusations, and repeated outbursts of weeping. Distraught, he set her free and pressed his face into his hands. Having wept and sobbed her fill, the girl asked in a tormented, but obviously curious voice, "Where were you... with her... tell me... where?"

"In Leppänen's sauna, mostly..."

"What did you do with her? Tell me everything... absolutely everything."

The boy's words came harshly and painfully, their harshness revealing the irrevocability of his misfortune. "Well I... talking won't help..."

The torment that made his voice break was strained to the point of tears. He did not regret having done wrong, but having caused Elina pain. She began to cry anew.

"I already know... Taking turns with Oskar... Horrible... both of you... you probably told each other about it... Pigs... animals... bucks... disgusting... disgusting animals. And even you..."

391

An ugly, angry expression came over Elina's face. She jerked at the ring on her finger, got it loose, then rose and left, throwing the ring at Akseli's feet.

"Take it to her... Put it on that slut's finger... that whore for everyone to ride... Take it..."

Elina was well supplied with terms of abuse from the discussions of her brothers and her father, and they poured out in a stream. Akseli ran after her and took her forcibly into his arms. As she struggled, he said, gasping, "If you go... Don't go... I'll kill myself... If you go..."

"You won't kill anything... you'll just go to the sauna with that slut... So go... just go..."

"I'll kill myself... don't leave me... goddamn, I'll kill myself..."

Frightened, Elina looked at his face and saw it distorted by a pain so great that she realized at once it was no idle threat. Her struggles ceased, and the certainty that this was all unchangeable and irrevocable caused her to sink nervelessly into Akseli's arms. There she wept, a long, despairing weeping, until weariness brought it to an end once and for all. Akseli said nothing. Staring fixedly over the girl's head, he kept on stroking her hair.

They searched for the ring, and when Akseli put it back on her finger, she looked away sniffling, drying her tears with a handkerchief.

"There's nothing to be done about it now. I would ask you to forgive me if it would help... but what is..."

"No... don't talk... don't talk about it any more... not tonight... later... don't talk now..."

They sat for some time in silence.

"Has Janne sent word if the beds are ready?"

"He, he... has..."

Her words were broken by a few after-sobs. Elina looked out at the lake. The landscape was beginning to darken, for the sun had set. But it was further dimmed by the final tear gathering silently in the corner of her eye, from where it slid down to the tip of her nose and stopped.

Life had dealt her a blow. Its first.

V

Of course Anna could tell by Elina's mood that something had happened.

"What's wrong with Elina?" she said to Otto.

"They must have had a fight about something."

"Is it starting already?"

"Already? It's been a long spell of sunshine, if you ask me. It's about time for a little rain."

It was hard for Elina to get over the matter. Akseli did his best to help. He openly assumed the burden of guilt and offered no defense at all. Once he did try to alleviate the fault by alluding to the common guilt of mankind.

"There are very few who haven't slipped in that way."

"I haven't."

"Well... You're a different kind of person."

That was some consolation to Elina. She was indeed different from Aune Leppänen. When it was getting on toward autumn, she became herself again. Sometimes she would still cry, after which she would sing a spiritual song, but happiness and laughter had returned to their former abodes.

Akseli was earning money. Man and horse were at their best, young, strong, and unruly. From Akseli's "sector," one heard a crashing as a load of logs came through the brush to the roadside. Both man and horse snorted in some kind of spell wrought by action. It was as if Poku understood the need for a bed, for tables, chairs, pots, plates, spoons, for a wall clock, and many other utensils. Earlier the boy had vied for the highest pay as a token of honor, but now there was another and sterner significance in the work. This winter there was no danger that anyone would challenge him for top earnings, as had sometimes been the case in the past. In the harsh severity of work, he could feel the pressure of the future. From his father's equally bitter life's work, he had been left only the right to till for rent a few meager acres of land. He had to begin with almost equally empty hands. This man, who drew the highest wages on the job, did not so much as have a wallet, for up to this time, he had never really received wages of his own. Now he would put the money into a jacket pocket, and when he was alone, he would count it over again. The button on the pocket had to be reinforced with a safety pin.

Father Jussi had once predicted that the boy would wreck many horse's gear in his lifetime, and he had been absolutely right. When a load was hung up, the boy was too impatient to determine the cause, but hooked his tongs into the binding chains and pulled along with the horse: "... the...ere, she goes..."

Poku would break the harness, for some part of it would fail. Then the horse, who had done his best, would feel a harsh tugging at the corners of his mouth as the boy jerked at the reins in his anger. There was a stump under the bunks of the sleigh. He would have to start chopping it out in an awkward prone position if he didn't want to dismantle the entire load. Someone would happen along and say: "Did you catch a stump?"

"I did, dammit. I didn't see it. Goddamn Joonas Castrén. Bastards like that should be hanged by the neck."

Poor Jonas Castrén had become for Akseli a species of bogeyman, behind all the troubles that afflicted him. Castrén had been one of the most heated opponents of all laws to regulate rents and working hours, or at least his words had caught the boy's eye in the newspapers.

In the end, Castrén was demolished from underneath the bunks of the sleigh, and the harness was duly repaired. Poku laid his ears back in fright, but when all was ready, the command to go came as mildly as a request for pardon: "Come on boy. Try it again."

If there was moonlight, it was late at night before Akseli returned home. The boys might already be asleep, but his parents were awake, his mother because of the food, and his father out of some kind of sense of honor. Jussi could not stand to be in bed when his son returned from work. On such nights, there was an oddly respectful and humble note in his words. "Don't worry about getting up for the stable chores in the morning. I'll see to it that he's fed."

Elina had to wait out the week. Akseli appeared only on the weekend, and there was little joy in his presence. Before long, he was asleep on Elina's bed. He snored unpleasantly, but the faulty aesthetics did not bother his bride. Quietly, she crept from the chamber into the main room.

"Has he left?"

"He's sleeping."

"Ha, ha. You have my sympathy."

Elina enjoyed taking offense as an adult on Akseli's behalf, and in return for his words, Osku got a certain grown-up's comments on just who was what in this world. There are real men, and then there are those who only look like men.

394

The wedding was held on Midsummer's Eve at the workers' hall. Rehearsal for the wedding waltz began a week earlier. Apparently it was mandatory — at least a couple of turns around the floor. Not that dancing the waltz was in itself such a complicated art form. The problem was one of attitude.

"Hell no. A grown man skating around the floor."

No one at the wedding took any note of the groom's difficulty with the feat. Some small clumsiness was forgiven him. In the wedding address, the vicar told of how pleased he was with the marriage.

"I have known you ever since you were a boy, and I wish you all success as you step into manhood."

As was natural on this occasion, the vicar's wife was also at the wedding. This time the couple stayed for a while, even after the dancing had begun. Everyone's uncle also gave a speech, and for the first time, Anna began to look with favor on the groom. Both speakers, the vicar as well as Halme, testified that Akseli was indeed an exceptional man. But the most eloquent speech Halme had ever given he addressed to Elina, a young woman about to assume the role of mother. He addressed her in such heart-felt terms that the old women sighed and whispered to each other: "It sure is sad Emma never got any children..."

As a wedding gift, the young couple received a fine edition of Scripture and a sum of fifty markkas from the parsonage. That fact was also influential in winning Anna's favor for her son-in-law. The boy seemed to be a favorite of the people at the parsonage.

There the two sat on the far bench at the workers' hall, a trifle stiff and embarrassed. Elina was not annoyed at the drunks who came up to whisper in secret to Akseli, as Sanni had been earlier. The first of them had received a polite but firm refusal: "Not now. Some other time."

Elina even laughed heartily at Elias, as he hung around them for a long time, mimicking Halme's words and giving them a twist of his own.

This time it was Janne who dodged around corners at the hall, slyly evading Sanni. He was the target of many offers, for he was no longer an ordinary tenant's son. He was Janne Kivivuori, a mason, a board member of the workers' association, a member of the "Aid" Co-op council, and secretary of the parish rental commission. Of course, his rapid rise had resulted from his father-in-law's smoothing the way for him, but his conduct on those governing boards soon made it clear that he was not a mere tool of his father-in-law. He absorbed new

395

ideas quickly, and the traits of a cold and clever schemer were soon apparent beneath a half-negligent surface. Despite his youth, people were beginning to fear him. In disputes, he was completely unruffled, quick to find his opponent's weak point and to attack it shamelessly. Mere acquaintances would approach him with a bottle, asking humbly: "Is a poor man's bottle good enough for Kivivuori?"

The bottle was indeed good enough, but when its bestower began to whisper his errand, a veiled look would come over Janne's face.

"It's a question of the rent. It's before the commission. If Kivivuori could sort of look after my interests."

"Of course I'll do what I can. But I'm just the secretary, and I don't take part in the decisions."

The man would thank him as humbly for his promise as he would a great man. Janne would then appear at Sanni's side, equally humble, and sigh, "So... how will the boy get along with the old man?"

A lively exchange in Swedish would follow, not out of any desire on their part to show off their refinement, but because what they said was not suitable for the others' ears.

Before the dance had ended, the young couple left for the Kivivuoris. They were not interested in a noisy departure; having paid their respects to the more prestigious guests, they disappeared. Together they walked along the village road on that morning after Midsummer's Eve, leaving behind them the din of music and dance and drunken chatter. A couple of wandering drunks met them on the road, and, smiling benignly, Elina and Akseli heard out their compulsory reiterations.

"We just happened to be here now, so don't get mad. Look, we're just a couple of little guys, but that's no matter. But we really have to congratulate you again."

Their hands would be shaken over and over, until they would finally free themselves almost by force and go on their way. The very last thing they could hear in the fading din from the hall was some drunkard's carefree shout: "By God, boys. 'The sweet voice of Väinö's kantele echoes among the pines...' Isn't that the way it goes, boys?" The cabin greeted them, squatting silent in the shadowless glow of the night. The door was unlocked, with only a dry stick thrust through the hasp. The broad planks of the entry floor creaked underfoot as they made their way into the parlor. Elina had already spent a couple of nights at the Koskelas when they had worked late getting the rooms there ready. Tomorrow she would go there to stay, and she said, as she removed her coronet of myrtle, "This is my last night in this room. I really don't feel like sleeping."

"Let's not, then."

Having undressed, they went to bed. Lying on their backs, they started to talk in whispers about the wedding and the people who had been there. The talk was of no consequence, but it kept them awake. Nor was it in any way attuned to the mood of the morning. Elina's whispers were long and rapid, with Akseli 's replies serving only to fill in the gaps. A small red glow began to appear on the wallpaper above the door. Somewhere the first cock crowed.

From the yard, they could hear the sound of footsteps and the drone of a voice singing, "Tampere Lempäälä Viiaala, Toijala Kuurila Iiittaalaa, Parola Hämeenlinna Tuurenkiii, Leppäkoski Ryttylä Riihimäki, Hyvinkää Jokela Järvenpää, Kerava Korso Tikkuriii, Malmi Oulunkylä Preetiksperiii, and then only Helsinki..."

The footsteps reached the entry and they heard Anna's scolding voice: "Heathen... Not even at your daughter's wedding..."

Elina and Akseli looked at each other and smiled. They did the same when the next couple arrived. There was no singing this time, but Sanni's angry whisper continued to be heard in the bake-room even after the creaking of the bed-springs had ceased.

The last to arrive was Oskar. He opened the door and said to himself, half-aloud, "Oh, darn it. They're hugging in every bed in this house. I got to go and sleep in the hayloft."

After fumbling around in the cupboard and swearing because the last of the cheese had been taken to the workers' hall, he left.

The whispering began anew in the parlor.

"I was thinking we might move the stove into the bake-room and make it a real kitchen. Then the main room could be more of a Sunday room."

"Let's do it. The only thing we need to do is move the stove."

"We can do it this summer already. Father can find time to do the masonry work."

"We could put wainscotting on the main room walls."

"Yes, but only halfway up. We'll have real wallpaper above it."

"Why not? But I don't think I can manage it this year. I have to have a new double-bunk sled. The old one won't do for next winter's hauling."

397

"Of course not until we can afford it. But did you notice how the vicar's wife chirruped when she congratulated us. She can really be sweet at times like that."

"Look, the gentry never show anything on their faces. They have been taught all their lives how to lie about anything, anywhere. That's what civility is, learning which face to show in what place. Although she's probably not such a devil underneath; she's just a climber. And you needn't worry about her. You have only those six help-days to put in, so you won't have much to do with them. But what's going to happen in 1916?"

"It'll work out somehow. But how did you like Sanni's dress? I didn't think it was all that pretty, even if it was supposed to be so fancy."

"I didn't really look at it. But you looked so good in your wedding dress, it hurt me to look at you."

The tiniest of chuckles mingled with the twittering of barn swallows. The light of day was growing stronger in the parlor windows. On the dresser were Elina's coronet and Akseli's starched collar. Draped over a chair was the white wedding gown, on which the rosy rays of the morning sun were dancing. It shone obliquely, casting a shadow from a stepladder onto the window. The subdued voices of the summer morning intruded into the room: the chirping of swallows, the crowing of a cock, the lowing of a cow for her milker somewhere beyond the rise of the yard.

Finland's summer is beautiful. But so very short.

398